Francesca's Foundlings

Kathleen Ferrari

Francesca's Foundlings
Lynton Series, Book 2

Any feedback about this published work is welcome at
feedback@roskerrypress.com.

ISBN 13: 978-0-9836354-3-7
Library of Congress Control Number: 2015958405

Credits:
Dorie McKeeman, Editor
Kristina J. Hickman, Cover Illustrator

DEDICATION

Michael O'Connor —"a chuisle mo chroí"

&

In memory of my little Cocker Spaniel, Grace, who kept me
company through the writing of much of
Francesca's Foundlings

ACKNOWLEDGMENTS

Thanks to my readers who urged me to continue Franny's story.

Special thanks to:

My daughter, Amanda, who encouraged me to keep writing.

In memory of my cousin, Robert F. Quinn, firefighter, who reviewed the fire scene for me. Any mistakes are mine, not his.

Susan Logan and M.G.C. for providing valuable insights to the contents of this book.

Dorie McKeeman for her patience and skillful editing. Kristina J. Hickman for drawing another wonderful cover.

My fellow writers in the Souhegan Writers Group: Cherie Konyha Greene, Sue Spingler, Luci Osborn, Michael Sills, Jenny Schuster, and Mike Robertson, for their friendship and support.

CHAPTER ONE

"Watch out! You're going to drop that baby!"

Franny MacCullough hurried across the room to where her sister, balanced precariously on a stool, was arranging dolls on the shelf above her head. Franny rescued the life-size baby doll that was dangling precariously under Sofia's arm and cuddled the doll against her shoulder.

Sofia shook her head. "You *do* know it's only a doll, right? You haven't totally lost it, have you?"

"Forget about the doll. You're going to end up on your ass if you aren't careful. Use the ladder, if you please." The orders came from Brid Sheerin, who stood, paintbrush in hand, across the room from the Chiesa sisters. "We don't have time to cart you over to St. Luke's with a broken neck. We still have too much to do here." She paused to study the painting on the wall in front of her, and, tossing this one last comment over her shoulder, added, "Besides, you know they are all 'babies' to Franny."

At forty-six, Brid was the eldest of the three women gathered in the soon-to-be-opened doll shop. She was not happy with the mural: under the name of the shop—Francesca's Foundlings—dolls played together in a world of flowers and small woodland creatures. It was too sweet for her tastes, but then her tastes did not include collecting dolls.

"What do you think?" she asked the other two women. "Does

this need something more? And do not say 'a unicorn.' I draw the line at unicorns." She continued to examine her work. "I never played with dolls, so I can't be sure what's missing."

Sofia snickered, "I suppose you played with guns," then pausing to make her point, she added, "Real ones."

Brid continued looking at the painting with a critical eye. "I never held a gun in my hand before Neil took me shooting last year." She faced Sofia. "I admit I do love shooting now, but when I was a girl, it was swords that I played with. *Robin Hood* and *The Three Musketeers* were my favorite stories. No stray stick or broom handle was safe. In fact, I took lessons in fencing when I went to college. I got to be quite good at it." Tall and as slender as she had been at eighteen, Brid practiced yoga daily and ran when she could find the time.

Still cradling the doll, Franny backed up to stand in the entrance of the shop. The painting that filled the wall over the glass case containing her antique dolls was the first thing customers would see when they came in the door. "It's wonderful—so much more whimsical than the one I stenciled on the workshop wall at home. I love it!"

Sofia hopped off her stool and stood next to Franny. Putting down her brush, Brid joined them. All three had dark hair. Brid's, black and naturally curly, surrounded her face like a halo. Franny and Sofia shared the chestnut-brown-colored hair with red highlights they inherited from their grandmother. Franny wore hers in a classic chin length bob. Sofia's was cut shorter in an elfin cap.

Brid made a face as she stared at the painting. "It does the job, I suppose; it certainly catches your eye and—"

"It's wonderful and you know it!" Sofia snorted. "You missed your calling. You should have gone into advertising."

Always mindful of the tension that bubbled beneath the surface between Sofia and Brid, Franny leaped to diffuse it, adding, "I think it's perfect. All it needs is for you to sign it." She looked at Brid expectantly.

Brid opened her mouth and then closed it. She was reluctant to put her name on the work. *I did not spend four years studying art to paint silly pictures of baby dolls,* she thought. Brid looked at Franny's beaming face. *Oh, what the hell.* Returning to her paint box, she chose a new brush, tested the bristles with her fingers and dipped it into the black paint. Bending down to the lower right corner of the mural, she printed her name, SHEERIN, in the block letters that branded her signature.

"There you are, then. You now own an original work by the great painter, Brid Sheerin." The hint of bitterness was discernible only if one listened closely.

"And I am thrilled! Thank you so much for doing this." Franny hugged Brid, whose eyes locked with those of Sofia, standing behind her sister.

"I am glad you like it. It's a little too cute for me, but then as I said, I never played with dolls."

Sofia groped in the pocket of her jeans for her cell phone. She frowned as she checked her messages. "Where are those guys? They said they were bringing dinner. I'm starving."

Not bothering to hide her annoyance this time, Brid shot back, "Do not text Brendan. They promised to bring dinner and I am sure they will. It's sleeting out, you know. The traffic is horrific. You don't have to micromanage everything." Wrinkling her nose, she added, "That fellow is a saint to put up with you. I certainly never would."

"No squabbling, ladies," Franny said, hoping to prevent an argument. "It's my fault, I've worked you both to the bone all afternoon and I should have had snacks here for you. It's just that if I keep that stuff around I eat it and—"

Always the peacemaker, Brid thought. Aloud, she said, "We didn't need any snacks, Franny. When was the last time you saw your sister snack?" It was true. Sofia was fanatical about what she ate, avoiding sweets and most carbohydrates; she seemed to live on diet soda and sugar-free gum. Her daily runs and strict eating policies kept her weight just under a lean one hundred pounds. Brid told Sofia, "Chew some of that disgusting gum you always seem to have in your mouth if you're so hungry."

Sofia was rarely speechless, but Brid could do it to her. It was not only the thirteen-year difference in their ages; it was the fact that in so many ways they were alike. Both hard-driving, intelligent women who had an innate distrust of the men around them, their reluctant bond was formed around Franny, whose sudden

3

widowhood had thrust her into a role she neither wanted nor was prepared to accept. Realizing that they each played a part in helping Franny reinvent her life, most of the time Brid and Sofia managed to avoid open warfare, but their differences were always there, just under the surface, waiting for something to spark them.

The buzzer at the rear door of the shop sounded loudly. Franny grinned at her sister, "Looks like you won't starve, after all. I'll let them in."

Brid watched her go. *It's about time*, she thought. She and Sofia listened as Franny greeted Brendan Feeney and Neil Malone. And then they heard her voice rise in surprise, "What have you got there? Oh, my God! I don't believe it." Brid smiled.

Neil's broad back appeared in the doorway as he and Brendan carefully maneuvered a large, wooden carousel horse into the front of the shop. "Hi, ladies," Neil said, greeting Sofia and Brid. "Now, where do you want me to put this guy?" He and Brendan lowered the horse to the floor.

"Right here, in the center of the bay window. We can group the dolls around him," Brid walked over to the large window facing Main Street to supervise the horse's placement.

"No, wait, set him down. I need to dry him off first." Franny said to the two men. She reached for the roll of paper towels they had been using to clean the display case. "You can't give him to me," she protested, her face clouded with concern. "He's yours, Brid. You can't —"

"I believe I just *did* give him to you and I'll hear no more about it." Brid cut her off. She nodded to the two men standing on either side of the horse. "When she's finished drying him off, carry him over to the window. He will fit nicely right there in the center." She watched as they lifted the horse in place.

"I'll tell you one thing, based on what he weighs, he's going to eat all your profits," Neil joked as he stepped back from the window.

"He's perfect! We could have looked and looked and never found anything better. Where did you ever find him?" Sofia's genuine delight was without the undertone of sarcasm that she normally used to address Brid.

Brid ignored the question. Nothing could be gained by letting

Sofia know where the horse had come from. Unlike her sister, Sofia had never been in Brid's apartment and did not know the horse had held a place of honor there. Let Sofia assume that Brid had discovered him through the Irish art gallery she owned.

"I'm going outside. I want to see what he looks like from the street," Franny said, opening the door and stepping into the sleeting rain without bothering to stop for her coat.

"She's going to get soaked," Sofia said, grabbing the umbrella next to the door and joining her sister on the sidewalk in front of the shop.

"Okay, I'm going back to the truck for the food before Sofia remembers that she's starving." Brendan headed toward the rear of the shop.

"You need any help?" Neil called after him.

"Nah, I got it. No point in both of us getting even more wet. I'll be right back."

Removing his wet coat and hanging it over the ladder Brid had used to paint the mural. Neil moved to stand behind Brid pulling her against him. She let herself melt into his solid bulk, realizing that she was tired; the women had been working since seven that morning. *Painting murals was for younger artists*, she thought ruefully. Neil's mouth was next to her ear. "That was a nice thing you did for her, but won't you miss him?"

"We've been together a long while to be sure, but now I think it is time we both moved on," Brid replied. "Old Bucephalus will be happy there in the window, watching Main Street. It will be much more interesting than being stuck alone all day in my flat." Neil nodded, saying nothing more.

Brendan returned with the stack of take-out boxes and a cloth bag filled with eating utensils and a selection of drinks, which he deposited on the top of the display case. He smiled at the couple standing so closely together. "I'll go get those girls before we have to send the Coast Guard for them."

Brid was surprised that Neil had not immediately stepped away from her, putting the proper distance between them, when Brendan had returned with the food. Neil was a private man, not given to public displays of affection. Their love affair, begun over the last two years—after having known each other for most of their lives, —had caught her by surprise and was for the most part a secret. A few people knew that they were going out, but nobody knew they were lovers. Standing there, comfortably leaning against him, she felt her desire flair and fought the urge to turn and kiss him. It was she who moved away as Brendan and the Chiesa sisters came back inside.

"It's wet out there, but at least it's not more snow!" Brendan said as he took off his dripping rain slicker adding it to Neil's hung over the ladder.

"I don't know, I think, at this time of year, the rain is worse," Neil said, looking out at Main Street through the water-streaked window. "At least you can shovel snow; if this freezes, we are going to be in trouble."

"I am so hungry I could eat that horse," Sofia said, eying the stack of boxes with suspicion. "What did you get?"

Brendan grinned. The food game was on. He began to take inventory of the boxes containing the food. "Let's see. I got…a box of greasy, crispy, fried chicken, French fries, onion rings, chips and—"

"Stop it, Brendan. You did not! Where is…"

Brendan took a box marked with an "S" off the top of the pile and handed it to her. "I believe that this is what you are looking for: salad, *no* dressing; plain, grilled chicken. Did I get that right?"

Mollified, Sofia smiled up at him. "Why do you insist on making me crazy? I don't eat crap, and you know it. Why does that make me some kind of freak?"

"It's fun teasing you, but I admire your discipline, and we should all watch what we eat." Brendan did his best to appear repentant. He probably would have pulled it off, if Brid had not snorted in disgust.

Sofia blew up. "You!" She scowled at Brid. "Like you have a clue what it's like to have to worry about what you eat. You could eat that horse and then a cow on top of that and never gain an ounce. You don't even *try* to eat responsibly." Sounding more like a judge than the lawyer she was, Sofia continued, "Thin or not, you will eventually pay for all the ways you have abused your body. And I can't wait to watch it."

"Enough, Sofia. We got you your salad, let the rest of us

destroy ourselves in peace." Neil did not raise his voice, but his tone let everyone know he was annoyed. Sofia flushed; as one of the founding partners at the law firm of Maguire, O'Shea, and Malone, he was her boss, after all.

"Let's eat in the back room." Franny picked up the boxes of food and carried them through the door to the room she planned to use for storage and shipping. The others trooped in behind her. Setting the food down on a packing crate, she opened the remaining boxes to reveal two large pizzas and a salad. Brendan removed bottles of soda and sparkling water, paper plates, plastic forks and paper napkins from the cloth bag he had retrieved from the display case and stood them next to the pizzas. "I guess we're going to have to sit on the floor," Franny said, realizing that there were no chairs.

"Do you still have that blanket in the truck?" Sofia asked Brendan.

"Good idea. I'll go get it." Getting up, he retrieved his rain slicker from the front of the shop and then retraced his steps to head out the back door to where the truck was parked.

"Ladies first. Help yourselves," Neil said, standing back for Brid and Franny to fill their plates. "The two slices with anchovies are for Brid." He smiled over at her.

"Who else would want the disgusting things, anyway? They're gross." Sofia sniffed, making a face.

Some days Brid really enjoyed the challenge of sparring with Sofia, but tonight she was tired. Not bothering to reply, she slid the two pieces of pizza onto her plate and, using her plastic fork, scooted some of the salad next to them.

Brendan returned, carrying a red plaid blanket under his coat. "All set for a picnic?" he asked as he unfolded the blanket and spread it on the wooden floor. "Everyone take a seat." He moved the pizza boxes and the salad to the center of the makeshift dining area.

Gracefully, Brid sank down on one of the corners, happy to be off her feet. She watched as Brendan held a salad and Diet Coke for Sofia, who settled herself diagonally across from her. *What a shame*, Brid thought, *that Sofia does not seem to appreciate what a great guy she is dating.* In many ways, Sofia treated Brendan like a faithful dog:

sit, come, wait, listen, be quiet—or some variation of them all.

At five-foot-ten and weighing one hundred and fifty pounds, Brendan had a slender build, but also the muscles required to do his job as a Lynton firefighter. A competitive runner like Sofia, he was as fit as she was, without needing to shove it in the face of everyone he met. He was a looker, too. Dark hair, blue eyes and a small scar under his left ear—a souvenir from his days playing hockey—gave him a roguish look.

"I think we're in pretty good shape," Franny said, covertly eying a third piece of pepperoni pizza.

"Mother of God, have the thing, will you?" Brid said, correctly interpreting her gaze. "You've burned about a million calories today."

"Well, I guess I could." Franny looked at Neil. "You guys didn't get any dessert, did you?"

Neil smiled. "We did not. Go ahead and have another piece. Nobody is counting."

As Franny reached for the slice of pizza, they heard the front door of the shop open and the sound of Lilah arguing with Franny's dogs, Lucy and Oliver. "Lilah's back with the dogs," Franny said. Before anyone could answer, two excited and soaked dogs burst through the door dragging Lilah behind him them at the end of their leads. Plunging into the center of the blanket, the black Lab shook, showering them all with icy raindrops. The springer spaniel took advantage of the ensuing pandemonium and inhaled the rest of the pizza in two gulps, one large paw planted firmly in the remains of the salad.

"Lucy—Oliver—Off! Get—off the blanket!" Franny commanded. The dogs grinned, in that way dogs do, back at her. Scrambling, Brendan managed to rescue two drinks before they were knocked over and drenched the blanket.

"I'm sorry! How was I to know you would all be sprawled on a blanket on the floor like you were having a picnic at the beach?" Lilah Patch, Brid's assistant at the Sheerin Gallery, shook her head at the devastation her two charges had caused. "Sit." Both dogs obeyed immediately, while continuing to eye the now empty pizza boxes.

Looking at her, Brid felt a flash of guilt. Poor Lilah—she had been running around all day for them—grabbing supplies, distributing flyers and walking the dogs. Standing there in her dripping windbreaker, sodden red Converse sneakers and stringy hair (no hat, of course), she looked chunky, and very young. She also, Brid realized, looked pasty-white. Brid was about to ask Lilah if she was feeling okay, when, without warning, the girl collapsed in a small heap, cracking her head on a file cabinet next to the door as she fell.

Brendan moved first. He was at Lilah's side before the others had even shifted. The dogs, realizing that something was wrong with one of their favorite people, forgot about sitting and nosed in around him. Brendan pushed them away as he checked Lilah's pulse.

"What do you need?" Neil asked, kneeling to Brendan's left.

"There's a first-aid bag behind the front seat of my truck. It's red, you can't miss it." Brendan said, already punching 9-1-1 into his cell phone.

KATHLEEN FERRARI

CHAPTER TWO

Lilah felt like she was drifting. It was Brid's voice, all high and Irish—a definite sign Brid was getting nutty—that made her open her eyes. Had she overslept? Was she late for work? Again? Brid would kill her. Her eyes met the steady gaze of a man she had never seen before.

"You got a pretty good bang on your head when you fell. You're gonna be fine, but we need to get you checked out first. We're getting ready to run you over to St. Luke's." He smiled encouragingly.

Oh shit, shit, shit, she thought, suddenly focused. *I can't go to the hospital.*

She tried to sit up. The man, who, based on the insignia on his shirt must be an EMT, gently pushed her shoulders down. She was surprised to find herself on a stretcher.

"I'm fine. Really, let me up. I need to ..." Lilah's voice trailed off. Her heart pounded. *I have to get out of here. I have to!*

She felt someone take her hand.

"Hey, it's okay, Lilah, we're all right here with you." Brendan squatted next to her. She could see Sofia and Franny peering anxiously over his shoulders. "I'm going to take a ride with you. You're going to need some stitches, but don't worry, I doubt they'll hurt as bad as getting your tattoo did."

Lilah felt her racing heart begin to slow down.

"You scared us out of our wits falling over like that!" Brid said, appearing on the other side of the stretcher. "Neil and I will be right along behind you."

"I felt a little dizzy, I'm fine now. I didn't eat..." She knew even as she said it, that there really was no point in arguing with Brid. You never won.

"We're ready to roll," the EMT announced. He told Brid, "Your husband is waiting in the car, behind the ambulance." Brid opened her mouth and then closed it.

Brendan rolled his eyes and grinned at Lilah, who, despite her panic, stifled a laugh. *'Your husband'—Brid must be lovin' that,* Lilah thought. *Brid should marry Neil Malone. He rocked. Poor Neil, though. Imagine actually being married to Brid and living with her all the time.* Lilah grimaced. It was hard enough working for the woman.

Brendan helped guide the stretcher for the EMT. An ambulance waited in the street, its flashing lights sweeping the shadows.

Lilah saw a short guy in an EMT uniform waiting by the ambulance. She had always thought the big, white, box-like vehicles were menacing. Icy rain stung her face, but the men moved fast so she didn't really get wet. As soon as the stretcher was latched in, the ambulance took off, siren wailing.

"Ever ridden in one of these before?" Brendan asked, sitting in the seat across from her. Lilah shook her head. He went on, "I did, once. I broke my ankle at a fire and caught a ride in one. It's a weird feeling."

Their trip was quick; St. Luke's was only seven blocks from Franny's shop. The three men unloaded the stretcher and pushed it into the ER, where a nurse directed them to one of a series of small treatment rooms. As Brendan and the shorter EMT shifted her from the stretcher to the bed, Lilah strained to hear the report the guy she had come to think of as "Head Dude" gave to the nurse: "... Apparently fainted ... BP hasn't come down at all ... needs sutures ..."

In a few moments, Head Dude was back. "I'm sure you're going to be fine. Next time you feel faint, look for a soft spot to crash."

"Thanks." Lilah managed to smile at him even though she felt like weeping. "I'll try."

Telling her that he would be back, Brendan walked out with the EMTs. Lilah already had figured out he knew them. First responders in Lynton probably all knew one another; it was not exactly a metropolis. And they had that brotherhood thing going on.

"Hi. My name is Sam. I'm going to be checking on you while you're here. So what exactly happened? Did you faint?" A nurse pushing a rolling cart with a computer mounted on it approached the bed. Lilah guessed the girl was only a couple of years older than herself.

Lilah admired the small tattoo of twined ivy encircling her wrist. The artist had been good. Lilah's eyes automatically searched for a pen; she would love to be able to sketch the design.

The nurse waited, fingers poised over the keyboard, for Lilah to answer.

"I didn't eat today. We're getting ready to open up a new shop on Main Street and I was rushing around doing things. It's no big deal." Lilah clenched her hands into tight fists under the blanket Brendan had tucked around her.

"A new shop downtown? That's wonderful. So many of the shops downtown have closed in the last couple of years."

"It's this lousy economy. It's hard to make a go of things." Lilah said.

Sam leaned over and gently checked the bandage on Lilah's face. "Looks like this is no longer gushing, but I bet the doctor will still want to stitch you up. You don't want a scar." Stepping back, she asked, "What kind of a shop is it? I mean, what will you be selling?"

"It's a doll shop," Lilah said.

Sam looked perplexed, "You mean a toy store?"

"Oh no—much cooler than that." Lilah warmed to her subject. "There are no other toys, only the dolls. Not new ones, either. Old dolls." She stopped to consider this. "Well, not ancient ones like with the painted china faces. You know, dolls like our moms and my Meme had—Madame Alexander and Suzanne Gibson and Ideal dolls—like those."

"I never liked dolls. I guess I was a tomboy." Sam frowned at the numbers on the monitor next to the bed measuring Lilah's

blood pressure." I hope it doesn't mean I'll be a lousy mother."
Her gaze swung back to Lilah as numbers on the monitor leaped.
"Hey, do some deep breathing. I want you to relax. Tell me more
about the kind of dolls you plan to sell."

"Franny—she's the owner—does this other neat thing, too. She
makes these muslin dolls and sells them on her website to moms
who want to dress them in their kids' old baby clothes. They sell
like crazy. I guess a lot of mothers save that stuff." Her eyes
searched the room. "Where's my backpack? Did they leave it at the
shop?"

"The EMTs usually put it in this cubby. Sam nodded toward a
narrow closet next to the door. Reaching for Lilah's wrist, she said,
"I'll grab it for you as soon as I check your pulse." Her eyes were
back on the monitor as she silently counted.

Gently placing Lilah's hand back on the bed, Sam opened the
cubby door and retrieved a battered green backpack. She handed it
over to Lilah, "Here you go."

Fishing down inside the bag, Lilah pulled out a card and handed
it to Sam, "Here, take this. The URL to the shop's website is on
there. Check it out." The card had a sketch of the shop's door.
Under it was her name and title: *Lilah Patch, Acquisitions.* Franny
had insisted.

"Thanks, I will. My mother has all our baby clothes in a big
trunk stuck in a corner of the attic. She thinks someday we're going
to put them on our kids." She shook her head in disbelief, "Like we
would ever put that old stuff on a helpless baby. But she might like
something like that muslin doll." Sam slipped the card into her
pocket and studied Lilah more closely. "I suppose everyone tells
you that your eyes are two different colors."

Lilah laughed. "Yeah, they do. Like I wouldn't already know it
or something."

Sam changed tactics, becoming more businesslike. "I need to
verify some info before the doctor comes in to check you out." She
looked down at the computer. "Do you take any regular
medication?"

"No." Lilah waited, her guard shooting up.

"No birth control?"

Lilah shook her head and watched the nurse type rapidly.

Sam smiled, "No guy, huh? Don't worry; they're out there. You have to keep looking. You smoke?"

"I did, but I quit. It got too expensive."

"I hear you. My boyfriend used to smoke and he quit, too. He was blown away when he realized how much it was costing him. Makes me happy because now I'm not always left sitting at the table alone while he's outside having a butt. You'll live longer."

"I have to ask you this, it's not personal. Do you drink or do street drugs?"

Lilah shook her head. "Look, I work as an assistant in an art gallery and do a little freelance web design on the side—not exactly making big bucks. I'm trying to save as much as I can for tuition to finish my degree. I have no money for drinking or drugging." She sighed. "And no time, either. I'm either working or I'm sketching."

"I get it." Sam stopped typing and looked at Lilah. "You know, with all this talk about the nursing shortage, people think that we're raking it in, but by the time I pay my rent and my car payment and my student loans, I'm eating frozen dinners and ramen noodles by the end of the month." It was Sam's turn to sigh. "I have one more question and we're done. When was your last physical?"

"I can't remember the last time I saw a doctor. I guess it was my physical for college. That was four years ago. I'm pretty healthy. I don't even get colds. Like I told you, I didn't eat today, that's all. There's nothing wrong with me." She pushed the blanket aside, preparing to get up.

"Oh, no. You're staying put," Sam said. She put a firm hand on Lilah's arm and took the blanket from her grasp. "You need a couple of stitches. You don't want a scar on your face. Doctor Sanjet will be in shortly. Is there anything I can get you while you're waiting?"

Lilah was already pulling her sketchpad and pens from her pack. "Let me see your wrist for a minute. I want to grab the way the artist filled in those leaves in your tatt. It's really nice work."

Flushing with pleasure, Sam did as requested, extending her hand to provide Lilah a better view of her wrist.

The curtain around Lilah's bed moved to reveal a petite Indian woman.

"Miss Patch? I am Doctor Sanjet. I am here to take a look at your face."

Lilah let go of Sam's hand, allowing her to move away from the side of the bed as the doctor scrolled through the information on the chart.

"This says that you fainted and hit your head on a filing cabinet when you fell." The doctor looked at her sharply. "Did someone push you?" She watched for Lilah's reaction.

"Of course nobody pushed me!" Lilah frowned. "I had just gotten back from walking the dogs and I got dizzy. The next thing I knew I was on the floor with freakin' blood dripping all over me. I didn't get a chance to eat lunch, that's all it was." She looked at Sam for confirmation.

Dr. Sanjet leaned over and took Lilah's chin in her hands, gently turning the girl's face to get a better look at the gash running along the side of her left temple.

"A couple of stitches will close this nicely and you should have almost no sign that it has happened. Your hair will hide any faint scar, but I am thinking you will not even have that." She straightened up. "However, I want to do a couple of other tests, too."

Using a small flashlight, the doctor checked to make sure that Lilah's pupils were normal. Holding up her right hand she asked, "How many fingers do you see?" When Lilah answered three, she smiled and said, "You are correct. Are you feeling nauseous?"

"I'm fine. I just didn't have lunch." Lilah protested.

"Just to be sure, I am going to order a CT. I want to rule out any complications from the fall." Lilah nodded glumly wondering how much that would cost.

Turning to leave, the doctor paused and said, "Also, do you think that you can produce a urine sample?" She extended a container wrapped in plastic to Lilah, who reluctantly took the cup. "There is a bathroom on the left just as you enter this room. I will be back in a moment to put in the stitches. Please go with her, in case she feels dizzy again," the doctor instructed Sam.

Down the hall, in the waiting room, Brid sat next to Neil fidgeting on one of the hard plastic chairs, wondering what minion of the devil had designed these instruments of torture. She badly wanted a cigarette. She looked around the room for the most likely candidate to beg one from. No one measured up. Besides, it would be too obvious. The simplest thing was to go outside to see if she could find anyone smoking. How she was going to slip away from Neil was something else. She was not *smoking*–not really. At least she no longer bought cigarettes. Sometimes, though, she needed one. Like right now. What was taking so long, and where was Brendan?

Franny and Sofia came through the door. Spying Neil and Brid, they threaded their way across the room and dropped into the two chairs across from their friends.

"What's going on? Is she okay?" Franny asked, leaning toward Brid, concern in her voice. Sofia began scanning her phone.

"Who knows? We haven't seen anyone or heard anything since we got here." Brid shook her head, annoyed. "I have no idea where Brendan is." She frowned at Franny and Sofia, happy to have found another target to vent her frustration on. "Where have you been? I thought you were right behind us."

Before Franny could answer, Sofia looked up from her phone and said, "Did you forget about the dogs? We had to take them back to Hiram's Forge. We wouldn't want them to be upset by having to wait in the car." She looked at her sister, "Right, Franny?"

"They *were* upset! They knew something was wrong with Lilah. Besides, they needed to be fed their dinner."

"Fed their dinner?" What about all the pizza they ate?" Brid asked.

Neil stood and stretched. "Do you want me to go ask the nurse if she can give us a status on Lilah's condition?"

"Would you please? I am getting ready to jump out of my skin," Brid said

Neil looked down at her. "Yes, I noticed."

At that moment, Brendan strode through the door and headed toward them. He moved so gracefully Brid was reminded that she'd always thought he should have been a dancer.

"What's going on back there?" Neil asked.

Before Brendan could open his mouth Franny chimed in with, "Can we go back and see her?"

"When will she be released," Brid asked before Franny had finished speaking.

"Whoa, there!" Brendan raised his hands in a mock attempt to fend them off. Sitting down in the chair next to Brid, he began to tell them what he had learned from the EMTs on the ambulance.

"She needs a couple stitches. There's a pretty deep gash about an inch and a half long on her left temple. She must have caught the corner of the file cabinet on the way down. Coming in, the EMTs were concerned about her BP. It was pretty high, but the poor kid was probably scared out of her mind." He looked over at Brid. "I bet she has no health insurance, does she?"

Brid shook her head. "Not from me—she's only part-time and I can't afford to give it to her. But I'll pay for this. She shouldn't be worrying about that now. When can we see her?"

"I should probably pay for it—she got hurt at my shop. She was working for me. You shouldn't have to pay," Franny insisted.

"Let's not argue. Let's agree that Lilah's hospital bills will be paid," Neil said smoothly. Looking at Brendan, he asked, "What happens now?"

"They'll numb her face, stitch her up, probably give her a tetanus shot and then we can take her home. It's a function of how busy they are back there. Lilah's condition is not considered to be critical, which is actually a good thing. She'll probably have to come back in a few days for a follow-up."

"Sounds like it was nothing too serious, then," Neil said.

"She probably just forgot to eat because we had her running around all day." Franny said.

At this last, Sofia said, "Well, she's definitely eating something."

"Lilah is not fat!" Franny said, rising to Lilah's defense.

"How could you tell, with those baggy clothes she wears?" Brid asked.

"Were you able to finish up at the shop?" Neil asked Franny, attempting to change the subject.

"Yes. I think everything is as ready as it can be. I am really nervous—"

"When was the last time any of you saw Lilah having a cigarette?" Brid asked, interrupting Franny.

"We don't exactly watch Lilah, you know," Sofia said. "What

does that have to do with a cut on her face?"

Franny frowned. "I can't remember when it was, Brid. I bet she quit. She probably didn't want to say anything because she was afraid it would make you feel bad because you were smoking again. Do you think that's why she was dizzy?"

Neil's eyes met Brid's and he shook his head slowly back and forth indicating he was not happy to learn she was smoking again. She shrugged.

"Maybe the question you should ask yourself is: 'When was the last time I, myself, bummed a cigarette from her?' Then you'll have your answer." Sofia said.

The two women sent daggers at each other, not realizing that a tall, gray-haired woman wearing a white coat and a stethoscope around her neck had come up to the group.

"I'm looking for Neil Malone and Brid Sheerin." She struggled over Brid's name, pronouncing it 'Bride' as people often did. She looked from one to the other, waiting for confirmation.

"I'm Neil Malone and this is Brid," Neil answered, extending his hand and ending Brid's name with the soft g sound, the way it was pronounced in Irish.

"I'm Doctor Harkey—the physician treating Miss Patch. Would you both come with me, please?" Without waiting for a response, she headed toward a door marked "Consultation."

Once inside the small room containing a table circled by chairs, Dr. Harkey said, "Please have a seat." She took a chair facing them. "Lilah gave me permission to discuss her case with the two of you once I persuaded her not to sign herself out against medical orders. She seems to have complete trust in you." The doctor paused. "And she doesn't appear to be a girl who trusts easily."

"What's wrong with her?" Brid demanded. "I thought she just needed to have her head stitched?" Neil reached over and squeezed Brid's hand.

"I'm admitting her. We need to get her blood pressure down as soon as we can. The best way I can make that happen is to enforce bed rest."

"Her blood pressure? How high can it be? She's a young girl!" Brid's voice rose anxiously.

"Her BP has been holding steady at 145/97." The doctor said.

"That's not so high," Brid argued, desperate to make the situation seem better than it was. "Mine has been higher than that and I've never been hospitalized."

"Dr. Sanjet, the ER physician treating Lilah called me down for a consult on her case. I am the head of Obstetrics here at St. Luke. Lilah is approximately twenty-nine weeks pregnant. What we are dealing with is a condition called gestational hypertension. Unchecked, this can lead to preeclampsia, also called toxemia. Untreated, her current condition is potentially fatal to both Lilah and her baby."

The blood drained from Brid's face. Neil looked at her with a baffled expression. "Pregnant?" Did you know that?"

"Of course not. She wears those damn baggy clothes and tunic things. She looked the same to me," Brid said.

Taking pity on her, the doctor smiled for the first time, "She is fortunate she had this accident. Apparently, she has been receiving no prenatal care and because she ended up here tonight, I believe we have caught this in the early stages where we can make a difference in the outcome."

"I should have known." Brid berated herself. "She stopped smoking weeks ago."

"She's to be commended for that," Dr. Harkey said. "Smoking would only make her situation worse."

"What exactly is the treatment, Doctor?" Neil asked.

"If we can keep her pressure where it is with diet and bed rest, she is home free. If not, and her condition should progress, by far the best treatment is to deliver the baby." The doctor paused, allowing them to process what she said. "Let's wait and see. As I said before, I think we have caught this early. If she's careful, and we can keep her stable for another seven weeks or so and then deliver her—we will end up with a healthy baby close enough to term to hopefully have few problems."

The doctor stood up. "As soon as she's upstairs in her room, you can go say goodnight. Right now she is upset about a cat. As I have already told you, I want to get her blood pressure down. Anything you can do to reassure her about the animal would be much appreciated." The doctor extended her hand first to Neil and then to Brid. "Good evening."

"Thank you, Doctor." Neil stood up and held the door open for her.

"What in the name of God are we going to do?" Brid asked, looking up from where she still sat at the table.

"I guess I am going to have to deal with the damn cat."

"Moaki." Brid said automatically.

"What the hell kind of a name is that?" Neil asked.

"Who knows? She probably made it up. She loves that cat."

"Apparently, so." Neil agreed.

"Don't say anything to Franny and Sofia. Franny is nervous enough with the shop opening tomorrow." Brid stood up, her mind still on Franny. "You know what she's like about babies. Especially one that might die."

"We shouldn't say anything. If Lilah wanted them to know she would have included them on the release form for her medical information. It's important we don't break her confidentiality. It's a legal issue."

Brid shot Neil a look of disbelief and stormed past him. "But of course, how could I have forgotten that." Pausing for a moment, she took a deep breath and opened the door.

KATHLEEN FERRARI

CHAPTER THREE

What's going on? Is Lilah okay?" Franny asked, searching Brid's face. Brendan and Sofia stood on either side of her, waiting to hear the answer to her question.

"She's fine, but they want to keep her overnight to settle her blood pressure down. They'll be letting her out tomorrow, to be sure," Brid said, having no idea if it was true.

"Yeah, the guys on the ambulance were a little concerned about that. You don't usually see BP that high in someone her age unless they're really overweight. The guys checked it a couple of times," Brendan said, confirming Brid's story.

"Lilah is not exactly the picture of health and fitness," Sofia carped.

"Well, as it happens, I am," Brid retorted. "And I have had high blood pressure at times, myself. Besides," she looked at Sofia, "Lilah is not fat. She's solid. She's probably as fit as any of us, especially the way she rides that bike of hers everywhere."

"Brendan, I think you should make sure the ladies get home. Can you walk them to the car?" Neil interjected, in an effort to prevent further arguing between Sofia and Brid. "Franny has a busy day tomorrow and I believe Sofia has an important client meeting at nine o'clock. We'll keep you all posted on what's going on with Lilah."

"That's probably the best plan." Brendan handed Sofia her

jacket. "Come on women, time to get you both tucked into bed. Tomorrow is the big day for the shop."

Sofia shrugged into her jacket, but Franny was clearly torn.

"I hate to leave without at least seeing her," she said. "I feel like this is my fault. I had the poor girl running around all day."

Brid thought quickly. She had to diffuse this before Franny insisted on going upstairs and checking things out for herself. "Don't be ridiculous," Brid scolded. "You certainly didn't tell the foolish girl not to eat. In fact, I believe we told her to stop and get something to eat when we sent her over to Home Depot."

"Actually, the doctor didn't want a crowd up there." Neil reminded them as he glanced at his watch. "It's getting late, so we won't be staying long." Smiling at Franny, he said in a teasing voice, "Tomorrow is going to be a busy day for you, Mrs. MacCullough. You need to get some sleep."

"You're right," Franny agreed. "But, Brid, promise you'll call me after you see her."

Brid knew when Franny had dug in. *The bloody woman will not move until I yield!* she thought. "I will call you when I get home. Neil and I have to see to the cat first. But, I promise to call you later."

"Let's go, you two. There's nothing more we can do here and I need to go over my notes for my meeting tomorrow." Sofia was not actually tapping her Prada-booted foot, but the impression she gave was the same as if she had been. "I'll see you in the morning." She directed this last to Neil before she leading the other two through the waiting room toward the door.

"Bloody bitch!" Brid hissed for Neil's ears only, thinking, *It is a damn good thing nobody's taking my blood pressure at the moment. I would land in the bed next to Lilah.*

"You won't even try to get along with her. You go out of your way to bait her," Neil said, shaking his head and adding before she could protest, "I'm going to ask at the desk where they put Lilah. She must be upstairs by now. You better do some of that yoga breathing before you self-combust."

She decided to follow his suggestion, breathing slowly and deeply as she watched him cross the room and chat with the woman at the reception desk, working his lawyer magic. He thanked the woman and pointed toward the elevators in the lobby to let Brid know he had the room number.

"You're one hell of a liar there, Poker Face," Neil said as they waited for the elevator to arrive.

"You'll be happy to know that your buddy thought so, too," she said, referring to her ex-husband, Drew MacCullough. "Where is she, anyway?"

"Maternity," Neil replied. They stepped into the elevator and he pushed the button for the fourth floor.

"Lovely, just lovely. You know how much I adore babies."

Moments later the door slid open, revealing the contented faces of what were obviously four happy grandparents. One grandmother was telling the other, "Really, I'm not kidding. He looks exactly like Daniel did when he was an infant."

Neil, being Neil, of course said, "Congratulations."

"Thanks," the men answered for the proud foursome. "Here," one said, "have a cigar on Ryan. "He's our first grandson."

"Thank you." Neil pocketed the cigar. "I'll enjoy this."

Brid slipped by the quartet with no comment, spying Lilah's name next to "Room 408" on the whiteboard on the wall behind the nurses' station. With Neil close behind, she swept down the hall until she was standing in front of the door. There she hesitated, her bravado gone, reluctant to face what waited for her inside the room.

"Everything's going to be okay," Neil said quietly. He knocked softly on the door, which stood slightly ajar.

They heard Lilah's subdued voice. "Come in."

Brid squared her shoulders, took a breath and sailed into the room. "Well, this is a fine mess you've landed yourself in, isn't it?"

Dressed in the cotton hospital gown with blue fleur-de-lis designs instead of one of her garish T-shirts, Lilah huddled in the bed, looking miserable. Now that Brid knew, the baby bump was obvious.

"I know you're really pissed, Brid." Lilah turned her head away. "I'm sorry. It was ... I'm sorry."

"Everything's going to be okay," Neil said, trying to reassure the two women.

Ignoring him, Brid continued, eyes only for the girl in the bed.

"What were you thinking, Lilah? You could have come to me. I would have helped you, but now … " Brid's voice trailed off.

The tears in Lilah's eyes spilled over, but she said nothing.

"And we're still going to help you—Brid and I," Neil said, filling in the silence. Both his tone and his stance warned Brid not to contradict him. "The most important thing is that you and the baby are okay."

Lilah smiled tentatively up at Neil.

He went on. "We'll work it out, if you cooperate by getting that blood pressure down. Do we have a deal?"

"But you don't understand—I can't pay for any of this! I don't have any money for doctors or hospitals. People have kids all the time. I thought it would, you know, like, just happen."

Brid exploded, "What you *should* have thought of was how not to let this entire thing *just happen!* What the hell were you—"

Again, Neil overrode her, his anger as clear to her as her own. "*I* will handle this."

Turning to Lilah, he said, "There are programs for young women in your situation. And for whatever other medical treatment you or the baby need, I will pay for it." He looked at Brid, who said nothing. "Brid and I will help you figure this out."

"But I don't know when or how I can pay you back." Lilah's voice broke into a sob. "I don't have any money … saved for this and I have to … finish my BFA. I *have* to."

Neil was comforting. "Of course you do. And you will. Let's get this baby safely born first and go from there, okay?"

Looking at how woebegone Lilah appeared, dressed in her ill-fitting hospital gown and her bruised face covered with butterfly bandages, Brid felt her anger begin to dissolve.

"Dr. Harkey said you were worried about Moaki. If you give me your key, we'll go feed her and make sure that she's fine." For the first time since entering the room, she smiled at Lilah. "Will that make you feel better?"

"Will you? She must be so scared. I'm always home by now."

I doubt it, thought Brid, considering what she knew about cats, as she watched the girl dig through her backpack.

"Here's my key. You know where my building is on Main Street, don't you? The number is 505. I'm on the fifth floor, apartment C, in the front corner of the building. There's a bag of cat food in the cupboard under the kitchen sink." She sniffed before adding, "Thank you so much for doing this."

A nurse stuck her head in the door. "Are you Lilah's parents?"

Brid sucked in her breath, aware of Lilah covering her mouth to keep from laughing.

Neil answered smoothly, "We're not lucky enough to have that honor. We're just friends."

The nurse smiled. "Either way, I'm afraid visiting hours are over and this young lady needs rest." She waited pointedly for Brid and Neil to leave.

"I will call you in the morning. And I'll tell Moaki that you'll be back soon." Brid started toward the door.

Neil hesitated. Brid sensed he was at a loss as to what to do next.

"Try not to worry, Lilah. We'll see you in the morning. Good night." He told the nurse, "Take good care of her, will you," and walked by Brid without a word, his face like a thundercloud.

"And just what is it that I have done to annoy you so much?" she asked in the hall, the sharpness of her tone masking her unease. Most of the time Neil was even-tempered, rarely allowing circumstances to outwardly ruffle him.

"You might have given the poor kid a hug when we left," he retorted, focused on the elevator, which unfortunately was on the first floor. Angrily, he punched the button.

"Given her a hug?" Brid's voice rose. The nurse at the desk looked up. Brid lowered her voice and hissed, "She works for me, remember? And I don't go around hugging people."

Neil was too much an Irishman to let that pass. "Well, you've been known to hug me on occasion." He smirked as he said it, his anger at her slipping away.

Brid laughed. "Only when you're naked," she answered lightly. She felt more relieved than she would have believed possible. Did she really care that much what he thought of her?

Turning bright red, Neil gasped, and looked around to see if anyone overheard her. Discovering they were alone in the hallway, he began to breathe normally once again. "For the love of God, someone might have heard you."

Continuing to tease him, Brid made a sign with her hand that she was zipping her mouth shut. Neil shook his head.

"Look, I know you're not demonstrative, but Lilah has no one else. She must be terrified."

"She damn well should be terrified. Being a single mother is terrifying. As far as her having no one else, we don't even know that to be true. She told me she grew up in Lewiston, Maine. She could have a huge family up there."

"I doubt it. Or if she does, she doesn't seem to want to have anything to do with them." His face took on an obstinate look she was coming to know well. "But I intend to find out."

I'll just bet you are, she thought, looking at his set expression.

They stepped into the elevator and rode down to the first floor. It was still raining but Neil didn't seem to notice as he led the way to his car. Brid followed, pulling up the hood of her jacket, her mind whirling with the wider impact of Lilah's hospitalization. She had intended to pop in and help Franny with the opening of the doll shop, but now the only way she could make that happen would be to close the gallery. *Well*, she thought, *I can do that if I need to*, but she knew it was hardly a great idea in this economy to be cutting business hours.

She waited while Neil, reaching around her without touching her, unlocked the passenger door of the car and opened it. He still insisted on this gesture; she had mixed feelings about it. God knows she had been opening her own doors almost all her life, but there was something so completely 'Neil' about it that most of the time she tolerated it. Tonight it irked her, yet another sign of his need to be in control, and she didn't bother to thank him.

"Where the hell is 505 Main Street?" Neil strained to see the numbers they were passing.

"I think it's across from the CVS on the corner of Crane Street. The brick building."

Neil looked surprised. "It's not the best neighborhood down there."

"Well, it isn't the North End, but I've been in worse. She lives on a shoestring." *I will need to pay her more now*, Brid thought. *God knows where it will come from.* But she knew she would find it somewhere.

Looking over at her, Neil studied her expression, correctly

interpreting the grimness he saw there. "This is not your fault. She's in a bad place. And we'll help her get out of it."

"Stop, this is it," Brid said, peering at the numbers on the buildings.

Five flights later, they stood in front of the door to apartment C. "At least she's getting her exercise," Neil said. He was slightly winded despite his daily walk and passion for skiing.

Brid didn't answer; the stairs hadn't fazed her. Opening the door, they stepped into the tiny studio apartment, which claimed a bit of instant charm with its sweeping view of the city below. Turning on the light revealed a surprisingly neat living space and one annoyed ticked-tortie cat, who immediately made her feelings known to them with insistent meows.

"Why, hello there. You must be Moaki." Neil squatted down to pet the animal, who was rubbing against his legs. Brid was already opening the cabinet where Lilah kept the cat food. She poured the kibble into the cat's dish. At the sound, the cat abandoned Neil to run over and start eating. Brid refilled the water dish and placed it next to the food.

She wandered around, closely examining the sketches that covered the walls. Most were in pencil, but here and there was a splash of color where Lilah had used pastels.

"It's a shame, really," she frowned. "She's more than good. And now, her life will be consumed with how she will support and raise this child, not her art." It amazed Brid how much the sketches had evolved since the last time Lilah had showed them to her.

"I can see that. I had no idea." Neil smiled. "But what's the problem? I think her work is wonderful."

"She needs to finish her degree and keep working on her drawings, not be having a baby. Look around you. What in the name of God is she going to do with a baby?" Brid shook her head, turning back to watch the cat, contentedly eating her food. "You be good, Moaki. She'll be back tomorrow," adding, more to herself than either Neil or the cat, "I hope."

Neil took a closer look at Brid's strained, white face. "Come on, soldier. I'll take you home." He pulled her close for a moment in a tight hug.

Brid's cell phone rang as they were getting into the car. 'Franny' flashed across the caller ID display. Brid's eyes met Neil's as she pushed the button to talk. "Hiya. We're just leaving Lilah's now."

Franny wasted no time. "Lilah's pregnant, isn't she?"

"Yes." Brid didn't dare look at Neil sitting next to her. She knew that he had heard the question. What was she supposed to do? Franny was not stupid. There was no point in lying; the pregnancy was obvious once you knew what to look for. Besides, Franny was going to find out soon enough.

"Oh, Brid."

"Yes, I know. I guess we shall have to wait and see what happens." Brid stole a look at Neil's set jaw.

"But why are they keeping her in the hospital? What's wrong with her? Is it because she hit her head or is it something to do with the baby?" Franny's fear seemed to rise in waves from the phone Brid held in her hand.

"She has gestational hypertension. Apparently the wretched girl has had no prenatal care. The doctor is concerned that it will progress to toxemia." Brid didn't bother to elaborate. She was sure that Franny, who had lost more than one baby, most likely knew precisely what that was. She was not mistaken.

"Oh, no! That can be fatal to both of them. Did they tell you the treatment is bed rest?"

"Yes, the doctor, I think she said her name is Harkey, did say that. If it gets worse, she said they would have to deliver the baby early." Next to her, Neil had begun to shake his head, clenching his jaw even tighter, something she would not have thought possible.

"We can't let that happen. How many weeks pregnant is she? She has to get to at least thirty weeks or the baby might not survive." The anxiety in Franny's voice increased with every word she spoke.

"Calm down, will you please. There is nothing you can do about this tonight and you have to get some sleep. The shop is opening tomorrow—you need to focus on that. Will you do that, please? Lilah is in the best possible place. They will take care of her over there at St. Luke's."

"I suppose you're right. But you need to promise that you'll let me know as soon as you hear anything new. And I—wait—that doctor who took you and Neil into the consultation room was

Marianne Harkey, right?"

"Yes. Dr. Harkey. She didn't give her first name. Why?"

"She's head of obstetrics. She's the best there is. If they called Harkey in, it must be bad."

Oh Mother of God, Brid thought, *this just gets worse.* "Was she your doctor?"

"No," Franny replied. "I see Stephen Kim. But when John was born, she came in to assist with the birth. I thought she looked familiar when she took you guys off to the consultation room."

The birth that almost killed you, you mean, Brid thought, recalling what she knew of Franny's final pregnancy.

"Well, there you go. You just said that she's the best. I am sure Lilah's going to be fine."

"I certainly hope so." Franny's voice was quiet.

"We are almost at my condo. I will pop into the shop in the morning. Please try to get some sleep. You've done all you can to make the opening a success."

"Good night, Brid. Thanks for everything you've done to help. And please, thank Neil, too."

"Bye, then." Brid pushed the End button as Neil pulled the Mercedes into the parking place in front of the converted Victorian where she lived. She waited for the explosion she was sure was coming.

Neil surprised her. He shook his head, a reluctant smile slowly lighting his face.

"So much for confidentiality."

"Oh, you and your confidentiality. You heard her; she guessed. Was I supposed to lie? It's one thing to blurt it out to her and quite another to lie to her face." Brid stopped, suddenly aware of the phone she held in her hand. "Or to her ear."

They were both tired, realizing as they climbed the stairs to her second-floor condo that it had been a long day. Neil took his key and opened the door, standing aside for her to precede him into the room. He reached down, his lips lingering on hers. Stepping away, he said, "I think I will go home tonight. We're both asleep on our feet." As his hands slid down her body, he added, "If I stay here, it will be a while before we get to sleep. I'll pick you up in the morning and drop you at the gallery."

Good idea on both counts, Brid thought, ignoring the surge of desire she felt and remembering for the first time that she had left her car there. She lightly returned his kiss. "Off with you, then. I will keep you posted," and, thinking of the opening of Franny's shop, she added, "on *all* our babies."

CHAPTER FOUR

S topping for a moment to admire the faint pink streaking across the gray morning sky, Franny juggled her tote bag and cup of coffee as she locked her car, which was parked in the small space allotted to her behind her shop. As promised by the perky weather girl on television, it was going to be a nice day— sunny and unusually mild for February in New Hampshire. The dreariness of the prior three days was gone.

"Why, thank you, Drew," Franny said, giving her late husband credit for the turn in the weather.

It was something, she knew, he would have done for her if he could. He had been dead two years this past December, but she still talked to him, often aloud like this when she was alone. Brid had told her to leave the poor bastard in his grave, but then had grudgingly conceded that, as long as Drew didn't talk back, there was probably no harm in it.

Franny headed toward the back door of her shop, still thinking about Brid, who missed Drew, too, but would never admit it. Franny was sure Brid was falling in love with Neil Malone, a fact, she was also certain, Brid had yet to realize herself. That was definitely going to be something to watch.

Depositing her bag on the floor, she remembered the picnic chaos hours before and was grateful she and Sofia had been able to clean it up so quickly. *A table would've prevented the whole mess,* she thought, making a mental note to get one. Still holding her coffee, she hastened into the showroom and stopped, transfixed by the sight before her. *Perfect*, she thought. *It's absolutely perfect.* Almost a year in creation, Francesca's Foundlings was no longer an idea in her head, but an actual place. She clasped her hands together with pleasure.

Everywhere she looked were dolls that little girls had loved for almost a hundred years. The display case opposite the front door held the older, more fragile ones. A row of Ginny dolls created by the Vogue Doll Company in Somerville, Massachusetts, posed in various outfits, surrounded by their accessories: leather-strapped ice skates, straw hats with velvet ribbons, small hat boxes and pink comb-and-brush sets. The corner of the case held a nursery display for Ginnette, Ginny's baby sister. The set—wooden crib, feeding table (painted white with scattered rosebuds) and baby bath—had been a real find. Searching online, Lilah also had managed to purchase six Ginnys in excellent condition. They smiled up at her from the case.

Franny walked to the bay window and looked out onto Main Street, just starting its day. She unlocked the door, stepped onto the sidewalk to admire the window she and Sofia had carefully arranged the night before.

"Pretty awesome, isn't it?"

Franny flinched, her heart pounding. She had not heard Sofia jog up behind her.

"You scared me to death," Franny said, her voice a little testy. Her sister, baseball cap pulled low on her head, could have been mistaken for a child. "You know something, Sofia? It looks exactly like I dreamed it would." She bit her lower lip, losing her smile. "I just wish …"

"He sees it, Franny." She hugged her sister for a minute and then stepped back. "And he's bragging his ass off about you to all the other dead guys up there."

Franny was surprised; Sofia was not usually outwardly affectionate. Smiling back at her sister, she felt herself relax.

"Oh yeah, I'm sure he is. Remember how he used to tell people his wife played with dolls? The looks they would give him when he said that," Franny shook her head. Drew really had been incorrigible.

Sofia focused again on the window. "I have to hand it to that witch, the horse really does make it work."

"Sofia! Please don't call her that. Brid has been wonderful and you know it."

"Don't get excited. She calls *herself* a witch half the time. It's better than 'bitch,' isn't it? And she *is* a witch." She continued before Franny could interrupt again, "She works her ass off, I'll give her that." Sofia frowned, "I wonder what Neil sees in her."

"Everything." Franny answered.

"What do you mean?"

Before Franny could elaborate, the McGonagles' van pulled up to the curb behind them.

"Morning, Franny. I guess today's the big day." Peter McGonagle hopped out the driver's-side door and opened the back of the van, revealing three large bunches of deep pink balloons. Franny had chosen this particular shade of pink—almost rose—to appeal to her customers.

"Good morning, Peter. I'm excited, but very nervous!"

"I think you made the right choice on the color," Sofia complemented Franny. "It pops without being too sicky-sweet. Let me get these." She took the first bunch of balloons from the man's hands. "I'm the sister, by the way—Sofia Chiesa."

Peter looked from one to the other as he handed Franny the second bunch of balloons. "Yup, I see it. Nice to meet you."

Franny had spent the past six months getting to know the other downtown merchants, dropping into their stores and attending their meetings with Brid. Under Peter's ownership, McGonagles had been doing a successful business in Lynton for more than twenty years. "Watch what he does," Bid had told her. "He's a very good businessman." And, Franny had decided, he was a nice guy, too.

Sofia led the others into the shop.

"Hey, everything looks great," Peter said. "You've created something really unique here." He examined the mural more closely. "Brid, huh? She's a piece of work, isn't she? It's kind of a shame that this isn't framed. Just painted on the wall like this, one day it will be painted over."

"Nothing lost if that's the case." With the door open, none of them had heard Brid come into the shop. "It's hardly an 'Old Master.' I just slapped it up there because Franny wanted some babies and bunnies on the wall."

She looks tired, Franny thought. *And why not? She works too hard and now this thing with Lilah has really put her in a bad position. There's no one to help in the gallery.*

"Good morning, Peter," Brid went on. "Do you believe this weather? Hopefully the weather gods will not remember it's February." She inspected the balloons nearest to her. "Franny, you made an excellent choice with this shade of pink. It catches the eye and lingers without being saccharine, thank God."

"I have one more thing in the van for you," Peter told Franny over his shoulder as he started out the door.

Calling after him, Franny said, "But I only ordered the balloons," She looked at Brid. "He must have confused my order with another one."

Peter returned, carrying a simple white vase of tulips that exactly matched the pink of the balloons.

"These are from the Downtown Merchants Group, welcoming you and Francesca's Foundlings to Main Street," he said, putting them down on top of the display case, "and wishing you the best of luck. We are all delighted to have you join us."

"Thank you so much. The balloons are perfect and the flowers are gorgeous." Franny's eyes filled with tears.

Seeing her distress, Brid changed the subject. "This shade of pink is quite unusual. Do you happen to have any more of them?"

Peter laughed, knowing her fondness for tulips.

"As a matter of fact, I might. The color sure is different. I had to hunt for it and wasn't convinced until I picked them up at the flower market yesterday that they were going to be the right shade. I got lucky." He reached for the door. "I got extras because the color is so different. I'll put a bunch aside for you. Have a great first day, Franny." He told Sofia, "Nice meeting you."

"Thanks, Peter." Franny said. "You've been great." Musing, she added, "I can't believe the Downtown Merchants Group sent me flowers. Everyone is being so nice."

"You will understand why they sent you flowers when you look at your profit numbers by the end of the month. Times are hard for the small brick and mortar merchants. The last thing we want on Main Street is an empty shop. We are glad you are here." Brid looked around the colorful little store. "You really have done a beautiful job; the reviewers are going to love it. We need to see if we can entice *Victoria* magazine to come and see this." She moved some balloons closer to the front of the shop so they were clearly visible from the street.

"I have to run, literally. I have a meeting at nine with one of our larger clients." As a member of the running club at the Y, Sofia started and ended her daily run, usually five miles during the week, from there. "Wishing you and the dolls tons of luck today. I will call you later." She glanced across the room, "See you, Brid," and was gone before Brid could open her mouth to reply.

With the shop to themselves, Franny's expression changed.

"Last night after you called, I checked out *toxemia* on the web and—"

"Holy Mother of God, I told you to go to bed! You have enough to worry about without adding Lilah to it!"

"Lilah is alone and we all have to help her. You can't do it by yourself." Franny said pushing back. "What are you going to do about help in the gallery?"

Brid grimaced. "I left a voice mail with a temp agency. I've used them before and they are good. A lot of competent people are looking for work. I don't really need an artist. Someone who can wait on customers and help me with stock will fill the gap until Lilah can come back." She sighed, "It's the website and the online business that has me worried. I can't do—"

"But I have the answer," Franny interjected. "I've been thinking about it. We both need Lilah to work on the e-business. You said that she doesn't have full-blown toxemia yet, only gestational hypertension, right?"

"Yes, but the danger is that it can advance to toxemia, which, from what that doctor said, is serious."

Franny's expression darkened. "It can kill them both." She shook her head and hurried on. "But it won't, if we take good care of her. Based on how fast they get people out of the hospital these days, I bet they will let her leave, if she goes to a place where someone can help her." She took a quick breath and announced with a rush, " She can stay with me. I can put a bed in the study so she won't have to climb the stairs—there's a bathroom next to it—she can work on the e-business in bed—I'll make sure she's eating correctly and doing what she's supposed to. It's perfect."

"Are you mad? You've only just started a business here. You have no idea what kind of work is involved, especially in the beginning. The very *last* thing you need in your life right now is a sick woman, to say nothing of a baby!"

Franny took a step closer to Brid and got right in her face.

"I wish you would all stop 'handling' me when it comes to babies. It's been over six years since my baby died. I am not going to crash into a depression, if I help some poor girl who happens to be pregnant. I would hope that, if nothing else, this last year has proved to you and Sofia that I am no longer fragile. So, please, just stop this right now."

Brid began to smile. "Well, you certainly have become very mouthy. You're right, you have changed, though—and thank God for that—but why can I not make you see that Lilah is not our responsibility? Sweet Jesus, I had this very conversation with Neil last night. Lilah is an employee. She is a talented artist and has always been trustworthy. We don't know much about her beyond that and," her voice took a momentary snide tone, "the fact that she feels the need to have rather nasty snakes inked on her. This baby must have a father somewhere. They all do, don't they? What about him?"

Brid glanced at her watch, not waiting for Franny's answer. "I need to go now. I will check back with you later." She took one more look around the shop. "It's brilliant, it really is. You should be proud of yourself. I am sure that ... " She stopped herself. "I'm off. I hope you have a great day. I'll stay in touch about Lilah."

Franny watched Brid march by the window, her face a storm cloud. *What is going on in her head?* she wondered. Underneath Brid's life-is-tough-and-only-the-tough-survive exterior, Franny knew Brid had a soft heart she kept well hidden. Certainly, after what Brid had done for her in the last two years, she knew that as well as anyone. What was up with this distancing from Lilah? Something about the situation was definitely scaring her—and Brid didn't scare easily.

The door opened; Franny shook herself from her pondering.

It was Mara Sorento, carrying a stack of plastic food-boxes and trailed by a wan little girl in a red ski jacket. Mara's old van with **Live to Eat Catering** painted on the side was parked where the florist's van had been parked earlier.

"Oh my God! What a completely sucky morning I've had." Small and slender to the point of sharpness, Mara wore her long, black hair in a braid down her back. A free-lance caterer, she ran her business out of her home. One perpetually happy customer was Desmond Sheerin, Brid's father, who bought Mara's appetizers and pastry for his Irish restaurant and bar, Ceol agus Craic.

"Here, let me help you." Franny took the top three boxes off the stack, lessening the chance of a catastrophe. She smiled at the young girl, who, having moved out from behind Mara, was walking on tiptoes around the shop, stopping in front of various dolls as she went. She was tall—all legs, ending in lilac boots with silver stars. She was not a pretty child; her face had too many angles and her mouth was too big. Her eyes, though—a true green you almost never saw—gave every indication that, with a little luck, she would grow up to be a beautiful woman.

"Hi," Franny said, placing the boxes on a small, round table covered with an Irish lace cloth borrowed from Brid. "Do you like dolls?"

The child nodded slowly as she studied the Vogue dolls displayed in the glass case. Taking her eyes from the dolls she said, "I do like dolls. Where did you find them?"

"Lots of different places. I have a friend who helps me look." Franny said.

Mara smiled for the first time since bustling through the door. "Sorry. Ava, this is Mrs. MacCullough. She's the doll lady I was telling you about."

Putting the last of the boxes on the table, she addressed Franny, frustration lacing her voice.

"What a morning. First, Dolce got into one of the cupcake trays, the canine thief. I heard this crash—he had the entire pan off the counter and was inhaling cupcakes as fast as he could. Thank you, St. Francis, they were not chocolate, because I did not have time to run him over to the vet, or the money to have his silly stomach pumped out. So I had to quickly whip up another batch. And then Ava woke up with a sore throat. I'm taking her to the pediatrician for a culture after this." She threw the girl a quick kiss. "She gets strep, but they won't even consider pulling her tonsils, yet."

Mara walked over and wrapped her arms around her daughter. "Ordinarily, I would have left Ava with my mother, but she's in Florida." She sighed, "So here we are." Then she brightened. "Take a look at the cupcakes. I'm really happy with the color of the icing; I think it's exactly the right shade. I hope you like it."

Franny peeled the top off the container and grinned as she admired the deep pink icing, which matched the color of the tulips on the table next to them. A white flower made from sugar, with a faint yellow center, sat on top of each pink cupcake.

"They're perfect. Thank you." She gave Mara a quick hug.

"I think you're ready," Mara said. "This place looks like something out of a magazine. You've done a great job. I hope you have lots of customers." Gently turning her daughter around to face the door, she said, "We're out of here. I'll stop by later to pick up the boxes."

"Wait, I have something for Ava." Franny reached into a basket next to the cash register and handed the girl a doll-shaped lollipop. "Good for your thro at."

The lollipops had been Lilah's idea; she had found a place that customized them.

The girl smiled as she took the candy. "Thank you. Lemon is my favorite."

"I hope you feel better."

Ava stopped on her way out the door. "I like your doll store. It's cool." She spun around and followed her mother.

"Thanks again, Mara," Franny called out. Mara was halfway to the van.

Franny stood holding the basket of candy, thinking about what Lilah had told her: "Give the lollipops to the kids on their way out the door. We don't want icky-sticky in here. It will keep them from screaming when mom or grandma refuses to buy them a two-hundred-dollar doll."

Clever Lilah, Franny thought. *I wish she were here.*

Franny walked into the rear room and retrieved her cell phone. Brid had been acting so strangely about Lilah this morning. Not completely sure she could rely on Brid to convey to Lilah her offer of a place to stay, Franny scrolled down her contact list. She found the number she wanted and made the call.

KATHLEEN FERRARI

CHAPTER FIVE

Lilah glanced up from her sketch, having heard the soft knock on the partially opened door of her hospital room.

"I thought I would pop up to see how you are doing this morning." Sam, the ER nurse, was standing in the doorway. "It's that no-birth-control thing that gets you every time." She dropped into the chair next to Lilah's bed, her weariness from an all-night shift written on her face.

"No way!" Lilah said, in a sarcastic tone. "I feel like such an idiot. I did learn that in Health Ed when I was in junior high. I suppose it will sound really lame when I tell you it was only once."

"We hear it all the time—unfortunately that's all it takes."

"Yeah, I get that now. I knew it, but I guess I thought I would get lucky." Lilah tore a page from her sketchbook and handed it to Sam. "Here you are. I hope you like it." Lilah preferred to sketch in a comic book style reminiscent of Japanese Manga. Despite the character's big eyes and wispy hair, Sam was clearly recognizable as the girl in the picture.

"This is totally amazing. You even got my tatt right." She handed the paper back to Lilah. "Please sign it. I'm so definitely having this framed."

Lilah took the picture and scrawled her first name across the bottom.

"I love your tatt. I may use it on one of the characters in the graphic novel I'm working on. If that's okay with you?" She passed the picture back.

"I would be flattered if you did. I love it myself. Be sure and tell me when I can buy your book." She stood up and stretched. "I'm beat, so I'm heading off to bed. I'll check back tonight to see if you're still here, but I'm betting they'll send you home today. I took a peek at your chart. Looking good."

"You think so?" Lilah's face lit up. "Oh, my God, that would be awesome. I have to get back to work; I can't pay for this place. I keep seeing dollar signs multiplying on the wall."

"Good Morning, Lilah. How are you feeling?" Brid strode through the door, balancing two cups in one hand and carrying her purse and a white bakery bag in the other.

"Hi, Brid." As her boss deposited her purchases on the tray table at the end of the bed, Lilah tried to determine how mad Brid was at her. "This is Sam—the nurse who took care of me in the ER last night." Nodding her head toward Brid, she continued, "This is my boss, Brid Sheerin. She owns the Sheerin Gallery on Main Street."

"I love your window displays; they are so awesome. I'm sure I could never afford anything in your gallery, but I watch for your windows. It's exciting when you change them," Sam said. "Here, take this chair— I'm heading out. I need to get to bed before I fall asleep on my feet."

"You should come into the gallery; I would love to show you around. Not everything is expensive," Brid said. "Lilah has a huge hand in decorating the windows."

Nice of you to say Brid, but it's not true, Lilah thought. *You're the genius when it comes to the windows, not me.*

"It's lovely to meet you." Brid sat in the chair Sam had offered.

"Bye, Lilah. Take care of yourself. I have the card you gave me. I'll watch for your book." With that, Sam left, her clogs smacking the floor as she walked away.

"I brought you one of those chocolate croissants you like from La Boulangerie." Brid took the tops off the cups and extended them to Lilah. "Coffee or tea? I wasn't sure what you were drinking these days."

Lilah reached for the tea. "I'm kinda off coffee."

"Well, as you know, I prefer coffee in the morning, so that works for me." She handed the bakery bag to Lilah. "Here's your croissant."

The women sipped their drinks for a few moments without speaking. Lilah broke off a small piece of the pastry, played with it nervously, but didn't eat it.

Inspecting Lilah over the top of her cup, Brid asked, "Have you seen the doctor yet?"

"No, the nurse said the doctor would be in this morning to see me, but she hasn't come yet. I guess she usually shows up between eight-thirty and nine o'clock."

Brid glanced at her watch. "Shortly, then."

Again, they sat in silence, each attending to her drink. When Brid could no longer stand it, she put her cup down and leaned toward Lilah.

"What in God's name were you thinking? I mean, when, precisely, were you planning on telling me about this?"

"I didn't know for a couple of months," Lilah protested in a rush. "I'm never regular and I wasn't paying attention—I was drawing." *Brid should at least get that,* Lilah thought. "And then I thought I had the flu. When I realized it had been, like, three months, I took one of those tests . . . " She looked away from Brid, not wanting her see how close she was to tears. "I was going to tell you soon. I didn't expect to have to tell you like this."

"What about the child's father? Have you told him? Where is he, anyway?"

"There is no father—"

"Everyone has a father, Lilah. Including this baby you're having."

"It's my problem and I'll handle it."

Before Brid could respond, Dr. Harkey walked into the room.

"Good morning, Lilah. How're you feeling?"

Grateful for the interruption, Lilah instantly felt relief. She liked Dr. Harkey and the way she made you feel like she had things under control.

"I feel *fine.*" Lilah tried to sound her most convincing. She felt she had to get home to Moaki and back to work. "Can I go now?"

"Not quite so fast." Then, seeing the stricken look on her

patient's face, Marianne Harkey softened her tone. "Actually, there is good news. Your pressure is holding steady around 140-over-90. You definitely have gestational hypertension, but there's no sign of protein in your urine. And that means you have not progressed to pre-eclampsia." She hesitated, "Yet."

"And that's good?" The girl watched the doctor's face for clues. *She has to let me go home,* she thought.

"That's Christmas and your birthday wrapped up in one box." Dr. Harkey smiled briefly before she continued. "And that's the way I intend to keep it."

"We need you on bed-rest and a no-salt diet for the next seven weeks. Assuming you got pregnant when you said you did—and I think you're right, based on the size of the baby—that brings us to thirty-six weeks gestation. I'd really like to get you to that point. It doesn't thrill me to have to deliver a four-week preemie, but we can usually handle that, and, if need be, we can transport your baby to the NICU at Mary Hitchcock in Lebanon. We'll have to see how it goes. We have every reason to expect a healthy baby and mom when we're through this," she paused, "*if* you do what you're told."

"Why couldn't the baby stay here? I mean, what could go wrong?" Lilah asked, her voice betraying her fear.

"Let's not get ahead of ourselves. Some babies who are delivered early do have some problems that require a level of care we can't provide here," Dr. Harkey said.

"What kind of problems?" Lilah persisted.

"Let me worry about that for now," The doctor looked at her sternly, "You worry about staying calm and keeping your blood pressure down."

"Can you tell us what you mean by 'bed rest'? She lives by herself in a five-story walk-up." Brid asked anxiously.

Shut up, Brid! Lilah thought. *You are not helping things at all.*

The doctor's immediate reaction confirmed this.

"A five story walk-up is out of the question. She can't live alone. 'Bed rest' means she stays in bed, so she's going to need help." She looked down at Lilah, "You can get up to use the bathroom and shower, but that's it. Hopefully, if we are careful, your blood pressure will not get any worse. If it does, there are things I can do." The doctor sighed. "I'd prefer not to have to do them."

The tears Lilah had been holding at bay since being wheeled into the ER slipped past the wall she had thrown up against them.

"Oh, God. I don't freakin' believe this. A million people have babies, with no problems. I have no place I can go. I just want to go back to my own apartment."

"What about going home to Lewiston?" Brid asked. "Is that completely impossible? Surely, your family would help you ... " Brid stopped as she watched a shocked look cross Lilah's face.

"I have a solution I think will be a win-win for everybody. Would you like to hear it?"

None of the women, engrossed in their conversation, had noticed Neil Malone standing in the doorway. Awkwardly, under his arm, he carried a stuffed cat, hastily bought at the hospital gift shop. Walking over to the bed, Neil offered the cat to Lilah. "This guy is a stand-in for Mookie. Not as good, I realize, but I thought he might cheer you up."

Lilah's smile affirmed his thought.

"*Moa*-ki." Brid said, in a tone dripping with ice.

"What?" Neil asked, meeting her eyes for the first time since entering the room.

"*Moa*-ki," she repeated, with irritation. "The cat's name is pronounced 'Moa-ki.' Not 'Moo-kie,' like a cow."

Neil had been a lawyer too long not to know when to back away from an argument. Ignoring Brid, he focused on the doctor, who was addressing him.

"Good morning, Mr. Malone. I am all ears and I'm sure Lilah is, too. Let's hear it."

Lilah stroked the stuffed cat, murmuring her thanks and, watching Neil's face, realized something felt wrong between him and Brid.

"I spoke to Franny this morning," Neil said. "She thinks it makes sense for Lilah to stay with her until the baby's born–says she has lots of room. She's going to put a bed on the first floor so Lilah doesn't have to climb the stairs." He paused a moment and, hearing no objections, went on. "She promised to make sure Lilah follows her diet and stays off her feet. In return, we are hoping that Lilah can continue to work for both Brid and Franny, using her laptop from bed." He addressed his next question to the doctor, "Is that feasible?"

"She can try it. If things remain stable, I don't see why not." The doctor considered Lilah thoughtfully before continuing. "Keeping your job might actually lessen your stress level, so, sure, as long as your blood pressure stays where it is, I'm fine with it."

Lilah started to say something to Dr. Harkey, but spoke to Neil instead.

"Really? I mean, you talked to Franny and she said this was okay? I could stay there?"

"I just got off the phone with her. She said she was sorry she couldn't be here, but to let you know she would see you tonight, at the house."

Why? She doesn't even know me, Lilah thought, amazed that Franny was willing to take her in.

"I think she just wants to help. She's a nice person," Neil said. "So, can we take her home today?" he asked Dr. Harkey.

"I don't see why not; I'll write the orders." Dr. Harkey spoke to Lilah as if they were alone. "Now, listen to me. If you want to stay out of here, you will do exactly what I tell you. Stay off your feet, no salt, and try to stay calm. The best thing you can do is keep that baby safely where it is right now, because its life and yours are what's important. If you need another reason, you would not believe the cost of six or eight weeks in the NICU. I want to see you in my office this Friday, so call and make an appointment." She started for the door and stopped, adding, "I'm waiving my fees, so you don't need to worry about how you're going to pay me." She nodded to the group. "I hope you all have a good day."

Before Lilah could thank her, she was gone.

"Okay, ladies, we need to plan." Neither woman answered him.

How can I just move in with Franny? And what about Moaki? Lilah thought. Aloud, she asked, "What about my cat? Can she come with me?"

"Well, actually, no. Franny doesn't mind taking Moaki," Neil made a point of correctly pronouncing the cat's name as instructed, smiling at Brid as he did so, "but she's pretty sure her dogs won't like it. She said the last thing you need is to get stuck in the middle of a dog-and-cat fight. Definitely would not be good for the baby."

Neil hesitated for a minute, seeing the distress in her face. "So, I thought we could board her. I am sure we can find a good—"

"I'll take the bloody cat." Brid spoke for the first time since her murmured 'goodbye' to the doctor.

Lilah stared at her boss in amazement; Brid didn't do animals. "But you hate cats," she said.

"I never said I hated them. I don't want to live with them. But, as this is an emergency, I think the cat will prefer staying with me to being shut up in a kennel for the next seven weeks." She smiled at Lilah. "I have never abused an animal in my life and I don't intend to start with your cat. It's not as if it is forever. So stop worrying."

With a definite edge to her tone, she addressed Neil, "You seem to have this all figured out." She glanced at her watch. "I have thirty minutes to get over to the gallery and meet the temp the agency is sending over. Once I get her sorted, this afternoon, I can go over to Lilah's, pack up what she needs and pick up Moaki and drop her off at my flat. Will that suit you?"

Lilah watched Neil's face anxiously as he answered.

"Sure. I'll wait with Lilah and drive her up to Franny's when she's released. Brendan's already gone up there to get the room ready. He's invited us all for dinner. Once we get her settled, I'll head back to the office. I asked Erica to cancel my meetings today. Fortunately, I had no court appearances scheduled, so it was not a problem."

Brid indicated the sketch pad that Lilah held in her lap. "I need more coffee for this; I am going down to the café. While I am gone, make a list of everything you want me to bring from your apartment. Can I bring you anything back from the cafe?"

Starting her list, Lilah shook her head. "No, thanks." At least Brid would understand the art supplies she needed to continue her work.

"Can I buy you a cup of coffee?" Brid asked Neil.

"Thanks, I'll take you up on that." Neil followed her out of the room, telling Lilah, "We won't be long."

"I know you're annoyed, but I think things will work out fine," Neil said as he fell in step beside her. Brid made no response. "I would think you would be happy. This way she can continue to work on your online orders and your website. Didn't you tell me that was what you were worried about—the damn website? Am I not correct?"

"This morning when I stopped by the shop and saw Franny, I did my best to get her mind off Lilah and her problems and back on her own, which include getting her shop up and running smoothly. I thought I succeeded." Brid stopped abruptly and faced him, paying no attention to the curious looks she was getting from people walking past them. "So what the hell did you do? Call her up and tell her she had to act like Mother Teresa in her spare time?"

"It might interest you to know that *Franny* called *me*, after she first called Brendan, who happens by chance to have today off. She told him to come get her keys so he could go set up a bed in the room Drew used as a study. My job was to invite Lilah and to break the news to you. For some reason Franny seemed to think you were not going to be happy about any of this. I told her I couldn't imagine why—it was a perfectly logical solution to a number of problems for all three of you." Neil lowered his voice and spaced his words carefully. "And I cannot for the life of me fathom what you are so upset about. Franny obviously knows you far better than I do."

Brid glared at him.

"Well, let me make it perfectly clear to you: I care about Franny MacCullough. She is my friend. The last thing—the *very* last thing—I want is to see her revert back to the woman she was when that bastard died. I believe involving herself with Lilah and this baby has a great chance of making her do exactly that." She hesitated for a moment and then, making up her mind, continued, "And, unlike you, I do not need to find myself some off-the-shelf daughter and grandchild because I have suddenly been struck with the realization that I will never have my own."

Neil flushed scarlet, the color racing up his neck and face and bleeding into his hairline. He opened his mouth and then shut it. Turning on his heel, he headed back the way they had just come. After a few paces, he stopped and faced her.

"This conversation is over. Tell Lilah I stepped out to make a call. I'll come back upstairs when I am finished. Maybe I'll see you at Franny's later. Or, maybe I won't."

He didn't wait for Brid's reply, but set off rapidly down the hall and away from her.

KATHLEEN FERRARI

CHAPTER SIX

The smell of Brendan's fabled spaghetti sauce simmering on the stove greeted Franny as she pushed her way into her kitchen, hugging two shopping bags and a bouquet of spring flowers in her arms.

"That smells wonderful. I'm starving." She deposited her load on the kitchen counter. "How are things going? Will that room work out okay, do you think?"

Brendan began filling a white ironstone pitcher with water. "Looks like it should. The bed fits in there fine. She's been online most of the afternoon. She said she was hunting for more dolls. Neil went to his office. He said he'd be back for dinner." Putting the flowers in the pitcher, he asked, "Where do you want these? Kitchen table?"

"Oh, no. I bought them for Lilah. That room is so masculine; I thought these would brighten it up. I'll go in and say hello and then I'll come back and help you. Thanks for putting them in water." She picked up the flowers. "You never cease to amaze me. My sister should snap you up."

Returning to chopping tomatoes for his salad, Brendan snorted with laughter. "I doubt Sofia would agree with you. I don't think she has any plans to do any snapping. She thinks I am way too controlling—at least when it comes to the subject of food." He pointed at himself. "Me, too controlling? She should look in the mirror."

"Then, she's an idiot." Franny shook her head. "Let me check on Lilah. Back in minute."

"Take your time. Everything is under control here. But we are going to have to talk about this no-salt thing. It's going to be tough."

Carrying the flowers in front of her, Franny made her way toward the room at the back of the house where Lilah had been set up, a self-contained suite that probably had been designed for either a nanny or an in-law. It had an attached bathroom complete with walk-in shower, making it perfect for its current use. Drew had appropriated the suite for himself as an office hideaway and grandly referred to it as his 'study.' Franny had rarely ventured in while Drew was alive and had ignored the room completely since his death, leaving it for her cleaning lady to deal with. She paused in the doorway to watch Lilah, who was focused on the laptop balanced on several throw pillows in front of her. The dogs, sprawled near the bed, announced Franny's presence by getting up and going to greet her.

"I was wondering where you two had gotten to. I take it you've forgotten that you even *have* a mom." Lucy's sturdy Lab tail beat back and forth, denying Franny's words, and Oliver grinned at her as if to say, "Whataya mean? I'm right here, at your service."

Lilah looked up as Franny placed the flowers on the table next to her bed. "Like they ever would. Those are pretty," she said, nodding at the flowers.

"It's so dark in here I thought they would brighten the room up. I have a pretty guest room upstairs, but we thought it would be better to have you on the first floor."

"Are you kidding? *Really*? I love this room. The colors are great." She looked at Franny. "Oh, I get it. You think that because I'm preggo I've gone all pastels? *Bor-ing!*"

Lilah laughed and Franny realized that she couldn't remember the last time she had heard her laugh. *Poor kid must have been drowning in worry*, Franny thought.

"Never happen; sorry to disappoint you," Lilah declared. "I'm a dark and brooding kind of girl." She settled back into more pillows that Brendan had pilfered from the family room couch. "Did you decorate this room? I really like it. I think I'm going to have to snatch that TV when I leave." She nodded toward the 52-inch flat-screen television on the wall.

"Not me. This was Drew's study. He had a clear vision of what he wanted—something masculine and very comfortable." The walls were painted a dark green accented with a light mocha trim. A deep burgundy Bidjar Persian rug covered the hardwood floor. Two leather recliners disguised as wing chairs were positioned to watch the television. "I guess he succeeded, didn't he?"

Ignoring the question, Lilah jerked her head toward a portrait of a young woman on the wall opposite the desk. "So, what's up with that?"

Franny flushed. She had forgotten about the painting. The hanging of the watercolor was a painful memory for her; she and Drew had fought bitterly over it. *Funny*, she thought, looking at it now, *how life changes*.

"It's Brid, isn't it?" Lilah waited for an explanation.

Franny realized Lilah sensed there was a story behind the watercolor.

"Yes." Franny pushed one of the leather chairs close to the bed and wearily dropped into it. "She painted it for Drew as a gift while they were married. I can't remember why, although he told me. His birthday, maybe? You can ask her. He insisted on hanging it in here."

She had begged him not to, but he had brushed off her objections, telling her that she never had to look at it. It was probably the reason she had always avoided this room.

Lilah cocked her head and evaluated the likeness. "Self-portraits are tough. Artists tend to make themselves look better or worse than they actually are. Knowing Brid, I bet she was prettier than that, especially when she was younger."

Franny stared at it, too. "You may be right. But *I* think she was gorgeous then and she's gorgeous now."

She turned away from the portrait to face Lilah.

"How are *you* doing? Are you okay with all this?" She opened her arms to include the room. "I mean, we practically kidnapped you and carried you off."

Lilah hugged herself for a minute before answering.

"I really just wanted to go home, you know? I guess I mean back to before, when I was the only one who knew about the baby." She stopped, blinking back tears. "But that Stormtrooper doctor was not going to let me out of Saint Luke's if I didn't have a place to go." She rolled her eyes. "I had to get out of there. I would be paying Neil back for the rest of my *life*. I'm so grateful to all of you for everything you've done for me. So this is cool, and I can still do my work for you and Brid. Hey, how did today go? Tell me everything."

Franny pressed the button that activated the footrest and sighed as the chair reclined.

"I am so tired, but it was such a great day." She reached into her pocket and handed Lilah her phone. "Check out the color of the balloons. Isn't it perfect?" She knew Lilah would like it.

Franny had wanted traditional nursery colors for the shop: pinks, blues and yellows in the palest of shades. Lilah had argued against the pastels, urging Franny to go with cream-colored walls accented by what Lilah called "a color with something to say." They had settled on the deep pink, a choice that had immediately won Brid's approval. Her reaction had been: "I like it. This is not a shop for children. That pink is a grown-up color. It definitely sets the tone."

Franny watched Lilah scroll through the pictures, enjoying the girl's exclamations of approval.

"Oh my God! Look at the cupcakes! The color of the frosting is perfect." She grinned at Franny. "Mara is totally awesome. She's an artist herself the way she decorates her pastries. How did they taste? I don't suppose you snagged one for me?"

"Are you kidding? I couldn't keep them on the plate. I had to call Mara at lunch and beg; she made me more for the afternoon. I didn't even dare take one." Franny smiled, remembering the way her customers had hovered over the mini-cupcakes before deciding to indulge. "I think people eat them because they're so small. You can convince yourself that they don't count." *I do it all the time*, she thought.

"But did you sell anything? Or were people only there to snoop around and eat free cupcakes?"

"Oh yes, people bought much more than I thought they would.

I was so excited. I have a list in my purse of what we sold, but wait until you hear this: all the Ginny dolls sold by noon. I couldn't believe it." It had been so much fun watching some of the customers' faces light up when their eyes settled on a certain doll. "We have to find more Ginnys, so can you work on that?"

"I bought four more on eBay today and I am debating on a fifth. The doll is kind of beat up, but the seller is asking almost nothing for her and I know how much you like a lost cause. I knew those Ginny dolls would go fast." She said smugly. "It's because they're small and you can slip them into your house and just say, 'Oh, yeah, she's not a big deal.' I think these dolls are like crack to some people. You should see the comments on the websites I visit."

"You already found more? You're wonderful. Definitely get the battered one. I hate to see any doll get tossed out."

Lilah typed something into the laptop and then looked up.

"I think you should pick a doll—one of the good ones—and raffle her off. We can put her in the window to get people's attention. They'll have to come into the shop to buy the raffle ticket. I'll also put it on the Foundlings' Facebook page and on the website. We need to get people into the store. People love to gamble." Lilah stroked the stuffed cat Neil had given her that morning as she thought about her idea. "And we can say that the proceeds from the raffle go to the Boys & Girls Club or some do-goody thing like that."

"What a great idea! It helps tie the Foundlings into what's going on in Lynton."

Brid came into the room carrying a stack of books. Her eyes took in the room before settling on Lilah. "It looks like you are happily ensconced. How are you feeling?"

Lilah sighed, "I keep trying to tell everyone. I feel fine."

"I brought you some stuff from your apartment." She deposited the books on the bed. "I thought you might want these."

"My art books! Thanks, Brid. You're awesome. About the only good thing I can think of coming out of this is that I should be able to get some work done on my sketches."

"And the baby—don't forget the baby! He or she will also come out of this." Franny looked from one stony-faced woman to the other. "Oh, you guys! Just wait: you are both going to fall in love." Before either Brid or Lilah could reply, there was a tentative knock on the door.

"Okay to come in?" Neil stood in the doorway, carrying a canvas shopping bag and suitcase containing Lilah's clothes. Arriving at the same time as Brid, he had insisted on bringing them in from her car. "Brendan said to tell you dinner is ready. We're just waiting for Sofia."

"I can't think why," Brid said. "She never eats anything."

"Oh, no. Dinner's ready? I told him, I would be right back to help and I've been in here sitting on my butt. Doesn't it smell wonderful? No Irishman should be able to make spaghetti sauce that tastes like Brendan's does. There should be a law against it."

"I hope they wait until after we eat to start enforcing it. I'm starving." Neil quipped. "Where do you want me to put these things?"

"Just leave them there on the floor by the bed. I'll put them away later." Franny said and then asked Lilah. "Unless there is something you need right now?"

Lilah shook her head and asked Brid, "Did you get Moaki? Is she okay?"

"Yes, I brought her over to my condo. The damn little púca is acting like she owns the place."

Relieved, Lilah asked, "Okay, so what's a púca?"

"A púca is a Halloween imp who makes mischief. And, by God, that's what she is. She runs around like she's hell-bent." At the sight of Lilah's woebegone face, Brid relented. "Well, she can't really be a púca, because Irish cats who are named that are always black."

When Lilah made no response, Brid lost her temper.

"Holy Mother of God, that cat is handling this better than any of us! She has a roof over her head, plenty of food and water and a clean litter box. She has even found a place to plant herself: when I left, she was sprawled in the bay window eying the birds in the feeder on the patio. She is *fine!*"

Brendan appeared in the door, carrying a food-laden bed tray. "I hope you're hungry. Here's your dinner." Franny removed the open laptop, so he could place the tray in front of Lilah.

Lilah stared at the plate: broiled chicken breast, baked sweet potato, steamed green beans and broccoli. She looked from her dinner to Brendan and back again.

"I thought you were making spaghetti and meatballs. I know I've smelled spaghetti sauce cooking all afternoon. And garlic bread. I smell garlic bread. What is this? No way am I eating all these vegetables."

With more than a hint of impatience, Brendan said, "Listen, Lilah—"

Trying her best to be diplomatic, Franny interrupted him, "Lilah, you can't have spaghetti sauce or meatballs. There's too much salt in those dishes. Dr. Harkey said 'no salt.' It makes your blood pressure go up."

Sounding like a sullen teenager, Lilah said, "Look at this potato; it's *orange*! I don't —"

"That son of a bitch!" Brid exclaimed. "I don't believe my eyes. Although no one knows better than I what that bastard was capable of." She stood before the portrait Lilah had admired earlier, having discovered it on the wall. "What in the name of God and His angels is *this* doing here?"

"Drew hung it there. He —" Franny began tentatively.

"What is wrong with you?" Brid, hands on her hips, thundered at Franny. "Did it not ever, even *once*, occur to you to tell that bastard to go feck himself? You don't let your husband decorate his man-cave—or whatever the hell this is—with a portrait of his ex-wife." She reached up and snatched it off the wall.

"Calm down, Brid. The picture is actually Franny's now and if she wants it ... " Neil stopped, seeing the look on Brid's face.

"Need I remind you that I wanted this picture at the time of the divorce, and you were supposed to get it for me. And you did not," Brid accused him.

"What I remember, *clearly*," Neil emphasized the last word as the others watched the sparring in awed silence, "is that Drew flatly refused to give it to you. Did you expect me to fight him for it?"

He and Brid glared at one another as she clutched the portrait between them.

"It is mine now. And I am taking it home with me." Finished with Neil, she told Franny, "I will replace it with something of equal value, which, come to think of it, is not much." Taking a deep breath she continued, "Let's eat. I am famished."

No one dared to argue with her.

With the painting tucked under her arm, she started toward the door, and then stopped. She said to Lilah.

"And you stop complaining and eat your dinner. You got yourself into this mess and now the least you can do is make sure that baby is born healthy." Holding her head high, she stalked out of the room, leaving the others to follow in her wake.

They found Sofia in the kitchen, peering disapprovingly into pots on the stove. "I hope there is at least a salad," she sniffed.

Arranging themselves around the kitchen table, the five focused on the steaming dishes of pasta Brendan called "Feeney's Finest Spaghetti." Even Sofia couldn't completely resist it. For a few minutes, the only sound in the room was that of cutlery doing its job, as everyone ate their dinner in a contented silence.

Neil leaned back in his chair. "This, my friend, is the best spaghetti I have ever eaten." He looked at Franny and grinned. "Sorry, Franny, but it is."

She laughed. "Don't apologize to me; I agree with you. It's definitely better than our sacred family recipe. Don't you think so, Sofia?"

Her sister looked up from the small helping of meatball-less pasta she'd placed on her bread plate. Her pasta bowl was filled with salad.

"If you mean those hockey pucks that Mom passes off as meatballs, then, yes, Brendan is an awesome cook."

"So how did a guy named Feeney learn to cook Italian food?" Neil asked, reaching for the garlic bread.

"My college roommate was Italian. I spent a lot of weekends with him. His grandmother lived with the family and, man, could she cook. This is her sauce, or, as she always called it, 'gravy.' "

"How did it go today?" Neil asked Franny.

"Excellent. I sold all the Ginnys and four of the large Madame Alexanders. Everyone who came in seemed to love the shop."

"How many customers did you have?" Sofia asked.

"I think about thirty-five," Franny said. "I know we sold twelve dolls."

"I would consider that a good start. Traffic will continue to build," Brid said. "I've got to get going. I have to check on the damn cat and I have some emails to answer tonight." She stood up and carried her dishes to the sink, rinsed them and tucked them into the dishwasher. "I'm going to say goodbye to Lilah and then I am out of here."

As soon as Brid was out of earshot, Sofia hissed, "What is her problem? I mean, she's always a bitch, but tonight she outdid herself. I could hear that whole argument over the portrait from the kitchen." She asked Franny, "You're not really going to let her take it are you? That picture was Drew's and he left it to you."

Franny sighed. "Sometimes I don't understand you. She painted that picture and, in case you've forgotten, it's of her." Franny glanced away from Sofia before adding, "Anyway, Brid's right. I never wanted it in this house. And you know that." She swallowed, remembering the heated argument she and Drew had had over the picture. "Drew's the one who insisted on hanging it in there."

"What do you suggest we do, Sofia?" Neil said, coming to the rescue, as he realized the effort required for Franny to argue with her sister had fizzled. "Wrestle it away from her?"

Before Sofia could answer, Brid returned, carrying the tray, which she placed on the counter next to the sink. "She's asleep. I logged her out of the laptop and shut off the light." Slipping her jacket on, she added softly, almost to herself, "I hope this was not a huge mistake."

"How can it be a mistake?" Franny locked eyes with Brid, feeling a rare annoyance with her. "Lilah is one of us and she needed our help."

Picking up her tote bag and the portrait, Brid headed toward the door. "Well, I hope you are right." She smiled at Brendan. "Thank you for dinner. It was a treat. My Irish genes rebel when I attempt to cook Italian food—which is unfortunate, because I love it."

"Anytime." Brendan said.

"Hold on. I'll come with you." Neil started to pick up his plate, when Franny stopped him.

"I'll get that," she said, not missing Brid's look of disgust as she did so. "You've done more than enough today."

Handing her his dish, Neil laughed. "It was a light day for me.

Comes from being the boss. I just sit around and attempt to look busy. I don't really do anything in there." Then, before Sofia could correct his claim, he added, "I was glad to help."

He opened the door for Brid and they both said good-bye. Franny anxiously watched them leave, not exactly sure what was making her feel so uneasy.

As soon as the door closed behind them, Sofia was up, hurriedly positioning herself behind the curtain to the left of the wide, multi-paned window that faced the street.

"This is not going to be good," she said, a hint of excitement in her voice.

"What do you mean?" Franny asked, joining her at the window.

"Neil's pissed. Couldn't you tell? He almost never loses his temper, but when he does, watch out."

Although the Chiesa sisters could not hear what was being said, they watched as an obviously heated argument, bordering on a brawl, unfolded in front of them in the driveway. Brid had carefully placed the portrait on the front seat of her Jeep, then hurled the tote bag in after it and slammed the door. She whirled to face Neil, her face blazing with high color. They were both shouting but the eavesdroppers in the kitchen could not make out what they were saying. For a moment, Franny was sure Brid was going to slap him.

Neil jabbed angrily around in his coat pocket. Finding the key ring he was looking for, he struggled to remove a single key, cursing as he did so. Grabbing Brid's hand, he deposited the key in her palm and closed her fingers around it. Turning his back on her, he marched to his car, parked behind hers in the driveway, got in, reversed into the street and drove off with tires squealing.

"Was that Brid leaving?" Brendan, busy scouring pots at the sink, his back to the window, could not see what had happened in front of the house.

"Neil. Not Brid." Franny said.

"No shit!" Still holding a pot, Brendan joined them at the window, where the three watched Brid slowly get in the Jeep and drive away.

"I hope they broke up." Sofia took a sip from the Diet Coke in her hand and then added, "She was never good enough for him."

"Shut up, Sofia." Franny and Brendan said together.

CHAPTER SEVEN

"Please answer," Brid said softly to herself.

It was not quite a prayer, but as close as she came to saying one these days. Brid clutched her phone as she waited for the call to connect.

"Dr. Deluca. How can I help you?"

"I am standing in the state liquor store at Exit 6. I have a bottle of Jameson single malt in my hand." She examined the bottle. It had not changed since the last time she held one. It felt good. It made her feel like she had come home.

"Put the bottle down, turn around, and start walking toward the door."

Despite the terror she felt, Brid almost started to laugh. Trust the doctor to remain calm, even if, in her own mind, making this call did signify the end of the world to Brid. Obediently, she put the bottle back on the shelf, feeling a pang of regret as she did so. She started walking toward the automatic doors leading to the parking lot.

"Are you moving?"

"Yes." Brid concentrated on doing exactly that, her eyes focused on her black leather boots marching purposefully across the speckled-tile floor, one determined step at a time.

"Good. So am I. I will meet you in fifteen minutes. Are you in the car yet?"

"Yes." Brid slid across the cracked leather seat, slammed the door shut, and hugged herself in an effort to stop shaking before starting the car. "I am just turning the key now."

"Good. Lock the doors."

Brid laughed, realizing she must sound slightly demented. "I can't lock the doors; the locks don't work." *Would I be locking myself in, or the Jameson out?* she wondered.

"Oh, for God's sake! When are you going to buy a new car? That damn Jeep deserves to be pronounced dead." The doctor's disgusted voice came through the speaker of the cell phone on the seat beside her.

Maybe so, Brid thought, *but this old car can still move when I need it to.* She was flying up the highway now—away, away from the best Mr. Jameson had to offer her tonight.

"Where am I going, then?" she asked,

"The Dunkin' Donuts at exit eight," the doctor calmly ordered. "I should be there at almost the same time you arrive. I am in Hiram's Forge—getting on the highway now. I just delivered the sweetest little foal. When you get there, order a large black coffee and don't let go of it."

Eleven minutes later, Brid steered the Jeep into the deserted parking lot. It was after eight o'clock; not a popular time for coffee and donuts. She ordered the black coffee, as instructed, and carried it to a corner table with a good view of the parking lot. Within minutes, a silver Toyota truck careened into the entrance and stopped abruptly. It seemed as if the driver was inside the coffee shop and striding toward her before Brid heard the truck door slam shut.

It was not the first time Brid realized that Georgia Deluca eclipsed any space she entered. It was the way she carried herself, with her aura of complete confidence. More times than Brid could count, the two of them had been someplace together when a stranger had approached them, certain that Georgia must be 'someone,' only to listen to Georgia graciously explain that she was not. Tall and lissome, with silver hair that defied coloring carelessly piled on top of her head and clasped in a silver hair clip, Georgia had once been a very pretty girl. Life had melted the soft roundness from her face and emphasized her high cheekbones and cornflower blue eyes, surrounded now by a web of fine lines. At sixty-six, she was stunning, even dressed as she was, in a strange mixture of debutante and derelict.

Georgia wore threadbare jeans and scuffed brown boots that looked like they had recently walked through a barn. Her twill corduroy-collared jacket, once blue, was faded to a soft slate gray. Diamond studs—not small ones—glittered in her ears; her mother's pearls adorned her neck. She always wore them. "So that I remember where I came from," she had told Brid during one of the long nights they had spent together, fighting their separate demons.

Sliding into the seat across from her, Georgia reached over to cover Brid's hands, still clutching the coffee cup, with her own.

"I have a cat," Brid said, and promptly burst into tears.

"And that drove you to drink? A dog I would understand, but a cat? Actually, if you think about it, you have a lot in common with cats."

Swiping at her tears, Brid was startled. "What do you mean, I have a lot in common with cats? I hate the damn things, as you very well know." Sometimes it amazed Brid that their friendship had endured with such depth, considering their jarring disconnect—Georgia's passion and her indifference— regarding animals.

"Cats are smart, aloof, independent, inquisitive, have great balance and can take care of themselves." Georgia paused, taking inventory of the woman sitting across from her. "Much more so than dogs, cats are survivors—hence the 'nine lives' nonsense. Sound like anyone you know?"

"Oh, that description fits me precisely, to be sure," Brid said. "Certainly the part about being smart. I've made such a brilliant mess of my life."

"Tell me what really happened." Georgia looked at her intently. "I know it's not the damn cat, although I admit I am curious as to how you, of all people, have ended up with one."

"Neil doesn't want to see me anymore." Feeling her eyes flood with tears again, Brid looked away. *Dear God and His angels, I have to stop this weeping.* She was not a weeper, never had been. "He threw my key in my face."

"Oh, Miss Brid. No, he did not."

Georgia had been living in the North for almost forty years. Her Miss-Mary-Georgia-Hicks, old-Virginia background rarely made its presence known these days. That it had now was a sign of how rattled she was; Brid took note.

This last week had had a nightmare quality that Brid was trying to avoid even thinking about, much less describing. The simplest explanation, she decided, would be to start with Lilah.

"Lilah has managed to get herself pregnant."

"Lilah? Who is Lilah?"

"The girl who works for me in the gallery. She has that horrible snake tattoo on her leg."

"Oh. Right." Georgia shivered. She was not a fan of snakes. "I'm surprised. Bright girl, isn't she? Oh well, as we both know, girls do that. Get pregnant, I mean."

Brid snorted. "She certainly has." It still rankled that Lilah had not told her sooner about the pregnancy. "The baby is due in about eleven weeks. They want to make sure Lilah stays pregnant for at least seven more." She took a sip of her coffee and made a face; it was cold. "We appear to have bonded together into a village of misfits to take care of her."

"Go on." Georgia waited.

"There are complications. She has this condition called gestational hypertension. Do you know what that is?"

"Yes. It's serious. It has to be treated aggressively."

"So Franny—of course, it would be Franny—has tucked the girl firmly under her wing. Today, she and Brendan moved Lilah into the room Drew used for his study." Her voice shook. For God's sake, she was not going to start crying again. She was *not*. "Neil is in his glory."

Georgia frowned. "What do you mean, 'in his glory'? What's he doing?"

"I'll tell you what he's doing," Brid said, her voice dripping with sarcasm, "he's running around acting like he is the girl's father, and he is not."

"Now it's all starting to make sense. I gather you found this threatening in some way?"

"Yesterday, the nurse at the hospital thought I was her mother!"

Brid protested. "Really? That's hilarious. You must have almost had a stroke yourself." Georgia started to laugh, but stopped when she realized Brid was not.

"My God, don't you see? It's what Neil *wants*—what he has always wanted—a nice, Catholic family, the kind that lines up in the pew at Easter with the boys in their blue jackets and bow ties and the girls in matching plaid dresses." Her voice broke again. She bit her lip to regain control.

"I don't think they do that anymore. And how would you know, anyway? When was the last time you were in a church at Easter?"

"Maybe they don't, but trust me, I do know this: if Neil had children, his would do that. And I knew from the start he was that kind of man." She slapped her hand on the table. "I knew it and, still, I let myself get involved with him."

"Maybe, but none of this explains why he broke up with you. There's something you aren't telling me. Go back to the part where he threw your key in your face—which I can't see him doing. He's too much of a gentleman."

"How would you know?" Brid said with exasperation. "You have met him *once* and all you talked about was football." She recalled the small dinner party she had hosted in early December, attended by Georgia, Franny and Neil.

Georgia remembered it, too. Usually guarded around men, she had been drawn to Neil from the start. They'd spent the evening chattering away about the Army-Navy game that had been played earlier in the day.

"Which was all it took for me to see that he was not the kind of man who would throw your key in your face. At least, not without extreme provocation." She paused, "I know the type."

Brid blinked. The women had known each other for fourteen years. Having met in Alcoholics Anonymous, they also knew each other's secrets. Georgia could only mean she was putting Neil in the same class as her late husband. Brid was stunned. She had never heard Georgia compare any man favorably with Rob Deluca.

At Brid's silence, Georgia continued. "So, exactly how did you provoke him? If you don't mind my asking?"

"I didn't do a thing, I ... "

Georgia waited, pointedly saying nothing, as Brid paused.

"I told him he was acting like a pathetic fool, which he has been."

Georgia kept her silence.

Brid's voice dropped almost to a whisper.

"I told him I was all wrong for him, that he should find some nice, Catholic woman who taught CCD and could still have babies, because he so clearly wants one." She frowned at Georgia. "It *is* what he wants." A sob caught in her throat. "I told him I didn't care if I ever saw him again." Tears streamed down her face. "What am I going to do? I think I might love him. I can't bear the thought of not having him in my life. But I can never give him those things, and you and I both know it."

"The first thing you are going to do is continue to stay sober." Georgia became again what she had first been to Brid before they had become friends—her AA sponsor. "You tell me how you plan on doing that."

Georgia, you can be so bloody intractable, thought Brid. *And thank God, because it might get me out of this mess.* "Go to meetings, eat right, exercise, get enough sleep, call you twice a day or more if I need to, avoid stress." She recited the mantra of recovery by rote.

"And?" Georgia folded her arms across her chest.

"Go to more meetings." Brid looked at her defiantly. "Which I don't have time for now, with Lilah no longer available to work in the gallery."

"Tough. Close the place for an hour." Georgia pushed her chair back. "You will lose it all anyway if you start hitting the bottle again." She stood up. "Come on, let's go. There's a Step Meeting at St. John's tonight. We can catch the end of it, if we hurry. You can drop your Jeep off and ride with me."

Brid followed the silver truck out of the parking lot and back to Lynton, where Georgia waited while she parked her car in front of her condo.

She tried to read Georgia's face as she buckled her seat belt, but couldn't get past the serene expression. Sometimes, Georgia could be an enigma; it was annoying.

"Wretched, disgusting beast," Brid said, swiping at the back of her neck, where Georgia's greyhound, lost in the shadows behind her, had just planted a wet kiss. "I should have known Gussie was here somewhere. Sit down, Gussie. I adore you, too."

Smiling a goofy greyhound grin, the dog settled back on the rear seat, satisfied that she had gotten Brid's attention.

"Do you never go anywhere without her?"

Georgia ignored the question, because, of course, Brid already knew the answer: Gussie was her shadow.

"Gussie must have heard you have somehow acquired a cat. She's probably just commiserating with you because she also lives under feline law."

"Is that what that moth-eaten pile of fur you allow to shed all over your furniture is? A cat?"

"You know very well General Armistead is a cat. And Ragdoll cats are *reduced* shedders," Georgia said, automatically coming to the cat's defense. "He's a bit past his prime, I'll grant you, but then so am I."

Georgia and her animals, Brid fumed to herself. It's a wonder she doesn't keep ducks in the bath.

Georgia went on. "How did you end up the lucky owner of a cat? Did you find the cat or did the cat find you?"

"Owner?" Brid retorted, horrified at the thought. "Who said I was her owner? The foolish cat is Lilah's. Franny didn't think her menagerie could tolerate another addition, so I said I would take Moaki until Lilah is sorted out. I think of the cat as *visiting*. But she's taken over the place like she's the bloody Queen of England."

"Well, I think it's a great idea. I should have thought of it myself." Georgia briefly took her eyes of the road to stare directly at Brid. "You need something in your life to love," she paused, "especially now."

Brid didn't reply, watching as the familiar spire of St. John's came into view. Georgia parked the truck under a light in the church's lot. She made no move to open the door. Instead, her eyes locked with Brid's. There was no trace of old Virginia in her voice now.

"Tonight was bad. But you called me, which was the right thing to do. And you didn't slip, but it was too close." She hesitated, deciding how much more to say. "You don't want to start drinking after being sober for this long. The climb back is too hard." Her eyes slid away from Brid's. "I know."

Instinctively reaching for Georgia's hand, Brid thought she saw a hint of tears.

"You know what to do," Georgia continued, "you just need to keep doing it. Focus on staying sober, and you will." She released the latch on the door. "And one more thing. You need to get this into that thick Irish head of yours: Neil Malone is not Drew MacCullough."

Before Brid could open her mouth to protest, Georgia silenced her by adding, "And he's not your father, either."

CHAPTER EIGHT

A flash of red outside the window caught Franny's attention. She was at the door in less than a minute, but the boy was gone, the silver bike he rode streaking south on Main Street. It was the third time this week she had noticed him peering in the window, his red bike helmet pulled down low and shading his face. Each time he had shown up around three o'clock. She guessed he was on his way home from school.

"What's wrong? You look upset," Neil asked, coming up behind her.

Franny spun around to face him. "Oh my God! You scared me!"

"I'm sorry. You were a million miles away. What's wrong?"

"Did you see that kid on the silver bike who was just looking in the window?"

Neil peered down Main Street in the direction she had been facing. "No, I wasn't paying any attention. Was he bothering you?" His eyes searched the front of the building. "Did he do something?"

"I don't think so," she said. "But this is the third time I've seen him staring in the window. He looks to be about ten, but I could be wrong. I don't know much about boys." She bit her lip, remembering her lost son. "What could he possibly want here? Boys could care less about dolls, right? I wonder if he's in some kind of trouble."

"I know a lot about ten-year-old boys. I was one. I used to race around this city on a bike, too. Usually up to no good." He shook his head. "God, it doesn't seem possible that that was more than forty years ago." His expression changed. "I'll bet he's planning something. Hopefully, it's nothing worse than soaping the windows or writing 'Fuck You' on the side of the building. Funny how times change. When I was ten, I knew that word, but I was damned careful to keep it to myself. My father would have killed me if he ever heard it come out of my mouth. And I'm not talking about one of these time-outs parents are so fond of now. You let me know if that boy continues to bother you and I'll deal with it."

Franny took a good look at Neil. It has been six weeks since the night of what Sofia insisted on calling "The Fight Scene." He looked terrible: his face was drawn and he appeared to have lost weight. He looked, she realized with a start, the way he had in the weeks following Drew's death.

"I'm sure he's only curious. Maybe his mother is into dolls." She took his arm. "Come on in. I'll buy you a cup of coffee."

Inside the shop, Neil slowly looked around, admiring what he saw, particularly something Franny had added: a white wicker Victorian rocking chair with Raggedy Ann and Andy perched next to each other on the wide seat. The dolls were her own and not for sale, but she enjoyed having them in the shop.

"I had one of these guys." Neil said, picking up the Raggedy Andy. He replaced the doll in the chair. "How's business?"

Franny looked up from the coffeemaker "Business is pretty good, considering the economy. Right now, I am the new kid on the block, so I get a lot of walk-ins, but that will change. Brid told me eventually things slow down. That's when I'll know if we have a chance of succeeding—if people keep coming back. I'm not in the red, but only because I don't pay myself." Franny reached for the bag of ground coffee *thinking, I should pay Lilah more.* "Lilah has been amazing, nosing out dolls for great prices. I think she views searching for dolls for our inventory as a quest—the kind of quest she writes about in her stories."

About to open the coffee, she hesitated. Seeing the electric kettle she kept filled with water sitting next to the coffee maker, she had a better thought. "You probably would prefer tea, wouldn't you?"

"I'd love a cup of tea, if you have it."

"Tea I have, for sure. It's mugs I don't have." She flipped the kettle's switch. Once the water began to boil, she made tea in a green pottery teapot. Handing Neil a delicate, flower-splashed, bone china teacup, she said, "You'll have to make do with this."

He laughed, even though she could see it was an effort for him. Taking the cup from her hand, he said, "I'll try not to break it."

"No worries. I pick them up at the Goodwill Store for next to nothing. Our mothers collected these and now we can't wait to dump them. But I think they go with the shop and I like being able to offer my customers a cup of coffee or tea." She paused to pour herself a cup. "You can get some great stuff at Goodwill—another find I owe to Lilah. I'm ashamed to admit it, but before she took me there, I had never been inside. I only went as far as the donation box outside." She wrinkled her face. "Funny, really, when you remember Drew and I loved to go antiquing. I guess we were too snobby to go to Goodwill."

Neil laughed, "I don't know about you, but he certainly was. His mother not only never stepped foot in the place, she probably had the housekeeper drop the stuff off." He put the cup down on top of the display case. "I came by to see if you would have dinner with me; I have something I want to talk to you about."

"I'd love to, but I can't. I have to get home to fix Lilah dinner."

"All taken care of. I asked Sofia if she and Brendan could bring dinner up there and she said she would be happy to. It turns out that she and Lilah both watch the same show on Thursday nights."

"Amazing to think that Sofia and Lilah have anything in common, but they both love that detective show. She and Lilah actually get along pretty well."

"Would you mind, then, if it was also an early dinner?" Neil said. "There's something I want to do afterwards."

"Not at all I like eating early. Where did you want to meet? Craic?" The minute the words left her mouth, she realized it would not be Ceol agus Craic—Neil would not want to run into Desmond Sheerin. She was not surprised to see a shadow cross his face. No, it would definitely not be Craic.

"I'm in the mood for lasagna. Nobody makes it better than Nona's. I thought we'd go there. Okay with you?"

"Are you kidding? I never turn down dinner at Nona's. I will have to steal the points from somewhere, but I'm in."

"Points?"

Franny shook her head. "It's a Weight Watchers thing. Be glad you don't have to know."

"Maybe you can tell me all about it over dinner. I could stand to lose a few pounds."

She studied him more closely. "I think you have lost weight since the last time I saw you. Are you feeling okay?"

"Time to get some glasses, Franny. It happens to us all—the eyes go as we get older." Neil's mask was back in place. "You close at five, right?" He looked around for the sign listing the shop hours. "Shall I pick you up?"

"I'll meet you there at 5:15. If I walk over, I can earn a couple of points and eat more."

"You really will have to explain this point thing. It sounds like advanced math to me. I'll see you at Nona's at 5:15."

Franny thought he seemed less morose as he headed out the door.

Then he stopped, adding, "Thanks, Franny."

Franny was in the workroom behind the main shop, opening a Fed-Ex shipment from the doll hospital in North Carolina, when the bell jangled. Returning to the front of the shop, she was amazed to find Elaine MacCullough waiting.

In that moment of surprise, Franny wondered: Was Elaine still her mother-in-law? *I'll have to Google that when I have a minute,* she thought. *"If your husband is dead, is his mother still your mother-in-law?"* She almost laughed as she pictured herself typing that. A quick glance told her that this was more than a social visit; Elaine wanted something. All the signs were there, including the smile that was not really a smile.

"Hello, Franny. How are you? It's been a while. I never see you at the club anymore."

Elaine's eyes swept over her; Franny felt herself flush. As always, when she was around Elaine, her clothes and her hair (both of which she had been pleased with this morning) felt wrong.

"You're looking well," Elaine concluded.

"I'm fine. I've been pretty busy getting the shop ready to open. I haven't had much time for anything else." She made no move toward Elaine. They did not have that kind of relationship. "What brings you in today? I know you're not a doll person."

This was an understatement. Elaine had made it clear to both Drew and Franny that she felt Franny's interest in selling dolls was a waste of time. Elaine had pressed her son, asking, "Surely, Franny can find something not based on a childhood fantasy that she can do to occupy herself? She *did* go to college, after all."

"I'm sure you must have read in the club newsletter that I'm the chair of the charity auction again this year." Elaine preened for a moment before going on. "At our first committee meeting today, Andrea Sanger suggested we approach you for a donation." Her glance searched the room as she continued. "A lot of the women knew about your shop; they couldn't stop talking about it. Although, why anyone would want an old doll..." Elaine's voice trailed off.

Franny silently counted to ten and dragged out her biggest smile.

"Vintage dolls *are* 'in' right now," she said, dismissing Elaine's tone. "The theory is that, because times are so economically grim, people are being drawn back to their past for comfort. It's great for business."

Elaine made no response. She continued to look around the store.

"Do you have a suggestion of which doll you would like to offer us? Or shall I pick one?" She reached into her bag, bringing out her wallet. "I would like it to be a substantial doll, not just a token." Elaine's eyes narrowed and her face, smooth and tight from what she discreetly referred to as "a tiny bit of work," was hard without the smile. "Of course, I'm prepared to compensate you."

Franny suppressed a sudden flair of anger.

"Don't be silly. I am glad to make a donation. You don't have to pay for the doll. And it *will* be a very nice doll—it only makes sense that Francesca's Foundlings showcase its best." *Not exactly what Lilah had suggested,* Franny thought, but similar enough and the publicity would be free. "Today was your first meeting, right?"

"Well ... yes." Elaine appeared to be taken by surprise. She was not used to being questioned, especially by Franny.

"So, you don't need to know the exact doll today. Right?" Franny's tone was agreeable, but behind the words was a clear message: Don't push me. "I do have a doll in mind, but I want to consult with my staff before making my decision. Francesca's Foundlings will be happy to donate a doll to your auction. I'll let you know by Monday, which should be more than enough time." Franny pictured the expression that would be on Lilah's face when she learned she was now Franny's "staff."

Elaine opened her mouth and closed it. Shifting her purse from one hand to the other, she started to leave as the silence grew between them. As usual, they had run out of things to say to one another.

Franny took pity on her. "I'll give you a call no later than next Monday and let you know which doll I have decided to donate. Will that work?"

"That's fine." Elaine opened the door to leave. "You've done a very nice job with your shop. It's almost like something you would find in Portsmouth. It's actually quite lovely. I'm sure it will be a success. Enjoy your evening."

A wave of sadness washed over Franny as she watched Elaine walk past the window. Her mother-in-law seemed less autocratic, almost human, today. Franny wished she felt a connection to the woman. They had both loved Drew. Elaine had tolerated Franny well enough when Drew was alive, and had considered her an improvement over Brid. But they had no real relationship and when Drew died, it was as if they were strangers unable to offer one another any comfort.

Still thinking about Elaine, Franny performed the routine she followed to close the shop, checking that the door was locked and the alarm was set. She removed the money from the cash box and placed it in the small safe Neil had insisted on. Most people paid with credit or debit cards, but every so often she had a cash customer.

The walk to Nona's was short: two blocks north then left onto Thaler Street and she was there. She arrived before Neil. The hostess seated her near the window, giving her a clear view of the approach to the entrance. She watched as Neil parked his car and strode toward the restaurant. He *had* lost weight. She could see it clearly now. It made his face seem less good-natured and somewhat haggard. He looked intent—on a mission. Entering the restaurant, he waved off the hostess and crossed the room to join her at the table.

"Thanks again for agreeing to have dinner with me," he said as he pulled out the chair across from her. "I really appreciate it."

"I was thrilled with the invitation. I don't get many, you know."

The waitress appeared, menus in hand. "I think we both know what we want," Neil told her and then looked across the table, "Am I right?"

"I almost always get the same thing. I'll have the spaghetti al tonno, please. And a salad with the house dressing on the side, too."

"Make mine the lasagna. Nothing beats your lasagna, as far as I'm concerned," Neil said.

"You guys are easy." Sliding the two menus under her arm, she asked, "Would you like something to drink before your dinners come?"

Franny shook her head. "Water's good for me."

Neil winked at the waitress. "She's a cheap date. I'll have an Irish whiskey, neat. Make it Jameson if you have some. Please."

The waitress nodded and left them.

Franny felt her mouth drop open. "Wow. I have never known you to drink Jameson before."

Neil fingered the large Boston College ring on his right hand for a moment before answering. "I only drink it when I need courage." He took a deep breath. "So how the hell is she?"

Franny's heart went out to him. She reached across the table and placed her hand over his. "Oh, Neil, I'm so sorry. What happened, anyway?"

"Come on, Franny! I know she tells you everything."

Franny considered this before answering him. "Everything, no. She told me that you threw her key in her face and you wanted a woman who could give you a family."

"Can you tell me why someone who is usually so rational has

completely lost her mind over this baby Lilah's having? I never told Brid I wanted a family." He closed his eyes for a moment and then, opening them, said, "You know, I don't think I ever did really want a family." He looked at her intently, "Because if I had, I would have made it happen. Twenty-five years ago, not now. And," he added indignantly, "I did not throw her key in her face."

Franny grinned somewhat sheepishly. "I know you didn't. Sofia and I were watching you guys argue. You put the key in her hand. I saw you."

"Thank God for that. There have been days these last few weeks I've felt like I was losing my mind."

"Have you called her?"

"No. Stubborn Irish pride, I realize, but I couldn't make myself do it."

At that moment, the waitress returned with their drinks. "You're in luck. We did have the Jameson. We just got it in for St Patrick's Day. Craic draws the crowds, but the bartender here stocks a couple of bottles for anyone who wants it."

"I am going to take this as a good sign," Neil said, raising the glass to Franny, "*Sláinte.*" He took a sip.

"What are you going to do now?"

"Do you talk to Drew?" He watched her face for her reaction.

She was surprised and then laughed. "All the time." Adding, with a straight face, "He never answers me back, though."

"I do, too." He took another sip of the Jameson and continued, a thoughtful expression on his face. "I talked to him about what to do about this mess."

He studied the glass of whiskey, turning it in his hand before going on.

"I suppose in a lot of ways Drew and I were completely different, which is why some people never understood our friendship. I have tried to live a dutiful life. The kind of life my parents expected me to live. For the most part, I have followed all the rules. I consider myself to be moderately successful. I have everything I want. I enjoy my work. I have season tickets to the Red Sox." He grinned at her. "This may surprise you, but I have never felt lonely." His face changed, suddenly bleak. "Until now. These last two years with her have been ... " His eyes filled with tears and he drained the glass.

"Did you and Drew ever talk about how you felt about Brid when he was alive?" Franny asked.

"Only once. Not that he would ever have remembered it. He was pretty far-gone. You know what I mean?"

Franny nodded. She did know.

"We were in Craic, sitting at the bar. It had been a long night. He and Brid had been divorced about nine months. Drew was a wreck. He looked at me and said, 'Make your move. You'll give her a good life. You can make her happy in a way I never could.' I didn't, of course. There was no point. Those two ... but after he died, things changed."

The waitress returned, bringing their entrees. She glanced at Neil's empty glass. "Another drink, or some wine with dinner?"

Neil looked at Franny. "Water's good," she answered, reaching for her fork. "I am not wasting any points on wine."

"You and those points." He told the waitress, "I think we're fine. The one drink was perfect. " He hesitated before adding, "You know, I would like a glass of water. Thanks." She nodded and left them to their meals.

"Anyway, to finish what I was saying, I've had your late husband's voice in my head since I handed back that key, telling me to stop being a fool and marry the damn woman." He took a bite, swallowed and continued, "And that's what I intend to do. I'd appreciate it if you would help me pick out a ring."

KATHLEEN FERRARI

CHAPTER NINE

"You're joking."

Neil grimaced. "Joking? No man jokes about asking a woman to marry him."

He offered her the breadbasket.

Ignoring the pull of the loaf of Italian Bread, Franny put it aside, her mind too full of this latest development to give it more than a glance. "Neil! Oh my God! Really?"

"More points, I suppose," he muttered, watching her dispose of the bread.

A horrible thought struck her. "What if she refuses?" she whispered.

A look of obstinacy settled on his face. "I'll have to convince her to say yes then, won't I?" He picked up his fork. "Let's eat. Dinner looks delicious."

Franny focused her attention on her plate of spaghetti al tonno. One bite and she was back watching her father cook in the red-and-white kitchen where she had grown up. His repertoire had not been large; he cooked the food he loved to eat. 'tuna spaghetti,' as she and Sofia had called it, was one of those dishes. It was a simple dish but, made right, it was unforgettable. The secret was the teaspoon of anchovy paste slipped into the sauce. She closed her eyes as she swallowed, savoring both the taste and her memories.

"Good?" Neil asked.

"Amazing. Almost, but not quite, as good as my father's."

"He was a good cook?" Neil reached for a chunk of bread and dipped it in the small plate of olive oil beside the breadbasket.

"He only cooked what he wanted to, and he made a horrendous mess doing it. His specialty was breakfast. He was known in the family for his eggs—he went to great lengths to make them exactly as ordered. He also made wonderful French toast, which he served with melted butter and powdered sugar, finished off with a drizzle of real maple syrup." She made a face. "I owe my passion for food to him, and the scourge of my weight, too."

"I can't say the same about my father. His sole talent with food was putting a teabag into a cup. And he did that rarely. My mother waited on him hand and foot."

"Was your mother a good cook?"

Neil looked up from his lasagna. "My mother was first-generation Irish. Do I have to say any more?"

"I know some very good cooks who are Irish. Look at Brid. She's a wonderful cook. I dream about her shortbread." Franny protested.

"Brid's mother was a great cook. It was Rosemary's cooking that packed Craic in the old days before the restaurant was renovated. I think she actually liked to cook, which my mother definitely did not. Brid gets it from Rosemary. Believe me, my mother—and don't get me wrong, I loved my mother and she was a good woman—was no cook."

In her head, Franny could hear Brid's description of Peg Malone: *"An Irish martyr and saint, if ever there was one."* Brid had told her, tartly, *"Peg's specialty was assigning 'tramp' status to whatever girl was hanging around her son."*

"Speaking of mothers, you will never guess who walked into the shop today, right after you left. You just missed her."

Neil's expression was wary. "No idea. Who?"

"Elaine MacCullough."

"There's a lady, I can guarantee you, who has never stepped into a kitchen and boiled water. Drew used to call her 'Her Highness, the Countess of WASP.' Remember?"

Franny shook her head. "Sometimes, Drew was not very nice about his mother. I always thought their relationship was superficial. I would never describe them as being close."

"It was certainly complicated. They say every man loves his mother. No matter what Drew said, I don't think he was the exception."

"Brid really hates Elaine," Franny said.

"Yes. I know. And she has good reason to hate her. Elaine was cruel to Brid and, even worse, she was horrible to Brid's mother. As I am sure you must know, Elaine comes from old Boston money. Her grandparents, no doubt, had Irish maids working for them who were straight off the boat. I'm sure that's how she viewed the Sheerins. Des never realized it, but Rosemary certainly felt it." He paused, then went on. "As a result, the more imperious Elaine was, the more respectful Rosemary became. She always called Drew's parents 'Mr. and Mrs. MacCullough.' It didn't help that Drew loved Rosemary Sheerin. And she returned that love. I imagine Elaine was wild with jealousy over that."

"Brid told me some of the things Elaine said to her. Elaine was usually indifferent to me, sometimes sarcastic, but never out-and-out mean."

Franny returned to her pasta, sliding most of what remained on her plate to the side before taking another bite. "I think she went out of her way to try and be kind to me after I lost my baby. She used to bring me macaroons from a French bakery in Boston when she went into the city shopping—she knew I loved them. And she never said a word to me about my weight. It had always been an issue before. I wonder why?"

"You're an easy person to be nice to, unlike Brid. When Brid is threatened or frightened, she gets nasty. She's a street fighter at heart. Think about the kind of comments she's been tossing out ever since she found out about Lilah."

Franny stopped eating. "Not even you get to say anything bad about Brid. Not to me. I don't know what I might have done without her help."

The waitress chose that moment to check on them, sparing Neil the need to answer. "How was your dinner?" she asked. "Everything okay?"

"Everything was excellent, as it always is," Neil said.

"Can you pack this to go for me?" Franny asked, indicating the half of her dinner still on her plate.

"Of course. Would you care for one of our desserts? We have them delivered daily from Boston's North End. I can bring the tray over for you to see, if you would like. They're delicious."

Neil looked at Franny. "Up to you."

"No, thank you. I'm sure everything is wonderful. The problem is I will want one of everything."

The girl laughed. "Okay. I know what you mean. I'll be right back then."

"So where are we going next, Romeo?" Franny grinned, enjoying watching the blush spread from under Neil's collar up his face and into his hairline.

"We're going to see my friend, Jack Blaine. We went to school together. He's a good guy. I trust him. Diamonds are not exactly my field of expertise."

"You're in luck, then. I actually know something about them. My grandfather worked in a jewelry store in Boston. Papa taught me a couple of things about diamonds."

"I thought you might have some idea as to what kind of ring Brid would like, but this hidden knowledge of gems is a bonus."

Before Franny could answer, the waitress returned. "Sir," she said, placing the leather folder in front of Neil. Turning to Franny, she put a small white box on the table. "And here's your al tonno. It's my favorite, too."

"Thank you. That will be my lunch tomorrow. It was delicious," Franny said.

Neil slipped his American Express card into the folder and handed it back to the waitress. He waited until she left the table to speak.

"I was with Drew at Blaine's the night he bought Brid's ring," he said, watching Franny closely.

He seemed to be expecting some kind of a reaction from her, she realized. Funny, she felt nothing. She knew that, of course, Drew would have bought Brid an engagement ring. Franny suspected Neil was trying to decide if the conversation was upsetting her. When she didn't react, he went on.

"It was a large stone—an amethyst if I'm remembering correctly—surrounded by diamonds. Drew paid a fortune for it.

I'm not sure she even liked it. She rarely wore it."

"I think I've seen her wear it."

"You have? When?" Neil was clearly intrigued. "I haven't seen her wear it in years."

"Do you remember the day I met Lorie Derouin for lunch?" Franny asked, slowly twirling the small take-away box on the table in front of her.

"Yes. If *you* remember, I told you to stay away from Lorie Derouin, but you refused to listen to me."

"You're right, I didn't listen to you." She looked at him steadily. "Did you really think I could just walk away from an invitation for a sit-down with the woman in whose arms my husband died?"

Neil sighed. "Come on, Franny. You don't know that. You only know she was with him."

Franny sniffed. "One thing I learned for sure at that lunch; she was definitely with him."

"You shouldn't have gone to meet her. All it did was upset you even more. What does this have to do with Brid's engagement ring? I'm really confused."

Franny laughed. "You have to listen carefully and then you'll get it. Brid came with me that day. I told her I was going to meet Lorie and I begged her to come. She didn't want to, but I think she must have realized I needed an ally, so she gave in and agreed to go with me."

She paused, remembering, "Brid looked spectacular that day. She was wearing a beautifully tailored black suit and killer high heels. I was shocked because it was so unlike her. I had never seen her dressed in anything but pants—usually jeans." She paused, and then added, "She was wearing that amethyst ring. It was the final detail in the picture she had created of a successful woman in control of her surroundings. I thought it was a beautiful ring and I knew Drew had most likely given it to her. I never asked her." Franny added softly more to herself than to Neil, "Of course, it would have been her engagement ring."

Frowning, Neil leaned toward her. "I'm re-thinking this. It was a mistake to ask you to come with me. I apologize for making you relive all this again. I have enjoyed our dinner, though. I don't get to talk to you often enough now that you're so busy running the shop."

Franny set her shoulders and folded her arms in front of her. "I am going with you to pick out the ring. I'm flattered you would ask me and also I think I can help you. Brid is very particular about her jewelry, which is why she wears the same pieces all the time. I know what she likes and, even more important, what she doesn't like." She bit her lip for a moment, trying to decide if she should continue. "Why do you think this would be any harder for me than it is for you? You said you were with Drew the night he bought her engagement ring. Why go back to the same store? You could go into Boston. There are lots of fine jewelers there." Curious, she waited for his reply.

"That's easy. At heart, I'm a cheap bastard. Jack Blaine and I go way back. He'll give me a good deal on a ring. As far as it being hard, I've been practicing law for almost thirty years. As a result, I've come to realize life is messy. Sure, at first glance, this might raise a few eyebrows, but when you take a step back, it really isn't that odd. Brid and Drew had been divorced for a long time when Drew died. And I want to marry her. I once handled a very messy estate where the deceased had divorced his wife and then married his daughter-in-law, who had divorced his son in order to marry him. *That* was strange. What I am about to do is not."

"You're kidding me," Franny protested.

"I'm not. It happened. Are you sure you're up for this? You can still back out if you want to. I'll understand."

The waitress returned with the receipt and Neil's credit card. She wished them a pleasant evening.

Quickly calculating the tip and signing the receipt, Neil tucked the card into his wallet. "I want to find a ring Brid will really like and want to wear. I think you know her pretty well and might have a better chance of getting it right than I will. I appreciate you taking the time to help me." He stood up. "Shall we go?"

Franny reached for the take-away box. "I can't wait. This is going to be fun."

CHAPTER TEN

"You can almost feel a hint of spring in the air," Franny said as she and Neil walked back toward Main Street.

"I know, but don't forget it's not even St. Patrick's Day. We could still get dumped on. It's New Hampshire."

They stopped in front of a multi-pane window under a sign that read, *E.M. Blaine, Fine Jewelry and Timepieces since 1908*. Considered the most exclusive jewelry store in Lynton, Blaine's always had enticing window displays—dazzling but never tacky.

Caught in the window's spell, Franny's eyes moved from one glittery gem to another. She and Drew had bought a gift for Sofia's graduation from law school at Blaine's. Drew had often shopped here but, as he liked to surprise her, he never invited her along. Her own engagement ring, a large, square-cut diamond, had come from Blaine's. She looked down at it, still on her finger.

Neil took a deep breath and opened the door for her. "This should be good. Where's your phone? Get ready to take a picture of Jack Blaine's face when I tell him why I'm here."

Blaine's was one of those shops where time seemed to have stopped. Burnished walnut display cases stood in the same places they'd held since Edward Blaine first opened his doors. Edward, Jr. had added the thick, dove-gray carpet, but the essence of the shop remained unchanged. Blaine's had a church-like air; customers seemed compelled to lower their voices once they stepped across the threshold.

"What brings you to Blaine's tonight, Mr. Malone?" A petite redhead stepped from behind one of the glass cases, addressing Neil in a low musical voice, her eyes widening slightly at the sight of Franny.

"Hi Patsy. Is Jack around?" Neil answered, neatly sidestepping her question.

"He's out back. I'll get him for you." Casting one more curious glance in Franny's direction, she disappeared toward the rear of the shop.

There was no bustle about Blaine's. The only sound breaking the silence was the ticking of the clocks lining the walls. Franny felt herself relaxing as she listened.

"And to what do I owe the honor of having you drop by, Counselor?" Jack Blaine approached them with the confidence of a third generation shop-owner. "Is the old Hamilton acting up again? Better behave itself or you'll be trading it in for one of those battery-operated sports jobs like the one Tom Brady is hawking these days."

Jack was largely responsible for keeping Neil's vintage wristwatch going. He knew Neil would never trade it in; the watch had belonged to his father and he cherished it.

Neil cleared his throat. Only then did Franny realize how nervous he was. His usual composure seemed to have fled.

"Jack, do you know Franny MacCullough?" he asked.

The smile on Jack's face slid away, replaced by a look Franny had come to recognize as the one people pasted on when they first encountered her after Drew's death. Brid called it the "Comforting-the-Grieving-Widow Face." Franny wished people would act normally. Jack reached for her hand.

"I think we met a few years ago when you and Drew purchased one of our watches." As Franny raised her eyebrows in amazement, he continued, "How are you doing? Drew's death was a shock to all of us who knew him."

"I can't believe you remember that, Mr. Blaine. We bought the watch for my sister's law-school graduation. That was a while ago." She removed her hand from his. "I'm doing really well, thank you.

I recently opened a doll shop here in Lynton."

"I wish you every success with it. I think you'll find you will come to either love it or hate it." He looked around his store. "Myself, I must love it—I have been here since the week after I picked up my diploma from Bentley."

"Don't let him kid you, Franny. It's working on the clocks that he loves. He puts up with the retail end of it so he can spend every spare moment he has doing that," Neil said.

"You may be right," Jack nodded. He had been fascinated by the inner workings of clocks and watches since he was a small child watching his own father's deft fingers make them tick. He grinned at his old friend. "So what can I show you tonight?"

"I need a ring. An engagement ring."

Neil seemed to have lost all the glibness of tongue he was known for in difficult conversations.

Suddenly, Neil's earlier comment about taking a picture made sense to Franny. The look of astonishment on Jack's face did make her want to reach for her cell phone.

"An engagement ring? Really?" The man was clearly flustered. His glance went from Neil to Franny and back again to Neil. "Well…congratulations. Let me show you—"

"Um…No. It's not her. She's here as ring consultant."

"Right. Of course." Jack mumbled.

Franny stifled a giggle. Obviously Jack had been surprised at the thought of Neil being involved with his own best friend's widow. *Wait until he finds out the bride is Neil's best friend's ex-wife*, she thought. She wondered if Neil would tell him.

"What price range did you have in mind?" Once more the salesman, Jack took a set of keys from his pocket and unlocked the case where the engagement rings were displayed.

"Doesn't matter. I want a ring I think she'll like and will wear. She's picky."

No kidding, Franny thought.

Jack put a tray of rings on the counter. "Here's the thing: it's all about the bling these days—as in 'my bling's bigger than your bling.' Girls today like platinum or white gold, like these, and they prefer large stones—often, *several* large stones." He pointed to a ring inserted in the white-velvet covered tray. "This is a beautiful ring and a great example of what I am selling to brides today. It's called a 'Bostonian' setting."

The subject of Jack's praise was a two-carat, square-cut diamond, flanked on either side by diamond baguettes. And they weren't small.

Neil peered at it uncertainly. *Brid would hate it,* Franny thought.

"Who's the girl who managed to lure you away from your happy life as a crusty old bachelor? Do I know her?" Jack asked.

Franny held her breath.

Neil squared his shoulders and leaned slightly over the jewelry case toward Jack. "It's Brid Sheerin." He paused and then added, "And I don't want to hear what you think about it."

Jack backed away from him, his face a mixture of shock and disapproval. "Oh, for God's sake. Are you crazy? She'll eat you alive."

"I love her." Neil's tone made it clear he was not going to discuss it. "I'm here to get a ring, Jack, not to ask for your blessing. Are you going to sell me one or not?"

Once again, watching the two men, Franny's fingers itched to grab her cell phone and snap a picture. She could see how they must have looked as boys, glaring at each other in the schoolyard. Neil had won this round.

"Fine. It's your life," Jack said. He looked at Franny, his face briefly registering bewilderment over how she might be involved with picking out an engagement ring for this particular bride. Then it was back to business.

"These are all beautiful rings. Most women would be thrilled with any one of them. I'll give you a twenty percent discount off the retail price on any ring in the store, Counselor. All you have to do is pick the one you want."

Neil nodded in acknowledgement of the offer. "Well, I don't know. They all look pretty spectacular." He asked Franny, "Which one do you like?"

"Can I see that one?" she asked, ignoring the tray in front of her and pointing to a ring in the rear of the case. A diamond solitaire in a yellow-gold Tiffany setting, it was almost hidden in the sea of sparkling white metal.

"The one in the corner?" Jack asked, as she nodded. He placed the ring on a red velvet cushion and positioned it in front of her. He smiled. "You have excellent taste. This may not be the largest diamond I own, but it's one of the finest. The color and clarity are excellent."

Franny studied the ring closely, picturing Brid's sturdy artist's hands.

"Do you want to try it on?" Jack asked.

"Oh, my God, no!" Franny backed away a step. "It would be bad luck."

"You think she'd like that one?" Neil looked closely at the gold ring on the red pillow. "It's really plain compared to these others."

"Yes." And that was the reason she had chosen it. "This is the one. I'm sure." And she was. It was a beautiful ring: a gorgeous diamond, as Jack had already told them, and, at the same time, not flashy. It would complement Brid. Franny smiled. This was the right ring. She was certain of it.

"It's yellow gold. That dates it." Jack's hand hovered over the ring.

"Brid only wears yellow gold. I have never seen her wear anything else," Franny insisted.

"You're right. Those hoop earrings she always has on are yellow gold." Neil reached for his wallet and handed his credit card to Jack. "Here. Write it up."

"Don't you even want to know how much it costs?" Jack asked.

"No. I told you, I don't care." He smiled at Franny. "If Franny says this is the ring, this is the one I want."

Jack shook his head. "You know, I think you may have lost your mind." He handed the ring to Patsy, who had quietly watched the entire transaction with great interest. "Polish this and put it in a box for me, please." Turning around, he ran Neil's credit card through the cash register behind him.

"Do you want me to gift-wrap it, Mr. Malone?" Patsy waited while Neil considered his next move.

"No, thanks. I don't need it gift-wrapped. A box would be great."

Jack handed Neil his American Express card and the credit slip to be signed. "I gave you twenty percent, although why, I don't know. You probably have your First Communion money."

Neil smiled. For the first time since stepping into the store, he seemed to relax.

"Thanks, Jack. I appreciate it." Quickly, he signed the credit slip, accepting from Patsy the small, silver bag embossed with the *E.M. Blaine* signature logo.

"Come on, Franny. I have another stop to make tonight." He held the door for her. Jack followed them out to the street.

"Hey, Neil. I'll take it back if she throws it in your face."

"Very decent of you, Jack. I'll keep that in mind," Neil said.

"Where are we going, now?" Franny asked, rushing to keep up with his long, confident strides.

"Back to the Foundlings. I've taken up enough of your evening. I'm sure you have things to do."

Neil appeared to Franny a different man from the one who had anxiously walked into the jewelry store. Leaving Main Street, they took the short cut down Kyle Street to bring them to the rear of Franny's shop, where she had left her car.

"I'm thinking of getting a new car. Did I tell you?" She unlocked the door of the silver Lexus that had once belonged to Drew.

"Any ideas on what you want?" Neil asked.

"If I were brave, I would get a Mini-Cooper. I just love them. Can't you see me tooling around in a yellow Mini? And I know what my vanity plate would be: 'Doll.' What do you think?"

Reaching past her to open the driver's door, Neil said, "I think you should get what you want. You're brave enough for anything."

"Are you going to Brid's now?"

"Not yet. I'm on the way over to speak to Des. It's traditional to ask the father of the bride for his daughter's hand." The expression on his face made him appear much younger than he had when he'd walked into Nona's earlier in the evening.

"I think you might just be the nicest person I've ever met," Franny said. Hugging him, she whispered, "Good luck tonight." She slipped behind the wheel.

"I'm sure you'll get a text—one way or the other." He shut the door and watched her start the car and drive away.

***

Craic was busy when Neil walked through its oak doors. Some

of the crowd was still waiting for the second dinner-seating. The dining room, designed to create a feeling of intimacy, was not large. Reservations were much sought-after and frequent diners had learned to call early for a table. Craic was the kind of place one saved for a special dinner or an important meal with a business client.

It was also *the* place to go for a drink in Lynton. Thursday nights were always busy; people liked to get an early start on the weekend.

Searching the bar, Neil's eyes found Des mixing an elaborate drink in front of a cluster of young women, who all appeared to be fascinated with what he was doing. Catching sight of Neil, he broke into a broad smile.

"Ah, Neil, let an old man buy you a drink." He passed the glass in his hand to his waiting customer. "Here you go darlin', drink it slowly." He turned back to Neil, "Will it be your regular you'll be havin'?" He reached for the Grey Goose even as he asked.

"Not tonight, Des. Make it Jameson—neat."

Desmond's hand froze a moment, then reached higher for the bottle of Irish whiskey. He poured the amber liquid into a glass and handed it to Neil. "Jameson, is it? And what's brought you to this, lad?" He added, "This was your father's drink."

And so it was, thought Neil. The image of his father carefully pouring a shot of what he called 'Irish' into a glass flashed across his mind. Just the one, Neil knew. John Malone, despite his heritage, was not much of drinker. As a cop, he'd seen too much of the devastation it often led to among his fellow Irishmen.

"Any chance you can break away and join me in the Snug? I have something I need to ask you." Neil was sweating even though the room wasn't hot.

"I can, lad." Pouring himself a glass to match Neil's, he called to the young man working the other end of the bar, "I am off for a break, Sean."

The bartender nodded at him. "Sure, Des, take your time, then."

Glass in hand, Des led the way down the hall to the small room behind the bar. The Snug resembled a cross between the library in a private home and a men's club. Seven tables surrounded by high back chairs upholstered in either chestnut-brown leather or dark green-and-gold-striped silk damask dotted the room. A gas fireplace glowed from the corner, flanked by two wing chairs. A portrait of the Irish revolutionary, Countess Markievicz, dominated the wall opposite the door. Diners waiting to be called into the nine o'clock dinner-seating occupied the tables, but the two chairs flanking the fire were empty.

Des angled his chair slightly toward Neil as he settled in. He took a sip of his drink.

Neil cleared his throat and then began. "I think you know Brid and I have been seeing one another."

Des chuckled. "I suspect the two of you have been doing more than gazing upon one another, but, yes, I did know that." He waited for Neil to continue.

Neil reached into his coat pocket and removed the small leather box from the silver bag. He flipped the top open and held the box between them. "I'd like your permission to ask her to marry me."

Des took the box from Neil's hand.

"Now that's a beautiful ring. Any woman would be lucky to receive it. As far as my permission goes, you have it, and my blessing along with it." He closed the cover and handed the box back to Neil. "Not that that means a damn thing. Brid is not one to seek permission from anyone, least of all from me." Des hesitated and then continued, "You're sure you know what you're about here? My daughter is not an easy woman to get along with, nor one who enjoyed the bonds of matrimony"—he looked steadily at Neil—"as we both know."

Neil stood up.

"What I know is that I have loved her for almost half my life. I should have asked her to marry me long ago." He laughed. "I probably wasn't brave enough." He extended his hand. "Thank you, Des. I appreciate your blessing. It means a lot to me."

Returning the ring to his pocket, he headed back toward the bar.

CHAPTER ELEVEN

Brid pushed the button in the ear of a furry, gray mouse with a bell at the end of its tail and placed the toy on the oak floor, facing the kitchen. It began to squeak. Moaki raced after it, leaping gracefully from the top of the coffee table.

Watching on Skype as the cat disappeared, Lilah giggled. She sounded younger than she was. *Far too young to be having a baby*, Brid thought. Although it was too late to worry about that now, as from the look of the girl, with her round face and swollen body, she was definitely having this one—and soon.

"Oh, my God. Don't make me laugh; it makes me pee my pants. Did you get that mouse for Moaki? See, you really do like cats." Lilah shifted in an obvious effort to get comfortable. "My back feels like crap today. This kid needs to learn how to just hang out."

Carrying the laptop, Brid followed Moaki, in order for Lilah to see the cat chase the mouse. The cat had managed to flip the toy on its side and stop its progress into the kitchen.

"I had to get the little devil a toy before she took her boredom out on my rug," Brid replied. Changing the subject, she asked, "Do you have any names for this child yet?"

Lilah had insisted on not knowing if the baby was a boy or a girl, saying she would find out when the baby wanted her to know.

"How can I pick out a name when we haven't met? I don't even name my characters until after they're around for a while. You know that." Lilah stroked her belly,

True, Brid thought. Lilah's heroes and villains often went nameless for weeks while she pondered what to name them.

"Where's Franny?" Brid asked, knowing that, by this hour, Franny was usually home and drifting in and out of the Skype calls Brid set up nightly for Lilah to see the cat.

A funny look came over Lilah's face: not quite guilty, but definitely shifty. Intent on following the cat, Brid missed it.

"Oh, go ahead and tell her. The man is not a criminal because he's finally come to his senses and stopped putting up with her. He can have dinner with whoever he wants to."

Grand, Brid thought, *Sofia*.

Brid was not in the mood for dealing with her—and what was she going on about now?

Lilah sighed, clearly unhappy to be the bearer of this particular news. "She's not home. She's having dinner with Neil. Do you want me to tell her to call you when she gets back?"

"It's not important. I'll stop into the shop tomorrow." Replacing the laptop on the coffee table, Brid bent down and scooped up Moaki, holding her in front of the screen. "Say goodnight to your wretched cat. And try to get some sleep. You look exhausted. From what I've been told, you had better sleep while you can."

"Bye-bye, wonder-cat. I miss you." Moaki meowed in response to Lilah's voice, tail twitching as she stared at the computer screen. "'Night, Brid. Thanks for getting Moaki the mouse to play with."

Brid reached over and shut down Skype. She pulled the cat close, brushing her lips lightly over the top of the furry head before dropping the cat gently on the floor. "Go on, then. And don't you dare even think about scratching my rug." The cat stared at her and then began to groom herself.

Brid crossed the room to her easel, where it stood facing the windows overlooking the garden. Cocking her head, she examined her work-in-progress: a portrait of Lilah curled among the bed pillows, as she had been tonight. In the portrait, Brid had taken the artist's license of adding the small, striped cat. The painting needed work, but she was not unhappy with it. She planned on giving it to Franny as a replacement for the self-portrait she had taken from the wall of Drew's study. This frame of mind was unusual for

Brid—she was never pleased with a work-in-progress.

She was contemplating how to capture the struggle between how she first saw the girl she had hired to work in the gallery two years earlier and the woman she was beginning to see in Lilah's face when the doorbell rang. Backing away from the easel while still focusing on her painting, she wondered who could be dropping by at nine thirty. *Probably Franny*, she thought, *reporting on Neil's latest strategy for rescuing Lilah.*

Her hand froze on the doorknob as she peered through the peephole. Neil Malone stood there. Squaring her shoulders, she opened the door.

"And what would you be wanting with me, at this hour of the night?" The lilt in her voice signaled how unnerved she was.

"Jesus, it's not even ten o'clock." Neil's face reflected the irritation in his voice. "Since when do you turn into a pumpkin at nine thirty?" Not interested in her answer, he continued, "Can I come in? There's something I need to ask you."

Brid hesitated, consumed by a desire to be in the same space with him again if only for a few minutes, she said, "Come in, then." She swung the door wide and stepped back, not wanting—or daring—any physical contact with him. He looked thinner to her, and tired.

"Have you lost weight?"

Neil shook his head, "Is that all women think about? I just heard the same damn thing from Franny. The answer is no, and I am not sick either, before you bother to ask." His eyes caught sight of the painting on the easel. "Very nice. Too bad you don't have any idea how good you are."

"So now you're an art critic, as well as a saint? And I thought *I* was the one with the BFA?"

"I know what I like when I see it. And I know what's good."

Brid could see from the way his back stiffened that her barb had found its mark. He had chosen to ignore it, too smart to strike back. Or to give her the satisfaction of knowing she had hurt him.

"God, I've missed you." He took a step toward her.

Feeling her heart begin to pound, she danced backwards away from him.

"Holy Mother of God, what is it that you want from me?" she

asked.

"I know you're mad at me, although I haven't a clue as to why."

Neil looked at her with a forlorn expression and her guard started to come down.

"I came here to ask you something. And, by God, I intend to do it." He shrugged his coat off and tossed it on the wing chair next to the fireplace.

"Ask away, then. I know I'll not get you out of here until you do." Her eyes flashed defiantly.

Neil's face softened. He seemed younger to her suddenly, and vulnerable. He reached for her hand. Reluctantly, she let him keep it. He studied it for a moment and then, with surprising grace for a man whose legs reminded him often that it had been thirty years since he had played football, he dropped to one knee. His eyes never left her face.

"Brid Sheerin, will you do me the honor of becoming my wife?"

Brid froze in place, staring down at the man kneeling in front of her. The most honorable man she had ever known, to be sure. But still, she could never marry him.

"Get up. I am begging you, for the love of God, get up."

Maybe it was the desolation in her voice, or perhaps a sense that he had gambled and lost that brought Neil awkwardly back to his feet. Brid's shaking hand found his face, briefly caressing his cheek, before she crossed the room and put six feet safely between them.

"You have no idea what you are asking. None at all." Her voice broke and tears slid down her face. Silently, she cursed herself. She was not a weeper, and yet this man had her nearly undone.

"What I am asking? God damn it! I know exactly what I'm asking. I can understand why you think I'm stupid. I know I've been stupid and a coward, too. I've loved you for more than half my life and not said a word. Never had the courage before tonight to ask you. I always thought you were beyond my reach." He stopped, his eyes attempting to read her face and then he went on. "I stood by and watched you marry my best friend and then continued to watch as the two of you came close to destroying one another and I still said nothing. No more! These last two years with you have been the best of my life. I won't give you up without a fight."

He closed the distance between them. Gently placing one large hand on either side of her face, his eyes searched hers. "I think you love me, too. You do, don't you? Brid, why are you so afraid? Tell me."

Brid was crying in earnest now, her slender body racked by sobs. Neil enfolded her into his arms as if she was a child. The fight had left her, her tears quenching her blazing anger. They stood holding each other for some time, the minutes ticking past, she weeping as if her heart would break, he murmuring endearments into her hair. The only other sound was that of the bell on the toy mouse's tail, softly jingling as Moaki tossed it the length of the old oriental carpet.

Shuddering, Brid gathered herself together and then, looking up into Neil's unhappy face, she smiled.

"Of course, I love you. Who could not? You are the dearest man." Then the smile left her face. "It was not supposed to happen though. I'm not good at love, it would seem. I smash it to bits."

"Do you mean Drew?"

"Certainly, Drew. And one or two others along the way, when I was drinking."

"How can any of that possibly matter to us? Now? Drew's dead. And as for the others, I don't see any of them here, either."

"You realize that, by every measure those nuns gave us, I'm not a good woman? And yet, sinner that I am, I have you, the most generous man in the world, standing in front of me."

Tossing her wild, black hair from her face, she reached up and kissed him. Nibbling first on his lower lip, she slipped her tongue into his mouth, her hands pulling at his shirt, desperate to touch his bare skin. Groaning, Neil entwined his fingers in her hair, tipping her head back to hungrily devour her mouth.

She struggled with his belt as they slid together to the floor. He was more intent on kissing her throat and her ears, alternating between extended visits to her mouth. Having been apart for almost six weeks, both were in a hurry. They were still partially clothed when Brid straddled him, startling the cat as she reached her climax. Waiting for that, underneath her, Neil groaned as he emptied himself inside her.

Moaki made them break apart. They had fallen asleep in each other's arms when the weight of the cat walking across them caused them to wake.

"Evil creature!" Brid complained, shifting her body so that the protesting cat on her back slid off.

Neil grunted and said, "As pleasant as this has been, I vote for adjourning to the bed. I don't know about you, but I'm too damn old to spend the night on the hardwood floor."

"I didn't hear you complaining about the floor earlier."

Despite her words, Brid began gathering up stray pieces of clothing. Leaning over him, her right breast swung enticingly close to his mouth, an opportunity he took full advantage of.

"Actually, I was distracted. And I seem to be again." He reached for her as he spoke.

"I'm for the bed. You're welcome to join me there," Brid said, pushing him gently away and getting up off the floor.

She was reading Yeats as she often did before going to sleep, a secret smile on her face when Neil, a glass of water in his hand, joined her in the bedroom about five minutes later. He handed her the glass of water. "I thought you might want this.

"You know I think I might like being betrothed," she said, taking a sip from the glass.

"What did you do with my pants?" he asked.

Without looking up from her poetry, she answered, "It's a little late for wearing your pants, isn't it?"

"Very funny. I need something in my pocket."

"Over there on the rocking chair."

With his back to her, Neil removed the small box and, concealing it in his grip, climbed into bed next to her. Looking down at Brid, he said, "Nice to be back." Gently, he took the book of poetry from her hands. "I asked you a question earlier this evening. I'm still waiting for my answer."

"Mother of God, can't it wait until morning?"

"I believe I told you I have been waiting more than half my life. I'd like to settle the matter now."

The blood drained from Brid's face, taking her look of contentment with it. "I'll give you your answer, but not before I also give you the opportunity to retract the question."

"I have no intention of—"

"Stop acting like a bloody lawyer and be quiet and listen," she said.

Neil closed his mouth.

"What do suppose I did after we had the fight in Franny's driveway?"

"No idea, and I don't care."

"Well you damn well should." Brid bit her lower lip, gathered her thoughts, and continued. "I drove directly to the liquor store. I had a bottle of Irish in my hand when I came to my senses and called Georgia."

"And then what did you do?"

"I told you to stop acting like a lawyer."

"Unfortunately for you, I am a lawyer."

Brid exploded. "And I am a God-damned drunk!"

"Answer the question. What did you do after you called Georgia?"

Brid sighed, not sure she was happy or sad as to the direction this was going. "I put the bottle down and then I drove to Dunkin Donuts to meet Georgia."

"And you never had a drink?"

"No. But I could have. It was so close, Neil. I could almost taste it. I wanted it."

"This is bullshit. Will you marry me, Brid? Answer the fucking question." His eyes never left her face.

The silence between them grew. Finally, she gave him her answer.

"Yes, you fool. I will." As long as she lived she would never forget the look of wonder that spread across his face.

"You will. Really? You said yes?"

"Yes. I will. Now, can we please go to sleep?"

"No. Wait. First I have to give you this." He flipped open the ring box and held it toward her.

"You actually bought me an engagement ring?" She felt her eyes fill with tears. Was she going to spend her life with this man doing nothing but crying?

"Do you like it? If you don't, we can get you another one."

"Another one? No! This is exquisite. I love it."

"Franny said it was the right ring. Jack liked another one—it had more sparkle. 'Bling,' he called it. But Franny said—"

"Wait. You took Franny MacCullough into Blaine's to pick out an engagement ring? For me?"

"Well, yes. I figured Franny would know what you would like. And you do like it, right?"

"I love it. But, my God! Jack's head must have blown off."

Neil chuckled. "It *was* pretty funny; you know Jack. Come over here, I get a kiss, don't I? In fact, we're officially betrothed now, so I think we're supposed to consummate our engagement." His hand began to slide up her thigh.

Brid leaned over and kissed him, her lips lingering on his mouth. "You have a short memory for a lawyer." Her eyes twinkled, "I believe what we did earlier on the living room floor counts as consummating our engagement. Can you wait until morning? I am about to turn into that pumpkin."

Neil let his hand drop and shut off the light. "You're right. It's been a helluva day. I love you, Brid."

There was no response for a moment. Then Brid said, "Neil, what would you have done if I had told you I had that drink?"

"I would have asked what I could do to help you. But you're stronger than you realize. I love you and that's all that matters. We'll deal with whatever comes."

Next to him, she sighed as he pulled her into the circle of his arms. And then she murmured words she thought she would never say again. "And I love you."

It was Neil, hurrying out of the bed, not the madly-ringing door buzzer, that woke Brid. The time on the clock next to her head read 3:47. Her heart began to race; something was wrong. Cinching the belt on her robe as she walked into the living room, she heard Neil speak into the intercom.

"Who is it?"

"Brendan. Let me in."

Brid reached past Neil and pushed the button to open the door. A look of amusement flickered briefly across Brendan's face as his glance took in first Brid and then Neil standing behind her.

"Franny thought I might find you both here. I think she was

hoping I would. Don't either of you bother to leave your phones on? We've been trying to reach you for the last hour."

"I shut mine off, I didn't want to be—" Neil started to explain.

"It's Lilah, isn't it?" Brid interrupted him.

Brendan nodded. "You guys need to get dressed. We have to get over to St. Luke's. When Franny called me I texted the ambulance crew—a buddy of mine was on call." Brendan hesitated before continuing. "They think she was heading into full-blown eclampsia. My friend said it comes on that fast."

"Give us five minutes," Neil said.

"Oh, Holy Mother, how could—"

"Not now, Brid, we don't have time. We need to get there. Lilah needs us." He added, "Franny's going to need us, too." Neil gripped Brid's arm and led her into the bedroom.

Brendan was on the phone talking to Franny when they returned to the living room.

"Okay. Sofia got there, right? Good. We're leaving now. Do you want to speak to them?" He handed the cell phone to Neil as they all hustled down the stairs to the street. Brendan's truck was running and double-parked.

"We'll be right behind you, " Neil told Brendan, the phone at his ear as he steered Brid toward his car parked at the curb.

"Neil, you need to pray," Franny was saying. "Lilah's in surgery now. They're not being very encouraging. Dr. Harkey and her team were waiting in the ambulance bay when we pulled in. They moved so fast. It was just like the night they brought me here." Her voice broke and Neil was reminded of both that night, when he had waited with Drew as Franny fought for her life, and of the morning she had called him to tell him Drew was dead.

"Hang on, Franny. We'll be there in fifteen minutes. This is going to be different. Lilah will be fine."

"I don't know. She looked ... " Franny's voice trailed off. "Promise me you'll say a prayer, Neil. I think God might actually listen to you. Promise me."

"I promise. We're coming we should be there soon." He disconnected the call, handing the cell phone back to Brendan. "Franny sounds like she's about to lose it."

"Don't worry about Franny," Brid snapped. "What did you

promise her just then?"

"She asked me to say a prayer." He shrugged, "I don't know why she thinks I have any influence with the Almighty, but for some reason she does."

The streets leading into Lynton were deserted and Brendan drove fast with Neil following close behind him. Less than ten minutes after leaving Brid's place, they pulled into the circular driveway of the hospital emergency entrance. Brid opened the door before the car came to a complete stop and leaped out. She raced toward the hospital's revolving door.

"It's Gerard," she called over her shoulder. "St. Gerard Majella. He's the patron saint of women in trouble in childbirth. My mother was devoted to him."

CHAPTER TWELVE

The Birthing Center on the fourth floor of St. Luke's was quiet. They approached a circular desk where a nurse sat reading a computer screen.

"Can I help you?" she asked, her smile dimming slightly when she caught sight of their faces.

"We're trying to find out the status of a friend of ours," Neil said. "She was brought in tonight as an emergency admission. Her name is Lilah Patch."

"She's still in surgery." Pivoting slightly in her chair, the nurse pointed to a door about twelve feet away. "You can wait in the family conference room. The others are there. As soon as we know something, I will let you know. It shouldn't be too much longer."

"Thank you," Neil said, reaching for Brid's hand.

The door to the small room was slightly ajar. Brid hesitated, not sure she could handle what awaited her. Neil, reaching over her shoulder, pushed the door open. The Chiesa sisters sat opposite one another, each huddled in a corner. Sofia was reading a legal brief. Franny, slumped in what appeared to be the most uncomfortable chair in Lynton, was watching the clock over Sofia's head.

"What in the name of God happened?" Brid demanded, carefully remaining at the end of the table in the center of the room. She feared that, if she got too close, Franny would hurl herself into her arms. "I just Skyped with her a few hours ago. She was fine." Even as she said it, Brid realized that Lilah had seemed a little off and had complained about her back.

"I went in to say good-night and I thought she looked funny. Her hands and face seemed puffy, especially around her eyes. At first, she seemed to be okay. She told me about Skyping with you and watching Moaki chasing some toy mouse you had bought for her. She complained about having a terrible headache—and then she started talking to Kren." Franny stopped and shook her head. "She told me Kren was sitting in the leather chair, surrounded by flashing lights. She started yelling at him."

"Holy Mother of God. She saw Kren?" Brid reached for the table to steady herself.

"Who the hell is Kren? The baby's father?" Neil looked from one concerned face to another, waiting for someone to enlighten him.

Stretching like a cat, Sofia answered him succinctly. "Kren is the villain in Lilah's graphic novel. He's a bad guy. Evil. Anyone would be afraid of Kren, except the point is—he's not real."

Rarely at a loss for words, Neil was, for the moment, speechless. Brid was pretty sure that he had never seen the graphic novel Lilah was working on. He probably had never seen *any* kind of graphic novel.

"But you said she was talking to him," Neil persisted.

Franny's explanation tumbled out in a rush. "When Lilah started talking about seeing Kren surrounded by flashing lights, I realized she probably had pre-eclampsia. It's one of the signs—that, and the sudden headache and the swelling in her face. It was all right there in front of me. I can't believe I was so stupid not to have realized something was wrong the minute I saw her! I called Dr. Harkey's answering service. She called me right back and said she was sending an ambulance." Franny's voice broke. Fighting for control, she continued. "The doctor asked for my cell phone number. She said to get Lilah into the car and start driving to meet the ambulance. She said—" Franny stopped again, breathless. She picked up the water bottle from the floor next to her chair and took a sip before continuing. "Dr. Harkey said we had run out of time. So, I got Lilah into the car and headed toward Lynton."

"Did you at least call a neighbor to ride with you?" Neil asked.

Franny shook her head. "There was no time. Harkey said,

'Move. Now.' She wasn't kidding around. As I started driving, a call from one of the paramedics on the ambulance came in over the speaker in the car, and that helped a lot. She was really nice and kept me talking, so I never felt as if I was alone. She knew Lilah could hear her so she was careful not to say anything that might upset her. Not that it mattered, Lilah was kind of out of it." Franny stopped talking and shut her eyes, as if she was trying to erase the memory of her ride from Hiram's Forge.

"Then what happened?" Neil asked, gently, attempting to hide his impatience.

Franny blinked and continued, once again focused on the conversation. "I could tell from her questions that they were worried about Lilah having a seizure, but she didn't have one. At least not while she was in the car with me. I met the ambulance at the intersection of Route 101. You wouldn't believe how fast they got her out of the car and into the ambulance. I followed them here. I could see them moving around inside, but not what they were doing to Lilah. I had a hard time keeping up with them. I have only driven that fast once in my life." Her eyes found Neil's. "The morning Drew died."

Franny looked at the clock. "They're done, you know; they've been done for a while. A Caesarian is one of the fastest surgeries performed. It usually takes less than an hour, start to finish, and when the baby's at risk, they move even faster." She twisted her hands in anguish. "Something's gone wrong. We should have heard by now."

Brid opened her mouth and then closed it without saying a word. What could she say? Franny knew from experience what she was talking about.

"You're right. We should have heard something by now." Sofia stood up and started toward the door. "I'm going to see if I can find out what's going on."

There was a soft knock; the door opened to reveal Dr. Harkey. Dressed in wrinkled scrubs, her face was gray with exhaustion. "Good"—she looked around the room—"it appears that you're all here."

Neil pulled a chair out. "Sit down, doctor. You look like you need to."

A grim smile flickered briefly across Dr. Harkey's face as she allowed herself to drop into the chair.

"Thank you. I think I will." Dr. Harkey sighed with pleasure. "It's great to be able to sit down."

Brid and Sofia moved to stand on either side of Franny, who had begun to tremble.

"Is Lilah going to be okay?" Franny asked, unable to control the shaking in her voice.

"I think Lilah will be fine," Dr. Harkey said directly to Franny; then she addressed them all. "She didn't have a seizure, which is good. She's upstairs in the ICU, and the staff is watching her closely. She's been lucky so far, and I am guardedly optimistic that her luck will continue. The same thing that put her at risk will most likely pull her through this."

"And what would that be?" Brid asked.

"Her youth." Dr. Harkey laughed, seeming to relax for the first time. "She's twenty-one. They bounce back pretty fast at that age." She looked more closely at Brid. "It would be a far more desperate story if it was you up there. Now, I suggest you all go home and get some sleep. I promise, Lilah is in good hands. You'll be able to see her tomorrow." The doctor stood up slowly, stretching her neck left than right.

"I have been in the business of delivering babies for over thirty-five years. Most of the time I love what I do, but not tonight. One night like tonight is one too many. It makes me look longingly at Dermatology."

Neil cleared his throat and asked, tentatively, "How is the baby doing?"

"Oh, Lord, I am getting too old for this." She shook her head. "Once I get them out and hand them off to the peds, I'm consumed with the mother. I'm sorry. It's a little girl—a very feisty, loud little girl. She was screaming even before I fully delivered her through the incision. She's in the NICU. My guess is the baby is only in there as a precaution, and both she and her mother will be in one of our regular birth-suites tomorrow. The baby's APGAR score was high, considering the trauma of her birth. Greg Mallet is her pediatrician. I imagine you'll still find him in the nursery." Her eyes swept the group. "Ask one of the nurses to point you toward the NICU. It's on this floor."

Franny, released from uncertainty and fear, burst into tears.

Brid wondered if she was reliving the stillbirth of her son.

Dr. Harkey crossed the room, and took both of Franny's hands in her own. "You listen to me. You saved that girl's life tonight and probably the baby's, too. You did exactly what needed to be done, and you should be dancing with joy—not weeping." Franny smiled tremulously and accepted the handkerchief Neil passed her.

"How much did she weigh?" he asked.

"Six pounds, four ounces. Quite credible for a thirty-five weeker." Dr. Harkey dropped Franny hands. "Greg can fill you in on the baby, but I think she's going to be fine. We like to get them to thirty-eight weeks, but with today's science, if all goes well, we are saving some of them as early as twenty-three weeks. Neonatology has made huge strides since I began my practice." The smile left her face. "Eclampsia, unfortunately, is still a killer. I am so glad we were able to beat that devil to the finish line tonight." She nodded to them. "I'm going to bed. You all go and see little Miss Patch."

Neil opened the door and, speaking for them all, said, "Doctor, we can't thank you enough—"

"Save your thanks for Mrs. MacCullough here; she's the heroine of this story. I will check on Lilah in the morning." Glancing at her watch, she sighed, "Well, *later* this morning, anyway. Good night." And then she was gone.

Dabbing her eyes, Franny said, "A little girl. We'll have so much fun with her. But wait—we don't even have a crib for her! Lilah insisted we not buy anything until the baby was born."

"We have plenty of time to get all that stuff," Sofia said. "What I'm interested in now is getting some sleep."

"I don't know," Brendan teased, "I think a guy would have been great. Don't you, Neil? We're already out-numbered by these women."

"I'm happy with a healthy baby. A girl is fine with me." He started out the door. "Let's go see her."

Sofia yawned, as if to prove her earlier point, "I'm heading out. I have to meet with a client in less than five hours. You all go check out the baby. I'll see them both tomorrow. See," she scolded

Franny, "all your worrying, and things are going to be fine. Sometimes, there *is* a happy ending. I told you there would be." She leaned down to retrieve her jacket from the chair. "Neil, I'll see you in the office tomorr—" Her eyes widened as she caught sight of Brid's left hand. "Is that an *engagement* ring?"

"Oh, my God!" Franny looked from Brid to Neil. "I'm so happy for both of you." Beaming, she pulled him into a hug.

"Really? You guys are engaged? Wow." Brendan shot his hand out to Neil. "Congratulations, man. I think that's great. When's the big day?"

"I just got her to accept my proposal tonight. That's why my cell phone was turned off; I didn't want to be interrupted. It was a dicey negotiation. We haven't got around to discussing a date yet"—his eyes met Brid's—"but we will. Now I want to go see this baby who has been such a troublemaker. Let's go find the NICU."

Sofia reached over and took Brid's hand, to get a closer look at the ring. "You've got great taste, Neil. It's a beautiful ring." Her tone was less than enthusiastic as she added, "I hope you'll both be very happy." Dropping Brid's hand before she could reply, Sofia started for the door. "I have to get some sleep. I'll no doubt see you guys later one place or another. Walk me to my car, will you please, Brendan?"

"Sure. I'm heading over to the firehouse. I'm on duty at seven; no point in going home. I'll stop by after my shift and check on both the Patches." He gave Franny a quick hug. "Great job tonight. Let me know if you get tired of the doll business, and I'll try to get you on the fire department payroll. We could use a cool head like yours."

Sofia tugged his arm, anxious to be on her way. "If we don't go right this second, you're going to have to carry me to the car," Sofia threatened. "Beside's we are keeping Franny from seeing the baby."

Allowing himself to be towed out the door, Brendan said, "Say hello to the new Ms. Patch for me."

"Come on," Franny said, almost giddy with excitement. "Let's go see that baby!"

They found the NICU tucked in a corner, not far from the birthing center. Franny rang the bell at the closed door and a nurse buzzed them inside.

"Which baby are you here to see?" she asked, studying them.

Brid realized that the nurse was trying to figure out who they might be.

"The Patch baby." Neil added, "We're friends of her mother's."

"I thought so. She's our newbie. Dr. Mallet's in with her now. Why don't you wait in here and I'll see if he can come out and talk to you." She ushered them into a small conference room and closed the door.

"Do you know this doctor? Is he good?" Neil asked Franny, deferring to her as they all did on issues of childbirth and babies.

"He's new—part of the Lynton Pediatric Group. Lilah met a girl in Dr. Harkey's waiting room who loves him. Lilah gave him a call, and she liked him, too. He agreed to take her baby as a new patient."

When the door opened to reveal the doctor, three words came to Brid's mind: *tall, young,* and *hot.* Greg Mallet was at least three inches taller than Neil (who, Brid knew, was over six feet) and the doctor appeared to be Lilah's age (which, Brid reasoned, he couldn't possibly be). She couldn't remember the last time she had seen a man so classically handsome. Whereas the late-night emergency call and subsequent birth-drama had been etched on Dr. Harkey's face, Greg Mallet looked as though he might have just left a Bruins game.

"You all must be Lilah's 'peeps.' " He laughed. "That's what she called you when she filled me in on her situation. Let me guess. You're Neil Malone"—he offered Neil his hand—"You were the easy one." He studied the two women and made his decision. "You're Franny MacCullough. So, you must be Brid Sheerin." Looking from one face to another, he asked, "How'd I do?"

"I hope you're as good a doctor as you are at guessing games," Brid said.

"Actually, I am. Let's sit down." He gestured toward the chairs grouped around the room. When they were all settled, he asked, "So what did Dr. Harkey tell you?"

"She updated us on Lilah, but told us to ask you about the baby." Neil replied.

"Those Patch girls have the angels on their side," the doctor began. "Based on my training, this should not have ended well, but I think—and I hope Dr. Harkey confirmed this, because I haven't followed up on Lilah since the birth—they are both going to be fine. I can tell you the one down the hall is going to be."

"Really, you're sure?" Franny asked, still not convinced it was true.

"Yep. We've got her in an incubator because, at thirty-five weeks, she's considered pre-term, but her weight is good. She's breathing on her own and is very alert. Unless something changes in the next few hours, I will probably move her out of the NICU sometime tomorrow."

"How much does she weigh?" Franny asked, not having paid attention to what Dr. Harkey had told them.

"Six pounds, four ounces. She's eighteen inches long. Not bad, considering she had five weeks left to cook."

Brid shook her head to clear the image of the baby in a pasta pot.

The doctor slapped his hands on the table, having told them everything they needed to know, and stood up. "Would you like to see her?"

"All of us?" Neil got to his feet. "I thought it would be limited to immediate family."

"From where I'm standing, you *are* the immediate family. We only have one other baby in here, so things are pretty quiet. Come on, we'll get you guys suited up, and you can meet her."

Dr. Mallet led them to a room next to the nursery that contained two sinks and several shelves of light blue, cotton gowns, booties and masks.

"Scrub your hands up to your wrists over there." He gestured toward the two large, stainless steel sinks. "The water turns on automatically when you stand in front of the sink. You'll need to wash for two minutes before each visit. A green light will go on over the sink you are using when the two minutes is up." He pointed to where the gowns were stored, "On the left are the 'Dad' gowns. One should fit you, Mr. Malone."

When all three of them were ready, the doctor opened the door to one of the small rooms that buzzed with equipment. In the corner, under a bay of lights, stood an incubator. The nurse who had greeted them—Katelyn, according to her ID tag—stood beside it, talking to the baby lying inside.

"Hey, look. Someone's come to see you." She smiled at the visitors. "It's about time. She was getting bored here with just me."

The doctor unlatched the incubator and opened the top. With practiced hands, he swaddled the baby in the pink blanket the nurse handed him and calmly lifted her, cradling her in the crook of his arm. "So, who's going to get the first cuddle?"

Wordlessly, Franny opened her arms.

Katelyn pushed a rocking chair to the center of the room. "Have a seat. Even though she's tiny, the first time you hold her can be a little bit overwhelming."

Franny sat as directed, and the doctor gently placed the baby into her arms.

"She's a little beauty," he said. Grinning he added, "I think she likes it here. She was screaming her head off in the delivery room but ever since we got her down here, she's been quiet, just taking it all in."

Focused so completely on the infant in her arms, Franny felt as though the two of them, rocking slowly together, were alone in the room.

Watching her, Brid understood how desperately Franny wanted a child of her own.

Franny had fallen in love.

KATHLEEN FERRARI

CHAPTER THIRTEEN

Franny kept checking her watch. The vintage, gold Rolex with its delicate leather strap had been her last birthday gift from Drew. Every time she looked at it, she was reminded of the grin on his face when he had handed her the watch in its gaily-beribboned gold box. For that reason, she made a point of wearing it, instead of relying on her cell phone, the way most of her friends relied on theirs.

She fussed some more with the clothes of the baby doll she was holding; the soles of its shoes had recently been repaired. The glue used to hold together the leather soles of doll shoes tended to dry out with age. Franny depended on a doll hospital in North Carolina for repairs of her dolls and some of their accessories. The work was usually very good, but sometimes, small things like shoes were overlooked. Her fingers traced the seams of the shoes to make sure the job had been done well.

Down the block, the bells of St. Peter's Episcopal Church rang three times.

Abandoning the doll, Franny moved swiftly from behind the glass case and crossed the shop, positioning herself near the door. She had to stop herself from craning her neck to check the sidewalk.

A silver bike sporting rings of blue and yellow on the frame, a baseball mitt hanging from the handlebars, appeared at the top of Main Street. The boy riding it wore a red bike helmet covered with yellow lightning bolts. Dressed in an un-zipped jacket and the pale-blue polo shirt and navy pants that were the uniform of Queen of the Angels Grammar School, he pedaled toward the shop as he had done every day after school for the last few weeks.

Today, Franny was ready for him, determined to find out what kept him coming back so routinely to inspect her window display. She was no expert on small boys, but guessed this one to be about ten. The bike glided past the door, slowing to a stop in front of the bay window. The boy let his feet touch the ground for balance as he leaned over the handlebars to peer in the window.

Franny stepped outside from her hiding place and put her hand firmly on the back of the bike seat. "What are you doing?" she asked. "Do you want something? Is it the horse?" she asked. "He's not for sale. See the sign?" She pointed to the sign at horse's feet stating he was not for sale.

"Yeah. I can read, you know." He twisted toward her, his eyes widening at seeing her hand holding his bike seat. "Let go of my bike. You can't keep me here. I'll yell that you're kidnapping me if you don't let go." He looked around to see if anyone was close enough to rescue him.

Despite his bluster, she could tell he was scared. *Probably remembering the 'Beware of strangers' warning drilled into him by his parents*, she said to herself. The color had drained from his face, making the splash of freckles across his nose stand out. *Cute kid*, she thought.

Franny removed her hand from the bike seat and took a step back. "No one's kidnapping you. Take off if you want to, but it seems like you keep looking in this window for something—and if that's true, I might be able to help you." She stopped talking, waiting to see what he would say. When he continued to eye her with distrust, she went on, "This is my doll shop. I've watched you come by every day and stop to look in the window. You don't seem like a guy who plays with dolls, so why don't you come in and tell me what you're hoping to find here." She nodded at him, and went back into the shop.

The boy hesitated a moment, then leaned his bike against the side of her building and followed her inside.

"Let's sit here by the window. We can check on your bike that way." She directed him to a small table with two chairs. They had a clear view of his bike through the carousel horse's legs. "Now we can talk without you worrying about it." Before he could sit down, she extended her hand. "My name is Franny MacCullough. You can call me Franny. Everyone does."

He stared at her suspiciously and then seemed to make up his mind. Grabbing her hand, he said, "I'm James."

Firm handshake for a kid, Franny thought. To the boy, she said, "Welcome to my shop, James." She watched him check out the room, taking in the rows of dolls and their assorted accessories. "What do you think of it?"

"Kinda girly, too much of that pinky color," he said. He shrugged his backpack off and set it on the floor. "But nice, I guess, I mean, if you're a girl. My sister would love it." He rolled his eyes. "Every single thing she has is pink." He looked at the window. "The horse is cool, though." Tentatively, he reached up to touch one of the prancing legs.

"A friend of mine gave him to me. His name is Bucephalus."

James' face lit up. "Like Alexander's horse?"

"Exactly. The man who rescued this horse was a big fan of Alexander." Franny was secretly delighted that this boy recognized the name of Alexander the Great's beloved warhorse. For just a second, she thought she felt Drew's benevolent presence, and then the feeling was gone. "Are you learning about Alexander in school?"

"Not really. My class is doing a project on military figures in history. I'm gonna do a report about Alexander. My dad and I are reading a book about him. Alexander's the best." His gaze travelled back to the horse. "He and Bucephalus were undefeated in battle." He grinned at her. "Pretty awesome, huh?"

Franny couldn't help but return the smile. "Pretty awesome. So, what is it that you want with my doll shop?"

James' eyes searched the faces of the dolls on the shelves and in the cases. He sighed.

"You don't have a doll like Juliette's." He waved his hand to take in everything on display. "None of these are like her doll."

"Hold on. Just because you don't see the doll here in the shop doesn't mean I can't get it for you." Franny reached for her notebook and, flipping open a fresh page, wrote the date at the top. "But before we start, should you call your mom? Is she at home waiting for you?"

James shifted uneasily in his chair, his eyes sliding away from hers. "I don't need to. She's not waiting for me. I go to my friend Henry's to hang out most days."

Franny nodded, not sure she believed him. "Well then, who is Juliette?"

"My sister." He stopped and then added, "She's a pest."

Franny smiled, wondering if all boys thought their sisters were pests. "Okay. So tell me about this doll you are looking for."

James bit his lip and then began to tell his story.

"Juliette has lots of dolls, but only one she ever played with. Last summer she lost it. She really misses it. Sometimes she cries because it's lost. I thought maybe I could buy another one like it here." His eyes drifted to the shelves again.

"How old is your sister?" Franny asked.

"Five, but she had the doll since she was a baby."

"James, do you understand that I sell *old* dolls?" Franny asked. "You probably can buy a doll like the one your sister had at the mall." She wondered why his parents had not already done so.

He looked at Franny as if she might be from another planet. "That stupid Baby Jullee *is* an old doll. She was my *Mom's* doll. Mom gave her to Juliette. See, they kind of have the same name."

"Wait, you said the doll's name is Baby Jullee?"

He nodded glumly.

"I'll be right back." Franny got up and hurried into the room behind the shop. She returned carrying the binder Lilah had put together, that contained detail-sheets on baby dolls. Flipping through the pages, she located the doll she was looking for and hoped, with a sinking heart, that she was wrong.

"Is this the doll?"

James' face lit up. "Yeah! That's her! Juliette's doll looked just like that, but not as new. How much would it be?" He leaned down and struggled to remove something from the rear pocket of his backpack. Wallet retrieved, he pulled out a handful of wrinkled dollar bills. "I have money." Carefully, he spread three dollars and seventy-five cents on the table in front of Franny. "I have a total of eighteen dollars and seventy-five cents saved up. I have fifteen dollars in my bank at home."

It would be Baby Jullee, Franny thought.

The dolls, manufactured in a small run between 1950 and 1953 by The Arlessey Doll Company, came dressed in a delicate, pink-voile dress and satin underskirt, white leather boots and a white hat covered in rows of white lace. Baby Jullee dolls rarely surfaced, and when they did, if they were in any kind of decent condition, they were expensive. Franny had seen one at a doll show, but had never owned one. *Oh, why couldn't it have been a more common doll?* she anguished silently, looking into James' excited face.

"Keep your money for now. I'm afraid it's not quite that simple."

The boy's face fell.

"I have to find one for you," she said, expressing more confidence than she felt. Looking down at the data sheet, a thought occurred to her. "Did you say this was your mom's doll?"

He nodded.

"Do you know where she got it?" Franny guessed that James' mother was probably around her own age. If so, given the years that Baby Jullee had been on the market, his mother's doll likely had first belonged to someone else.

James furrowed his brow, searching for a memory. "It was Mimi's doll. Her name is Julie, too. Mimi gave it to my mom when she was a little girl and then my mom gave it to Juliette."

"Mimi's your grandmother?"

"Yes." He looked down at the wallet still clenched in his hand.

This kid is hiding something, Franny thought.

"Okay, James. I have a doll detective who tracks down dolls like Baby Jullee for me; she's really good at it. And I am going to look for Baby Jullee, too." Lilah would love being called a "doll detective."

"Awesome. When can I come get her?" James was almost bouncing in the chair.

"Sorry to tell you, but this doll is going to be really hard to find. The company only made them for three years, and they didn't make a lot of them."

James slumped back.

Franny tried to be encouraging. "I can't promise you I will be able to find one, but we will do our best." She picked up her pen.

"What's your telephone number? I'll call you as soon as I find a doll." She waited, watching his face.

"Uh, that's okay. I'll just keep stopping here on my way home from school to see if you've found one." James reached for his backpack and slipped it on.

The sense she'd had earlier, that he was not telling her everything, returned. Why didn't he want her to have his phone number?

James stood up, started for the door and then stopped. He smiled shyly. "Thanks, Mrs. Mac—I mean Franny. I'm glad I met you." He was out the door, on his bike and riding by the window before she could answer.

Sipping from one of the teacups she kept on hand for customers, an open box of cookies within reach, Franny was intently staring at her computer screen when Brid walked through the door. Franny looked up, "Hi Brid, you're —is that a *goat* sticking out of your bag?"

"What's wrong with a goat?" Brid pulled the offending stuffed animal out of her bag and waved it in Franny's face.

Franny went back to her research. "Nothing. I just don't think of goats as being especially cuddly."

"This baby will get enough cuddling from the rest of you." Brid gave in and laughed. "He's a grand goat—in fact, he is a spectacular goat. I got him from a fabric-artist I know." She held the toy up to admire it. "I hope Little Miss No-Name doesn't puke all over him."

Franny raised her eyes from the screen and looked more closely at the felted black-and-white toy in Brid's hand. He was certainly not your average goat.

"Lilah said she would know the baby's name when she met her. We'll probably find out what it is when we see them tonight. The goat really is cute. I'm sure the baby will love him."

"I hope Lilah realizes where he comes from." Brid answered. A calculating look came over her her face. "That is the third cookie you've shoved into your mouth since I walked in the door. You only eat like that when something is bothering you. So, what is it?"

"Oh, crap. Really?" Franny reached over and snapped the cover of the box shut. "Mara gives me samples to try out on my customers. But then *I* eat them. I have to stop. These are today's offering—they are so good."

Brid moved to peer over Franny's shoulder. "Why are you searching for some doll called 'Baby Jullee'?"

"I finally managed to talk to the boy on the bike who's been coming by, looking in the window. He told me the sweetest story."

"Neil mentioned some kid who's been hanging around here. What exactly did he tell you?"

"He's looking for a doll to replace the one his little sister lost. She was really attached to this one doll. He pulled what appeared to be his life savings from his pocket and offered it to me to find this doll."

"Baby Jullee, right?"

"Unfortunately, yes."

"Why is that unfortunate? What's the problem with Baby Jullee?" Brid sat down in one of the wicker chairs.

"They're impossible to find. They were only made for three years in the early fifties, and the company went out of business in 1962. Baby Jullee dolls almost never come on the market. I have seen one only once—at a doll show."

"And they are very expensive, like all items that are hard to find?" Brid waited.

"Well"—Franny hedged, knowing exactly where Brid would take this— "usually, yes, they are. Of course, it depends on the shape they're in. If I were to find one dressed in her original clothes, in the original box, it wouldn't be cheap."

"Not cheap?" Brid persisted.

Like a dog with a bone, Franny thought, realizing there was no point in trying to evade Brid.

"The closest I have come to actually locating any in cyberspace was one that sold two years ago for fifteen hundred dollars."

"Does this kid have a credit card, do you think?"

Franny closed the search, logged off her laptop and shut the cover with a decisive snap.

Funny, Brid, Franny thought. "He told me he has eighteen dollars and seventy-five cents saved up." She stood and slipped the laptop into the tote bag next to her chair. Bracing herself for what she knew would be Brid's reply, she declared, "If I find James the doll, I'll sell it to him for what he has in his pocket," and further asserted, "As we both know, I can afford to take a loss on this particular sale."

"Holy Mother of God! How many times do I have to tell you? You are attempting to run a retail business here—you are no longer playing with dolls in your attic."

Franny couldn't help herself; she started to laugh.

"What do you think is so funny, if I may be so bold as to ask? I promise you, it will not be funny when you go bust."

"You. You're funny. I'm not sure if you sound more like Sofia or Drew."

Brid scowled. "On rare occasions, your sister makes sense, but do not *ever* tell me I sound like that bastard we both were stupid enough to marry. *I* do not sound like Drew MacCullough!"

"Sorry, but he's the one who used to accuse me of playing with dolls."

"Give the boy the damn doll, then—with my blessing. But, I am warning you against it. Remember *that*, when you are living in a cardboard box in the alley behind my gallery."

"You know you would let me live in the back of your gallery and not make me live in the alley. You're not as mean as you pretend to be," Franny replied, unfazed. "Let me grab my coat and lock up so we can go. I can't wait to see Lilah and the baby."

On the street, a dark-green van with **J.A. Benincasa and Son, Plumbing** written in cream-colored letters on the side came to a lurching, double-parked stop in front of the shop. The driver left the hazard lights on as he slammed the van's door shut and marched toward the shop.

"Did you call a plumber?" Brid asked, watching the man bearing down on them.

He was through the door and in the room before Franny could answer. Her first impression was that of an angry bull about to charge: solid and full of energy. He was not a tall man—maybe five-nine—and had dark, curly hair. His deep-brown eyes, she would realize only later on reflection, he had bequeathed to James. He wore tan pants and a dark-green shirt that matched the color of his van. The name "Nick" was embroidered in cream-colored thread over his left breast-pocket.

"Which one of you is Franny?" He looked from one woman to the other.

"I'm Franny MacCullough. This is my shop. How can help you, Mr. —?"

He took two steps forward, so that his face was right in front of hers.

"I don't know what game you think you're playing here, but I'm warning you, stop trying to scam my son." He reached into his pants pocket, pulled out a twenty-dollar bill. He slapped the money down on the top of the display case.

"If you are so damn hard-up for money that you have to prey on little kids, let me donate to the cause."

Brid stood up so fast her chair fell over backwards with a crash. "Listen, you ejit, who the hell do you think you are talking to?"

Ignoring Brid, Franny focused her attention on the man in front of her.

"Mr.—*Nick*. Your son asked me to help him find a doll to replace one his sister lost. Look around you. I buy and sell vintage dolls—as you could see, if you'd stop insulting me for a moment. James came to the right place for help."

Despite the fact that they were now close enough to hug one another, Franny took a step forward. Nick stumbled back.

"I took no money from your son"—her tone was even, unrushed—"nor any credit card information." She added the last bit to amuse Brid, who, Franny sensed, was standing behind her, coiled and ready to strike. "If I'm lucky enough to find this doll—and odds are that I won't—I will deal with James, not you." She took another step forward and, in the same motion, she snatched up the money from the top of the case. Her eyes were level with the man's mouth. She stuffed the twenty into his shirt pocket. "Now, take your money and get the hell out of my shop before I call the police and have you thrown out."

Nick backed his way toward the door. "I'm warning you, lady. Stay away from my kid." And then he was gone.

Franny shook her head. "What an asshole. All I can say is that sweet little boy's mother must be an angel to have genetically wiped out *that* Neanderthal." Aware that Brid was grinning, she asked, "And what are you smiling at?"

"You. What did you do with Mouse-girl? I thought you were going to smack the guy in the face."

Franny lifted her coat from the rack next to the door and shrugged it on. "God, I wanted to, but then I would have ended up in jail, and poor Neil would have had to bail me out"—she grinned—"and, *he's* got enough on his hands dealing with you." She picked up her tote bag. "Grab your goat and let's go see our baby."

CHAPTER FOURTEEN

L ilah studied the sleeping baby tucked in the crook of her left arm, marveling at how perfect she was. At the sound of the door opening, she looked up and smiled dreamily at Brid and Franny as they walked into the room.

"Look who's here? More aunties to visit you," Brendan told the baby from his seat by the window, where he'd been reading the newspaper. Catching sight of the bag Brid carried, he added, "And they brought presents. We accept all donations, don't we?"

Franny had eyes only for the baby. Her breath caught as she gazed down at her.

"She's so beautiful. Look at her face. Her skin reminds me of one of those creamy tea roses tinged with pink."

"She's definitely a rose. I told you I would know what to call her when I met her. Say 'hi' to Rose Malone Patch." Lilah offered the sleeping infant to Franny, who reached out with eager arms to cradle her.

Lilah shot a quick, anxious look at Brid, who had sat down in the chair next to the bed. *Please don't be mad*, Lilah thought.

Aloud, she said, "I asked Neil if it was okay to use his name; he said he would be honored." When Brid was silent, Lilah continued, her words tumbling over each other in a rush. "I like the way it sounds. I wouldn't have just, you know, used his name without asking him if it was okay."

"Why must you always do things the hard way, Lilah?" Brid asked, watching with a slight frown as Franny sang softly to the baby in her arms. "You could have had a child without almost killing yourself going about it. I believe that's what most people do." Holding out her arms, she said to Franny, "Let me see the little troublemaker."

Reluctantly, Franny handed over the baby. As Brid lifted her up, the infant opened her eyes and stared into Brid's face.

"You are a beauty, Rose Malone. Rose Malone is a grand name for you." She looked up and smiled at Lilah. "Rosemary was my mother's name. Did you know that?" Mouth open, Lilah shook her head, indicating, she did not. Brid gently tapped the baby's chest. "It would seem we are starting out with me owing you a favor. Maybe if you take Neil's name, it will lessen the sting when I tell him that I am not."

"What do you mean, you're not taking his name? Why would you—" Lilah winced slightly as she shifted toward Brid and craned her neck. "Let me see your hand!" she demanded.

Behind Rose's downy head, Brid wagged the ring finger of her left hand.

"Oh, my God! That is so totally sick! When did you decide to get married?" Indignantly, Lilah added, "And when were you going to tell me?" She looked from Brid to Brendan, "Did *you* know about this?"

Brendan hid behind the newspaper.

"Neil asked me to marry him the night you were busy scaring us all out of our collective wits. As for telling you, here I am. Telling you." The baby began to fuss. "Away you go," Brid told her, handing her back to Lilah. "I have exceeded my expertise on the subject of babies. When they start to cry, they have to go back where they came from."

"The nurse said to try and feed her when she cries. She latches on pretty well, but it takes her a little while to get the idea that she needs to suck."

"TMI," Brendan said, standing up. "And that's my cue to step out. I'm going to track down Sofia. She went off to make a phone call an hour ago." He folded the paper, placed it on the chair and ambled out of the room.

Rose snuffled around for a few minutes and then began to nurse steadily. Lilah adjusted her body to accommodate her.

"How are you feeling?" Franny asked Lilah, her eyes still on the baby. "Have you been out of bed yet?"

"Oh yeah, the nurse had me up first thing this morning."

"And how did that go?" Brid asked.

Lilah laughed. "Awesome, once I figured out that my guts weren't going to end up on the floor. The nurse promised me it gets better."

"It definitely does get better, but the first time is not fun. And that's exactly how it feels—like your entire insides are going to fall out. I remember," Franny said, grimacing at the memory of the pain.

"When can you come home?" Brid asked.

"Dr. Harkey said she may release me Saturday, if I am going to a place where someone can help me."

"You and Rose are coming home to Hiram's Forge to stay with me." Franny said, firmly, looking first at Lilah then at Brid. "Well, she is, isn't she? I already know exactly what we should do for the nursery. I think we should have lots of bunnies."

"I think that's a grand plan for an interim next step," Brid replied, "but I would not worry too much about a nursery until we figure out where she is going to be living."

Franny frowned. "I thought Lilah and Rose could stay with me. I have the space and I would love to have them. We need to get a crib, though, and other things."

"Rose doesn't need a crib yet—do you?" Lilah interjected, thinking, *I can't live permanently with Franny.* The baby continued to nurse contentedly. "She can sleep with me. It will be easier to nurse her."

"Oh, *no,*" Franny said, horrified. "She can't sleep with you. You might roll over on top of her and smother her. All the books say —"

"We can get her one of those Jericho baskets. That should solve the problem nicely for the moment, and Lilah can carry her about in it." Brid's tone dared either woman to contradict her.

"It's a *Moses* basket. Jericho was something else. Read your Old Testament," Sofia informed them from the doorway. "It's a great idea, though. Rose won't need a crib for ages." She looked from one face to another. "I mean, they don't grow that fast, do they? I thought we could make a list of things she'll need right away like, you know, diapers. Brendan and I will run over to the mall and pick them up. I'm sure we can find a Moses basket at the baby store there." She looked around. "Where is he, anyway?"

"He left a little while ago to go find you," Franny said.

Sofia advanced into the room, smiling at the baby, when her eyes fell on the felted goat sticking out of the bag at Brid's feet. Pointing, she asked, "What is that?"

"A goat," Brid said. "He's a gift for Rose Malone."

"Really, Brid? A goat? Who gives a tiny baby a prickly, old goat?"

Lilah's eyes followed the direction of Sofia's finger. "Let me see!" she cried. "Is that really for Rose?"

"Yes, and if it appreciates the way I believe it will, it might pay for her first year of college." Brid, shooting Sofia a venomous look, handed the gift to Lilah.

"Are you serious? Is this an Aoife Molloy?" Lilah reverently removed the small black-and-white goat from the tissue paper. "Oh my God! It *is* one of Aoife's!" she said, finding the artist's signature on the animal's underside.

"I am delighted motherhood hasn't completely destroyed your brain. Aoife's collection this year is entitled 'Animals from the Farm.' And this"—she gestured, palms up—"would be the goat."

"I still think it's a weird toy to give an infant." Sofia continued to eye the gift with suspicion.

"It's not a *toy*," Lilah protested. "Aoife Molloy is one of the foremost fabric artists in the world." She told Brid, "I can't take this; it's worth *way* too much. The ostrich from the 'Animals from Africa' collection sold last year for twelve thousand dollars!"

"I didn't give it to you; I gave it to *Rose Malone*," Brid said. "All *you* are supposed to do is say 'thank you' for her, as she cannot. Write me a nice note, if it makes you feel better."

"But you can't afford to give her this." Yet, even as she said it, Lilah knew how badly she wanted Aoife's special goat for Rose.

"Wait—how do you know this Aoife person?" Sofia asked Brid, clearly ready to see the little goat in a new light. "Have you shown her work in the gallery?"

"We roomed together when I was at school in Boston. She

used to come out and help me wait tables at Craic on the weekends, when we were both poor students living on ramen noodles." Brid shook her head, a wry smile on her face. "A long time ago. She had a problem with her visa at one point, and Da pointed her to someone who made it all come out right. She's never forgotten that. I have shown a few of her smaller pieces in the gallery but her work is too expensive for my clientele." She shrugged. "We are old friends. Whenever she is in the area she comes out to see me. She met Lilah when she was here last year."

Brid told Lilah, "When I told Aoife that I wanted a piece from 'Animals from the Farm' as a present for your baby, she practically gave him to me. In fact, consider it a gift from us both. It turns out he was her favorite. There's always one piece in every collection that she's especially fond of, and she was delighted to send him off to a good home."

Lilah had been paying attention, but Brid, detecting a bit of sleep in the girl's eyes, said, "You must be getting tired. We should probably leave you and the baby to get some rest."

"Oh, before we go, I almost forgot." Franny took the laptop from her tote bag and placed it on the table next to the bed. "Do you feel strong enough to do some work?"

Lilah perked up and rolled her eyes.

"Definitely. Rose sleeps most of the time, and I get so bored, I could scream. Kren is not behaving. And the other characters aren't either. They can be a bunch of pigs. I should draw them to *look* like pigs." That was not a bad idea, she realized. She made a face at her sketchbook sitting on the high rolling-table at the end of the bed. "What do you need?"

"I was hoping you could do some research for me. In fact, I told this customer you were a doll detective. Can we put that up on the website? I think it would be funny, don't you?"

"Wow! 'L. Patch—Doll Detective.' I'm stoked. I'll do that, but I need to find a decent picture of myself to post with it. Maybe I'll take a new one." She was already thinking of a new color for her hair.

"This is the doll we're looking for." Franny handed Lilah a small white card.

She read it and whistled softly.

"You realize, I would have better luck finding the Baby Jesus than Baby Jullee, right?"

"Lilah, you can find anything. Besides, we have to try. This customer is special," Franny insisted.

Lilah continued to frown at the card. "I hope he or she has a lot of money. If I find this doll—and that would be amazing—it won't be cheap. I think the last one I saw on eBay went for fifteen hundred dollars. It could have been even more. Of course, that one was in perfect shape."

"Ah, don't give that another thought," Brid said, waving her hand. "The customer is loaded. Franny thinks he has about eighteen dollars saved up, isn't that so?" She pointedly looked at Franny.

Brid's words hung in the air a moment.

Lilah looked from one face to the other. "So, what are you guys talking about? Does someone really want to buy Baby Jullee or not?"

"Brid is just being mean—" Franny began.

"No way! Not Brid." This came from Sofia, who had been listening with growing interest.

Franny ignored them both, directing her words to Lilah. "Do you remember I told you about a boy who kept coming by the shop and staring in the window?"

Lilah nodded.

"I met him today. His name is James, and he's a cutie-patootie. It turns out he has a little sister named Juliette, who had a Baby Jullee that originally belonged to her grandmother. Somehow, Juliette lost the doll. James was checking out the window to see if we had a replacement. I promised him we would try our best to find him one."

"Ask Franny about young Mr. James having a raving ejit for a father, Lilah," Brid suggested. "He showed up at the shop just before we came over here and accused her of trying to take advantage of the boy. He told her to stay away from his son."

"What?" Sofia exploded. "Did he threaten you? Did you call the police?"

"You would have been very proud of your sweet sister," Brid said. "She threw him out of the shop, almost on his ass. It was impressive, to be sure."

"Are you crazy, Franny? He could have hurt you! Guys like that hurt people every day. We can get a restraining order taken out on him, you know." Sofia pulled out her cell phone, ready to make notes. "What—exactly—did he do?"

"Oh, here you are, Sofia," Brendan said, walking into the room on the tail end of the conversation. "What did *who* do?"

"The guy is an asshole—one of those short guys with thick necks that are all mouth. I'm not worried about him. He works for Benincasa Plumbing. He came storming out of one of their vans. They have a great reputation. I'm sure they would not employ a psychopath," Franny said flatly, dismissing the incident. "All I can say is that his wife must be a saint, because James is a very nice boy."

Wow, Lilah thought. She had never heard Franny call anyone an asshole. "A complete jerk" was as far as Franny usually went. Brid had a really bad mouth on her when she was mad, but not Franny.

"Hey, wait a minute. Are you talking about Nick Benincasa?" Brendan interrupted.

"Well, 'Nick' was embroidered on his shirt. You mean he's the *owner*?" Franny's surprise changed to a scowl. "Brendan, do you know this guy?"

"Listen, I don't know what happened at the shop today, but Nick's a great guy who's had some rotten luck. I can tell you, he's very protective of his kids. He's an amazing dad; his two kids come first. And as far as being an asshole, you've got the wrong person. His ex-wife, Jenn—*there's* a world-class asshole. Nick's been picking up the pieces from that mess for the last four years." Brendan paused, frowning. "I think what you two have going on here is a huge misunderstanding."

The color drained from Franny's face as she listened. "Oh, God. What happened with his wife?"

"Nick and I have worked on more than a few jobs together. I met Jenn at a party when she was pregnant with their daughter. Pregnant—and pissed as hell that she was having another kid, I might add." He shook his head in disgust. "Jenn Benincasa believed she was meant for better things than Lynton. She took off before the baby was a year old. Just up and left. Nick's been juggling the business, the kids, and the house ever since."

"Now it all makes more sense. I feel awful." Franny said, remembering how evasive James had been about his mother waiting at home for him.

"I don't know why," Brid said, clearly unmoved. "Remember, I was there. Nothing Brendan's just told us justifies the guy barging into your place of business and jumping all over you the way he did."

"Maybe," Franny reasoned. "He must be so raw about it all that he's hyper-concerned about everything to do with his kids. He probably feels terrible that Juliette lost the doll, and now poor James feels *he* has to do something about it. It must have made the guy feel like a bad father, and, clearly, from what Brendan says, he's not."

"Time for you all to head out." At the door, a nurse standing with her hands on her hips looked none too happy with the crowd around her patients. "In case you have forgotten, these two were in ICU yesterday."

Calling goodnight to Lilah, Brendan and Sofia filed out of the room.

Franny leaned over and gave Lilah a hug. "Get some sleep, and if you feel up to it tomorrow, see if you can find Baby Jullee. Just keep track of the time you spend."

"No problem. Like I said, I am pretty glazed here when Rose is sleeping." She grinned. "A doll detective, huh? I'll put out some feelers to my peeps tomorrow. Maybe we'll get lucky."

Brid was the last to leave. She made no move to hug Lilah, but bent over the baby, sleeping now inside her bassinet next to Lilah's bed.

"I am not big on babies, but I do believe you have done a lovely job with this one. I think we will have some fun with her." Gently, she tapped Rose's small fist. "You let your mother get some sleep. She has to get out of here and back to work."

CHAPTER FIFTEEN

B rendan Feeney pushed open the glass door to Caroline's Kitchen, the smell of frying bacon and fresh-brewed coffee hitting his nose. It was not quite seven o'clock in the morning. The red vinyl stools along the counter in front of the open kitchen held Caroline's regulars, mostly blue-collar workmen who needed the kind of breakfast that would carry them through a long day. By unspoken agreement, they'd left vacant the booths in front of the windows facing Main Street and the tables in the center of the restaurant. These were guys who liked to keep an eye on their food as it was cooking.

Looking up from refilling a cup of coffee, Caroline Nealy smiled and called out a greeting.

"Well, if it isn't young Mr. Feeney. Been a while since we've seen you in here. You must have a girlfriend who's feeding you in the mornings."

Brendan felt his face grow hot. He and Sofia had been spending most of their nights together at her place or his, although she certainly wasn't feeding him. On the contrary, it was he who tried his best to get some food into her.

"Hey, Caroline. Shifts have been crazy." His eyes searched the profiles of the men at the long counter until he found the face he was looking for. Fortunately, next to his quarry was an empty stool. Brendan walked over and straddled it.

"Nick, how's it going? Haven't seen you since the Lawton property last fall. Been busy?"

Nick Benincasa glanced up from the *Lynton Ledger* sports page.

"Hi, Brendan. I guess that's right. How're things? Where are you working these days when you're not out fighting fires?"

"I'm doing some custom kitchen cabinets for a couple who are restoring an old place on Latimer Street. I had to do some research to find the style they wanted, so the project was a little slow getting started. It should pick up now that I know where we're going with it. You?"

"I do okay. Can't outsource a blocked-up sink." He grimaced and added, "Or worse."

"I guess we're both lucky that what we do requires someone to be there to do it." Brendan reached for the coffee Caroline delivered, nodding his thanks.

"Yeah, true." Nick's eyes wandered back to his paper.

"How are the kids? They must be getting really big," Brendan said, tiptoeing toward the conversation that was the reason for his mission.

Nick Benincasa had what women described as a sweet smile. The mention of his kids almost always put it on his face.

"They're good—really good. Next year Juliette will be in school all day. She's in kindergarten this year. Spends half the day in school and the other half in the extended-day program they have there. James is in fifth grade, and all he cares about is baseball. He's a catcher, if you can believe that." Nick laughed, "Pretty damn good one, too."

"Ready to order there, Brendan?" Caroline asked, pen and pad in hand.

"Sure. Two eggs over easy, bacon crisp, English grilled, and thank you."

"Be up shortly." Caroline pulled the slip from her pad and clipped it to the revolving order-wheel behind her.

"So, what happened the other day between you and Franny MacCullough?" Brendan asked Nick.

"How did you hear about that?" Brendan had Nick's attention, his newspaper abandoned.

"She's a friend of mine." Brendan took a sip of his coffee to buy time and then continued, somewhat reluctantly, "I'm dating her sister. So I've gotten to know her pretty well."

Nick opened his mouth to speak, but Brendan cut him off.

"The thing is, I feel like I know you both pretty well, and what she told me happened the other day just doesn't add up. I'd like to hear your side of it."

Nick grunted as he considered the invitation.

"Okay. I have to go back a bit, though, for you to understand. Juliette had this doll called Baby Jullee. It was her mother's— although what Jenn was doing with a baby doll is beyond me. She has to be most the non-maternal female on the planet. I can't see her *ever* playing with dolls."

He looked away from Brendan, the subject too painful to continue. *Wow, he's still really pissed,* Brendan thought. "Anyway," he shook his head, "it was Jenn's doll and she gave it to Juliette when she was a baby. Then, as you know, Jenn left. And Juliette carried that doll everywhere. It was funny—and sad, too—because she didn't do that with any other doll. Or toy, for that matter. Only Baby Jullee." His voice strained in frustration. "Last August I took the kids over to Nantucket on the ferry. I thought, you know, it would be fun for them. Make some nice memories."

He stopped talking as Caroline set Brendan's breakfast before him. Brendan cut his eggs with his fork and began eating, waiting patiently for Nick to go on.

"What a nightmare. The doll went off the side of the ferryboat—Juliette was hysterical. She didn't stop sobbing the entire weekend. Sometimes, I think I should have gone in after the damn thing." He ran his fingers through his thick hair. "It wouldn't have made any difference if I had; the doll disappeared pretty fast. I remember thinking: 'Thank God it isn't Juliette in the water.' James felt awful about it, too. So much for making a nice weekend of memories."

"Did you look for another doll like it?" Brendan asked.

"I didn't, but my mother-in-law did. With no luck. Baby Jullee had been hers to begin with—and that's part of the problem. The doll was made in the fifties by a company that wasn't in business very long. I guess they didn't sell a lot of them, so the dolls are hard to find. And according to my mother-in-law, not cheap."

"Yeah, she mentioned something about that when she told me what happened, but I'm still not clear what she did that made you so mad at her—?"

"She promised James she would find him another Baby Jullee—actually told the kid she has a doll detective who works for her." Nick groped in his pocket for his wallet. "So now he's convinced he's going to bike down to her stupid shop and pick up a doll he can bring home for his sister."

Brendan slid his empty plate away from him.

"What you're telling me matches pretty closely to Franny's version of the story. What you need to know is that she didn't pull James in off the street. He's been checking out her shop window pretty regularly for the last few weeks. She couldn't figure out what a boy would want in a doll shop, so the other day she confronted him. He told her he was looking for a doll for his sister. And she took it from there."

Nick was quiet. He seemed to be taking in the new pieces of the story.

Brendan continued. "As far as having a doll detective working for her, I think she put it like that because she felt it would be easier for James to relate to, rather than calling the person who works for her a 'researcher.' " Brendan couldn't keep the grin off his face as he thought of his last sight of the doll detective. "I know the girl who sources the dolls, and she is amazing at hunting down the hard-to-find ones. Franny told me she warned James she might not be able to find the doll. Whether he heard that part of what she said is another story, but I know she would never have deliberately misled him."

Brendan dropped a ten on top of the check Caroline had left for him. He debated internally for a moment, then decided he wanted Nick to understand Franny's intentions—as a person as well as a business owner.

"Look, I don't have kids," he said, "but I do get a sense of how much you love yours, and I think I understand why this upset you. But you should know that Franny MacCullough was only trying to help James—and it isn't about the money. Her husband died suddenly a couple of years ago, and life hasn't been easy for her. She's crazy about kids and wasn't able to have her own. She would never do anything to hurt James."

Nick frowned. "Maybe I over-reacted. It's a hazard of being a single parent. There's only me to look out for them, you know?" He shrugged. "I had no idea that James had been haunting the place—of course, he didn't tell me *that*. All he said was this nice lady had promised to find him a doll for Juliette, and he was saving up his money to pay for it." He crumpled his paper angrily. "Ah, shit," he muttered, feeling miserable.

Brendan extended his hand. "You were just being a good dad. Franny and Lilah are pretty tenacious. If there's a Baby Jullee out there to be found, they'll track her down. I have to get over to the station. It was great seeing you."

"Hold on a minute. Was that the doll detective who was in the shop when I was there the other day? She had some kind of accent?"

"Definitely not the doll detective; she's in St. Luke's. Just had a baby." He thought for a moment. "An accent … oh, yeah. That would have been Brid Sheerin. She's Irish, although you only hear her brogue when she's upset. I bet she was mad, huh?"

"I thought she was going to kill me. But the MacCullough woman stepped between us."

"Probably good that she did. Brid *might* have killed you. She watches out for Franny." He checked the time on his cell phone. "Hey, I really gotta go. See you around."

* * *

Standing behind the display case and facing the door to the street, Brid studied the porcelain baby-doll swaddled in a cloud of pale-pink tissue paper in front of her. "So what is it worth?" she asked.

Opposite Brid on the other side of the case, Franny smoothed the smocking on the ivory-colored dress the doll was wearing. *Trust Brid to be hung up on the money*, she thought. "Not as much as you think," she answered, her attention focused on getting the doll to look just right. "This is not the original dress. I had to recreate it from pictures. Lilah found this doll on craigslist, when we were gathering inventory before we opened the shop. They should probably start the bidding around one hundred and fifty dollars. I think they'll be able to make that without …"

Franny had half-expected a comment from Brid at hearing the dollar figure, and, noting the silence, looked up to see Brid stiffen and the color drain from her face. She was vaguely aware of the sound of the bell above the door. She turned around to see what could have caused Brid such a state of shock.

"Oh, Franny, I want to thank you again for letting us come and take a picture for the auction catalog." Ashlyn Medford had flung open the door and swept into the shop in all her President-of-the-Women's-Auxiliary-of-the-Lynton-Country-Club glory. She had an imposing-looking camera dangling from her neck. "Is that the doll you're giving us for the auction?"

"Yes, it is, hi Ashlyn," Franny said, while at the same time, trying to remember if Brid had ever mentioned Ashlyn to her. Did she not like the woman? That might account for her strange behavior.

"Do you want her displayed in the window or in the box? Actually, I had this made to stand behind her in the window, to help advertise the auction." Franny reached for a poster that Lilah had designed and held it up.

Getting no reaction from Ashlyn, she left it on the top of the case.

Ashlyn continued to coo over the doll. "She is really lovely, much more impressive than I expected. I think we should consider her for the cover of the catalog. What do you think, Elaine? This doll could be the top bid."

It was only then, with a sinking heart, that Franny realized the real reason Brid had gone as still as a wild animal run to ground. Elaine MacCullough stood just inside the door. Brid must have seen her following a few steps behind Ashlyn.

"I hardly think so, Ashlyn. We're offering a trip for two to Tuscany, after all," Elaine said.

"Of course, you're right," Ashlyn bubbled on. "But I still think this doll would definitely punch up the cover." She looked at Franny and grinned as if they were fellow conspirators. "I just *love* dolls. I always have. I may bid on her myself. She would be sweet on the bed in my guest room."

"Why don't you take some pictures in the box and then we can put her in the window? That way you can decide which arrangement you like best." Franny carefully fluffed the pink tissue and made sure the satin bow on the doll's bonnet was not hiding her face.

Brid moved from behind the case to the side of the room to avoid the photo shoot. Unfortunately, Elaine still blocked her escape.

Ashlyn appeared to know what she was doing with the camera, taking several shots from different angles. Franny took the opportunity to try to get Elaine out of the doorway.

"Hello, Elaine. Can I get you a cup of tea? I have some lovely meringues ... "

"Thank you, no. I don't eat sweets, as you should know." Elaine kept her eyes on Brid. Ashlyn picked up the doll. "Right. I think I've got some good ones of her in the box. Shall we try the window?"

"Go ahead, I'll set it up for you," Franny said, tucking the poster under her arm and gently taking the doll from Ashlyn. She moved to the window, arranging the scene as Ashlyn brushed past Elaine and out the door, oblivious to the battle lines forming behind her.

Elaine spoke first. "Rod brought home an ugly rumor the other day." She looked pointedly at Brid's left hand, stepping into the room for a closer look. "I am so sorry to see that it's true."

"Brid, don't you have to take that book over to Lilah?" Franny asked from across the room, nodding at a reference book on top of the display case, fabricating an errand as casually as she could. "She's waiting for it, isn't she?"

"I'm going just now."

Brid picked up the book and started to leave, when Elaine spoke again.

"I am so glad that Neil's mother is dead. This would have broken her heart. It certainly broke mine when you married Drew."

Franny gasped. "Elaine!"

"I doubt you would have recognized Peg Malone if you had run into her on the sidewalk. And we both know if you *had* recognized her, you would have looked the other way." Brid took a step toward her former mother-in-law and then stopped, checking herself. "As far as your 'heart,' Mrs. MacCullough, you never had one to break. No one knew that better than your son."

She moved past Elaine and out the door, almost breaking into a run as she headed toward the gallery, leaving the two women inside stunned in her wake.

Franny bit her lip and said, "I'm sorry she said that, but you shouldn't have pushed her. She loves Neil."

Elaine let out a deep breath and her color slowly returned to normal "I see nothing has changed. She always was a terrible person." Elaine considered Franny thoughtfully and said, "You, on the other hand, are not. I can't imagine why you have anything to do with her." Speechless, Franny stared at her.

Finished with her photos, Ashlyn backed in the door.

"I hope I didn't chase away a customer."

When neither Franny nor Elaine responded, she continued, "Okay, I think I managed to get several keepers. I'll be back the day before the auction to pick up the doll."

She smiled brightly at Franny, "Thank you so much for contributing the doll to the auction. All the proceeds will go to our signature project: fostering children's literacy in Lynton. It's such a good cause. Don't you agree?"

Franny pulled her thoughts from Brid and focused on what Ashlyn was saying. "Yes, I do, and I am happy to be a part of it."

"Okay, then, I think we're finished here, aren't we, Elaine?"

"Yes, I believe we are. We better let Franny get back to," Elaine paused and looked around before continuing with a sweeping hand gesture, "whatever it is she does here. Oh, and Franny, we should have dinner. I know Rod would love to see you. Give me a call and we can set something up." *That'll never happen*, Franny thought as Elaine walked out, leaving Ashlyn Medford to follow behind her.

Hands shaking, Franny speed-dialed Brid on her cell phone She bit her lip when it went to voice mail. "Brid, it's Franny. I need to talk to you."

Putting the phone down, she debated closing early to run down to the gallery; the look on Brid's face when she'd left the shop was worrying her. The bell over the door jingled. Franny looked up to see Peter McGonagle carrying in a vase of pale pink roses.

"Hi, Franny. I have a delivery for you." He placed the vase of flowers on the top of the display case.

"For me? Really?" She couldn't imagine who might be sending her flowers—especially roses. Her mind turned fleetingly to the red roses Drew had sent her the night before he died.

"They're for you. There's a card." Peter nodded toward the small white envelope tucked into the flowers. "Looks like you might have a secret admirer."

Franny snorted. "I doubt that. They're probably from my sister."

"Enjoy them, whoever sent them." Peter said, already on his way out.

"Thanks, I will. They're beautiful," she called after him.

Franny picked up her phone and called Brid again. Still voice mail. Distracted, she plucked up the card and absentmindedly opened it, expecting to see a quirky message from Sofia. Instead, she read:

I'm sorry. Please let me apologize by taking you to dinner. Nick.

He had attached his business card to be sure she would know how to reach him.

KATHLEEN FERRARI

CHAPTER SIXTEEN

Neil opened the door to the flat and was greeted by the sight of Brid's back. She stood at an easel across the room, concentrating on the painting in front of her and giving no sign she had heard him. The stiffness of her shoulders, though, did not bode well. Usually, she lit a fire when she came in from the gallery, but not today. He felt a distinct chill in the air. Not all of it was due to the temperature in the room.

He set his briefcase on the oak sideboard by the door. He liked the sight of it sitting there; it made him feel he belonged here. He was about to call a greeting when Brid spoke, without turning around.

"There's no dinner. I'm painting."

Before Neil could answer, the cell phone lying next to his briefcase buzzed with a text.

Where r u? U ok?

"There's a text for you from Franny," he said.

Brid stabbed at the painting with her brush. "Ignore it. She's being a pest."

"I'm going to make a pot of tea. Would you like some?" he asked. She shook her head.

Pondering what might be going on, Neil walked down the hall to the kitchen. As he flipped the switch on the electric kettle, his eyes fell on a round loaf of soda bread wrapped in a starched linen napkin. *Now when did she find the time to make that?* he wondered. *It wasn't there when I left this morning.* He located the serrated bread-knife and cut a generous slice. Waiting for the water to boil, he enjoyed the bread, allowing himself the disloyal thought that it was better than his mother's.

Reaching for the kettle, he poured a cup of the now boiling water into a Beleek teapot, swished it around to heat the pot, then emptied it. He had lingered over the tea before selecting Lapsang Souchong—Brid's favorite—and bypassing his own: good, solid Barry's Original. He added the tea and covered it with water from the kettle, allowing it to steep as he prepared a tray.

Despite Brid's supposed lack of interest, he included a mug for her; he'd been raised to believe a cup of tea would cure anything. Making room for the soda bread, he surveyed the tray and was satisfied. He carried it through to the living room, depositing it on the coffee table in front of the fireplace.

"So are you going to tell me what this is all about, or are you going to make me guess?" He slipped his arms around her, pulling her close while burying his face in her hair.

"For the love of God! I am trying to paint." She wriggled out of his grasp.

"You're not painting, you're attacking the thing. You're only going to have to fix it. Come over here and join me in a cup of tea. Are you feuding with Franny?"

"Don't be ridiculous. Of course I'm not fighting with Franny. I just don't happen to feel like talking to her now. Or to you, either."

Unfazed, Neil removed the brush from her hand and placed it in the holder on the side of the easel. "That's a shame, because I feel like talking to you. Come and sit down."

At that moment, the door buzzer sounded, startling them both.

"Are you expecting someone?" Neil asked.

"I give up. It's Franny—who else? Let her in." Brid absentmindedly poured a cup of tea.

"Who is it?" Neil asked, facing the intercom by the door.

"Neil! Thank God you're home. Can I come in?" Franny's anxious voice filled the room.

Brid threw up her hands as if to say, "I told you so."

"Of course." He said, and opened the door.

Franny's worried look matched the sound of her voice; she attempted to see past him. "Is she here?"

"Yes, she's here." Brid said, answering for him. "Come in, so the two of you can both fuss about, and then I can get back to my painting."

Franny almost shoved Neil out of the way in her hurry to get across the room.

"Brid! I've been so worried. Why didn't you answer your phone? I've called you about ten times." She sat next to Brid. "Are you okay?" She searched the other woman's face as if she could find the answer there.

"Holy Mother of God! You are a *plague*. I just want to paint in peace. Leave me alone." She shook her head in disgust, looking from one to the other. "Why don't you go out to dinner and wring your hands together?"

"That may not be a bad idea," Neil said. "I am more than happy to take you both to dinner wherever you would like to go; first, I want to know what the hell is going on here." Watching the two women, he took a sip of tea and waited for a reply. When none was forthcoming, he added, "Franny, would you like a cup of tea or coffee?"

She shook her head, eyes on Brid, wanting her friend to speak first. When Brid remained mute, Franny reluctantly began.

"Brid was in the shop today when Elaine came in and said something…" she paused, seeing that Brid's face had become even stormier.

Neil put his Belleek coffee mug down abruptly. Franny winced as the Parian china met the coaster.

"What the hell happened with Elaine MacCullough?" he demanded. "I don't understand why you two can't accept that she is a lonely, old woman who has lost her only son. You both know she has problems."

Brid stood up, hands on her hips.

"Even *vipers* get old. I may be wrong, but I don't think it makes them any less dangerous. If you think I have any intention of sitting here listening while you weep over that evil witch, you are greatly mistaken. I'm going for a run. Spin Franny the tired tale of how the poor, old hag was devoted to her darling son." Her eyes flashed, glaring at Neil. "You forget; I was there."

Without a backward glance for either of them, she grabbed a

hooded sweatshirt draped over a chair and was out the door, closing it with a resounding slam.

Neil reached for his cooling tea, taking a long, thoughtful sip. He put the mug down again, this time more gently.

"That went well." He shook his head. "Elaine, huh? What happened?"

"Brid stopped by the shop this afternoon. I knew that Ashlyn Medford—do you know her? President of the Lynton Country Club's Women's Auxiliary? Anyway, I knew she was coming in today to take a picture of the doll I am donating for their annual charity auction." Franny sighed, "But I didn't realize that Elaine was coming with her. Brid was behind the display case when Elaine showed up." Franny faltered, still stunned by the memory. "It was the strangest thing. Elaine never came very far into the shop—just stayed in the doorway, like she knew she had Brid cornered."

"Come on, Franny, she's what? Seventy-six, seventy-seven? I hardly think she is as malevolent as Brid makes her out to be," Neil said, disbelief in his tone.

Franny's voice dropped to a whisper. "She was really cruel to Brid. It was awful."

Neil's skepticism wavered. He was not sure he wanted an answer, but knew he must ask.

"What did she say?"

Franny filled him in, almost verbatim, her story punctuated by Neil's reactions: a strangled growl; covering his face with his hands; an explosive "God, *damn* it!" that accompanied his hurling a magazine across the room. Mostly, his face and body registered grief. When she finished, he shook his head as if to clear from his mind the ugly scene her words had painted.

"Neil, why would she say those things to Brid?" When he didn't answer, she gently coaxed, "Neil?"

He sighed. "That was unfortunate. I'm sorry you had to witness it."

"But why does Elaine hate Brid so much? I mean, she and Drew—that was a long time ago."

Neil got up and walked over to the French doors. He stared out into the garden for a moment, before facing her once again.

"I imagine it's as simple as Elaine having been jealous. The old 'mother-son' thing."

Neil ran his fingers through his hair, more gray now than chestnut. He deliberated how much to tell her; she was Drew's widow, after all. That fact rarely came between them, but this was one of those times that it did. Slowly, he began to tell the story.

"From the moment Drew walked into Craic, he was besotted with Brid. And she was something to behold"—he grinned, despite himself—"all long legs, flashing green eyes and attitude. When those two came together it was like a conflagration. And to think I was the one who brought him in there." He paused, lost in his memories. "Elaine wanted Drew to marry the right kind of girl: a debutante from what she would have deemed a good family. Hell, Elaine wanted him to marry a girl just like herself, not some fiery, Irish beauty with an artistic temperament. And especially, not one who'd grown up over a *bar*, a girl with a hell of a mouth on her." His eyes met Franny's. "Drew didn't give a damn what his mother wanted and married Brid anyway."

His glance drifted toward the door. *How long has she been gone, anyway?* he wondered, absently checking his watch.

"You know, this might surprise you, but Elaine was good to me. They both were. Rod MacCullough was a class act, and he would never have made me feel unwelcome. Elaine was another story. She was raised to believe she was better than most people and she never forgot it. She could have made my life miserable. But she never did. I have no idea why."

"Oh, Neil," Franny smiled at him, "you must have been such a nice boy. How could she not like you?"

"I was Drew's shadow, a freckled-faced Irish kid whose father was a city cop. I was in and out of that house from the time I was nine years old. The MacCulloughs lived in another world from the one I came from." He shrugged. "They never treated me any different from Harry, who was one of them," he said, referring to Drew's childhood friend. The three boys had established an enduring friendship. "When I graduated from high school, they gave me a check for a thousand dollars—a hell of a lot of money, especially then. My father wanted me to return it, but my mother said that would be an insult, and if the MacCulloughs thought that highly of me, I should keep it."

"But why would Elaine make stuff up about your mother hating Brid?" Franny pressed.

Neil snorted. "What do you mean, make it up? It's true. My mother would turn in her grave if she knew I was marrying Brid Sheerin."

Franny stared at him. In a voice hardly more than a whisper, she asked, "But—why?"

"I'm not sure it makes sense if you're not Irish. I guess there must be some version that goes on in every culture, but, my God, Irish women can be hard. They have these two buckets: 'good girls' and 'bad girls.' " He smiled, remembering the sight of seventeen-year-old Brid Sheerin Irish step-dancing on top of the old, oak bar on St. Patrick's Day. "And Brid was definitely a 'bad girl.' "

"What did she do that was so awful? I know Brid can be difficult, and she always tells you exactly what she thinks, but … " Franny's voice trailed off in confusion.

Neil sighed, not sure he wanted to have this conversation.

"Okay," he said, "I will try to explain it to you. When I was growing up, girls from Irish families were supposed to be modest, emulate the Blessed Mother, and aspire to be some man's wife in order to bless him with a lovely family to be raised devoutly in the church. They were supposed to be 'nice girls.' It's not like that today, which is good, but it sure as hell was when Brid was a teenager. Does any of that sound like Brid?"

Franny shook her head.

Neil went on. "She broke their two cardinal rules: she got drunk in public, and she flipped off the church." His mouth tightened, remembering his mother going on about "that one," as she always had referred to Brid. "It's not that Irish women don't drink, because, believe me, they do. Alcoholism is not only a male plague among the Irish. But the women of my mother's generation drank, for the most part, in private or amongst themselves. If they made a spectacle of themselves in public, their reputations were done-for."

He took a sip of his tea before continuing. "I'm not saying Brid was sitting *at the bar,* drinking. Let's just say, she knew where to find the stuff, and from the time she was a teenager, she helped herself. Like many true drunks, Brid could hold her liquor for a long time—until she couldn't. So on a night when she was waiting tables, you wouldn't notice that she had been nipping—until the evening was almost over, and then, you definitely would. There were nights she would get into it with her father, and the air would turn blue. It was common knowledge among the women that she was a party girl; she was a topic of discussion in the corners at the Sodality meetings and the church suppers at Our Lady's. When Brid Sheerin married Drew MacCullough, the air was thick with gossip: what those good women called 'the scandal' of it." He remembered his mother going on and on about it.

"What about her parents, didn't they try to stop it?"

Neil laughed. "Not so that I recall, but then Brid was, as she is now, a force of nature—and pretty much unstoppable."

Neil watched Franny process what he was telling her. *Where is Brid?* He hated the thought of her running in the dark.

"I've been wondering," Franny said, "how do you deal with Brid's position on the church? I mean, isn't it a problem for you?"

"Not for me." He studied her for a second. "Was it a problem for you?"

Franny seemed mystified by his question.

He continued, "Did it bother you that Drew didn't go to church?"

"Drew?" She looked surprised. "Well, to be fair, he *did* go to church at Christmas and Easter. But you know Drew—he didn't really need to go to church."

Neil snorted.

Franny tried to explain. "I mean, there was a lot going on inside Drew's head. Nobody understood that better that you." Her voice dropped almost to a whisper as she confided, "I never even pray for him. Is that bad? I know he's in a good place and doesn't need it, because despite everything that happened, he was a good person."

Neil nodded, his ears straining for some sound that Brid had returned. He thought about the prayers that he said for Drew, not at all convinced that his old friend was in such a 'good place.'

The door opened and Brid slipped into the room. Her faced was flushed; the tension had left her shoulders.

"Did I give you both enough time to gossip about me?" There was no sting in her tone; her anger was gone. She went over and sat next to Neil, her hand sliding along his thigh to lace her fingers with his.

"We weren't talking about you," Franny answered quickly, but felt her face burn at her blatant lie.

"Actually, we *were* talking about you. You look like your run helped. I was starting to get worried." Neil brought her hand up to his lips.

Brid snatched it back. "Ah, the two of you act like a pair of old women. I'm not that feckin' fragile. And I have been fending off that old witch for more than twenty years. Anyway, we have more important things to talk about. We need to decide what to do about Lilah."

"I told you, she and Rose can live with me." Franny's face had taken on a stubborn look. "My plan is for them to stay with me until Lilah finishes school. I can help take care of Rose."

Neil began gently, "Well, I am not sure that's—"

"No, that won't work. Once she's fully recovered, we have to find her a place of her own." Brid minced no words in overriding Neil's mild objection.

"I don't see why!" Franny insisted. "I have the room, and, like I said, I can help with the baby." She looked at Neil, her eyes pleading with him to side with her.

"I think I have a solution," he said.

Brid's face became wary, but she held her tongue.

"Why not have Lilah and Rose move into my house? It's a short walk to the bus stop. Once the weather turns warmer, she can walk downtown to the gallery or ride her bike."

"And where might you be moving to?" Brid asked.

"Oh, I thought I would officially move in here. The way things are, I'm here more than I am there. I know how much you love this place, and we can see if it's big enough to hold the both of us. If it isn't, we can look for something larger after the wedding."

"You would leave your *mother's* house?" Brid asked in a tone of disbelief.

"Did you really think I expected you to live there? I thought we would eventually sell it, but for now it's a good place for Lilah and Rose. And the market is depressed. It would be a good solution."

"But you've lived there your entire life," Brid protested.

"Sounds pathetic put like that, and remember, I did live in Boston when I was at BC and first began practicing law. But it's time—actually, it's past time. So, can I move in here?" He put his arm around her and pulled her close. "I'll be good, I promise. I do dishes."

"Do you think Lilah will be safe living there alone with the baby?" Franny asked.

Neil nodded. "I do. It's a mixed neighborhood in every way, with very nice people. Andrea Grayson—the girl directly across the street—had a baby in December. I know she'll be a great help to Lilah. And," he added mischievously, "Lilah can have her cat back."

Brid's eyes drifted to Moaki, curled among throw pillows on the antique fainting-couch that had taken Bucephalus' old spot in the bay window.

"Don't look so worried. We'll all be over there, helping her one way or another," Neil said in an effort to placate Franny.

She stood up. "I have to get home now and feed the dogs. Lilah and Rose are being released tomorrow, and I need to check that I have everything ready for them." She started toward the door and stopped.

"I forgot to tell you: Nick Benincasa sent me a gorgeous bouquet of roses today. He wants to take me to dinner to apologize for what happened the other day."

"Go. Tell him yes." Brid said.

"But you said he was an *idiot*." Franny protested.

"I know I did but Brendan insists I have been hasty and I trust his judgment." Brid said. Besides, I am all for anything that gets you out of your 'widow's weeds.' "

"Roses? Always a nice touch," Neil said., attempting to follow the conversation between the two women. "Who is this guy?"

Franny sighed, "It's a long story. Brid can tell you later. He's a plumber. His name is Nick Benincasa."

'Wait. I know Nick Benincasa. He's done work for me. He seemed like a nice guy—he's a good plumber." Neil looked at Brid and asked, "What am I missing here?"

Ignoring his question, Brid addressed Franny.

"Promise me you will go to dinner."

Franny looked from one face to another and then surrendering, shrugged.

"I'll let him buy me dinner. Maybe I will have some news about finding Baby Jullee by then. I would give anything to find that doll for James."

"That's grand, then." Brid smiled. "Thanks for checking up on me. Promise you will keep me posted on the dinner with the plumber." She added, "Just do not take any crap from him."

Franny smiled, "Okay. I promise. No crap. See you guys later."

Neil started to get up.

"No. Sit. I can see myself out," Franny said.

As soon as the door shut behind Franny, Brid raised her fists in triumph.

"Yes!" she said. "Finally, that girl is going in the right direction."

CHAPTER SEVENTEEN

N ick Benincasa was almost twenty minutes late. Franny sat at a table in front of the windows facing Thaler Street, wondering if she had lost her mind. She and Nick had agreed to eat at Nona's; the food was good, the atmosphere not too fancy. Refolding her napkin in neat little triangles for the fourth time, Franny wondered what had possessed her to meet this guy for dinner? He had called fifteen minutes earlier, apologizing and saying he was on his way.

Initially, she thought she might be late herself. She was just closing the shop when Sofia dropped by.

"Listen," Sofia had encouraged her, "Brendan says this Nick person is a great guy. Please try and have a good time. Try not to scare him away." Not certain that she had made her case, she'd added, "Drew would want you to."

Franny had been tempted to reply, "Oh yeah, I couldn't care less what Drew would want." But that only would have gotten Sofia in an uproar—the last thing Franny needed—so she had just smiled at her sister instead.

Walking to Nona's from the shop, Franny repeated to herself, *This is not a date. This is not a date. This is not a date.* The problem was, it felt like one. Her last date had been with Drew, almost sixteen years ago. And she remembered it felt exactly like this.

A sudden, loud stream of Italian followed by a burst of laughter shook Franny's thoughts back to the present. She craned her neck to see what was going on at the front of the restaurant. A petite woman, her silver hair cut short and slightly edgy, was almost waltzing Nick Benincasa toward Franny's table.

"And here is your young lady waiting for you, Nicola." She pulled out the chair opposite Franny. As Nick sat down, the woman spoke sharply to him in a burst of rapid Italian. Franny watched the color flood his face.

"Enjoy your dinner," she said to Franny and, without another word to Nick, hurried off into the kitchen.

"I apologize for being late," Nick began. "I don't go out much at night. The kids were pestering me about where I was going and why. It took longer than I thought it would to get out of the house … " His voice trailed off. "I'm sorry, Mrs. MacCullough; you don't care about all that. I'm afraid I'm really only fit company for little kids and broken toilets."

"Please, call me Franny," she laughed. "Obviously, you have a big fan right there." She inclined her head toward the kitchen.

"I'll call you Franny if you'll call me Nick." He picked up the menu and then put it down. "I've never met anyone named Franny before. Is it short for Frances?"

"Francesca."

A wary look came over Nick's face. "Francesca's an Italian name. What's your maiden name?"

"Chiesa. Francesca Chiesa. I was named for my great-grandmother."

So you're a *paisan*? Do you speak Italian?" He seemed to be holding his breath as he waited for her answer.

"Not really. Only a few words here and there," she replied.

Nick relaxed.

"My father was fluent," Franny went on, "but my sister and I never learned the language. I am only half-Italian. My mother's family came here from Germany in the early 1900s. Based on your conversation with the lady who showed you to the table, you speak it fluently. Am I right?"

He nodded. "My father's parents came here from Sienna right after the Second World War. My mother's parents were first generation. So both my parents spoke Italian growing up. They thought it was important that my sister and I learn it, too. We spoke it at home when I was a kid."

"Wait, the lady who seated you. She said something to you about a *puttana*. I actually do know what *that* word means. Did she say I was a whore?"

Nick looked appalled. "Of course not!" He sighed. "You don't even know me, and now I'm going to have to air all my dirty, little secrets to you. What Tizzy said was, 'Finally, you are here with a beautiful woman. It's about time you get over that whore.' The 'whore' in question is my ex-wife."

"I see," Franny said, although she really didn't. *A whore? Brendan has said nothing about that.*

Changing the subject she asked, "Who is Tizzy?"

"Tiziana Rinaldi. She's the owner."

Franny asked. "You mean she's 'Nona?'"

"Actually, no. 'Nona' was her mother. Tizzy is my godmother. She feels that that entitles her to comment on my personal life." He laughed, "Or lack of it."

"Your godmother? Really? How is that?" Franny asked. "I'm intrigued."

"The restaurant has been here for years. I think it opened in the early fifties. My mother used to work here when she was in high school. She and Tizzy became really close. Mom had four brothers, no sisters. When she married my dad, Tizzy was her matron of honor. It's customary for that same person to be godmother to the firstborn child. So I got Tizzy."

"Did she really say I was beautiful?" Franny asked, unable to stop herself.

"Yes." Nick looked at her quizzically. "You must already know that. Don't you?"

Flustered, Franny picked up her menu to hide her embarrassment. "I don't know why I bother to look, I always have the same thing at Nona's."

Nick grinned. "You do? So do I—the spaghetti Bolognese. It's the best you'll ever have anywhere. It's my grandmother's recipe."

"You're making that up," Franny said. "Why would Nona use your grandmother's recipe?" she asked. "I'm sure she must have had her own. If there is one thing I *do* know, it's that Italian cooks are very proud of their Bolognese recipes."

Nick laughed. "They sure are, but based on the stories I've

heard, Marianna Marotta— that's Tizzy's mother—was, first and foremost, a shrewd businesswoman. Her pasta, her cannoli, her fagioli were all to die for. Her Bolognese was not. And she knew it."

"How did she get your grandmother's recipe?" Franny leaned forward, caught up in the story.

Nick shrugged. "They played poker for it, and my grandmother lost."

"What? You're kidding me, aren't you?"

"If the old stories are to be believed, they loved to play cards. My grandmother and Marianna were part of a group of women who played poker on Monday nights. The restaurant has always been closed on Mondays. It was late in the month, and nobody had any money, so they were betting with other things. My grandmother's Bolognese recipe was famous, and they all wanted it. She thought she had a killer hand, so she bet on it, but Marianna was holding better cards, and she won. The Bolognese here at the restaurant improved immediately thereafter. Or so the story goes."

"It's a great story." She laughed, "I'm not sure I believe you, though."

Nick smiled, clearly enjoying himself. He seemed much nicer to Franny than the angry man who had stormed into her shop.

"It's true, I swear. I'd get Tizzy back out here to confirm it, but I'd rather not, if you don't mind. I try to keep her out of my business. It isn't easy. Ever since my mother died, Tizzy feels she needs to watch out for me. She means well, but she can be a pain in the ass, as you saw for yourself." Noticing the waitress heading for their table, Nick asked, "So what is it you always get?"

"I adore their spaghetti al tonno. It's the closest I've ever found to my Dad's."

"Your Dad cooked? So did mine. Must be an Italian guy-thing."

"Hi. I'm Pam." She spoke to Franny. "I'm your server tonight." Then, she smiled and said, "Hi, Nick. Can I get you something to drink first, or do you want to put your dinner order in?"

Nick checked his watch and said, "Hey, Pam. I think we can do both. I've already kept the lady waiting." He looked at Franny. "What would you like?"

"I'll have the spaghetti al tonno, please, and salad with the house dressing. You can serve the salad with my dinner." Franny passed the menu across the table to the waitress.

"Anything to drink?"

"Water's fine, thanks."

The waitress turned to Nick and asked, "Do you want your usual?"

"I do, and a Moretti La Rossa." Nick said.

"I'll be back with your beer and put your dinner orders right in for you." Slipping the menus under her arm, the waitress walked back toward the kitchen.

"I want to apologize again for being late. I thought I was on track, but when I started to leave, Juliette got whiny." He sighed. "She's usually pretty good about my going out on the rare nights that I do, and she likes the sitter. When she gets like that, it usually means something happened during the day to upset her, so I took a few minutes to try to find out what it was."

"Did something happen?" Franny asked.

"Yup. Her best friend didn't wear her red shoes with the glitter to school like they had planned. Juliette took this as a sign they were not friends any more, and it escalated from there, I guess." He shook his head. "Guys don't do this kind of thing. Or, they didn't when I was a kid. Everything is different now."

"I'm sure it's really hard being a single dad. Do the kids see their mom on the weekends?"

"Yeah, right," he answered in a tone laced with disgust. "The kids haven't seen their mother in person for almost two years. She Skypes them when her schedule permits, which is about every three weeks." He laughed bitterly. "Real *quality* time though."

Impulsively, Franny reached across the table to touch his arm. "I'm so sorry, Nick. I can't imagine …"

The waitress placed their drinks on the table. Franny drew back her hand wondering what the girl might report back to Tizzy,

"Thanks, Pam," Nick said. He picked up his beer and took a sip.

"Don't feel sorry for me. It's my own fault. I created the situation—and you know what? I don't regret it. I got two awesome kids out of the deal."

Franny nodded, waiting for him to continue.

"Jenn and I dated in high school. We were pretty hot and heavy, and then, after high school, we went our separate ways. I got a wrestling scholarship to Lehigh and she went off to NYU. End of story."

Franny reached for her water, hoping that it hid the shock on her face. This was not the picture of the slightly trampy wife she had dreamed up based on what Brendan had told her.

"Surprised you, didn't I? I suppose you didn't think plumbers went to college, but now most of us do. Anyway, I graduated, came back here to Lynton, got my New Hampshire plumber's license and took over as the 'son' in Benincasa and Son." He took another sip of his beer. "By then, Jenn was almost finished with her MFA at Yale. The spring before her graduation, she was back here visiting her mother. We ran into each other in the bar at Craic." He shrugged. "One thing led to another, and suddenly James was on the way."

"Just like that?' Franny asked.

"Just like that. To give Jenn credit, she could have chosen not to tell me about the baby and gone off and had the abortion she wanted." He studied his beer and then took another drink. "But she did tell me. I talked her into marrying me. Promised her the moon. And to be fair, for the first couple of years, she was kind of into me. James, not so much. She never wanted to be a mother. She felt she had been robbed of her dreams of starring on Broadway, and she resented the hell out of it. When James was four, she got really sick. She was on a lot of medication for a while, even after her symptoms had disappeared. The doctor never thought to tell her that sometimes other medications cancel out the effects of the birth control pill. She was almost sixteen weeks pregnant with Juliette by the time we figured that out."

"Oh, my God," Franny said, no longer able to contain her rising anger.

"What?" Nick asked, confused.

"So she got pregnant by accident *twice* and had two babies that she never *wanted*?" She tried—and failed—to keep the heat out of her voice.

"Exactly. The first time we were stupid, playing with fire, but Juliette was a complete surprise." He sighed, "And not a pleasant one for Jenn."

"I'm sorry. I know we are all different, but I tried for *nine years* to have a baby. We wanted a child so badly! I had four miscarriages—it was devastating. And my last pregnancy was going fine until, suddenly, it wasn't. My little boy was born dead." She felt her eyes fill with tears. "Look, I'm sure your wife or ex-wife or whatever she is, is a very nice person, but to me, a live, healthy baby is a gift to be cherished." She wiped furtively at her eyes, afraid she had really offended him.

"Hey, I'm sorry. Brendan told me you wanted kids and couldn't have them. I should never have told you all this. I don't know why I did." He covered her hand with his, squeezing it gently before letting go. "I usually don't talk about this stuff. But there is something very comforting about you. You need to know that I consider both my kids to be miracles. I'm not the most religious guy in the world, but I do thank God every day for both of them. I'm sorry I upset you."

"I get a little emotional about babies. If you don't believe me, just ask my sister. It drives her crazy. Sofia is not into babies."

"No problem. And for the record, my *ex*-wife is *not* a nice person. She's a bitch."

Nick took another drink of his beer. "Enough about my sordid past. So, what made you open a doll shop? Did you major in dolls at college?" He grinned to show he was kidding her.

"I majored in education. Somehow that got me an internship my senior year in the training department at Chayne. They offered me a job after graduation. That's where I met my husband."

"And the dolls?" Nick persisted.

"Do you really want to hear all that?" She was afraid he was being nice.

"I wouldn't ask if I didn't."

"I've always loved dolls. When I started collecting them, I was probably not much older than your daughter is now." She leaned forward, warming to her subject. "Eventually, I started going to doll shows, buying and selling out of my home. It was fun. I collected for years."

"What made you decide to open a retail business? You must have had a lot more security working for a company like Chayne."

"After I lost the baby, I quit work." She twirled her half-full water glass on the table, not sure how much to tell him of the deep depression she had fallen into. "I was really not able to work; I was too sad. After a while, Drew, my husband, built me a workshop and showroom in the house, and I sold and traded dolls again. I did it for fun, not to make money."

"What changed?"

"Drew died," she said flatly, no longer smiling. "Nothing seemed to make much sense to me after that."

"Until you came up with the idea of opening a doll shop?"

"That's right. At first I thought, 'I could never do that.' Certainly, Drew would never have believed I could do that." She made a face. "But then, I remembered he was not there to object, so here I am, the owner of a doll shop in the middle of a recession."

"MacCullough," Nick said, thoughtfully. "Any relation to Rod MacCullough, the retired banker? Lives in that big house in the North End?"

Franny sighed. "Uh-huh. His son."

"I've been in that house. Actually, had my head in the toilet, directed there by either the maid or the housekeeper."

"I'm not surprised. I don't think Drew's mother has any need for a toilet. She probably has no idea where it is."

Across the table Nick Benincasa stared. Then he threw back his head and roared with laughter. Despite herself, Franny began to laugh, too.

At that moment the waitress returned giving them a curious look.

"Here are your dinners," she said, placing the al tonno in front of Franny and the Bolognese in front of Nick. She jockeyed the plates and glasses to make room. "And your salad, ma'am. Can I get you anything else?"

"Not for me, thank you." Franny said, struggling to keep a straight face.

"Looks great, I'm set." Nick said, nodding at his heaping plate as if nothing was funny.

Hungry, they dug in and conversation ceased. After a few minutes, Nick forked some pasta onto his bread plate. "Now, taste this, and tell me if it's not the best Bolognese you've ever eaten." He slid the dish to Franny.

She twirled the spaghetti expertly with her fork, using her spoon as a bowl.

"Okay, but I warn you, I'm going to be honest with you. Your feelings may get hurt."

Nick smirked. "You wait. You're going to be blown away." He sat back in his chair and watched her.

Franny put the forkful of spaghetti into her mouth. Her eyes widened; he was right. She savored the taste for a moment, then swallowed the pasta. "Oh, my God. What's in it? It's fantastic."

"I can't tell you that. Tizzy would kill me. It's a secret. Tastes great, huh?"

"It's *so* good. It's even better than Brendan's and *his* is the best I've ever had. Until now."

"You're kidding me. Feeney makes decent Bolognese? That's just wrong. He's not even Italian. There should be a law against it."

Franny rose to Brendan's defense. "His sauce is awesome; next time he makes it for us, I'll ask him to invite you over, too."

"I'd really like that," Nick said, sounding like he meant it.

"Great. Let's plan to do it soon." Franny wondered if she was being too forward. They both turned their attention back to their dinners.

"How is the doll detecting going?" Nick asked, breaking the awkward silence that had fallen between them."

Franny made a face. "I wish I had something to report, but I don't. Baby Jullees are few and far between. But Lilah is looking, and if there is one out there, she'll find it."

"I'm not surprised. I always thought it sounded too good to be true. I'll break the news to James that you probably won't be able to find one."

"Wait, won't you give us a little longer before you say anything? I think it's so sweet that he wants to find the doll for his little sister. I hate to disappoint him."

"James is a good kid, but he's not that sweet. He feels guilty, and I haven't done much to make him not feel that way."

"Why would he feel guilty because Juliette lost her doll?"

"Given as he started all this when he threw it off the ferryboat,

I think he *should* feel some guilt. Don't you?"

Franny was stunned. "He threw Baby Jullee off a ferryboat? Why?"

"Do you want dessert?" Nick asked. "Nona's cannoli is memorable. You really should have one."

"No, thank you. But you have to finish the story about James," Franny answered.

Before he could answer, their waitress was back. "Can I interest you in dessert?'

"I think we're set." He looked at Franny, "Unless you've had a change of heart?"

"Oh, no. I'd like to take the rest of this home, please," Franny said, indicating the remains of her dinner.

"Sure," Pam said, removing her plate. She picked up Nick's empty plate, too.

After the waitress left, Franny continued to press him for the story. "So, what happened?"

"Last summer, I took the kids over to Nantucket on the ferry. James brought a buddy with him. James and this kid, Henry, thought it would be great fun to play catch using the damn doll. I get that. I had a little sister, too. Unfortunately, Henry can't catch."

He reached for the blue folder holding the check and continued. "It was a horror show: Juliette screaming, people yelling and grabbing the two boys—who were half-over the railing, pointing to where the doll went down." Digging out his wallet, he opened the folder. "It was ... Oh, shit." He looked up. "Tizzy!" he roared, his voice echoing through the almost-deserted restaurant.

"Nick, what's wrong?" Franny asked.

Their waitress reappeared, carrying, two small, white boxes tied with red and gold ribbons as well as a larger box with Franny's leftovers.

"Tizzy told me to tell you that a godmother can buy her godson and his beautiful lady-friend dinner, and she doesn't want to hear any more about it." She placed the boxes on the table and said to Nick, "This is for the kids." She said to Franny, "And this is for you. Tizzy said she hoped you enjoyed your dinner."

Nick scowled at the girl. Franny fumbled for a reply.

"Please tell her it was wonderful. I love to eat here," she finally managed.

"I'll tell her. Have a good evening." Not daring to look at Nick, the waitress left.

"What happened?"

Nick pulled some money from his wallet and slapped it on the table.

"Tizzy happened. She comped the meal. She won't let me pay when I bring the kids in either." He smiled. "Jeez. I can pay for my own dates, you know. Are you ready to go?"

"Date." *So*, Franny thought, *he considers this a date*. She looked around. They were the only people left in the dining room; the wait staff was busy setting tables for the next meal.

"I guess we should. I had no idea it was after nine o'clock."

Nick checked his phone and grinned. "Two texts from James wanting to know when I'm coming home. He says, 'Say Hi to Franny.'" He looked at her. "Shall we go?"

Franny followed him to the door, where he stepped aside to let her go first. On the sidewalk, she stopped and faced him, the awkwardness from earlier in the evening returning. "Thank you for a great dinner," she began.

Looking around, Nick interrupted, "Where's your car?"

"I walked over from the shop."

"I'll walk you back."

"Don't be silly. You don't have to do that," Franny said, surprised by his insistence. "It's just a couple of streets over. I can walk back by myself."

"Are you kidding? Tizzy's no doubt watching us right now. If I let you walk down that street alone, she'll come after me with a butcher knife," Nick said. "Besides, I would worry about you walking alone in the dark." With that, having tucked the small box for the kids in his jacket pocket, he grabbed her free hand and started toward Main Street.

Franny was conscious of how her hand felt swallowed in his larger one as they walked along. It was a strange feeling. She couldn't remember the last time a man held her hand; Drew had not been big on it.

Nick broke the silence as they reached the alley leading to the parking lot behind her shop.

"Here, can you hold these while I find my keys?" Franny asked dropping Nick's hand and giving him the two boxes she held in her other hand. Digging around in the purse looped over her shoulder, she came up with the keys.

"I love Lynton. I've lived here all my life. The Benincasas have worked in most of these buildings at one time or another. But it's not the same, sleepy little city it was when I was a kid. You shouldn't be walking around at night by yourself." He traded her the boxes of food he was holding for her keys, pushed the button to unlock the car door, and then held it open for her. "Here you go, Madame," he said, standing back so Franny could get in.

"Thank you so much for dinner. It was great. Next time I'm in Nona's I'm going to order the Benincasa Bolognese."

"Don't thank me, thank Tizzy. Remember, I didn't buy your dinner," Nick said.

Franny started laughing, her sense of awkwardness gone. "Thank you for *wanting* to buy me dinner, then. I had a really nice evening."

Nick's face softened. "You know what? So did I. I would like to take you to dinner again—this time to a place where they let me pay for it."

Then he kissed her. As kisses went, it was neither memorable nor insistent. Instead, it was sweet. And it took Franny completely by surprise.

He stepped back, returned her keys, and said, "Get in and lock the door. I'll tell James you're still looking for the doll."

Franny did as she was told and started the car. Nick watched as she backed out and drove away.

CHAPTER EIGHTEEN

Lilah sat cross-legged on the floor and studied the blank, white wall of the room destined to be Rose's nursery. She was surprised to find herself alone in the house—except for the baby, asleep next to her in the Moses basket, and the cat, sprawled in the sunlit kitchen window. It was nice. At heart, she was a loner.

The house had bustled with activity for the last three days. Neil and Brendan, along with a couple of Brendan's friends from the firehouse, had first moved out the belongings Neil wanted to store or take with him to Brid's condo. After that, they had moved Lilah's meager possessions into the house. Franny, Sofia and Brid had argued about which-dish-should-go-where, and did-Lilah-need-this-or-that. *Like I give a crap*, she had thought, listening while they'd chattered on as though she wasn't in the room. She had lived on ramen noodles and cereal for years, getting by with almost nothing in the way of kitchen stuff. Her attitude back then had been: Why bother cooking when you could sketch?

This morning after feeding Rose, she had walked around the neat, brick house touching things. Her fingers trailed along the chair rail in the dining room and traced the beveled edge of the fireplace mantel. It was the nicest place she had ever lived. She was amazed to think she and Rose had all this space to themselves. Even better: there were no drunks or druggies across the hall or downstairs. She was lucky that she had been renting her old place as a month-to-month tenant. She didn't think Neil could ever really understand the gift his offer of this house had been.

Neil had approached her as though she'd had lots of options, which, she remembered thinking at the time, was a joke.

"Listen," he'd said, last week, sitting across from her in Franny's homey kitchen, "would you consider doing me a favor?"

Doing you a favor? she had thought.

She already knew there was no way she could ever repay his kindness. He had negotiated somehow with the hospital business office to get most of her and the baby's expenses "taken care of" and had paid for the rest himself. She planned to pay him back as soon as she could, and had tried to give him some of the money she'd made doing web work for Brid and Franny. But he had brushed the offer away with a vague, "We'll get to that once you and Rose are settled."

Then he'd come to the real reason for the conversation.

"Would you consider house-sitting for me until I figure out what to do with my house?" he had asked. "Of course, I'll pay all the utilities and take care of any maintenance issues that crop up."

She'd been speechless. He must have thought she hadn't wanted to consider the offer, because he kept talking, telling her what was good about the house.

"It's just up the street from the bus stop," Neil had gone on, "and when it gets warmer, you can walk or bike downtown. The neighbors—"

"I would love it," she'd interrupted. "It sounds wonderful. How much would you want for rent?" She had held her breath. She'd been pretty good at living lean, but now she had Rose to consider and, even with the WIC vouchers, it was going to be really tight.

"I should probably be paying you, but I thought we could make an even swap," Neil had said casually. "You and Rose will live in the house rent-free and make sure that nothing goes wrong, and I won't have to pay a caretaker. It would be an even exchange. Will you do it?"

Huh? she'd thought. *An even exchange?*

She hadn't gone to fancy schools like Franny and Sofia, and she wasn't as smart as Brid, but she had understood what Neil was trying to do. She hadn't thought she could like him any more than she already did, but the sweetness of his offer—devising a way for her to protect her pride—had blown her away. She'd hated having to take the handout, but now she had to think of Rose. So, she had played along with him.

"Okay. Sure. If it will help you out for me—and Rose—to stay there, I would be glad to do it."

Neil had seemed relieved, as if that was one thing he could stop worrying about: where he could stash Lilah and Rose.

"That would be great. I want you to consider the house your own. Decorate it the way you want. Make sure you do a good job on Rose's nursery. Franny's been talking about how important that is for months." When she nodded in agreement, he smiled and said, "Good, we have that settled, and we can focus on this wedding."

Lilah knew Brid well enough to know that she could not care less if they got married, but Neil, he was an old-school guy, and he wanted the wedding.

Now, she and Rose were here.

Lilah looked at her sleeping daughter and almost hugged herself, she was so happy. Franny thought the house needed more stuff and wanted to bring over things "to make it more welcoming." Lilah loved it the way it was. She was not a fan of piles of cute crap with no purpose other than to fill up space.

"Have you decided what you want to do?"

Brid stood in the door of the room, a box of paints in her hand, Moaki twining herself around her ankles and meowing for attention. Lilah had not heard her boss come in. Setting the box on the floor, Brid dropped to a squat next to the baby. The cat purred, rubbing her head on Brid's thigh.

"I think you might have gotten an excellent child here. How that could have happened, I don't know." Gently she stroked the baby's cheek. "What's with all this pink?" she asked, taking a closer look at the delicately-smocked sleeper with rosebuds on the collar and toes.

Lilah sighed. "That's one of about seven zillion pink things Franny bought for her. I'd have to change Rose ten times a day for her to wear it all before she outgrows it."

Brid continued to watch the baby, who began to stretch and whimper. Lilah reached over and scooped her up.

"She wants food, but first I think I'll change her. She's wet."

Brid watched as Lilah quickly changed the diaper and then opened her shirt and offered the baby her breast. Rose had worked herself into a hissy and latched on fiercely. Slowly the baby's face relaxed as she began to suck. Her long lashes lowered as her eyes began to close.

"See? She's happy again," Lilah said. "All she ever does is sleep, eat and poop."

Brid said, "You seem to handle it like an expert. Where did you learn so much about babies?"

Lilah lifted the baby to her shoulder and began to rub Rose's back in a circular motion to get her to burp. "I did a lot of babysitting when I was younger." In an effort to avoid more questions, she added, "Didn't you?"

"Me?" Brid replied, raising her eyebrows. "I never babysat. I'd rather have cleaned the men's room in the bar than babysit. I don't like babies."

Rose chose that moment to burp, spitting up as she did so. Lilah wiped her daughter's chin and turned her to face Brid.

"But I am considering making an exception for Rose Malone," she said, leaning in to smile at the baby. "Aren't I, now?"

Rose began to squirm in an effort to face what she considered to be the right side of Lilah, who obliged by putting her on the other breast. Lilah loved the way Brid always called the baby 'Rose Malone.'

Brid gently tickled Rose's foot. "Don't make me reconsider." Leaning back on her heels, she asked, "Where are the sketches?"

Lilah nodded toward her sketchbook propped up under the window. "Look on the last two pages."

Brid retrieved the book and flipped it open. She looked closely at the pages filled with sketches: studies of Moaki prancing, stalking, slinking, sleeping, rolling on her back, and acting like a fierce jungle cat.

"Moaki, the little fiend," Brid murmured. She cocked her head as she considered the drawings. "And how do you see us painting her?"

"I want us to paint the figures just above the baseboards, so that when Rose starts crawling, she can see and touch them."

"It's brilliant," Brid said, taking another look. "I haven't your talent, but I can do the outlines for you, and you can finish them."

"No way. There's too many, and you know you paint as well as I do. You take one side of the room, and I'll do the other. You do your version of Moaki, and I'll do mine. They don't have to look exactly the same."

Lilah had Brid pretty much figured out, but this lack of confidence in her painting made no sense to her. Brid was good— really good. The portrait she had done of Drew MacCullough was so lifelike, you kept waiting for him to open his mouth and say something. When Lilah had made that observation to Brid, her answer had been, "Be glad that he can't." Lilah thought it was weird that Brid had given the portrait to Neil and not to Franny, but then again, she thought it weird that Brid and Franny were even friends.

Brid picked up the cat and rubbed the animal's face with her own, something Lilah never thought she would live to see. The cat rumbled happily in response. Watching them, she understood why Neil was worried about Brid having to give Moaki back. He had confided this to Lilah the day he had first shown her the house, asking her what she thought about getting Brid a kitten. Although Brid had handed the cat over yesterday, saying Moaki was a plague she was glad to be rid of, her fondness for the animal was obvious. Lilah felt a pang of regret. She owed Brid and Neil so much; maybe she should have let Brid keep her. But she and Moaki had been together for three years. Lilah had found her, a starving kitten living in an alley, shortly after arriving in Boston. They were a team, and she needed them to stay together. And she wanted Rose to have a cat.

"Have you broken it to Franny that you aren't doing bunnies?" Brid asked, opening the top of her paint box and removing a charcoal pencil.

Lilah made a face. "Not yet. Franny's great and everything, but we don't like the same stuff, you know?" Lilah lowered her voice in case Franny came walking through the door. "I hate all this pink shit. I think Rose looks great in bright colors, like cerulean and azure blue. But I would never hurt Franny's feelings. Thank God for Nick-the-Plumber. Since he starting hanging, she's been a little less intense about Rose."

Brid stopped working on the cat sketch and put down her pencil. Her face took on the intense expression Lilah loved to sketch: the one she had given to the witch in her graphic novel. Not that Lilah had shown Brid those pictures. Brid's green eyes changed to slits, and her lips formed a smile that was not quite a smile, more feline than human.

"Nick Benincasa is 'hanging?' 'Hanging?' Precisely what does that mean?" She waited expectantly.

"He texts her all the time. She's gone out to dinner with him twice. The second time, Franny was all dressed up. And she looked great. I mean, not like some dumpy, old widow like she usually does. She had a sexy black dress on—with some skin showing— and she borrowed a pair of slinky shoes from Sofia. She really rocked it. They went to Craic. And you know what *that* cost."

"Really? Da never said, the wretch. I've wondered when Franny will bring him around to meet us." Brid said.

"But you did meet him. The day he came into the doll shop and yelled at Franny. She says Nick's afraid of you."

"As well he should be; he acted like such an ejit. But that hardly counts." She stopped talking and then smiled broadly, delighted by an idea that had suddenly occurred to her. "I'll tell her to bring him to the damn wedding. God knows we need something to divert people's attention. It's a farce worthy of Shakespeare."

The wedding. Lilah was happy that Brid mentioned it. Much as Lilah wanted to hear about it, she certainly was not going to bring it up—not to Brid, anyway.

"So how's that going?" she said casually, as she placed the sleeping baby in her basket.

Brid was working again on her cat. Without bothering to turn around, she answered, "We have a date, a church—and glory be to God for *that*—a place to hold the reception and, if Neil gets his way, a priest. What more do I need?"

Lilah was outlining her own cats along the wall opposite Brid, but this made her stop.

"Duh. Like, *your* dress and *Franny's* dress? You know it takes a while to find those. Have you thought of that?"

"I don't care what I wear. I've already pranced down the aisle dressed like a wedding cake in that church once. Don't you think that's enough?"

"You can't just show up in your jeans and sweater, you know," Lilah said, looking pointedly at what Brid was wearing.

"Oh, but you're wrong, I could. Unfortunately, Franny is off looking for dresses, so I probably won't. I have warned her though: no white, no bustle, no flounces and, absolutely, no damned veil."

From the front of the house the door slammed and Sofia called, "Where are you guys?"

"Back here, in the nursery," Lilah answered.

Sofia marched into the room, followed by Brendan, who was sliding a large, flat cardboard box along the floor in front of him.

"What's in the box?" Lilah asked craning her neck to better see what was printed on the side.

Before Brendan could answer, Sofia began to lecture, "Lilah, you really should keep the door locked. I know this is considered a good neighborhood, but you're a ten-minute walk from downtown. Anybody could walk in here and murder you and the baby!"

Lilah bit her tongue. *Yeah, Sofia, like you've ever lived in a dinky apartment with paper-thin walls and a door requiring four locks,* she thought. *This house is security-Nirvana compared to that.*

Sofia glanced over at what Brid was painting. "Cats? Really? Wait—" She momentarily regretted not putting in her contacts. Without them or her glasses—which she only wore in the office or to court—Sofia was half-blind. Squinting, she looked closer. "Ah, those are Moakis. Cool." She grinned. "So, which one of you is going to break it to Franny that the bunnies got tossed?"

"I know Franny wanted bunnies, but I decided it would be more fun for Rose if it was, like, an animal she knew," Lilah said.

"For the love of God!" Brid exploded, putting down her brush and pivoting on her heels to face them. "Those silly, white bunnies with their pink noses and swishy whiskers are insipid. Do we want Rose to grow up to be the kind of woman who likes *bunnies?*"

"No!" Sofia and Lilah chorused together, causing Rose to open her eyes and look around.

"Grand!' Brid said, emphatically. Adding, as she returned to her painting, "Hares would have been lovely, but not those fools."

Hares would have been kind of cool, Lilah thought. *Biggish, brown ones with a spot here or there, even a scar or two for character. Maybe I'll draw one and frame it, or, even better, get Brid to—"*

The doorbell chimed, followed by Franny's voice asking to be let in. Lilah's face must have reflected her surprise, because Sofia shrugged while offering up her defense. "I locked it after we came in. You have to be careful."

"I'll go. You ladies continue your bunny-bashing," said Brendan, heading toward the front of the house. A minute later, he followed Franny into the room.

Clutching a white box covered in purple violets, she announced, "I found her. You are not going to believe this, but she's perfect!"

"Let me see!" Lilah dropped her charcoal pencil and rose from the floor. Taking the box from Franny, she inspected it carefully, noting, "Even the box is mint." As the other women crowded around, she lifted the top and then parted the light purple tissue paper to reveal the baby doll it protected.

"She's really sweet," Sofia said, her fingers gently touching the pale-pink, voile dress the doll wore. "Look, her shoes are real leather. I bet she was made here in the United States and not in some sweatshop overseas."

"How much did you say your little friend, James, had saved up? Wasn't it eighteen dollars? I bet she cost *all* of that," Brid said.

You can bet your ass she cost that, Lilah thought as her eyes met Franny's.

Franny chose to ignore Brid, saying instead, "I called Nick. His mother-in-law is going to stop at the shop tomorrow after work to see the doll and make sure she's the same as the one Juliette lost." Franny crowed. "But I know she is. I can't wait to see James' face."

"And this little gem cost you eighteen dollars?" Brid persisted.

Franny hesitated, "This doll is a find. They only made three hundred, and this is one of them. If Nick doesn't want it, I know we can sell it to someone else."

"And perhaps make some money," Brid muttered under her breath.

"Hey, what's in the box?" Lilah asked Brendan, again, pointing at the box he had lugged in earlier, hoping to divert Brid's attention.

"Oh, you picked it up? Awesome." Franny said, relieved they

were no longer focusing on the doll. "It's a crib for Rose from all of us." She reached down and scooped up the baby. "Now she'll have someplace to sleep when she outgrows this basket"—she dropped a kiss on the baby's forehead—"won't you?"

KATHLEEN FERRARI

CHAPTER NINETEEN

Franny could not keep her mind on the spreadsheet in front of her. Nick had texted that his ex-mother-in-law would stop by on her way home from work—any minute now—and she was worried the woman might not like the doll she had found.

Focus, Franny! she told herself sternly, returning her attention to the computer as the bell over the door jingled. She pasted a smile on her face, as two women almost a foot apart in height stepped into the shop.

"You must be Franny," said the shorter one. "I'm Julie Canon, James and Juliette's grandmother. Nick said you may have found us a doll for Juliette."

"Welcome to my…Franny started to reply when suddenly she realized who the other woman was.

"Maggie? What are *you* doing here?" Franny blurted out, ignoring the petite blonde who had just introduced herself.

Julie Canon's tall, dark-haired companion flung open her arms.

"Franny Chiesa! I had no idea this was your shop. Come here and give me a hug!"

Franny flew around the display case. After a moment, the woman held her at arm's length and searched her face. "You look happy; I'm so glad."

"Maggie, what are you doing here?' Franny asked. "I knew Julie was coming but…" her voice trailed off.

Recovering from her own surprise, Julie started to explain, "Maggie and I are going out to dinner. We are old friends and try to meet once a month. How do you know one another?" she asked.

"Franny was Cookie's roommate at Wellesley," Maggie explained to Julie. She laughed—"How's that for the universe reaching out to us?"

Franny felt her dread of Julie Canon slip away. True, she was Jenn's mother, but if Julie was a friend of Maggie's, she was definitely someone Franny wanted to know.

"I'm so sorry for being rude, Julie. It's just that Maggie has always been one of my favorite people, and I was so surprised to see her. Let me get the doll, I know that's what you came to see."

She went back around the case and reached down for the violet-covered box. Julie appeared to catch her breath as Franny lifted off the cover and gently parted the tissue paper surrounding the doll inside.

"Oh! It really *is* Baby Jullee! I can't believe you found her. I searched everywhere after Juliette lost her doll." Julie touched the doll's face before adding, "I mean, everywhere. I called doll shops, scoured online, went on craigslist and eBay, looked at the ads in the back of doll magazines. How did you ever find her? You're amazing." Tears glistened in the older woman's eyes.

"She looks exactly the way she did the Christmas that Santa brought her," Maggie said. Dropping her tone to a fake whisper, she confided to Franny, "I was so jealous. She's such a beautiful doll. I think that's when I knew I must really be a naughty little girl, because I didn't get Baby Jullee under *my* Christmas tree."

"But I shared," Julie protested. "I even let her spend the night at your house."

Maggie gave her friend a hug and said to Franny, "She did," adding, "You always were a great sharer."

Julie continued to examine the doll, a slight frown on her face. "The problem is, I'm not sure how we are going to pass this doll off to Juliette as being the doll she lost last summer." She looked up at Franny. "She's too perfect. I doubt this doll has ever been out of the box. Our Baby Jullee was a lot more loved."

"Don't you mean *abused?*" Maggie asked. "Remember the time Robbie and Dan Callahan kidnapped and buried her?"

"Yes. And it took three days to make them tell us where she

was."

"My father was livid. Remember? He made them buy you three doll outfits and write a formal letter of apology." Maggie smiled at the memory of her misbehaving brother and his friend.

"Which I could barely read, because I was only seven. I remember that your mom knitted Baby Jullee a sweater and hat, too. I loved your parents. They were great."

Listening to the two women revisit their childhood delighted Franny. It happened all the time when the topic was dolls. She believed those memories were the reason so many women held onto their dolls all their lives.

Hating to interrupt the two friends, she began hesitantly, "Ladies, I think it really will come down to how much Juliette wants this to be the doll she lost."

"What do you mean?" Maggie asked.

"If she really wants her doll back, she will tell herself this is her doll." As the women stopped to consider this, Franny rushed on, "We'll have to come up with a story to help convince her, but in the end, it will be up to Juliette to decide."

"What kind of story, exactly?" Julie asked.

Franny thought a moment. "We could tell Juliette that when Baby Jullee fell off the boat, the waves swept her to an island where she was found by a kind fisherman, who took her to a doll hospital. The doctors and nurses there took very good care of her, and that's why she looks so good."

"A fisherwoman. Make it a fisherwoman." Sofia stood in the open door. They had been so absorbed in their conversation that they hadn't heard the bell.

Franny thought, *Trust Sofia—always with the feminist thing.*

"Julie, this is my sister, Sofia"—she gestured to both women— "Sofia, this is Julie Canon, Nick's children's grandmother." Grinning at Maggie Kennedy, she asked Sofia, "I know you must remember Cookie's stepmom, Maggie?"

"It's nice to meet the original owner." Sofia said, extending her hand to Julie. "All Franny has talked about lately is finding Baby Jullee." She turned to Maggie. "What a surprise to see you, Mrs. Kennedy. How is Cookie? Still saving the world in faraway places?"

"For the moment, yes, but"—Maggie's eyes were shining—

"she's coming home in June."

"Home?" Franny almost clapped her hands with excitement.

Drawn first to the Peace Corp after college, Cookie had spent the last fifteen years serving as an aid worker for various NGOs in one remote place after another. She had made it to Franny's wedding, but not Drew's funeral.

"Yes. Or probably to Manchester," Maggie said. "She's taken a job as a social worker there."

"I've been really bad lately about emailing her; this place just *eats* time," Franny said, looking around her shop. "We chatted on Facebook right after Christmas, and she told me she was thinking about doing something different, but she never mentioned coming home. I can't wait to see her."

Maggie smiled, "Me, too."

Franny put the cover back on the doll's box. "I guess now that you agree the doll is the right one, I should let my customer know I've found Baby Jullee for him."

"You mean James? He will be ecstatic." Julie replied. "He's the one who lost the doll," she told Maggie. "He has been one guilt-ridden boy. Nick and I are so grateful you found another one. Nick is going to get together with you to figure out what happens next. It was so nice to meet you, Franny." She seemed about to say more, but stopped, extending her hand, she finished with, "I hope I get to know you better."

"I'm thrilled things worked out. We got lucky. Please come in again, and bring Juliette with you. I would love to meet her." Instantly Franny regretted her request. Who was she to suggest meeting Nick's daughter?

Julie smiled and said, "Oh, I will. She would love this store."

Maggie hugged Franny again. "So nice to see both you girls. When Cookie gets back, I hope we can have a 'girls' night' like we used to." Turning to her friend, she added, "You can come too, Julie. It will be a blast."

As the two older women stepped out to the street, Maggie asked Julie, "How is Nick doing, anyway?"

Sofia watched them go. "Wouldn't you just love to hear the answer to *that* question?" she mused. "Even more important, how are *you* and Nick doing? Any action there?"

Franny felt her face turn red. Sofia never minced words.

"Look at you!" Sofia hooted. "What has our hot-tempered plumber gotten up to?"

Trying to regain her composure, Franny busied herself closing the spreadsheet she'd been working on. "We've had four dates. Nothing has moved past the goodnight-kiss stage. Are you happy now?"

"Hmmm. Maybe you should be a little more … aggressive?" Sofia pressed. "It's the twenty-first century, you know. Women go after what they want."

"Oh, my God. The guy is still trying to figure out which end is up. He's raising two little kids by himself and running a business." Franny shut down her laptop, preparing to close the shop. "We're just friends"—she sighed—"and I think I like it that way."

"Sure you do. It's safe."

"What about you? Are you going after Brendan?" Franny snapped, tired of Sofia's superior attitude. Her sister's face went flat, and Franny was happy to see that her jab had hit home.

Sofia walked toward the window, but not before Franny saw her blush. *That's a surprise*, thought Franny. Sofia rarely let her feelings show.

"I really like Brendan," Sofia began. She was silent as she considered what to reveal to Franny. "It's just, he has no passion. You know?"

Franny couldn't stop herself. "And you've been with him for what, almost three years? Really? No passion? I'm surprised."

"Oh, my God, Franny! You know I don't mean *that* way. He's awesome in bed, okay?"

Franny was sorry she had brought up the subject. She was not one of those women who enjoyed discussing sex—certainly not with her younger sister.

"He doesn't feel any need to do more, to be the best—at least not at anything that matters," Sofia complained. "I don't even think he wants to be a fire captain, or chief, or whatever they are. In ten years, he will be exactly where he is right now."

"Don't you think that's because he's happy with who is?" Franny rushed to Brendan's defense. "He's good at so many things. And he *is* passionate about his running."

Sofia considered this. "I guess that's true, but, even there, he doesn't compete as much as he should."

"You mean, he doesn't compete as much as *you* think he should?"

Before Sofia could answer, the bell over the door rang and Nick Benincasa walked into the shop.

Franny felt a smile begin to light up her face. Sofia noticed and turned to find the source. Extending her hand, she said, "You must be Nick. I'm Franny's sister."

"That would be me. It's nice to meet you. Sofia, right?" He took her hand firmly in his.

"Good memory. And I doubt she talks a lot about me."

"I know Brendan Feeney pretty well. We've worked together and hung out a few times. He mentioned you, too."

"Yes, and he defended you to me."

"Defended me ... ah ... you must know that other woman who was here the day I met your sister." He made a face. "I don't think she liked me very much. I admit it was not my finest hour."

Sofia laughed. She had a boisterous, big-person laugh, not at all what might be expected from someone not quite five feet tall. It never failed to catch people by surprise. Nick took a step back.

"You think?" Sofia deliberately stepped forward to match the step he had retreated, and pressed on. "I'd watch my back if I were you. Being an enemy of Brid's is not something to take lightly."

"Sofia, stop." Franny protested. She smiled at Nick in an effort to reassure him. "She's kidding you."

Sofia reached for the door. "I'll see you later, Franny," she said, adding to Nick, "I'm sure I'll see you again, too."

"She's not what I expected at all," Nick said, staring after her.

"I know. She's smaller, thinner, in much better shape, prettier and smarter—but we really *are* sisters."

"I don't know about all that, but the 'prettier' is definitely not true."

His eyes met hers. She was the first to look away, busying herself with opening the violet-covered box on the top of the case.

"You did it, huh?" he said. "Julie told me it's definitely the right doll. The combined Benincasa family will be eternally grateful to you. Let me see this baby." Gently lifting the doll, he examined it carefully. "So this is what she looked like new, huh? I can see what you meant when you said she was in mint condition. Juliette's doll never looked like this."

"Your mother-in-law and I have already talked about that. We might have a solution. We decided to tell Juliette that her doll has been in the doll hospital getting fixed up, and that's why she's been gone so long. It will be up to Juliette to decide if this is really her doll. What do you think of that idea?"

Nick continued to look over the doll in that matter-of-fact way men have. His large hands poked at the smocking stitches on the dress and prodded the leather shoes, with no thought to the details he was seeing.

"Julie's my *ex*-mother-in-law. She's been amazing, and I don't know if I could have pulled off this 'single dad' thing without her. But we're no longer related." He studied the doll and said, "I think we should let Juliette decide. You can tell her that you found this doll and thought it *might* be the one she lost. My daughter is nothing if not pragmatic. She's had to be." Putting the doll back in the box, he pulled his checkbook from his pocket. "I rather not tell her a blatant lie. How much do I owe you?"

"I agree with you. We'll let Juliette decide." Franny finished repacking the doll in the layers of tissue paper." You owe me nothing. Remember? My deal is with James"—she put the box back behind the display case—"and he owes me eighteen dollars and seventy-five cents."

The smile disappeared from Nick's face.

"Come on, Franny. This doll cost a lot more than that. Julie told me to expect to pay over a *thousand* based on what she discovered during her search." He opened the checkbook and pulled a pen from his shirt pocket. "So, what's the damage? You can charge James eighteen dollars and seventy-five cents—in fact, I insist you do—he needs to cough up for being such a thoughtless jerk to his sister." His face darkened. "But there's no way you're eating the rest of the cost of this doll. You've just started your business. You can't afford it."

Franny felt her anger rise, along with the bile in her throat. Always some guy telling her what she could or could not do. Implying she was too dumb to know what she was doing. *It's my business*, she thought, *and I know far better than you what I can afford to charge for a doll.*

"Sorry," she said. "Like I told you before, I made the deal with James, not you."

For a moment Nick was speechless. Then he jammed his checkbook back into his pocket. "Listen. You can *keep* the doll. Juliette's gone this long without it, so it really won't matter. I don't need your late husband's charity. I can buy my own kid a doll."

He stormed out, letting the door slam behind him.

She swiped angrily at the hot tears that, unbidden, filled her eyes. Her "late husband's charity"—where had *that* come from? She shook her head: she would not cry over Nick Benincasa. She would not. She had promised herself she would never cry over a man again. Brid was right: Nick was an idiot. *Well*, she thought, *maybe he's not an idiot, but he's clearly damaged*—she sighed—*as most people are*. As she was, herself, she knew. Bending over, she slid the laptop into the tote bag at her feet and started to close the zipper.

Behind her the door's bell jingled. Coming to her feet, she stared into Nick Benincasa's face. He closed the door and turned the lock. He said her name once and then he was across the room.

He gathered her in his arms as if he intended to keep her there forever. The kiss was not like any they had shared before. This one felt as though he was trying to pull her inside himself. It sent a current of passion from her tongue to her core that those previous, almost-chaste pecks had not prepared her for. His voice was husky with desire.

"I'm sorry. I'm such a jerk. I'm just scared. I am so damned scared."

He kissed her again, and her hands found their way into his hair.

"I can't fall in love with you. I can't," he murmured. He searched her face, his eyes filling with tears. "But, goddammit, I have."

He swung her into his arms and carried her through the rear door and into the storage room.

CHAPTER TWENTY

Neil paused in the doorway of his office before announcing himself, watching Lilah study the framed picture she held in her hands. Dressed in her ragged jeans, star-splashed Dr. Martens, a worn denim jacket, and a purple and black scarf, she seemed strangely incomplete without Rose. The baby was usually in a sling across her chest or asleep in a carrier swinging from Lilah's hand. He wondered where Rose was. No doubt staying with one of her "aunties."

"Lilah, we had an appointment?" He had been surprised to find it on his calendar this morning.

Carefully, she returned the picture to its place on the mantel, next to the one of a man in a police uniform.

"I'm sorry. I didn't mean to snoop. She's your mother, right? She looks strict."

"Yes, but that photo makes her look tougher than she was." He laughed, "I was her only child, so she spoiled me, too. She hated having her picture taken, so there aren't many of them. She was about forty-five in that one. Younger than I am. The other picture is of my father." He gestured with an open palm and a nod of his head. "Have a seat."

Stepping over her backpack where she'd left it next to the chair, Lilah perched cautiously on the edge of the client chair.

Neil took his own chair, behind the mahogany desk that had once been his grandfather's. His elbows on the armrests, he leaned back and waited, not uncomfortable with the silence.

There was something different about Lilah today, and it was not just the absence of the baby. *Ah*, he realized, *it's her hair.* He remembered Brid calling it Lilah's 'mad hair', referring to the many color-and style-changes Lilah showed up with at the gallery. Today, she appeared to have hacked it off into layers, and the color was new. The front pieces were—he looked closely to be sure he wasn't imagining it—turquoise, fading to almost white at the tips.

"New hairdo, huh?" he asked.

"Yeah. I did it while Rose was asleep yesterday. It was driving me crazy. I read online that you shouldn't dye your hair when you're pregnant—it might not be good for the baby—and for so long it was, like, so boring I couldn't stand it. Yesterday was the first chance I had to do it."

"It catches your eye, for sure," he said, in what he hoped was an enthusiastic tone. He thought it looked awful; if God had wanted people to have blue hair, he would have created them that way and done a better job, at that.

"Don't worry," she said anxiously, "the color didn't stain the sink or anything. I made sure I got all the blue out. You can't even tell I did it."

"I'm not the least bit worried about the sink," he said graciously. "I want you to be comfortable in the house. Treat it as if it's your own. Because, right now, it is." From the look on her face, his attempt to reassure her didn't appear to work.

"Where's Rose? You could have brought her in with you. She would have been a big hit."

"She's over at the Foundlings; I wanted to talk to you without her fussing. I fed her, and she was sleeping when I left. She usually takes a pretty long nap. Unless Franny wakes her up." Lilah made a face. "Sometimes she does that."

Neil frowned. "She should have had her own kids." He glanced over at the portrait of Drew, hung opposite his desk. "Losing that baby was cruel. She and Drew would have been great parents." He sighed. "Raising his child would have been a great comfort to Franny."

Lilah looked at the portrait Brid had painted and got up to examine it more closely. She studied the dark hair streaked with gray at the temples, the unusual aquamarine color of the eyes, the lazy grin and the determined chin.

"So this portrait looks like him? I mean, Brid showed it to me when she finished it, but I didn't know him, so I can't really judge."

"It looks *just* like him. Sometimes I find myself talking to it as if he's standing there." Neil shrugged. "It sounds crazy, I know, but I miss him."

"Brid is a talented artist, although, for some weird reason, she doesn't know it."

"She's her own worst critic. She once had some idiot professor tell her that her work was 'mediocre' or some bullshit like that. That didn't help her confidence."

"I suppose she must have known him pretty well, didn't she? Being married to him?" Lilah asked, continuing to stare at Drew's likeness.

"I think she probably knew him as well as he allowed anyone to know him."

"Except for you?" Lilah persisted.

"Drew was my closest friend. We met when we were nine years old. I knew him as well as I know myself"—he chuckled— "maybe even better. In some ways, he was more predictable than I was— than I am. He could be counted on to always 'act like Drew,' as outrageous as that sometimes was. You know what I mean?"

Lilah slipped back into the seat across the desk from Neil. She thought a moment and then asked, "So is it, like, weird for you? I mean, to be marrying Brid when she was married to him first?"

Neil considered brushing her off. It was none of her business, but to be fair, she had found herself stuck in the middle of them all—her cobbled-together, found family. Instead, he decided to turn the question back on her. "Does it seem weird to you?"

"Yeah, it does. Totally."

He considered this, impressed by her honesty.

He looked across at the picture. "It's a pretty easy story to follow: we both fell in love with her when were young, and she fell in love with him. There was no mistaking it; she was crazy about him."

"And what about him? Was he crazy about her?" Lilah asked, her face a combination of skepticism and curiosity.

Neil played with folders on his desk, taking his time before answering. Finally, he said, "Drew liked women. He was drawn to them. And they liked him right back. If he really loved any one of them, it was Brid. The two of them just couldn't live together. They fought constantly."

"And Franny—did he love her?"

Neil hesitated and then answered truthfully.

"She thinks he did, and that's all that matters. Drew took care of Franny—both when he was alive and after he was dead. Being able to do those things fulfilled a basic need for him, something Brid never really allowed him to do."

Lilah nodded, her eyes meeting his in acknowledgment that what he had said was their secret.

"Do you think he would be happy you and Brid are getting married? Would he be jealous, or mad at you?"

He realized with a start that she was the first person to have asked him that, even though he would bet a lot of people would love to hear the answer.

"Absolutely not. Drew had a generous heart. One of his greatest strengths was that he never held a grudge. And he knew how much I loved her. I think, wherever he may be now, he's delighted."

Neil crossed his arms over his chest. "So, what brings you in here this morning? I don't really think it's to determine my fitness as a husband."

Lilah sighed. "Crap. I hate this. I feel like all I've done for the last few months is ask you for something."

Neil waited, saying nothing. He knew she would get to it eventually.

"I ... I've been doing some research. If I get what I'm reading online, if something were to happen to me, without me naming a legal guardian for Rose, she would become a ward of the state. Is that true?"

"Not exactly, but certainly it's better to have an estate plan in place, including naming the person you would want to raise Rose," he said.

Lilah snorted. "Estate plan? You mean like a will or something?"

Neil nodded.

"Why would I make a will? I've got nothing to leave her except my bike and my art supplies."

"I see your point, but you probably should name a guardian. The judge doesn't have to abide by it, but unless someone contests the designation or there is a clear case to be made that it is to the child's detriment, the choice of the parents usually stands. These things can get complicated. Is that why you're here? You would like me to draft the documents for you?"

Neil opened his drawer and removed a yellow legal pad. His younger colleagues would reach for their laptops at this point, but he still preferred to use paper and pen for the first draft of his legal notes.

Lilah shifted nervously in her chair. "Yeah ... but I need something more than just that."

Neil lowered the pen in his hand.

"Will you be Rose's guardian?" When his face showed what she thought was dismay, she rushed on, "I know it's a lot to ask. Really, I do. It's just, well, there's no one else ... "

Neil considered this before responding. "There is an obvious solution," he said, trying to keep a grip on what suddenly felt like a shifting boundary. "I've never pushed you on this before because, as your friend, I didn't think it was any of my business, but if I were speaking as your lawyer I would have to ask you: Who's Rose's father? He should be the one you name as her guardian, not me."

In the past, when asked first by Brid and then by Franny, Lilah had stubbornly replied that Rose had no father. That answer would not fly here. She bit her lower lip and refused to meet his eyes.

"He's not in the picture," she whispered.

Neil was pretty sure he already knew how she would answer his next question. "Does he know about Rose?"

In a voice barely audible, she replied, "No."

Finally, it all made sense to him. "You never told him you were pregnant?"

Lilah shook her head.

"It's something you can fix pretty easily, isn't it?" he asked.

"I don't know where he is right now."

Neil decided to try a different tack. "You must have family? In my experience in these cases, family always trumps outsiders."

"I don't think of you as an 'outsider,' " she protested, "I trust you. I know you would make sure that Rose is okay"—she gripped the arms of her chair—"There's no one else. Really. No one."

Neil sat back and absently rotated his pen through his fingers. More than once, he and Brid had speculated about Lilah's background and where she'd come from.

She had answered a request for a gallery assistant that Brid had sent to Massachusetts College of Art and Design, her alma mater. Lilah's story had been that she'd run out of money. She had provided references from two professors Brid knew. And she was good, both artistically and administratively. She had created a website for the gallery, improving foot traffic and creating an online business. Brid trusted her, and they shared a taste for the unusual in art.

It was only recently that Neil had learned Lilah was working on some kind of novel filled with creatures not quite human. She had always been closemouthed about her personal life, sharing as little as possible.

"I'm sorry. I need more than that," he said finally. "What you are asking is a huge responsibility and, even more than that, if anything were to happen to you, what would I tell Rose about her mother? Now, about all I could say is that you were a gifted artist who rode a purple bike with pink-and-green polka dots and a brass bell."

Lilah didn't answer. The minutes ticked by as she shifted uneasily in her chair avoiding his eyes.

"I get it." She took a deep breath. "I was born in Lewiston, Maine. My father died when I was three. He was killed when his truck hit a tree. I was told beer was involved. I have an older brother. He's doing time for armed robbery and some kind of drug connection. My mother died when I was fifteen. I spent the next two years with my grandmother. She died two weeks before I left for school in Boston. There really is no one else who could take Rose. Please say 'yes.' "

"Let me talk to Brid and then—"

"No!" Lilah protested, a look of panic on her face. "You can't say anything to Brid—you can't. She won't let you do it. Nothing's going to happen to me, I promise." She reached across the desk and took his hand. "Really, this is just a precaution. Brid doesn't ever have to know. It will be between you and me." She stood a moment longer, then released his hand and sat back down.

"I can't imagine keeping something like this from Brid." Even as he said it, Neil began to consider the possibility. They were not married yet. And it wasn't the first secret he had kept from her. His eyes traveled briefly to the portrait of Drew across the room. Why bring something to her attention that would only upset her? Lilah was right: it was only a precaution. Besides, as things stood, if anything did happen, who else was there to step in and take Rose?

"I am going to ask you to sign a formal client-contract, Lilah. Once I have that on file, I will go ahead and draw up a simple will and the necessary guardianship documents."

He picked up his phone and pushed a button. "Hi, Erica, can you bring me a new-client contract, please?"

He rested his chin in his hands, considering the situation.

"I can justify not telling Brid under the guise of attorney-client privilege"—he removed his reading glasses and pinched the bridge of his nose—"but I don't like it, and God help us both if she ever finds out."

"I can never thank you enough. I don't know what—"

"Brid tells me you're going back to work next week," Neil cut her off, waving away her thanks. "What have you decided to do about the baby?"

"Oh, it's so perfect," she said, smiling. "Andrea Grayson—you know, she lives across the street in the yellow house? Duh, of course you know that. Anyway, she's been really nice. She brought dinner over the first night I was in the house. Her little boy, Mason, is four months old, and she offered to watch Rose for me while I'm at work. She said 'two is no more work than one.' I hope she doesn't find out she's wrong. Babies are a *lot* of work. I'll pay her, of course, but it's so much better than having to leave Rose at a day care center full of snotty toddlers with people I don't know."

"I'm glad you like the Graysons," Neil said. "I've always thought they were a nice couple. It sounds like things are working out."

"I love the house. It's the nicest place I've ever lived. I need to get back to work so I can start paying you back."

"I would rather you worry about finishing your degree. I am not worried about you paying me back."

"I am. And I want to start." She sighed, "And now, I will owe you even more."

After a short knock at the door, Neil's administrative assistant, Erica, breezed into the room, papers in her hand. "Here you go," she said, placing them in front of Neil.

"This is Lilah Patch. She works for Brid at the gallery," Neil said, knowing that Erica would find a way to figure out who this less-than-conventional client was, anyway. He could see her checking out both the outfit and the hair. He told Lilah, "Erica really runs this place. We all just do what she tells us to."

"Mr. Malone will take good care of you." Erica said as she started to leave. "Wait"—she turned around—"I know who you are. You're the mom of that beautiful baby whose picture is on Sofia's desk. Little Rose, right?"

The dimples stood out in Lilah's face. "Yup, I'm her mom." Bashfully, she ducked her head, "She is a cutie."

"You can say that again," Erica gushed. "I never thought I would see the day Sofia Chiesa would get excited about a baby. But she certainly is in love with yours. Mr. Malone, let me know if you need anything else." On her way out the door, she told Lilah, "It was lovely meeting you. Enjoy your baby."

"She's right about Sofia—a woman usually focused only on her work." Neil thought for a minute. "No—to be completely accurate, her work *and* her damn running. But she and Brendan are definitely a part of Rose's fan club."

"What do I need to do now? I mean, for you to get started?"

Neil positioned the document so she could read it. "This states that you are engaging me"—he pointed out his name on the 'attorney' line—"in the performance of legal work for you. You need to sign it here and then date it."

Lilah took the pen he offered and signed her full name, Lilah Clemance Patch, and then added the date. She handed the contract back to him.

"You have an unusual middle name," Neil said, as he read her signature.

"Yes, it's an old French Canadian name—my grandmother's." She seemed anxious to move away from the subject of her family. She stood up and reached down for her backpack. "Can you start now?"

"Yes. As I told you, this is all really very simple. What we call 'boilerplate.' I do want you to think about making a list of anything you have that is of value. Things like jewelry or silver."

Lilah looked at him like he had lost his mind. "Yeah. That's easy. It'll be a short list." Straight-faced, she added, "I'll make sure to include the gold."

"We only have one thing left to do," Neil said. "Do you have a dollar?"

"A dollar?" Lilah asked, surprised. "Sure." Awkwardly she unzipped the backpack balanced on her hip. After hunting around inside, she located a dollar bill. She handed it to Neil.

Accepting it, he said, "Thank you. Now you have a lawyer."

"Oh, I get it. I just hired you, right?" She laughed, the tension gone from her face. "Thanks so much." She hoisted the backpack over her shoulders. "I better go rescue Franny, Rose is probably awake and yelling her head off." She left the door open behind her.

Neil scowled at the contract on the desk in front of him. *Thank God, Sofia is with a client in Bedford,* he thought. The last thing he needed was her snooping around. Once again, he pushed the button to summon Erica.

Seconds later she stood at his door. "Yes?"

"Close the door, please. Can you sit down for a minute?" he asked, noting her surprise. He did not usually ask her to take a seat.

"Of course, what's up?"

"It is very important that no one but you and I know that Lilah is our client." His eyes met hers. "That would include Sofia."

He could see from the look on her face that she understood. Erica Mayhew was no dummy, which was why he trusted her. Underneath her banter and her efforts to mother them all, she was detail-oriented and conscientious. But above all else, she was discreet. He handed her the contract.

"I'll put this in with your confidential files. And as for that girl, I never saw her, because she wasn't here today."

"Thanks, Erica," Neil said, "I appreciate your sensitivity with this one."

"Of course, Neil," she said, addressing him by his first name now that the client was no longer present. "No problem." Contract in her hand, she left the office.

Finally alone, he began to contemplate what he had done.

CHAPTER TWENTY-ONE

Franny checked her hair in the storeroom mirror for the third time in twenty minutes. Scowling, she wondered what Juliette would think of her, and how soon the girl would figure out that she and Nick were more than friends.

What, exactly, *was* her relationship with Nick Benincasa? Had they become "friends with benefits?" She had never slept with someone just because he happened to be available, but she knew people who did. It made no sense to her. Why complicate a friendship with sex, if it was never going to be anything more? What she and Nick had was too intense to fall into that category, anyway. She wasn't sure they even were friends. Her mind wandered back to the day they met. They were certainly *something*. But what?

She heard the bell over the door chime. It was too early to be Nick. He had told her he would send a text when he was on his way. She had debated closing early today, but had decided against it. A sale was a sale and, in this economy, every one counted. Sticking her tongue out at her reflection, she walked out into the front of the shop, only to stop abruptly beside the display case. Her heart began to race as she stared at the back of the tall, strawberry blonde who was closely examining the carousel horse in the window.

"What do *you* want?" Franny asked reaching out a shaking hand to grip the edge of the case for support.

She had dreaded this moment for almost two years. Lynton was a small city; it was surprising that she had not run into her late-husband's girlfriend before this. Now, here she was. *I doubt you're in the market for a vintage doll*, Franny thought.

Lorie Derouin turned and faced Franny. She looked older than Franny remembered, despite the colorful embroidered vest and ripped jeans ending in short, black, stiletto-heeled boots. Shadows hung under her eyes, and the laugh lines at the corners of her generous mouth seemed deeper than the last time Franny had seen her.

"That horse *has* to be Bucephalus. I'm right aren't I? It's the horse Drew restored, isn't it?" Lorie waited for Franny to answer. When she didn't, Lorie added, "He told me all about that horse. It looks fabulous there in the window; just the thing to make people stop and peek in." Suddenly her smile shifted to a calculating look. "He also told me how Brid stole it from him. How did *you* ever get hold of it? You're not still hanging around with her, are you?"

"What do you want?" Franny repeated. As she heard her own voice, she thought, *I have been ruder to this woman than I have been to anyone I have ever met.*

Lorie reached up to tuck in a lock of hair that had escaped from the tortoise-shell clip at the nape of her neck. The silver charm bracelet decorated with angels she wore tinkled with the movement.

Ah, the angels, Franny thought, recognizing the bracelet. Franny fought the urge to push the woman out the door onto the street, choosing instead to remain still and silent.

"I'm leaving New Hampshire, and I wanted to let you know." Lorie searched for some sign of encouragement, but Franny's blank look remained unchanged. "I could have emailed, but I really wanted to see you. And ... well, I wanted to say goodbye"—she took a step forward—"Come on, Franny, we used to be friends."

No, we've never been friends, Franny thought. They had been a team, she realized. A team designed to make sure Drew MacCullough's life ran smoothly. *He called you his 'office wife'*—Franny's thoughts raced on—*and I, I must have been the other wife, the one in charge of clean underwear, starched shirts, homemade pasta*—bile rose in her throat—*and domestic sex when he wanted it.* Franny felt her face begin to burn, remembering how much she had trusted Lorie, how much she'd told her. What a fool she had been.

"Goodbye," Franny said, looking pointedly at the door. On the counter behind her, she heard her phone beep, signaling the arrival of a text message. *Nick,* she thought.

Lorie's smile finally vanished, taking with it the illusion of youth she tried to cultivate with her clothes and makeup.

"Steve and I are getting divorced and I'm moving to the West Coast. To Cali." She shrugged, "I suppose it was inevitable. We've been having problems for years."

I know, Franny thought, *Drew told me. I can't believe I was in— what?—a triangle with this woman? And I didn't even know it,* she admonished herself.

"Anyway," Lorie was saying, "I got the letter from Neil Malone about the trust. The money is a game-changer for me. I wanted to thank you before I left."

"That money's not for you. It's for Alex, so that he can go to school where he wants and not have to worry about how to pay for it." Franny rallied all her energy to make sure her voice did not reveal the turmoil she felt.

"I know that," Lorie said, "but you must realize that not having to worry about how to pay for Alex's education gives me freedom. It's an amazing gift." Her smile was not quite as bright as the ones that had come before it.

"That money has nothing to do with you. Do you understand?" Franny said, silently willing Lorie to leave.

Lorie nodded. "Oh, I almost forgot," she said. She began to scramble through her large, satchel-like purse, finally coming up with her phone. "Would you like to see some pictures of Alex? He's getting so big." She swiped her finger across the phone, scrolling for photos.

The store bell saved Franny from the need to answer. Lorie's face held a questioning look; she was waiting for Franny to take the phone from her outstretched hand.

"Franny, did you really find Baby Jullee?" James burst through the door, his eyes sweeping the room. "Is she here?"

"Hang on, buddy. Let Franny finish helping this lady," Nick cautioned, coming in behind his son.

"We're finished here." Franny saw James' smile dim at the

sharpness in her voice and adjusted her tone. "This lady is leaving." She looked at Lorie. "You are. Aren't you?"

"Um … yes. I am. Thanks again." She dropped her phone into her purse and nodded encouragingly at James as she passed him on her way out the door.

Franny watched her leave.

"Do you know her?" Nick asked. "You weren't too friendly. I thought for a minute you had turned into your friend, Brid"—he laughed—"You sure didn't look happy while she was in here. I take it she didn't buy anything."

Kneeling behind the display case, Franny didn't answer. She stood up and held out the box containing the doll.

"Here you go, James. Tell us what you think." She avoided looking Nick in the eye, hoping that, by ignoring his question, the subject of Lorie Derouin had been forgotten.

"Awesome. It really is dumb, old Jullee." James' face was one huge grin. Taking the doll out of the box and turning it around, he added, "She sure looks a lot better than Juliette's doll, doesn't she, Dad?"

"Do you think that Juliette will think it's her doll?" Franny asked James.

"She's five. She believes in all kinds of stupid stuff." As if to settle the matter, he added, "Juliette still believes in Santa." James put the doll back in the box, tucking the tissue paper around it. "Can we go give it to her now?"

"Don't you have a transaction to complete?" Nick raised his eyebrows at James.

"Oh, yeah. " James dug into the pocket of his pants and took out his wallet. Carefully, he removed a twenty-dollar bill and handed it to Franny. "Thank you for finding Baby Jullee for us."

Franny opened the cash register. "I owe you … "

"Nothing." Nick said, firmly. "You owe him nothing." He looked at his son. "Tell her, James."

"Well, see, I told my friend, Henry, that you found Baby Jullee, and he told his mom. And she said"—he paused to take a breath—"he had to split the cost with me." He smiled at Nick. "So, my dad said, why didn't we make it an even twenty dollars, because you had to go to a lot of work to find the doll. Ten dollars is from me and ten is from Henry." He seemed to make up his mind about something and then went on, "Henry was there when Baby Jullee got lost, and he feels sort of like it was his fault, so he was glad to chip in."

The image of the two rambunctious boys playing catch with the doll on the deck of the Nantucket ferry came to Franny. She struggled to contain a giggle.

"Now it's costing me less money than I thought it would," James said, clearly delighted with the deal.

"Okay, then. That works for me. Shall we go see what Juliette thinks?"

After setting the alarm and locking the door, Franny hurried outside to where Nick stood, holding open the passenger door of a white, double-cab truck. James was already sitting in the rear seat; next to him was the box with Baby Jullee inside.

"Wow. How come I've never seen this monster before?" she asked, stepping up to get in.

"Didn't want to scare you," Nick said, before shutting the door and going around to the driver's seat.

"So is the truck new?" Usually they travelled in the green Benincasa-and-Son van.

"No. I've had it a few years. It's a gas-guzzler; I don't drive it much. I generally use the plumbing van when it's just me. I needed it to get the kids places. Not even James is supposed to ride in the front seat of a regular truck, hence this monster. "

Ah, thought Franny, *the things I don't know about kids—or the man behind the wheel, either. No mini-van for him.*

Leaving Main Street, Nick headed south several blocks before turning into a residential area consisting of neat ranches and wood-shingled capes. He swung into the driveway of one of them and honked the horn. A short Asian boy wearing round, black-plastic eyeglasses and a Yankees cap came flying out, as if he had been waiting for them. He wrestled the heavy door open and climbed inside next to James.

"Hello, Henry," Nick said, backing the truck out of the driveway.

"Hi, Mr. B." Henry asked James, "Where's Baby Jullee?"

"Right here." James pointed to the box on the seat between

them.

"And that's Franny," James said. "She found her."

"Mrs. MacCullough," Nick corrected him.

Franny looked over the back of her seat and smiled at Henry. "'Franny' is fine. I've heard a lot about you, Henry. I'm happy to finally meet you."

"Yeah ... I'm the one who didn't catch her." Henry offered, glumly.

"But we got her back. Take a look." James opened the box and parted the tissue paper.

"It really is her." A look of wonder spread across Henry's face at the sight of this miracle. "I mean, she looks a lot better than Juliette's doll but it's definitely her."

"Remember, she looks so good because she's been in the hospital *resting*," James said as he closed the box up.

"They have a whole story they made up to tell Juliette," Nick told Franny. "They are either going to grow up to be hackers or scam artists." He shook his head. "Either way, it's jail for sure."

Looking into the mirror, he spoke to the two boys in the rear seat. 'Remember, we are not saying this is definitely Juliette's doll. She has to decide for herself." Behind him the boys nodded in agreement.

Nick pulled the truck in behind the familiar green van, which was parked in front of a neat cape. "We're here," he said to Franny. The two boys spilled out of the truck, calling for Juliette. James had the box with the doll tucked under his arm.

Suddenly, she was there, pausing on the top step, balancing on one pink ballet shoe. Franny caught her breath, unprepared for the elfin blonde child wearing a pink tutu and silver leotard. She could find nothing of either Nick or James in the little girl whose gray eyes studied her inquisitively.

"Stop being so loud, James. It hurts my ears," she said sternly, covering them with her hands to make her point. "You, too, Henry." Having admonished them, she concentrated her attention on her father. "Daddy, you're home early." She raced past the boys to wrap her arms around Nick's thighs.

"Hey, Jules. You're looking very pretty." He bent down and hoisted her into his arms.

"Who are you?" She eyed Franny from where she was nestled against her father's collarbone.

"This is—" Nick began.

"I'm Franny. I'm a friend of your dad. And of James," she interrupted, not wanting to get into the 'Mrs. MacCullough' debate with this clever little girl.

"Franny is my friend, too," Julie Canon said from the doorway. "Why don't you all come inside?" She told Henry and James. "I made some gingersnaps. They're on the kitchen table."

"Awesome, Mimi," James said. He and Henry hurried into the house.

"Come on in," Julie smiled sympathetically at Franny, sensing how nervous she was.

Franny followed Julie inside, followed by Nick, who was still holding Juliette. Franny's first impression of the house was of light and space. The sage green walls, white woodwork and satiny hardwood floors were not what she had expected. Instead of the sports posters, bobble head collection and massive TV she had envisioned, she found jewel-colored Oriental rugs and Shaker-style furniture. Spicing up the plump, beige cushions were throw pillows that took their colors from the rugs and the eclectic collection of art on the walls. Looking around, she said, "Brid would love to see this. You have some stunning pieces of art."

"Thank you," Nick replied. "I can't afford anything really expensive, but if I see something I like, I buy it if I can." Gently, he put Juliette on her feet. "Let's go find the boys. I think they have something they want to give you."

"James! What do you have for me? Let me see!" Juliette took off toward what Franny assumed must be the kitchen.

"Keep your fingers crossed." Nick said to Franny as he followed Juliette.

James and Henry, who now sported milk mustaches, were seated across the table from Juliette. James pushed the box toward her. "Here. This is for you."

"What's in it?" She picked up the box and shook it.

"Hurry up and open it." Henry urged her, his black eyes glowing with anticipation.

Juliette lifted the cover and peeked in.

"Oh … Baby Jullee," she said softly. She pulled the doll out of the box.

"See, Jules," James began his story, "what happened was, Franny has a doll shop, and one day I asked her what happened to dolls that got lost, and Franny said"—he looked at her for encouragement—"that sometimes they get found and put in the doll hospital. So she called the hospital and asked if they had a Baby Jullee there, and they did. We think she might be the doll you lost. What do you think?"

Juliette poked a tentative finger at the doll's dress. "She has new clothes."

"Yeah, that's because when she showed up at the doll hospital, she had no clothes on," Henry chimed in, eager to play his part.

"But what happened to them?"

"We don't know." Franny spoke for the first time. "The nurses gave her these clothes. Do you like them?"

After considering this for what seemed like forever, the little girl nodded slowly.

"She does look very pretty, especially in her new hat," Franny said.

Juliette held the doll out in front of her, studying it closely. The look on her face gave nothing away.

Julie crouched down, slipping her arm around her granddaughter's waist. "Do you think this is your Baby Jullee? Are you glad to have her home, honey?" Julie asked.

"Yes, Mimi. My heart feels better. It's not broken anymore." Juliette hugged the doll to her chest. "I'm going to take her to my room so she can see her friends. They missed her, too."

"Juliette, don't you have something you want to say to Franny?" Nick asked.

With her doll clutched firmly in both hands, Juliette walked over to Franny and carefully placed it on the floor between their feet. Dipping into a curtsy, she said, "Thank you so much for finding my doll." Then, scooping up her restored treasure, she skipped out of the room.

Once she was gone, the two boys high-fived each other, clearly relieved to have the Baby Jullee saga behind them.

"Why don't I order a pizza and hold down the fort here, and

you two go out to dinner?" Julie said. "I think Franny deserves a great dinner for all her hard work, don't you, Nick?"

"Say no more. We're out of here." Grasping Franny's arm, Nick steered her toward the front door.

"Nick, wait," Franny protested. "Really, Julie, we can order a pizza for all of us."

Julie shook her head. "Have fun, you two. And, Franny, thanks again for finding that doll."

***

Franny twisted one of the dark curls on Nick's chest around her finger. "Your mother-in-law would die if she knew we were here instead of eating dinner."

"What makes you think she doesn't?" he asked, nuzzling her neck.

"Oh my God! How could she?" Franny sat up, pulling the sheet around her as though she expected Julie Canon to come through the door to her bedroom.

"She's not *blind*. She could see that I was about to ravage you on the kitchen table."

"Stop. You're so not funny." Franny said, playfully pulling away from him to show that she really thought he was.

"But, I'm right though," he said, reclaiming her. "Are you hungry? I could throw on some pants and raid the kitchen." He dropped a kiss on her head. "The dogs are outside in their pen, right?"

"You and the dogs. Yes, they are, but they would never hurt you." Her finger drifted down from his chest. "Don't go. I like you with your pants off."

"Do you? Well, if I don't scrounge us up some food, I'm not going to be able to keep them on. That should make you happy." He held her close for a moment and then in a thoughtful voice, added, "So what was the deal with that woman in your shop today? I've never seen you like that. You weren't even that cold to *me* the first time we met."

Franny sighed, extracting herself from his arms, her desire gone. "I have to get dressed, it's getting late."

"Who was she? What did she want?" He persisted, searching her face for clues. "Not a doll, I take it?"

"She's into angels, not old dolls." Franny said, slipping out of bed and beginning to dress.

"Angels? Did she think you carried those in stock, too?"

Dressed now, Franny felt less vulnerable. Nick, his pants on, hunted through the bedclothes for his shirt. She watched him, consciously having to stop herself from reaching out and touching him. She decided he deserved some kind of answer.

"That was Lorie Derouin. She was … " Her voiced thickened with emotion.

He looked up, surprised at the change in her tone, the shirt dangling from his hand.

Taking a deep breath, she continued, "She came in looking for me. She worked for Drew."

"You seem to be pretty upset. Is she a good friend?" Nick asked.

Franny sighed. She looked at him steadily for a minute and said, "After he died, I found out they were lovers."

The next minute felt like it lasted a long time, and then, dropping the shirt, Nick put his arms around her. "Whoa. That's a pretty tacky move."

"They were together when he died. At first, I believed the story she was telling me. She said he had asked her to come to the hotel for an early morning meeting, but then, during their 'meeting,' he claimed he wasn't feeling well and had a heart attack. She was at the hospital when I got there."

"There must have been more to it than that to make you think he was cheating with her?" Nick said.

She stepped away from him, now regretting telling him anything. She knew she didn't have the strength to relive with him the whole story. Not now.

"Lorie's getting divorced and moving to California with her son. She came to see me today to say goodbye."

"That's crazy, " Nick said. "Why would she think you'd care *what* she does, under the circumstances? Unless—I guess you guys buried the hatchet the last couple years and ended up friends?"

We definitely did not end up friends, Franny thought.

"She also wanted to thank me, because I once gave her son a pretty generous gift." She began to make the bed.

"You what?" Nick took the pillow from her hand and made her look at him. "I thought you told me she was Drew's *girlfriend*."

"She was. And now, with any luck, I will never have to see her again."

"I hope you're right," he said, pulling her into a hug.

KATHLEEN FERRARI

CHAPTER TWENTY-TWO

"**N**eil thinks you miss the cat. Do you?" Georgia asked. Struggling to make her hair behave, Brid began to fire off a flippant answer.

"Of course I don't miss the damn cat, I'm ... "

Who was she kidding? This was Georgia, after all. The very heart of their relationship forbade their lying to one another. Only truth worked between member and sponsor in AA. Their friendship had come later, but the rules set down at Tuesday night meetings in the basement of St. John's still applied. Giving up on her hair, she plopped down beside Georgia and leaned forward to hug her knees.

"Okay. I miss the little púca. I guess Neil is correct. That feline and I do seem to have a lot in common. I like the way she never backs down once she takes a stance."

"Like you."

"You make me sound like some kind of wild woman"—she made a sour face.

Trying another tack, Georgia said, "Neil thinks you're lonely."

Brid supposed she should be angry that Neil and Georgia had discussed her behind her back. But she was beginning to accept the fact that anger required too much energy—energy she needed for other things and no longer wished to squander.

"Holy Mother of God! Two years ago, I might have agreed to at least consider the idea, but how can I be lonely now? I am surrounded by this clutch of women, all of whom seem to need or want something from me." She ran her hands through her hair, undoing any progress she'd made earlier with her brush. "And what about Neil? Isn't my relationship with him supposed to keep me from being lonely?"

"Of course. Although I'm no expert on the benefits derived from being in love."

Oh aren't you now? Brid thought as Georgia continued.

"You are so self-contained, I would bet that, even with Neil, you hold a piece of your heart back." Georgia reached down to stroke Gussie, curled in a gray semi-circle as close to Georgia's feet as possible. "One thing I know for sure is that, with animals, you can open your whole heart and let them in. How else do you think I have stayed sane and sober for the last forty years? I think you fell a little bit in love with that cat, and you miss her."

"You have added head-shrinking to your practice, now? I already admitted that I miss the damn cat. She was good company."

"You know perfectly well that the only human-psych course I took was PSYCH 101, to meet my Gen Ed requirement—probably the same one you took. I know what I see. Neil believes that girl would have let you keep the cat."

Brid sighed. "He's probably right. Lilah feels so indebted to us. Really, to Neil. I think she would have done anything for him, including giving up Moaki. But I could never take her cat. Lilah found the cat when she was a kitten—rescued her from some alley in Boston. She loves that cat. I would never take her from Lilah."

"For someone who calls herself 'a cold-hearted bitch', you do look out for the girl's best interests, I'll grant you that." Georgia paused briefly. "I need a favor. There's this—"

"No. Absolutely no. It's true, I am fond of Moaki, but that does not mean I want—or need—another cat." She stood up and retrieved their coats from the closet. "We have to leave if we are going to get up to Hiram's Forge by seven-thirty. I don't know why Franny wants you to look at the dog, anyway. She has her own vet." She handed Georgia her coat.

"I'm betting she's not happy with what she's hearing from her vet. Lucy is an old dog. It's never easy when they start down this road. I imagine Franny wants a second opinion. I don't mind, but it's unlikely I will be telling her anything different from what she's already been told."

"I suppose you're right. It's nice of you to do it. She's a great cook; you'll get a good meal out of it. I told her no meat. We had better go, or we will be late."

"It's not a cat." Georgia said, returning to their earlier discussion as she slipped on her coat.

Halfway out the door, Brid stopped.

"Not a cat?" She stared at Georgia. "You must be mad. It's a dog? You know how I feel about dogs. As you may recall, I *had* a dog." The image of Boru, the Irish wolfhound puppy Drew brought home the first year they were married, flashed through her mind. As always, it was a painful memory—one she'd made a habit of moving past quickly. "It did not work out."

Georgia didn't answer as she followed Brid out the door.

***

Sofia picked up a milk-glass candy dish filled with chocolate truffles wrapped in deep-purple-and-gold foil, moving it from the end table to the coffee table. "This was Mom's, wasn't it?" She held up the dish and examined the markings on the bottom. "It *was* Mom's. How did *you* get it?"

Franny giggled despite herself. "She gave it to me. I didn't sneak into the house and steal it."

"You know, just because you got married first doesn't mean that I don't intend to, someday. I might actually like to have some of this stuff, too."

"Take it with you when you leave. I hope it's okay to still use it tonight, but if that's a problem, I will find another dish, and you can stuff it into your Louis Vuitton bag right now."

Slightly embarrassed, Sofia said, "Of course not. You can keep it. I don't eat candy." She sniffed at the truffles and wrinkled her nose in disgust, adding, "You shouldn't either."

"Give it to me." Franny whipped the dish out of Sofia's hand and set it back on the end table. "I wouldn't want you to gain any weight from *holding* it. Now, go over to that basket and pick out your headpiece."

"My what?" Sofia arched her eyebrows.

"Headpiece. In Ireland, these celebrations are like our

bachelorette parties, except that there they call them 'hen parties.' At a Hen, everyone gets dressed up in fancy costumes and headpieces, and they have a party to celebrate the bride." She nodded toward the basket on the floor. "Pick yours out. Lilah found them on an Irish-wedding website. And look at this!" She opened a bag next to the basket and pulled out a purple T-shirt. Across the front, written in gold, were the words: *I was at Brid's Hen.* "I got one for each of us."

"You really have lost it. Brid is almost fifty. A little long in the tooth for all this bride stuff, don't you think? To say nothing of the fact that it's her second marriage." Sofia selected a headpiece and dutifully, though reluctantly, put it on. "There are only six of us. I guess if you count Rose, then, seven. Not exactly a bash. And finally, there is no wine or anything *else* that looks like an adult beverage being served."

"I'm not going to serve alcohol when the guest of honor is a recovering alcoholic. I don't think the rest of us need it, do we?"

"No, I suppose none of us do, but a bachelorette party without the booze? Really?"

Lilah appeared in the doorway, carrying a wrapped package in one hand and the baby carrier with Rose asleep in the other. She had ridden up to Franny's with Mara Sorento, who was busy unpacking their dinner in the kitchen.

Franny moved toward the baby, only to be warned off by Lilah.

"Oh my God! Don't wake her up! She's been so fussy the last two days, I almost left her on the steps of some church." Setting Rose's carrier down and placing her gift among those already piled on the floor, Lilah reached for the basket of headpieces. "Awesome—they got here in time. Let me see." She selected one with a quartet of sparkling, gold hearts set on a purple headband. "I'm taking this one." She promptly put in on, the shimmering hearts accentuating the blue stripes in her hair.

"Stop picking on Franny," Mara said, bringing in hors d'oeuvres from the kitchen. "I think the party's a great idea." She placed a platter of mini quiches and asparagus-wrapped-in-prosciutto on the table, next to a plate of assorted cheeses and fruit. "And I wouldn't let Brid hear you say she's almost fifty"—she bent over and rearranged some of the quiches—"because she's not. And anyway, we *all* should look so hot. I'm going to wait until they get here to serve the soup and breads. We want the soup to be steaming."

"Let's eat in the kitchen," Franny said. "It's only us, except for Brid's friend, Georgia. And I don't think she'll mind. I bet she's a kitchen-person."

"I doubt she'll care, given what she does all day," Sofia said. "She's a vet, right? I mean, half the time she's up to her knees in horseshit, isn't she?" Sofia disapprovingly eyed the food on the table, particularly singling out the quiches for her most disdainful look. "Don't you have any veggies, Mara? Or something without scads of fat in it?"

Before Mara could answer, a car door slammed.

"Quick! Everyone put on a T-shirt and pick a headpiece!" Franny pulled on her own shirt and grabbed a headband with intertwined wedding bells, making sure the others followed suit. The sound of the kitchen door opening and closing reached the now-silent living room. Lilah smothered a giggle.

"Franny? Where are you?" Brid called out as she made her way through the house toward the decorated hens-in-waiting. "Where are the dogs? We have Gussie with us."

"I'm in the living room; come on in. The dogs are upstairs."

Brid stopped in the doorway, her mouth hanging open at the sight: four cheery women posing in identical, bright-purple T-shirts, topped off with garish headpieces.

"Surprise!" they sang out. Sofia began to video the scene with her cell phone.

Behind Brid, Georgia, shadowed by Gussie, smiled, clearly delighted that Brid was surprised.

"Oh, look—it's a party! Do I get to have one of those, too?" Georgia pointed to the frippery on their heads. Lilah passed her a T-shirt and headpiece, and Georgia immediately adorned herself with both.

Franny retrieved the last headpiece, a band with 'BRIDE' spelled out across it in white and silver spangles. She handed it to Brid. "This is yours."

"You people are mad. Completely daft. Ever since I met you"—she glowered at Franny—"my life has also been insane." She stuck the headpiece haphazardly on her head.

Franny smirked. "Don't be such a grump. We're having a Hen for you, like they do in Ireland."

Brid shook her head in wonderment. "I am hardly a blushing bride and, last I checked, we are not in Ireland."

"Don't be silly," Franny said, leading Brid to a chair decorated like a throne and covered in purple and gold streamers. "Of course you're a bride."

Brid shook her head in protest.

Ignoring her, Franny continued, "We can pretend we're in Ireland, if you want."

"Let's open the presents," Lilah said, handing the one on top of the pile to Brid, who was now seated like a queen at court.

"I see you've done your hair," Brid said, looking closely at Lilah for the first time since stepping into the room. "Bizarre, but interesting."

"I know. Awesome, isn't it?" Lilah asked Mara, who was crouched in front of the baby carrier, admiring Rose, whose eyes were focused on Gussie. "*You* like it don't you, Mara?"

"Totally. It's fun, and I think it suits you." Rising gracefully to her feet, she extended her hand to Georgia. "I'm Mara, by the way. You must be Georgia."

"Pleasure," Georgia nodded.

Brid groaned, "Mara, for the love of God, don't encourage her, or it will be chartreuse tomorrow."

"Let's do the gifts," Franny said, anxious to get the conversation back to the party.

The five women crowded around Brid like they were at a junior-high slumber party. Settling back into her throne, Brid slowly relaxed, turning her attention to the large box wrapped in gold paper and tied with purple ribbons in her lap.

"That one's from me," Sofia said as she chewed the side of her finger, a sure sign she was nervous.

"I actually wanted one of these." Brid said, lifting a pasta maker from the wrappings. "How did you know?" She seemed amazed that Sofia would give her a gift she liked. "Neil has suddenly developed a passion for Italian food. Thank you."

"Brendan has that same model. He said to tell you he'd be glad to help you figure out how to use it."

"That will be grand, as I am genetically preconfigured to make a total disaster out of cooking Italian food."

Franny's gift was a set of plush towels in deep cinnamon, each with a cream-colored monogram. "These are lovely. The ones I have now have seen better days," she said, stroking the thick fabric.

"Everyone needs new towels on a regular basis, but no one ever takes the time to go buy them. Lilah helped me choose the color." Franny handed the three remaining presents to Brid.

Mara's gift was a catered dinner for two to be delivered to their door. "I will make anything you want."

"In that case, I want all desserts," Brid said.

Franny was pretty sure Brid's answer was designed to provoke a response from Sofia. If that was the case, Brid was not disappointed.

"You would. I don't know why you never gain an ounce." Sofia folded her arms in front of her.

"Luck of the Irish, I guess." Brid reached for the package Lilah was holding out to her.

"From me and Rose."

Brid parted the tissue paper and revealed a small oil painting of Moaki. She held it up for the others to see. "This is really well done, Lilah. The brush work is amazing."

Lilah's face flamed bright red and she ducked her head. "I'm glad you like it."

"I do. I like it very much, and I know that Neil will, too." Brid stood up and placed the picture on the mantel. "Let's leave it here for now so nothing happens to it. Thank you all very much. This was ... " She paused a moment to gather her composure, then said, "Something smells wonderful. Why don't we eat?"

"Wait. There's one more." Franny handed Brid a small box tied with a white satin ribbon. It appeared to have no card.

Untying the bow, Brid lifted the lid and looked inside. She raised her eyes and found Georgia's.

"What is it?" Sofia shifted around Franny, trying to see.

Brid removed a circle of rolled-up red leather that had a buckle on one end, holding it tightly in her hand. She still hadn't said a word.

"Is that a dog collar? It is. It's a dog collar," Lilah said, the incredulity in her voice speaking for all of them.

"No way." Sofia said.

"I need you to take this dog for me. I have no one else who can." Georgia spoke softly, her tone belying the apprehension she felt in making the appeal. She watched Brid closely.

Brid nodded, slowly dropping the collar back into the tissue paper. "I will have to ask Neil. He's never had a dog. He may say no."

Georgia smiled, serenely. "Of course. Ask him. But please be sure to tell him this is a lovely dog. He will be absolutely no trouble to either of you. In fact, you can take him with you to the gallery; he'll like that a lot."

Brid sighed. " 'Absolutely no trouble.' Right."

"What kind of a dog is Brid getting?" Franny asked.

"Thatcher is a Tibetan terrier. He's eight. A real gentleman."

"A 'gentleman,' huh? I will have to bring Dolce over to play," Mara said. "He's a holy terror. Maybe the gentleman's good manners will rub off on him."

The others were already familiar with the many ways Dolce had earned his reputation and his nickname, "The Destructor."

"Now ladies, if you want to head into the kitchen"—Mara gestured with a sweep of her hand—"the soup is served."

***

"This dog is not a rescue-situation. Georgia went to great pains to tell me that he is what they call a 're-homing case.' "

Brid was in the kitchen, making tea. She put the teapot and two Beleek mugs on the tray and carried it all back into the living room, where Neil was reading a legal brief. She thought he looked tired. Putting the tray down on the table in front of him, she poked his foot with her boot.

"You have not heard a word I've said. Not one word."

"Not true." He pulled her down next to him. "There's a dog, and Georgia wants you to take it. He's 'not a rescue'; he's a 're-homing case.' Whatever the hell that is. Right? What did I miss?"

She leaned back against his shoulder, taking comfort from his closeness.

"A rescue is one of those poor, little waifs that's kicked and beaten to hell and back," Brid explained. "I hope the bastards who

212

do that go to a very deep and hot part of hell, and stay there. A dog that needs to be re-homed—or so Georgia says—is a much-loved dog whose owner can no longer keep him." She paused, sighing. "And this dog's owner can no longer keep him because the man was found dead in his bed on Monday morning. He was a teacher at one of those prep schools up north near the White Mountains. Died in his sleep and had no family. The school's headmaster called Georgia—his mother's dog is one of her patients. You know what Georgia's like about animals: she went up the next day and got him."

Neil said nothing. She knew he was waiting for her to go on.

"Georgia says he is grieving and will be no trouble. She is worried about him, and she wants him settled in a new home as soon as possible"—she shook her head—"and I told her I would have to ask you. I explained you have never had a dog."

Removing herself from his side, she poured their tea and waited for him to say something.

Neil looked up. "It's fine with me. I like dogs."

Sighing, she remembered: he did like dogs. She could see him in her mind, racing down three flights of stairs from the apartment she had shared with Drew, attempting to keep up with Boru the Wolfhound, who was straining on the leash. She should have known: Neil was not going to be her way out of this.

"Georgia has never asked me for anything for herself," she said. She looked around at her beloved apartment and her easel containing the unfinished painting of Lilah, her eyes coming to rest, at last, on the man beside her. She shivered thinking how very close she had come to having none of it. "I owe her my life. I know it sounds dramatic, but it is true."

Neil put down the paper and gave her his full attention. "Brid, it's only a dog. We can cope with a dog. It might be fun. What's this guy's name?"

She began to laugh and was suddenly aware she was sounding slightly unhinged. "His *person*—Georgia insists on calling this poor, dead soul that—was a devoted Anglophile. He taught English History, among other things, to these rich little darlings. The dog's name is Thatcher."

Neil looked at her. "Thatch—"

He threw back his head and roared. He tried twice to speak, only to start laughing again, tears streaming down his face.

I might kill him, she thought.

"My God! Thatcher! As in *Margaret* Thatcher?" He collapsed in gales of more laughter.

"Apparently so." She frowned as she continued, "I believe she was the one who said something about the Irish all being liars."

Neil pulled himself upright and rearranged his face in an attempt to appear serious. "Well, it can't be that hard to change the dog's name. We can call him 'Collins,' or something like that."

"Are you mad? I am not changing the poor animal's name. Especially when that woman called us liars. How would you like it if I decided suddenly to call you 'Luigi'—or worse, 'Tony Blair?' Georgia suggested we call him 'Thatch.' She said he would answer to that."

Brid slumped down next to him. Neil picked up his highlighter and resumed reading.

"I don't know what the hell happened to my life," she mused. "Grieving widows, pregnant girls barely out of their teens, a newborn—and now, a damn dog. None of which I asked for. Next thing you know, someone will show up with a ferret."

"I draw the line at ferrets," Neil said, still highlighting his document. "I don't like them. No-o-o ferrets." He looked up at her, "You seem to have forgotten me; I hope I fall in the *asset* column."

Brid put down the mug in her hand, very gently; it was her mother's Beleek, after all.

" 'Asset?' " she cried. "You are an *ass!*"

With that, she threw herself into his arms.

CHAPTER TWENTY-THREE

Neil strode confidently through Boston College's Gasson Hall, feeling very much at home and grateful that the latest renovation had left the building's integrity intact. He loved the old, Gothic structures, preferring them to the new development that had appeared on the campus since he had been a student. Brid, walking next to him, was not as impressed.

"You are not humming 'For Boston' under your breath, are you?" The Boston College fight song was close to the top of the list of things that drove Brid mad about Neil's beloved "BC."

He smiled and reached over, pulling her to his side. "You're such a wiseass. Do you know that? You're practically in church in this building, so do not blaspheme."

Brid snorted in reply.

"I'm warning you," he threatened. His barely-contained smile told her he was kidding.

Neil slowed his pace. "Here's what I'm thinking: I go in and break the news to him, alone. After I have revived him, I bring you in, and we have our chat. What do you think?"

Brid's fingers itched for a cigarette, which, unfortunately, she did not have in her possession. Not wanting to be tempted to sneak off for a quick smoke, she had left her hidden pack of cigarettes at home. She could only imagine the ramifications of lighting up in this stuffy, old fortress dedicated to the past glory of the male Boston Irish. Setting the place on fire wouldn't help her cause.

"Fine," she said. "Whatever you want to do. I haven't seen His

Arrogance since your mother's wake."

Neil opened his mouth and closed it. Only the slightest shake of his head betrayed his disagreement.

They stopped in front of a closed door, its nameplate— **THOMAS CARMELLO, S.J.**—slightly obscured by a yellow Post-it with "Fr. Tom" scrawled across it.

Neil leaned down and surreptitiously kissed her. "It's going to be fine."

"I will wait here with MacNeice to console me," she said, waving a well-read book of poetry in his face. "You just stick your head out and whistle when you want me to make my appearance. I will creep in and kiss his ring."

"It's the Cardinal's ring you have to kiss. Last I heard, Tom hasn't been tapped for that," Neil answered.

"He already *thinks* he is one." Brid walked toward a bench under one of the long, narrow windows across the hall.

Neil knocked on the door and waited.

"Come on in," came the reply from the other side.

Stepping into the office, Neil couldn't find the source of the voice at first. Then, from somewhere behind him, he heard, "So, this must be bigger than your usual plea to get one of the deserving students from our illustrious hometown admitted here. You usually pull that off over the phone."

Tom Carmello, dressed in baggy khakis and a paint-spattered BC sweatshirt, was standing on top of a high ladder, holding a paintbrush in one hand and a small can of paint in the other.

"What the hell are you doing up there?" Neil said. "I would think, now that you Jesuits finally have your own pope, you would have staff to do that."

Tom chuckled. "You haven't been paying attention, my friend. Francis would probably want to be holding the ladder *for* me. The Holy Father is not a fan of extraneous staff. He expects us to work for a living. Imagine that?" He paused to examine his efforts. "This stain has been driving me crazy. Every time I look up, it hits me square in the face. It was a slow morning. I thought I would take care of it."

He studied Neil with suspicion. "So, what is it? Coming down here from Lynton is quite a hike in the middle of a work week."

Dipping the brush in the paint, he reached up and continued working on the offending spot.

Below him, Neil swallowed hard before answering, "I'm getting married. It would mean a lot to me if you would perform the ceremony."

On top of the ladder, the priest paused to decide where to place a final white dab, his paintbrush hovering in the air.

"Married?" he replied absent-mindedly. "I always thought there was only one woman you would ever consider marrying ... " A second later, he swung around to stare down into Neil's upturned face. "Oh, shit. No. Tell me it's not her."

The brush slipped from his hand; they watched it fall with a splat on the polished oak floor. For a moment, neither moved. Then, they simultaneously leaped into action.

"Quick! Grab those paint cloths from the shelf over there"— Tom clambered down the ladder—"Thank God, it's latex." He carefully placed the paint can on a bookshelf to avoid further disaster and easily caught the cloth Neil tossed him.

On their knees, in silence, the two men scrubbed at the stain on the floor until it had disappeared. The priest leaned backed and looked at Neil.

"Not Brid Sheerin. Please tell me it's not Brid."

"Come on, Buzz. You sound like Jack. I expected more of you." Neil unconsciously used the name he had called his friend when they were young boys.

Tom's face softened. Groaning, he pushed himself to his feet. "You know, you're the only one left, except for my sister, who calls me that. Seems like a long time ago we were raising hell together, doesn't it? I'm surprised to hear that you're running to Jack Blaine for advice. Jack was always an ass."

"Well, in this case, you and he happen to be in complete agreement. So what does that make you?" Sensing the need to state what, to him, had seemed obvious, Neil said, "I bought the ring there."

"At least, I hope he gave you a decent break on it."

"He did. Although for a minute, I thought he was going to refuse to sell it to me. He also gave me *his* version of what an idiot I am."

"Knowing you," Tom said, "I'm pretty sure it's not a trinket. No way was Jack going to pass on making a buck. He was always a greedy bastard."

Neil gave the floor a final swipe. "I think we got it all. I hope that means they won't throw you out of here." He struggled to his feet, inwardly cursing his creaky knee. "I'd love to know why you guys think I'm such a fool when it comes to women. Just because I've never married one doesn't mean I haven't come close once or twice."

"It's not you. It's her. There was always something of the sorceress about Brid Sheerin. For God's sake, Neil, you must remember all that drama with Drew MacCullough." Tom shook his head.

"Well, I'm not Drew," Neil said, waiting to hear the comeback.

"No, you're not. You're no fool, either. I realize you've been in love with her for years," Tom said. "I haven't seen her since your mother died, but I don't imagine she's changed much. She was always something to look at."

"You noticed that, did you?"

"I'm a priest; I'm not dead." He gestured toward a pair of chairs in front of the desk. "Have a seat. I need to get some information from you, then we need to set up a time when I can meet with both of you. I'm supposed to do six months of Pre-Cana counseling, but in this case, I can use a little clerical discretion to waive that."

"Let's do it now. She's outside." Neil said, walking to the door.

He stepped into the hall to find Brid sitting on the floor in the lotus position next to the bench, reading the tattered copy of Louis MacNeice's poems. "I think you're up next," he said.

"Grand," she said, rising to her feet with none of the effort both he and Tom had needed to get off the office floor. She tucked the book into her bag and joined him. At the door, he stood aside to let her precede him into the office.

Tom stood behind his desk. Despite his lack of clerical collar, his rigid posture and stern expression left no doubt he was a Jesuit. "Good afternoon, Brid. It's been a long time. I understand that best wishes are in order: it seems you've managed to land yourself a big fish." The smile on his face did not go all the way to his eyes, and he did not offer her his hand.

"It's so nice to see you again, Father. You are looking well. May I sit?" Brid asked. "You are one of the few people who seem to remember you are supposed to congratulate the groom and wish the bride well. I am impressed."

As she had promised, Brid was on her best behavior. Watching her, Neil could see the influence of both her mother and the Sisters of Notre Dame de Namur who had educated her. She was a member of the last generation of girls who had been given strict instruction on how to behave in the presence of a priest.

Tom seemed to Neil to be slightly less sure of himself than when they had first entered the room. *What was he expecting?* Neil wondered.

"Of course, sit. You, too, Neil." He took his own seat behind the desk and removed a pad of paper and a gold pen from the drawer. "I need a few details to get this into the pipeline. Do you have a date in mind?"

"June eighteenth, Wednesday. Six o'clock in the evening," Brid answered. "Of course, we hope that date will work for you."

Her tone sounded dangerously sweet, in Neil's opinion.

"I think it should be fine. Let me just check my calendar." He scrolled through his planner on a laptop in front of him. "It looks like the date is open"—he began typing—"I am putting it in: Malone Wedding." He stopped and looked up. "At Our Lady's in Lynton, I assume? Not here, right?"

"Yes, Our Lady's. We're having a small reception after the ceremony, at Craic," Neil said, anxious to get the conversation over.

"Great. It's been a while since I've eaten there. The food is always memorable." Tom picked up his pen. "Who are the witnesses?"

The stillness grew as the full implication of the question occurred to the three of them. It should have been—would have been—Drew, and only Drew, who stood with Neil on his wedding day. They all knew it. Neil had served as best man the day Drew married Brid.

"I suppose I'll ask Harry." Neil answered at last, filling the lengthening silence.

Tom looked up. "Remind me what Harry's name is?"

"Elliot Winslow," Neil said.

Tom nodded, making a note. "And for you?" He looked at Brid.

She said nothing.

"What about Lilah? Or Georgia?" Neil suggested, knowing even as he did what her answer would be.

"Franny." Brid was firm.

"Fine. But I need her legal name," Tom said, scribbling something.

Brid lifted her chin. "Francesca MacCullough."

The pen stopped moving. Tom raised his eyes. "MacCullough?" He shook his head slightly, not sure he had heard correctly.

"Yes." Neil said quickly. "I know this must strike you as beyond the pale. I'm marrying Drew's first wife and she's having his widow as her attendant. They became friends after Drew's death. Close friends." He shrugged.

Brid remained mute. She was content to watch the two men stumble through the conversation.

"I see." Tom answered, although, clearly, he didn't. "Well, I need a few minutes alone with Brid. So, why don't you go take a walk? Say some prayers. Come back in about fifteen minutes."

Neil hated leaving Brid alone with Tom.

She's only here because she loves me, he thought. He took a quick look at her face. She gave no clue as to what she was thinking.

"Your turn to wait outside," Brid said.

Neil hesitated, reluctant to leave.

"Go. This is not the first time I have been called on the carpet by a priest. I will survive." Cocking her head, she gestured toward the door.

"It's Tom I'm worried about. Don't hurt him." He raised his hands in surrender. "Okay. I'll be outside if either of you needs me."

"We won't. Close the door." Tom said, impatient to talk to Brid alone.

As soon as the latch clicked, they both dropped their masks.

Tom glowered at her as he leaned across the desk. "What the hell is going on here?"

Brid's eyes narrowed and her demure expression disappeared.

Lilah could have told him that neither was a good sign.

"It is pretty simple," she said. "We are getting married. Neil wants to be married in the Catholic Church." She sat coiled in her chair. "You and I both know that loyalty is bred in his bones, so he wants *you* to marry him. 'Give me the child until he is seven, and I will give you the man.' Is that not the Jesuit credo? In Neil's case, you succeeded. Be glad. You won." She waited for him to speak. When he didn't, she added, "What is it that you find so confusing?"

"And you—do you want to be married in the Catholic Church?" Tom waited for her answer, his trap baited.

Such a smug bastard, but then, most priests are, Brid thought. *How stupid does he think I am?* Aloud, she said, "I want Neil to be happy, Father. Being married in The Church is important to him. As you should know."

"And if I refuse to marry you?"

Then we will get dear, doddering Mike Hannigan at Our Lady's to do it, she thought. *He would do anything for Da.* Containing herself, she replied, "On what grounds? I am a cradle-Catholic, baptized, confirmed, and married the first time in The Church. I have all the papers with me"—she reached for her leather satchel—"Would you like to see them?"

"I'm sure you do. My objections go much deeper than your Catholic pedigree. Let's start with Drew MacCullough."

"You may have me there. I am not clear on how The Church currently views a marriage that ends in divorce." With a straight face, she added, "They seem to be a little desperate of late."

She moved in toward the priest, who was still halfway out of his chair. Their faces were eight inches apart.

"But I can tell you this"—her voice was level—"Drew is dead. I know. I was at the wake. Quite dead. As in 'until death do you part.' Which means he's gone."

"And the widow? Francesca?" He resumed his seat.

Brid settled back in her chair. Some of the stress slipped from her face.

"Maybe when you meet Franny you will understand how it happened that we became friends. She sees the best in everyone—and though you may find this hard to believe—that includes even me." *I would kill for a cigarette*, she thought. "It certainly was never my intention for us to become friends. The truth is, I felt sorry for her. And why wouldn't I? I'm sure I will get no argument from you; Drew and I deserved one another. We were equally matched in both cruelty and selfishness."

She let that sink in, noting the surprise that flickered across his face, then went on.

"Franny didn't deserve any of it and was in way over her head trying to cope. She came to me when nobody, including Neil, would help her unravel the mess that Drew left behind. As I am sure you must realize, I know something about surviving Drew MacCullough. We discovered we really like one another. And we became friends."

Tom threw down his ace. "And the booze? Where are you with that?"

Brid got up and walked over to the window, standing with her back to him, staring out at the campus.

The silence in the room grew and, behind her, the priest said nothing, refusing to be the one to end it. In her mind, she was once again in the liquor store, the bottle of Jameson heavy in her hands. How close she had come to losing everything. She turned from the window to face him, her confidence shaken.

"I am a drunk. Some people in AA prefer 'addict' or 'alcoholic,' but I stick with 'drunk,' because that is the truth of it. I have been sober for sixteen years and twelve days. Not long ago, I came close to slipping. It was the first time in all these years that it was such a near thing. I called my sponsor and she talked me back from the edge."

She walked back to the chair and sat down.

"Neil and I had had a fight. I told him I did not want to see him anymore." Her voice broke. She stopped talking, fighting for control. "I knew then: I loved him; I could not imagine my life without him. Loving him terrifies me, sometimes." She sighed, "I am back at weekly meetings."

"Does Neil know?"

"What do you take me for?" Her attitude flared back. "Of *course* he knows. I told him. I also told him he was insane to want to marry me. He says it doesn't matter"—she shook her head—"I believe my smoking bothers him more than the fact that he could

222

wake up to find a drunk in his bed."

"And what about children? Would you agree to raise them in The Church?" Tom had his pen in hand again.

"Are you daft?" she asked. "I am going to be forty-seven and Neil, as you should know, is almost fifty-two. Who the hell do you think we are, Abraham and Sarah? I cannot have them, anyway."

"You swear to me you won't try to come between him and The Church?"

"I over-estimated you. How could you think that any*thing* or any*one* could ever come between Neil and his faith? He is like my mother in that. At times, I envy them. The Faith runs through his veins as sure as his life's blood. Even Drew understood that."

"Ah, the fabulous Drew MacCullough. I find it amazing that, even though he's dead, we still find ourselves talking about him."

The bitterness in his voice startled Brid; her face showed a flicker of surprise.

"I was always jealous of Drew," Tom admitted. "I'm not proud of it, and I've confessed it, but it's true. Neil and I shared a playpen; we grew up in each other's kitchen. He was my best friend. Once he met Drew, I lost something very special. We remained friends, but it was not the same. Drew MacCullough was a pied piper. But of course, you would know that better than me."

A shadow crossed his face; he looked sad. "At one time, I thought Neil and I might go to seminary together." He stood up and walked to the door. "Didn't happen. I probably give Drew too much credit for ending that, though. Neil is his own man."

He studied Brid for a moment longer and then smiled.

"God has his own plans," he said. "You may be what Neil needs. I hope so. I really do. I'll be happy to marry you"—he opened the door—"Let's get him in here and tell him the news before he wears out his knees."

KATHLEEN FERRARI

CHAPTER TWENTY-FOUR

The Bride's Room, located in the basement of Our Lady Queen of the Angels Catholic Church, started life as a storage room. In an effort to compete with their parish's upscale Episcopalian neighbors at St. Peter's, the Ladies' Sodality had converted the utility closet into a comforting space in which a bride could prepare for her walk down the aisle.

Brid sat staring at her reflection in a large mirror, one ornately framed in gold leaf and decorated with dancing cherubs. It had been the gift of some romantic parishioner who had hoped to provide the appropriate mood for young women during those last, dear moments of maidenhood. In the glass, Brid could see a painting of St. Elizabeth of Hungary, the patron saint of young brides, hung on the opposite wall. The saint appeared none too happy. *No doubt, she thinks I am too old for all this nonsense*, Brid thought, staring back at Elizabeth's disgruntled face. *And she is right.* Brid sighed.

Meanwhile, Franny fussed with the baby's breath woven through Brid's hair.

"I look ridiculous," Brid scowled at her image. "We could have stopped in at City Hall and then gone out for pizza. Of course, that would have been far too easy, right, Thatch?"

At the sound of his name, the dog, sprawled on the floor behind her chair, raised his head and barked once before resuming his watch on the door.

"And, of course, we need the sacrament, don't we?"

Thatch cocked his head, attuned to the tension in her voice.

"If only he could tell you how beautiful you look; you might listen to *him*," Franny said, adding one last touch, a tiny blue violet, "something new" and "something blue" hidden in Brid's dark hair completing the elements required to bring the bride luck. "Is he staying down here during the ceremony?"

"Ronan is coming to pick him up and take him over to the bar"—Brid glanced at the wall clock—"he should be here soon."

"It doesn't seem possible that less than a month ago you and Neil didn't have Thatch," Franny mused. "He's so devoted to both of you. It's like he's been with you forever."

Brid looked down at the dog. "He is a good boy. We are all about the same age and have the same interests: a soft bed and a treat now and again. He could have landed in a worse place. Georgia believes he is doing fine." She pondered this. "Neil believes he is still grieving for his old friend. I am sure Neil is right, but Thatch is a stoic, and he doesn't complain. Neil does his best to make it up to him."

A tentative knock followed by Ronan's "Okay to come in, then, Brid?" brought the dog to his feet, his tail curled over his back and swaying happily. Ronan, whose job these days as maître d' at Craic covered almost everything involved with running the place, was one of Thatch's many new friends. Franny opened the door and peered out, making sure it was only Ronan and not someone who was not supposed to see the bride.

"Ah, you're a sight, you are, Brid. Your man's a lucky fella, for sure." Ronan stood in the door, clearly uncomfortable in this sanctuary for women.

"Full of the blarney, as usual. But thank you for that. How are things over at the bar? Are we set?"

"We are as ready as we can be. We have a sign on the doors saying we are closed to the public—not that the public is too pleased about it. We've had more than a couple of people peering in and banging on the door." He laughed. "I guess the ejits can't read. Or they aren't big on marriage. I left Mara cursing at the cake. Something about it tilting."

"No!" Franny put her hand to her mouth.

"I don't care about the bloody cake. Neil wants the cake. It can tilt all it likes as far as I am concerned."

"You have nothing to worry about there," Ronan said. "Mara will make it all come right. She's stubborn, that one." Watching his face, Brid wondered, *Is there something going on between those two I've missed? Ronan and Mara?* It was an intriguing thought.

Crouching, Ronan called the dog over to him. "Now then, Thatch, there's a good lad," he said as the dog attempted to lick his face. "Let's you and me be off and leave the ladies to their primping." He reached for the leash hanging on the doorknob, clipped it to the dog's collar and started out the door, the dog trotting happily next to him. "We'll be seeing you later—and don't be losing the ring," he cautioned over his shoulder.

"Oh God! The ring!" Franny's eyes searched the small room. "Where is the ring?"

"In my purse, over there in the corner," Brid said. "You need to take some deep breaths. We are not about to perform open-heart surgery."

Franny's face crumpled, and Brid silently cursed herself. *When will I learn to hold my tongue?*

She stood up and put her hands on Franny's shoulders. "I'm sorry. You know I have a nasty tongue when I am nervous. I should never have agreed to this farce. If you were not here, I might walk out the door."

"You can't mean you've changed your mind about marrying him?" Franny said, shocked at the thought.

"No, never that. I love him. More than I thought it was possible to love anyone. Sometimes it unnerves me." She sighed and then made a face at the mirror. She reached down to smooth a crease in the dress caused from sitting. There was a faraway look in her eyes. "I can't wait for this to be over. You will never know how grateful I am for all you have done. Without you, I know I would have lost my mind. It is a great comfort to me that at least I am not dressed like a fool, and that is thanks to you."

Franny blushed, embarrassed by the complement, rare as it was, coming from Brid. "Oh, it was fun. I couldn't have done it without Mara." Franny and Mara, between them, had pulled this wedding together, working around Brid's surly lack of enthusiasm.

Franny had found the dress Brid was wearing. Obeying the

command that it not be white, Franny had chosen a green so pale it appeared almost ivory in a certain light. The soft cowl neckline of the sleeveless, floor-length sheath draped gracefully just below Brid's shoulder blades. Stunning in its simplicity, the gown might have been designed for her, so perfectly did it fit. She wore Georgia's pearls, "borrowed" at Franny's insistence in order to meet that part of the traditional bridal rhyme. Handing them over, Georgia had affirmed that the necklace also covered "something old," as the pearls had once belonged to her mother.

"Are you remembering the first time you were married here?" Franny asked.

"Yes. I was thinking about my mother," Brid nodded. "She was certainly happy that morning, and she looked so beautiful. I remember she told me she picked the color of her dress—a lovely shade of blue—in honor of Our Lady. Mammy was not much older than I am now." To her annoyance, Brid felt her eyes fill with tears. She quickly brushed them aside.

"The wedding was here, right? In this church?"

"Yes, same aisle, same church. 'Here Comes the Bride' and all the rest. Thank God I drew the line at that sappy music this time."

"Did you wait down here with your mother?" Franny pressed.

Why the persistence, Brid couldn't imagine.

"Down here?"—she looked around—"Oh, no. This is all new. Or at least new since I was married here. Back then, I got dressed at home in my parents' apartment over the bar—Elaine loved that. I should have thought to add it to the wedding announcement in the *Ledger*. Her face looked like she was sucking lemons through the entire ceremony. I burned the pictures, or I would prove it to you. I went from the car to the altar, no stopping downstairs."

"Does it feel odd to be marrying Neil in the same church where you married Drew?"

"I imagine it might, if I was still the girl I was then, but as I am not, it doesn't. That wedding feels like it happened to someone else, and this one feels unnecessary. I would have been happy this time, as I said, going to City Hall."

The sound of the organist beginning to play drifted down from the main church above them.

"We are here," Brid went on, "because Neil very much wanted this: the church, the flowers, the music, the Mass with bloody Tom Carmello officiating. I have not been in this building since my mother's funeral, but this church has been central to Neil all his life: his baptism, his First Communion, his daily attendance at Mass. It is only natural that he wanted to be married here."

She reached for the single cream-colored rose she planned to carry. "I understand that. I love that part of him. Who am I to deny him? God knows he puts up with enough from me."

A determined knock made them both turn; Lilah peeked in the door. Rose was asleep in the carrier that dangled from Lilah's right hand, a sight so familiar to everyone by now.

"I just want to wish you good luck," she said. "Oh, wow, Brid, you look totally beautiful. Franny, her dress is awesome. I was afraid it would be, like, too bridey. No offense, but you like such girly things."

Lilah's own wedding ensemble consisted of a shiny, purple tunic worn over fuchsia-colored tights, which she'd coordinated to match the fuchsia polka-dot bows on her black ballet-flats. She studied Franny in her rose-colored dress, picked as the perfect foil to the one Brid wore.

"You look amazing, too," Lilah observed. "I hope "The Plumber" appreciates you when he sees you. I saw him upstairs. He cleans up well."

Franny's face turned red.

"Go!" Brid said. "And if that ejit priest goes on too long, pinch Rose Malone, will you?"

Both Franny and Lilah looked horrified.

"Don't say that! I just fed the little piglet, and I want to her to sleep. If she cries, she'll wreck everything. See you." Lilah waved goodbye.

"Brid ... " Franny's voice trailed off.

Brid waited, expecting some comment about Rose, but the far-off look on Franny's face confounded her. *Something is definitely going through her head*, Brid thought. *The Plumber, most likely.*

"What? Are *you* getting nervous now?" Brid asked.

"Do you feel him?" Franny looked around her.

"Who?"—she laughed—"Holy Mother of God. Drew?"

Franny nodded.

"I do not! And we can be thankful for that one small favor." Brid stopped laughing. "Please don't tell me you feel him hanging around."

"No, I don't, and I would have thought he would be here." Franny said woefully.

"You think too much about that bastard. Still! I told you to stop talking to him. He's dead. You do know that, right? Although, if it were possible for him to join us from whatever corner of Purgatory he's having a drink—and, mind you, I don't put it past him to try—he would not be down *here.*"

"But ... "

"He would be up there, with Neil, as he always intended to be. If anyone is feeling his presence, it will be Neil. He—"

The sound of voices, one in particular rising above the others, cut her off.

"Dear God, now it begins." Brid closed her eyes.

"Brid, where are you, darlin'? You're going to be late. " Desmond opened the door with a flourish.

Brid took in the sight of him in his top hat and tails. It was clear he had already been into the Irish, no doubt celebrating this wondrous day. Despite that, he looked distinguished, not at all like the old devil he was. It was the height—which he still had, despite the stoop—and the bones. The Sheerins had good bones.

"Look at you, Da. Doesn't he look grand, Franny?"

Before Franny could answer, Des spread his arms to encompass them both.

"Here they are, then, MacCullough's women. I bet he's smiling down on the both of you—one no more beautiful than the other. I only wish your mother was here to see this day." He reached for Brid's arm, "Come on, then, we are going to be late."

"She was here for the first one, and that made her happy. Stop fussing"—behind his back, Brid rolled her eyes at Franny—"they can't start without me. Not even Tom Carmello can pull that off."

Opening her purse, she removed the plain, gold wedding band Neil had selected and handed it to Franny. "Here. Put this on your finger, so you can find it when you need it."

Upstairs, in the sacristy, Neil asked Harry for the fourth time, "You have the ring? Right?"

Dutifully, Harry dug it out of his breast pocket. "Haven't lost it since you asked me five minutes ago. I've done this a few times before, you know." He asked Tom who, vested for Mass, was watching the clock on the wall. "I don't suppose you let people smoke in here?" Before either man could reply, Harry put up his hand. "I didn't think so." He sighed. "When I see Drew MacCullough again, the first thing I'm making him do is buy me a drink. He owes me one for doing this." He walked to the door, which provided an excellent view of most of the church.

Down the aisle, to the music of Pachelbel's Canon in D Major, Brendan was escorting Georgia to her place in the front row next to Lilah and Sofia.

"Looks like people are in their seats. It must be almost show time."

Neil dabbed his face with his handkerchief, wondering for the first time if he would make it through his own nuptials.

Tom looked at Neil, ready to speak.

"Don't say it. I mean it. Don't," Neil said.

As one man to another, Tom extended his hand and smiled, "Good luck, my old friend. It's time." Then, as Father Carmello, he raised his hand, made the sign of the cross over Neil's head and offered his blessing. Adjusting his vestments, the priest strode out to the altar, followed by the other two men.

At precisely six o'clock, the organist began the first notes of Bach's "Jesu, Joy of Man's Desiring" and Franny MacCullough stepped into the nave from the narthex of the church. As he caught sight of her, Neil also noticed Nick Benincasa seated in the second row, who was craning his neck in her direction. Nick seemed like a nice guy, although Neil had only talked briefly to him the night before, at the rehearsal dinner. He watched Nick's face as Franny came into the light; she looked beautiful. From Nick's expression, Neil realized that he thought so, too.

Maybe something will happen there, he thought. *Franny deserves a guy who looks at her like that.*

And then, he saw Brid walking proudly toward him, and nothing else mattered. If he believed in reincarnation—which he did not—he could almost imagine that she had once been a Celtic warrior-queen, so regal did she look proceeding down the aisle on her father's arm.

Franny approached the men at the altar. Smiling at Neil, she positioned herself on Tom's right.

A moment later, Des guided his daughter to Neil's side. Kissing her tenderly, he then faced Neil, and reached for his hand. "The luck of the Irish be with you both," he said in a voice thick with emotion. He stepped back and joined the three women in the first pew.

Brid slid her hand into Neil's, her face relaxing into the smile he loved.

"Hello there, Counselor. I believe we have met here on this spot before, haven't we?"

"We have, my love"—he squeezed her hand—"but this time, we are standing in the right places."

CHAPTER TWENTY-FIVE

"You look really good in that dress," Nick said, his eyes devouring Franny. "It makes me wish we were someplace I could take it off you."

"You look pretty hot yourself. I've never seen you in a suit before. I like it."

He did look hot. She stopped herself from touching him. It wasn't easy. Allowing sex back into her life had also left her craving to be touched and to touch in return. She studied the way his shoulders filled his dark suit jacket and thought of his embrace. When he held her, his body felt different from the way Drew's had felt—more solid. She found that fact strangely comforting. Everything was so new, yet, at the same time, so familiar.

"Thank you," Nick said, blushing at the complement. "It feels good to put on a tie. I should take you more places that require me to do it."

"Brid is the one who is the center of attention today. I think she looks beautiful, don't you?" Franny said, unwilling to be distracted further from the wedding festivities taking place around them.

Nick looked over to where Brid stood sipping a glass of ginger ale and chatting with Erica Mayhew and another woman from Neil's office.

"She's beautiful, I'll grant you that," he agreed. "But she doesn't do it for me. She's either fire or ice, and I'll bet that you never know which one you're going to get. I like my women a lot more rounded and a lot more predictable, like the one I'm with." He covered her hand, which was resting on the bar, with his own; Franny felt her heart beat faster.

"Is this a private party, or can we join you?" Sofia asked as she and Brendan slipped onto the bar stools on either side of them. "I think I need to get to know the new man in my sister's life a little better, don't you, Nick?"

"Nothing to hide here—I'm an open book. Just ask your date." He reached around Franny to shake Brendan's hand.

Sofia kept her thoughts on her sister's date to herself. "So, Brid finally pulled it off." She tipped her glass, some kind of "tini," toward Brid in mock salute.

"What do you mean by that?" Franny asked, always ready to come to Brid's defense, particularly against Sofia.

"She's been trying to snag him for years," Sofia smirked, taking another sip of her drink.

"That's so not true, and you know it. *Neil* has been in love with Brid for years. Drew told me so." She waited to see what Sofia would say to that. Usually, whenever Franny brought up Drew, Sofia seemed to feel the need to correct whatever she said. Surprised that, this time, Sofia said nothing, Franny added, "I think she fell in love with him after Drew died."

"Nah, I think she fell in love with him when he took her to the shooting range. Nothing like seeing a man with a gun to turn a woman on." Brendan said.

Franny appreciated what she felt was his attempt to lighten the conversation.

"Neil Malone owns a gun? That's a surprise," Nick said, raising his eyebrows. "He doesn't look like the type to me." He searched the room until he found Neil, laughing with the priest and the best man. "I would have pegged him for a gun-control liberal."

"Neil's father was a Lynton police officer; he taught Neil to shoot when he was a kid," Franny said. "He's been shooting all his life." She thought a moment, adding, "He probably is a liberal, though. I can't imagine him ever shooting anyone."

"Brid is the one who fell in love with shooting. Didn't Neil buy her a gun for Christmas? How romantic—just what *every* woman wants from her lover," Sofia said. She placed her empty glass on the bar, signaling the bartender she wanted another. "Always scary, the thought of Brid with a gun."

"Stop—you're just trying to frighten Nick," Franny protested. Looking at him, she added, "Neil did teach Brid to shoot. He told me she's getting to be an excellent shot."

"Well, *that* totally makes me feel safer." Sofia muttered under her breath as she smiled at the two men. "Can you guys entertain yourselves for a few minutes? I need to talk to Franny about something. Will you excuse us?"

She linked her arm with Franny's, pulling her sister none too gently off the bar stool, and walked her toward the door leading into the Snug. Once they were out of earshot, she backed Franny into a corner by the door.

"What's going on with Lilah?" Sofia demanded. "She's acting weird."

"What do you mean, 'weird'? How weird?"

"Have you seen the outfit she has on today? And the hair?" Sofia gestured toward the loveseat where Lila sat talking to Georgia.

"Oh, that. Lilah just likes to look edgy. A lot of young artist-types dress like that. I thought you were serious, and something was really wrong." Franny started to return to Nick and Brendan.

Sofia grabbed her arm tightly. "You know she's stopped nursing the baby? Do you think she's on drugs?"

"Drugs! Are you crazy? To start with, where would she get the money? She's living on next to nothing. I don't know what she would have done if Neil hadn't offered her his house rent-free."

Sofia cocked her head, considering this.

"Maybe, but something is definitely off with her. You're probably right, though. She's never really seemed like a druggie. Just weird." Sofia thought some more. "And very secretive."

"I keep telling you, she's an artist," Franny said. "I know some of them do drugs, but not all of them. Besides, as we both know, lots of people do drugs, not just creative types. Not everyone can be an attorney and dress like you. You're way over-reacting on this one."

It was impossible to dislodge an idea from Sofia's mind once it was stuck there, but, even knowing this, Franny continued to try.

"Lilah said she stopped nursing the baby because she's going to take a course or two this summer. She'll have to go into Boston, and she thought it would be easier for both the babysitter and for Rose. The first three months are crucial for the baby, and she's nursed her close to that. I suppose it makes sense. I know she feels badly about it. She told me so."

Sofia didn't argue, but continued to watch Lilah, who appeared to be deep in conversation with Georgia.

When Sofia didn't answer, Franny persisted in her effort at persuasion. "Lilah's a great mom; anyone can see that."

Sofia focused her attention once again on Franny. "Your plumber is smokin' hot. Brendan told me he wrestled at Lehigh." Sofia looked back to the bar, where Nick and Brendan were laughing about something. "He's definitely got the body for it. Not much like Drew, is he? I think he's really into you."

Franny felt her face start to burn. She hated discussing guys with Sofia, who talked about them so casually. The only person Franny knew who was more closed-mouth about sex was Brid. Ignoring the reference to Drew, Franny said, "I need to get back to Nick. He's a little out of his element. It's not fair to leave him stranded."

Sofia looked around. "I can't imagine why. I bet he's had his head in the toilets of half the people in the room. He seems to be holding his own. Besides, he and Brendan are buddies." Chewing on her lip, she glanced once more to where Lilah sat across the room and shrugged. "Oh well, you're probably right about Lilah. Let's go see if the bartender made the drink I ordered."

"But she likes kids, doesn't she? I mean, she doesn't hate them, or anything like that?" Lilah bit her lip, waiting, with a growing sense of dread, for Georgia's answer.

Pausing in the midst of playing "This Little Piggy Goes to Market" with Rose, who gurgled happily on her lap, Georgia seemed shocked by the question. "Hate kids? You're kidding me, aren't you?"

Lilah was serious. She had heard her boss on the subject of children more than once—barely controlling herself when the "brain-dead parents" let their "feckin' rugrats" run all over the gallery, threatening to wreck everything around them. And then, for further evidence, there was Brid's own life, from which Lilah had drawn her conclusion: Brid had never had any children of her own, even though she could have.

Hell, Lilah thought as she waited for Georgia's reply, *Brid's marriage to the dead guy had lasted long enough for her to have a couple of kids, if she'd wanted them. It's not a silly question.*

Georgia continued to tickle Rose's toes a moment before answering.

"Brid keeps her emotions pretty tightly shut down. She is very careful about who she lets herself love." Georgia glanced across the room to where Brid stood laughing in the circle of Neil's arm. "Which is why today is such a miracle. But, I've never had the feeling she hated children. I don't know if there have ever been any in her life. Until this one"—she looked down at Rose and adopted the higher-pitched voice women use to address infants—"and we know how she feels about *you.*" Smiling down at the baby, she leaned in closer to her.

Rose grabbed at the gold earrings she suddenly found swinging in front of her.

Lilah twisted around in order to see what Georgia had been looking at. "She does seem to be into Rose, doesn't she?" Lilah mused, studying Brid's face, radiant with happiness even at this distance. "And I think she's really in love with Neil."

Lilah looked down at Thatch, lying sprawled like a dark mop next to Georgia. Barely visible through the fringe of hair covering his face, the dog remained focused on the baby in Georgia's lap. The dog behaved as if it was his job to keep all threats away from Rose. "It's funny, I didn't think she liked dogs either, but she's really into Thatch, too."

Before Georgia could comment, Des walked to the center of the room and signaled for attention by tapping a knife against the side of a Waterford goblet in the "Colleen" pattern chosen in Brid's honor when they had renovated the restaurant. The buzz in the room gradually died down, as the guests faced the beaming father of the bride, his face flushed and his tie askew. Des loved a party.

"Now, this is a happy day, a very happy day. I only wish Brid's sainted mother had lived to see it. I want to welcome you all to

Craic. I'm told it's my job to introduce the best man who will offer a toast on this fine day to the bride and groom." Des waved Harry out into the room and, smiling at one another with mutual admiration, the two men shook hands.

Lilah liked Harry Winslow; she knew that he and Neil had been friends since they were little boys. For an old guy, Harry was not bad—if you went in for the not-quite-dirty-old-man type. She could see that he must have been pretty hot twenty-five years ago. His silvery-blonde hair and perfect smile still held up. He was always nice to her. And not in a sleazy, "Do you want some candy, little girl?" way, either. She'd been shocked when he had given her a card with a crisp one-hundred-dollar bill in it after Rose was born. She leaned forward, anxious to hear what Harry would say.

"Thanks, Des." Harry looked around the room, appearing to take a silent roll call. "I know that almost everyone here realizes that I inherited this particular job because the guy who should be standing here is no longer with us." He paused as if to gauge the impact of his words, which seemed to surprise no one, least of all the bride and groom. "No one in this room regrets that fact more than I do. I miss him." He took a deep breath. "I gave a lot of thought to the words that Drew might have offered tonight, and what came to my mind was 'It's about time.' And it is." He raised his glass to Brid and Neil. "Here's to a long and happy life."

The words "a long and happy life" echoed around the room as Neil crossed to where Harry stood and enveloped him in a hug. When the two men separated, Brid stepped in with her kiss, saying something in Harry's ear that made him chortle.

Intent on watching the scene in front of her, Lilah was distracted as Mara suddenly appeared next to Franny. Gesturing wildly, she whispered something in her ear. Together, they headed back toward the kitchen.

Leaving Rose asleep on Georgia's lap, she followed them. There, in the center of the room on a rolling table in front of the stove, stood the three-tiered wedding cake, covered in emerald-green marzipan shamrocks. Mara and Franny huddled next to it.

Lilah's first thought was: *Brid is going to hate that.* Her second was: *No way this cake is making it out of this room in one piece.*

From behind her came a shrill voice.

"Oh, my God, it looks like the Leaning Tower of Pisa!" Sofia, flanked in the doorway by Brendan and Nick, rendered her indictment. "I mean, really, Mara, it's going to fall over before they can cut it."

"Stop it, Sofia. You're not helping," Brendan snapped. 'I'm pretty sure they get that."

"I don't know what to do," Mara wailed, ringing her hands. "I've never had this happen before—and I've made a *lot* of wedding cakes. I used Neil's mother's recipe for the top tier, and I think it's just too heavy. It's almost like a pound cake. It upset the balance of the rest of the cake."

"It's okay, Mara. Brid told me she doesn't even want a cake," Franny said, walking around the cake and studying it from a different angle.

"But Neil does! And he wanted the top tier made from his mother's recipe." Mara said, biting her lip to keep from crying.

"Based on what I've heard Brid say about his mother, that could be the problem right there. Her ghost probably cursed it." Sofia said, happy to be the one to have delivered this pronouncement.

"Shhhh!" Franny said, turning quickly to check the door. "He might hear you."

"Well, you know it's true. You've heard Brid say it." Sofia held her ground.

Ignoring the squabble between the two women, Nick stared at the cake.

"You could take the top tier off and have Brid and Neil cut that for the ceremony," he suggested. "While they're doing that, we can cut the rest here in the kitchen and nobody will have a clue that it almost tipped over." He grinned at Mara. "I mean, from what we're hearing, Brid didn't want the full-blown wedding cake in the first place."

Relief began to lighten Mara's teary face. She hugged Nick. "You're a genius. Of course that will work. I should have thought of it myself."

Whirling around, she handed Nick a large cake plate and then pulled two long, flat knives from a drawer under the counter. Skillfully, she slipped the knives between the layers, lifting the top one to the plate that Nick held. Once it was safely transferred, he set the top tier carefully on the long, wooden prep station.

"But what about the way the bottom of it looks? You can't bring it out like that!" Sofia said, frowning at the ragged edge left by Mara's abrupt amputation.

"Fixing it now," Mara said, reaching for the pastry bag she had brought for the last-minute touchups that cakes always seemed to need. Deftly, she applied great swirls of white buttercream to the bottom edge of the cake and announced, "Good to go!"

"Okay, let's switch this with the one on the table. I'll plate that while Brid and Neil are cutting the smaller cake." Nick said, stepping in to help Mara lift the remains of the larger cake onto the prep station.

"Be careful that you don't get any frosting on your jacket," she said, eyeing him anxiously.

"Where did you learn how to schlep wedding cakes around like that?" Brendan asked, obviously impressed by this new side of Nick.

"I worked summer weekends in the country club dining room when I was in college. I helped set up, move, cut and plate more wedding cakes than I can count." He grinned, "Never dropped one."

Mara looked up from meticulously arranging the restored top tier of the wedding cake next to some plates, utensils and a beribboned knife. "You must have been damn good at it, Nick. Let me know if you ever want a job." Turning to Ronan, she let out an anxious breath. "Okay, I think it's ready; you can take it out." As he pushed the table toward the door, she added, "*Carefully.*"

"Do you need some help cutting and plating that? Be glad to," Nick asked.

"No, no. You guys get out there, and watch them cut the cake." Mara heaved a sigh of relief. "I really don't know how to thank you."

Before Nick could answer, Lilah waved them all to join her. "Come on, you guys are going to miss it."

"Here's the cake for our bride and groom to cut," Ronan called out as he wheeled it into the room. Seeing the look on Brid's face, he added, "We're plating the rest for you in the kitchen. You'll be having it shortly."

Moments later, with everyone gathered around them, Neil and Brid stood in the center of the dining room, facing the topmost tier of their wedding cake. Brid brandished the pearl-handled cake knife as though it were a sword and then cut a small, neat piece that she slid onto a plate. She held the plate in mid-air for a moment, an impish grin on her face as she approached her new husband.

"Watch her, she's going to smash that right into Neil's face, just wait," Sofia said out of the side of her mouth to Franny and Lilah.

"No. She won't," Lilah said. "Watch."

Delicately, Brid offered Neil a forkful of cake. Then he took the plate and fork from her hand and returned the favor. The room erupted in applause as the wait staff began to serve the promised wedding cake to the guests.

Des was persuaded to take a seat at the piano. The crowd enthusiastically sang the traditional Irish songs he was famous for playing, ending in a rousing rendition of "The Irish Rover" that brought them to their feet.

Once again, Harry had the microphone in his hand. "Okay, now it's time for my favorite part of the reception. Ready? The bride is going to throw her bouquet. All single ladies out on the floor."

When no one stepped forward, Brid walked over and took the microphone from Harry. "Franny, Sofia, Lilah, Georgia and Erica, get out here."

The ladies in question all looked at each other sheepishly, but began to gather in the center of the room.

Lilah realized that they all knew they had no choice—not unless they wanted to live with Brid's wrath. Brid had wanted no part of a toss-bouquet, which is why she had chosen to carry a single rose down the aisle. "Absolutely feckin' ridiculous!" she had told Franny when the subject had come up. Doing her part, Franny had argued on behalf of "all the single girls who would be disappointed." When Brid had demanded to know who these girls were, Franny had presented her with the names of the women Brid had just summoned. A couple other women Lilah did not know joined them.

Brid said something to Neil, and he swung her up onto the bar. Clutching the bouquet Franny had ordered solely for this purpose, she surveyed the group clustered in front of her.

"Where's Mara? She should be out here, too"—her eyes sought out Ronan, standing near the kitchen door—"Ronan, go get her." He returned with Mara, who protested even as he hustled her into the circle.

"All right, then," Brid said. "Anyone else? And the woman who catches these fine flowers will be the next one wed, am I right?" She looked at Harry for confirmation.

"So they say." Harry replied, a grin splitting his face.

She'll throw it right to Franny, Lilah thought.

Brid lifted her hand and, with unerring aim, tossed the flowers directly into Sofia's arms.

CHAPTER TWENTY-SIX

B rid studied the small oil painting of the port of Dún Laoghaire and thought longingly—not of Ireland, but of Paris. Four days in the City of Light for their honeymoon had not been long enough. She could have spent four days without ever leaving the Musée d'Orsay, surrounded by the sensory reactions of the Impressionists to life going on around them. She and Neil had promised each other they would go back for a longer stay—and very soon—but in her heart, she doubted they would.

"Life never works like that," she told Thatch, who was curled in his bed next to her desk.

Despite the best of intentions, it had taken her almost ten years to get back to Paris again.

Thatch raised his head and looked at her with his gleaming-black, button eyes.

"Well, it doesn't!" she insisted. The dog swished his swoopy black-and-white tail back and forth in agreement.

Much to Georgia's surprise, Thatch adored Brid. Georgia had been convinced that, having spent his first eight years with a man, the dog would attach to Neil, but it was Brid he shadowed, following her from room to room and sprawling next to her mat when she did yoga. Sometimes, much to her amusement, he did his own version of downward-facing dog.

Her cell phone began to ring. Still absorbed in Dún Laoghaire's details, Brid propped the painting on her desk and reached for the phone, not bothering to check the ID.

"Hello," she said, expecting to hear either Neil or Franny.

"Brid?" A woman's voice asked, tentatively.

"Yes. Who is this?" Brid leaned her hip against her desk as she concentrated on placing the voice.

"It's Andrea Grayson. Neil's neighbor." When Brid didn't respond, she added, "I take care of Rose."

"Of course. I am so sorry. I had forgotten your name." Brid waited, puzzled as to the reason for the call. Fear rose in the back of her mind that something might have happened to the baby.

"Um ... Are you going to be picking up Rose soon? It's after five o'clock."

"I? Picking up Rose?" Brid was at a loss.

"This morning Lilah said you would be picking her up today."

"She must have forgotten to tell me that." Brid shot a glance at the clock on the wall. *Damn, Lilah. Where are you?* she silently cursed. She had no time to be playing nursemaid. "I can be there in twenty minutes. Will that do?"

"That would be great."

Brid heard the relief in Andrea's voice.

"Rose has already been fed. I'll have her ready to go. See you then."

Steaming, Brid scanned her phone's favorites and stabbed at Lilah's name. The call went to voice mail. Pausing only long enough to send a brief text asking Lilah where she was, Brid rushed to close the gallery, taking care to remove the cash and set the alarms. The dog watched her, waiting for the command he knew would follow.

"Come, Thatch. It seems now I am being asked to be an au pair for my sales help." She bent down, pausing to gently push the thick, black bangs out of his eyes and cup his fuzzy nose in her hand before snapping on his leash. Going through the back door, Brid stopped, bewildered for a moment not to see her battered Jeep waiting for her. She scowled at Neil's wedding gift, a four-year-old, dark-green Volvo station wagon, the result of a hard-won compromise.

She shook her head remembering the week before the wedding, when she had found herself in the parking lot of the Mercedes dealership, arguing with Neil—in front of the salesman, no less—that there was nothing wrong with her Jeep.

"Nothing wrong?" Neil was incredulous. "There's nothing *right* with it! It's an eyesore, totally unreliable, and probably not even safe to drive. They only let it pass inspection because of your good looks. I am buying you a new car—today."

Neil was generally a frugal man, but as far as he was concerned, there was only one car worth driving, and it was a Mercedes.

"Let's take a look at the smaller SUV. I think you'll like it. I came down the other day and drove one. It handles like a dream."

Brid snorted. *Men and their car dreams,* she thought with disgust.

Before things could precede any further, she spotted a Volvo parked at the end of a line of cars that were obviously not new. "I want to look at that Volvo," she said and began marching toward it.

"Oh, but that's one of our previously-owned vehicles," the salesman called after her, striding hurriedly alongside Neil. The salesman, realizing he was losing a deal he had all but closed with Neil, breathlessly threw out his final pitch when the two men caught up with her. "I think your fiancé," he panted, "wants to buy you a new Mercedes."

But she persisted. She liked the look of the Volvo—somewhat boxy, and determined. She didn't need a flashy car. Although the men she married apparently did: before Neil's Mercedes, there had been the Corvette Drew was driving when she met him. Nevertheless, she decided, if she was going to have to get something, the Volvo was going to be it. Following a bit of negotiation, the deal was done.

She still found herself surprised to find the Volvo parked where her Jeep once stood.

"Here I am then, Thatch: with a dog, a station wagon and, now, a baby to pick up. I am a regular soccer mom." Thinking about this, she made a face as she opened the rear passenger door for the dog. He jumped in next to the baby seat Neil had installed. "Trust me, we'll need it," he had told her. *Right again*, she thought.

Brid found Andrea Grayson waiting at her door, a fretful Rose in her arms.

"I am sorry for the confusion," Brid said. "I called Lilah, but the call went to her voice mail. I also sent her a text."

A funny look passed over Andrea's face.

Brid reached for the baby, who smiled at her, grabbing for one of her hoop earrings. "Oh no you don't, you little thief." She unhooked the earrings and dropped them into her purse.

"Uhh … Brid? About the phone—Lilah doesn't have it with her." Andrea scrabbled around in Rose's diaper bag and came up with Lilah's cell phone. She handed it over without further comment.

The cell phone had been Neil's idea. He had insisted on it when they had learned Lilah was pregnant, going so far as to put Lilah on their wireless plan and buy her the phone. Lilah never wanted it.

"She also left you a letter."

This Andrea tentatively extended to Brid, as though she was afraid that Brid might bite her hand. Sighing, Brid ripped the envelope open. She quickly read the note, refolded the paper and shoved it into her jacket pocket.

"It appears your mother is off on a quest," she told the baby, "and you will be staying with Neil and me for a little while." She raised her voice slightly to catch Rose's attention. "We will have lots of fun while she is gone. Won't we, *a leanbh*?" The baby chortled at her seeming to understand the Irish term of endearment.

Turning to Andrea, Brid continued, "What time can we drop Rose Malone off in the morning?"

"Any time after seven-thirty is fine. Lilah usually feeds her first."

"One of us, most likely Neil, will bring her by in the morning."

Andrea hesitated and then asked, "Wouldn't it be easier for you to stay at Neil's house?" When Brid made no response, she added, "I mean, all of Rose's things are over there."

Brid looked across the street at the neat brick house with its black shutters and bright copper roof-flashing. A red geranium stood in a white wicker planter on the doorstep. Neil had done a nice job; it was a welcoming house.

"Did you know Neil's mother?" she asked Andrea.

"Oh, no. Mrs. Malone had passed away by the time we moved in." Andrea seemed baffled at the question.

"Well, I did." Brid continued to stare across the street, offering no additional clarification.

Rose began to fidget against Brid's hip.

"I have formula and extra diapers and some of her clothes at my flat," Brid said, addressing Andrea's original question. "We have a portable crib, too. It's still in the box but how hard can it be to set up? I think we will be fine. We can pick up whatever else she needs later." Becoming increasingly fussy, Rose continued to squirm in her arms. "Thank you. I am sorry I was late. It won't happen again. One of us will see you in the morning."

***

Neil and Harry met for dinner at Craic on Wednesdays. It was Brid who had suggested it. Neil knew, even though she had not said so, that it was her attempt to help the two men fill the hole left by Drew's death. Both men had come to look forward to it.

"So how was the honeymoon?" Harry asked, eyeing Neil across the table. "Need any little blue pills?"

"Somehow I managed to rise to the occasion on my own. But thanks for asking." Neil said, adding with a straight face, "What can I say? It was Paris." Inside his jacket pocket he felt his cell phone vibrate. Frowning, he pulled it out to read the text.

"Oh fuck it."

"What is it? What happened?" Harry asked, rising halfway out of his chair. Neil almost never used the f-bomb. "Who died?"

"Nobody died"—Neil read the text again—"yet. It's from Brid. Lilah has apparently taken off."

Harry sat down. "Wow. I bet you didn't see *that* coming." He sat in silence as Neil focused on his phone.

Quickly, Neil texted Brid a question and, within seconds, his phone buzzed again with her answer.

"I realize Lilah's got to be a little flaky, looking the way she does," Harry said, "but she seems to be devoted to that baby. I'm surprised she would uproot her from such a good situation. It was generous of you to let Lilah have your house rent-free."

"She didn't take Rose with her." Neil muttered, his mind elsewhere.

"What do you mean? Then, where *is* she?" Harry asked.

"Brid has her. Lilah told the sitter this morning that Brid would pick up Rose. When Brid didn't show up on time, the sitter called and asked when she was coming."

He pulled two twenties out of his wallet and put them on the table. "I've got to get home. No doubt, Brid has called Franny and Sofia, and they are all over there trying to figure out what to do next. Unfortunately, I have a piece of information they don't. God help me."

"Doesn't Lilah have any family? Wouldn't they be responsible for taking Rose in?"

"Lilah has been very closed-mouth about that. I do know both her parents are dead." He stood up.

"So, with no named guardian, the state steps in, right?" Harry had the sense that he was missing something.

"In most cases, yes. In this case, Rose *has* a named guardian." Neil pushed his chair in.

"That's good. Just contact them, and they can pick her up tomorrow. End of problem."

"Yes. Except that I'm Rose's guardian."

Harry's eyes widened. "Oh, shit. Brid doesn't know, does she?"

Neil shook his head. "Can you settle up? I'll call you."

"Sure," Harry said, gathering up the money from the table. "Hey," Harry called after him, "you can bunk with me when she kicks you out."

Neil was already halfway across the restaurant. Turning around, he said, "Two men and a baby? Sounds charming, but you forget I still have a house. Your night's sleep is safe."

***

Neil opened the door to the flat to find Brid sitting on the floor, sketching a sleeping Rose, who was cradled nearby in Franny's arms. Sofia sat in the wing chair texting on her phone. *The calm before the storm,* Neil thought.

"Hello, ladies," he said. "I thought I might find you here."

He bent down behind Brid and studied her drawing, his fingers squeezing the knotted muscles in her shoulders. *Not a good sign,* he thought, wryly perceiving the irony: the very large elephant in the room was in fact, a tiny infant. "She has long eyelashes for such a little girl, doesn't she?"

"She does, at that—poor, abandoned little mite," Brid said, looking up at him, her face unreadable.

"Oh, I don't think Lilah abandoned her. She says she'll be back." Franny rushed to Lilah's defense, her face a reflection of her anguish at the thought.

"Let me see the note she left for you," Neil said.

"On the sideboard, next to my phone," Brid said, her pencil busy once again.

He picked up the note, reading rapidly.

Dear Brid,

Please don't be mad. I was wrong not to tell Rose's father about her and now I have to fix it. So I am going on a quest. I promise not to be gone long. I totally mean it. I know you and Neil will take good care of her. I will be back as soon as I can.

I'm sure she'll be good.

Lilah

"What the hell—a quest?" Neil said.

"All it means is that she is off searching for Rose Malone's father. 'Questing' is what the characters do in those fantasy novels she reads"—Brid paused in her drawing—"usually after they have made a total mess of everything, as is the case here."

"You *do* realize Lilah totally planned this? I told you she has been acting weird." Sofia said in a condescending tone. "But I had no clue she had it in her to do something like this."

The others looked at her with mixed expressions on their faces.

"You make her sound so cold-blooded. This is her *baby* we're talking about," Franny protested, pulling Rose closer.

"Precisely." Brid closed her sketchbook and rose from the floor. "Surely, you must have realized by now that, beneath all the primary-colored hair and garish tattoos, Lilah is as smart as they come. She misses nothing."

She reached for the sleeping baby who, whimpering in protest at being taken from the warmth of Franny's arms, promptly settled against Brid's shoulder. "As for this one, Lilah made sure that Rose Malone would be safe, before taking off on her 'quest.'"

Sofia stood up and pocketed her phone. "If there's no named guardian, Child and Family Services will step in tomorrow and find a foster home."

For a moment neither of the other women could say a word and then, in a rush, they spoke simultaneously, Franny's voice rising above Brid's.

"Foster care! I hope you're kidding. Rose is *not* going to—"

"You really are a cold-blooded bitch, aren't you?" Brid said, her contempt clear.

Sofia flushed. "Don't blame me. It's what happens when there is no named guardian. It's the law. Why does that make me a monster?" She snapped at Brid, "As for being a bitch, take a look in the mirror, why don't you?"

The two glared at each other.

"I think it's time you ladies went home," Neil said. "Getting into a catfight is not going to improve things. And besides, Rose has a named guardian." He braced himself for what he knew would follow.

"She does? Who is it?" Franny asked. "I mean, Lilah never said there was anyone—"

"Problem solved then," Sofia said, slinging her purse over her shoulder. "Come on, Franny. I'll buy you a salad on the way home."

"But, who is it?" Franny persisted.

"I am not really free to say who it is, yet. Rose will be taken care of. There's no need to involve Child and Family Services." Aware that Brid, holding the baby, was keeping her thoughts to herself, Neil forced himself to smile. "Don't worry about Rose, she—"

"—Is, at this moment, going to bed," Brid said, giving notice that she, too, was done with the discussion. "Thank you both for coming over and setting up the crib. I never would have figured it out, and she would have had to sleep in a drawer "—she adjusted Rose's weight on her shoulder—"and also, Franny, for getting the little terror to sleep." Brid headed down the hall with a final "Say goodnight, Rose Malone," tossed back over her shoulder. Thatch followed closely behind her.

Neil opened the door for Franny and Sofia, even though Franny's reluctance to leave was evident.

"I hope she's not going far away," Franny said, in an effort to ferret out more information. "I would miss her so much. They will let us see her, won't they?"

"Don't worry about it," Neil told her for the second time. "Everything's going to be fine." He was desperate to close the door behind both of them. Hand on the doorknob; he pointedly waited for them to leave.

"I hope Rose lets you get some sleep. I'll see you tomorrow," Sofia said, walking past him.

Franny followed, stopping long enough to give Neil a quick hug. "Tell Brid to call me if she needs *anything.*"

Thanking her, he shut the door behind them and sighed. The most difficult part of the evening was yet to come.

Neil was slumped on the sofa, his face in his hands, when Brid returned from putting the baby to bed.

"I bet you regret your silly rule about not keeping a bottle about the place, now," she said, sitting next to him.

He looked at her. A jolt of desire seized him, despite—maybe even *because* of —the mess he was in. He leaned forward, elbows on his knees, to quash it.

"If I've told you once, I've told you ten times: I don't need a drink to solve my problems. I am your *second* husband, not your first."

"Thank God for that. A big help he would be," Brid said. The ghost of a smile played around the corners of her mouth.

"Where's your friend?" Neil asked, realizing suddenly that Thatch had not returned with her.

"That fickle hound? He is only my 'friend' when Rose Malone is not about. Otherwise, he is only concerned with her."

"Funny, isn't it?" Neil said. "Living at a boys' school with a crusty, old bachelor—I bet she's the first infant he's ever seen."

"Who knows? She owns him now, soul-to-tail, make no mistake." She looked at him thoughtfully, and said, "Who is this guardian, and when will he or she be coming for Rose Malone? I told Andrea one of us would drop her off in the morning."

Neil looked at her but he said nothing. They sat together in silence for several minutes before Brid's hand reached for his.

"Do you know why I fell in love with you?" she asked.

"Actually, no. I have never understood it. But I do know not to question a gift from God." He realized that they were both, suddenly, very serious.

"Because you are the best—I mean, the very best—man I have ever known." She paused. "I had stopped believing there was such a thing as a good man, and then I realized you had been right there in front of my eyes almost all of my life."

"Well, I have certainly fooled you, haven't I?"

"So, when were you going to tell me that we are Rose Malone's guardians?"

Neil opened his mouth to speak and then he stopped, as he groped for the right words to answer her, "Not 'we,' Brid. Me. *I* am her guardian. I may be manipulative, but I would never do that to you. Legally, I couldn't, without your consent." He was shocked to think she believed such a thing was legally possible. "It was before we were married. Lilah came to my office and asked me if I would be the baby's guardian. She said it was only a precaution. And she was right; there always should be a named guardian." He leaned back and shut his eyes for a moment. "I never thought she would take off and leave the baby. Never. Even Harry was surprised."

"Hmmm. As much as I am loath to agree with Sofia, in this case, she is right. Lilah planned this very carefully, starting with her decision to wean the baby when she did. It never made sense to me, because I knew she loved nursing her. Now, it does."

Neil reached over and pulled her into his arms, resting his chin on the top of her head. "I'm sorry, my love. I seem to have landed you here in this mess of domesticity right beside me. I know you especially never wanted dogs and babies in mix."

Brid moved away from him and looked into his face. "Ah, well, it makes a change from Da and the bar. You can't blame yourself for the dog. That was Georgia." She stood up and placed her hands on her hips. "It's not like we have a choice; we couldn't let strangers take her. Besides, it won't be forever. Lilah would never abandon Rose Malone. And she knew the baby would be safe with us." She stopped talking, thinking over the situation. "I hope she gets back here before the child needs to be house-broken."

The tension Neil had been holding broke, and he roared with laughter. "I am pretty sure it's referred to as being 'potty-trained' when you are talking about children."

Brid waved her hand. "Ah well, it is all the same, isn't it?" She reached for his hand and pulled him to his feet. "Come on, you old guardian, let's see if you can perform your husbandly duties quietly and not wake the baby. Maybe then I might consider forgiving you."

KATHLEEN FERRARI

CHAPTER TWENTY-SEVEN

Frowning at her laptop, Franny hunted for an Alice in Wonderland doll, knowing that, if Lilah had been doing the search, she already would have found it. The woman who wanted the Alice doll was a serious doll collector and a good customer, and Franny didn't want to lose her business. Pushing down the rising anger she was feeling toward her missing doll-detective, Franny continued her online search.

"Hey, Franny. Here are tomorrow's cookies." Mara popped in the door left propped open to admit the rare August breeze. Handing over the box, she said, "You don't look happy. What's up?"

"I could strangle Lilah." As soon as the words left her mouth, she was sorry. *Poor Lilah,* Franny thought. *She probably felt like she had no other choice.*

"At least she didn't dump her baby on you, like she did to Neil and Brid," Mara said, her tone indicating what she thought of that.

"Neil is Rose's guardian. I offered to take her; I have plenty of room. But Neil said she needed to be under his care."

Franny realized Neil was choosing his words carefully. It had happened before with him. He never told an outright lie, but he was not above selecting words that hid the truth. She wasn't stupid. She knew he and Brid worried that she would become too attached to the baby.

"I can't see Brid doing the Mommy-thing at all. She's not someone I would ever think of as being into babies. Ronan told me the staff gets really nervous when she shows up at the restaurant. I know you love her, but Brid can be kind of bitchy—know what I mean?"

Franny did know, but she never criticized Brid. She shrugged her shoulders instead of agreeing.

Mara continued, "She must have pitched a fit."

"Surprisingly," Franny admitted, "she didn't. How did you find out, anyway?"

"Brid stopped by the restaurant the other day and had Rose with her. Des brought the baby into the kitchen when I was dropping off my raspberry pies. He was so sweet with her. You can tell he would love to be a grandfather. Rose is a little dumpling."

Franny nodded as she opened the box of cookies. "Oatmeal?" She took a small bite, swallowed and said, "Wow! What makes them so different?"

"I add coconut and sprinkle them with salt just before I bake them. I know the salt sounds weird, but it works. Let me know what your customers say." Mara helped herself to one. "Tell me—how are Brid and Neil coping with the baby?"

"They seem to be enjoying her. She's fun to watch. Neil usually drops her at the sitter on his way to work, and Brid picks her up at night. Rose is a good baby, and it's easy for them now because she's not walking yet."

"No kidding. Once they walk, you need eyes in the back of your head to keep track of them. Ava climbed out of her crib, out her bedroom window and onto the porch roof. She wasn't even two! I almost had a heart attack. I still get goosebumps thinking about it." Mara grimaced at the memory. "I have to run; I have a bunch of desserts to bake tonight for a luncheon at the country club tomorrow. See you later."

"Thanks, Mara."

Mara was always in a hurry, and today was no exception. Franny knew it wasn't easy to be on your own and, she imagined, being a single mom made it worse. Mara worked hard, and her catering business seemed to be thriving. Franny was glad for her.

She returned to her search for the elusive Alice. "Dammit, Lilah, why didn't you leave me your contact list before you took off," she muttered aloud. She continued to plug the keywords into her search engine. There were lots of Alices, but most were new. None was the one she wanted.

"Hey, do you have a minute?"

Franny had been so engrossed in her search that she was startled when she looked up to find Brendan standing in the open door.

"What a nice surprise," she said. "I don't think you've been in here since the night before I opened—the night Lilah fainted." She spread her arms. "What do you think?"

"Everything looks great. I knew you would be a success," he said.

"I'm glad you believe that. There are days I'm not so sure," Franny said. "I love it, though. There's nothing else I would rather be doing."

"Funny you say that. I feel the same way." His face darkened into a scowl. "That's one of the reasons I stopped by. Do you have a few minutes to talk?"

Franny looked around the empty shop. "As you see, I'm swamped with customers. But for you, I'll make the time," she smiled. "Can I get you a cup of tea or maybe some coffee?"

"You looked like you were really into what you were doing when I came in. Are you sure I'm not interrupting something important?" Brendan asked.

"You'd be doing me a favor. I'm trying to find a doll, and I am not having any luck. A distraction right now would be a blessing." She logged out of her laptop and came out from behind the display case.

"Another Baby Jullee?" Brendan asked.

"Alice in Wonderland. The maddening thing is that this doll is no Baby Jullee. Alices are out there—lots of them. I have to keep sifting through them. Lilah would have found the right one by now. Come and sit down," Franny said, indicating the table and chairs under the window. "Can I get you something?" she offered again.

He eyed the open **Live to Eat Catering** box as he sat down. "Nothing to drink, but I wouldn't say no to a cookie."

Franny brought the box to the table and sat opposite him. "Help yourself."

"Have you talked to Sofia today?" he asked.

"Not today; we texted last night. She was on her way to meet you. She said you were going out to dinner."

Brendan chewed the cookie for a while, lost in thought. The look on his face made Franny nervous.

"Why?" she asked. "Is something wrong?"

"You might say that—although I'm not sure Sofia would agree," he said. "We broke up."

"You mean you had a fight," Franny guessed. She had heard this before. "You'll patch it up. You always do."

"Not this time." He pressed his lips together and swallowed hard. "That's why I stopped by; I hope you and I can still be friends."

"Still be friends?" she echoed, going pale. "Don't be silly. I hope we'll always be friends. You're one of us." She clenched her hands, bringing them together in two fists under her chin, leaning on them. "I could kill that girl. How can she be so smart and so stupid at the same time?"

Brendan laughed. "I never thought I would say this, but you sound like Brid."

Brid. Oh, shit, Franny thought. "Brid will pitch a fit when she hears about this," she said, remembering Mara's earlier comment.

Shifting in his chair, Brendan said, "Sofia couldn't care less what Brid thinks. Anyway, you're not being fair to Sofia. Your sister's definitely not stupid. If she's anything, she's a little too smart." He sighed. "But she knows what she wants, and it's not me."

"That's not true. She *doesn't* know what she wants," Franny argued.

"You're wrong. She does. We spent most of last night discussing what Sofia wants. She wants someone who is going to bring his 'A' game."

Franny heard the bitterness in his voice.

Slowly, Brendan got to his feet. "I'm a municipal firefighter. I'm going to be thirty-five. I want a wife and a couple of kids"—he took a long breath—"but those things fall under the category of 'B minus,' according to Sofia. She said something about my living a 'pedestrian, blue-collar life.' Trust me"—he gripped the back of his chair—"we're done. Our conversation didn't end well. She definitely un-friended me—big time."

Franny stood up and pulled him into a hug. "I'm so sorry."

"Don't be. I'm okay." Brendan returned her hug and then let her go. "It's for the best. I'm glad I never showed her the ring I had in my pocket. I'm sure she would have thought it was pedestrian, too."

"Really? You were going to propose? You actually had the ring with you last night?" Franny asked, her eyes beginning to fill with tears.

"Sure, did. Don't cry though. I'll live and so will she." He pulled her into a brotherly hug and then let her go.

"I feel awful," Franny said, attempting to smile at him.

"Don't worry. I'll be around. Now, I've got to go get some sleep before my next shift"—he shrugged ruefully—"I didn't get much last night." Brendan started to leave and then he stopped. "Franny, promise me something, okay?"

She nodded, not sure she could find her voice to answer him.

"If you ever need anything—anything at all—you'll call me? And don't be mad at Sofia. Your opinion really matters to her, even though she doesn't let it show."

Franny watched him walk down the street until he disappeared around a corner. She felt like running after him, wailing the way a child would, but instead she reached for another cookie for comfort. She pulled her phone from her purse, but found no text from Sofia.

Lost in her dark thoughts, she wandered around the shop moving the dolls around and fluffing their dresses.

"You don't look very happy for someone who's had her dreams come true." Cookie Kennedy stood in the doorway. "What's wrong, Franny? Can I help fix it?"

"Are you real, or have I conjured you up out of sheer desperation?" Franny asked.

She burst into tears and threw herself into Cookie's arms. They clung together—Franny crying, Cookie patting her shoulder. Spent at last and more than a little embarrassed, Franny stepped away.

"Let me blow my nose," she said. "I'll be right back."

She returned from the bathroom to find her former roommate admiring the Ginny dolls in the display case.

"Let's sit down and catch up. I promise I won't cry," Franny said.

"I love this shop," Cookie said as they sat down at the table in front of the window. "You've done an incredible job with it." She took a long, speculative look at Franny. "So, what's wrong? Guy problems? Is Nick not behaving?"

Franny realized with a start she hadn't thought of Nick—not once—since Brendan told her about breaking up with Sofia. *Is that a bad thing?* she asked herself. Shaking her head, she said, "It's not Nick. That's all good. At least, I think it is. What are you doing here?"

"I flew in yesterday. I couldn't wait to see you"—she looked around—"and your shop. Maggie told me all about it. She said you found some lost doll for Julie."

"I really found the doll for Nick's son, James. He kept coming by, looking for it in the window."

"And that's how you met Nick?"

Franny scowled as she remembered their first meeting.

"I wouldn't describe it as a meeting made in heaven, but, yes, that's how we met, because James asked me to find the doll." Looking at Cookie, something occurred to Franny for the first time. "So, if Maggie and Julie have been best friends forever, you must know Julie's daughter, Jenn. Am I right?"

"Yep. I've known her since we were kids." Cookie bit her lip, a sure sign she was uncomfortable.

"And? You're not going to tell me more?" Franny waited with a growing sense of dread. *Please don't say you like her,* she thought.

"I love Julie. She's a super person. She and Maggie grew up together. When Maggie and my dad were first married, Maggie and Julie tried to get Jenn and me together, in the hopes we would become friends." She shrugged. "It would have been really nice for them, you know? The four of us could have done things together."

"But it didn't work out?" Franny asked anxiously.

"Ha! You might say that." Cookie made a sour face.

"You didn't like her?" Franny persisted.

"No, I didn't like her. Not that it mattered, because—trust me on this—*Jenny* Canon, as she was called then, sure didn't like me."

"Everyone likes you," Franny protested.

"Not Jenny. She was a mean girl even then. From what Maggie says, she still is."

"I guess she must be. Nick says she's a bitch," Franny said. "He's pretty bitter about her."

"He probably has every right to be. Maggie said even Julie is disgusted with the way Jenn walked out on those two little kids. I gather she treated Nick like a piece of crap."

Franny looked closely at Cookie for the first time since she had come in. "How do you do it? You never change. You look exactly the same as you did the first time I saw you in our room in Caz," she said, referring to the room they had shared in Cazenove Hall their freshman year at Wellesley.

"Even if that were true—which it isn't, by the way—how can that possibly be a good thing? If you remember, I was fat, dumpy and completely clueless." She helped herself to a cookie. "Annie says I have absolutely no sense of style," she said, looking down at her faded T-shirt and wrinkled khakis.

Your sister's right, Franny thought. Cookie—with her thick hair, creamy skin and perfect smile—could be so pretty if she would only try. But she didn't care about her looks. She had no interest in clothes and often pulled her lustrous, auburn hair haphazardly through the opening in her Red Sox cap. Her glasses were smudged from frequently being pushed back in place when they slid down her nose.

"Wow. These are wonderful," Cookie said. "What makes them taste so different?"

"They are good, aren't they? I asked the girl who bakes them. She adds coconut and salts them before she bakes them."

"See if you can get her to give you the recipe. I would love to try making them," Cookie said as she lightly touched the salt on the one in her hand.

"Since when do you listen to Miss Newbury Street?" Franny waited for the answer, her chin resting on her hands.

Cookie considered the question. "I don't really *listen* to Annie," she hedged, "not about style, anyway. I just let her think I do." She grinned. "It makes her happy."

Franny knew that Cookie was all about making her younger half-sister happy.

"What's she doing now, anyway?" Franny asked.

"She's a junior associate at my dad's law firm. As you can imagine, he's in his glory. At least one daughter's not wasting her *very expensive* education by being a 'do-gooder.' "

"Is it true that you're going to stay put and start doing good here?" Franny asked hopefully.

"I'm not sure about 'doing good,' but I have accepted a job as a social worker working in Manchester. I start in two weeks. And—wait—you still haven't told me why you were crying. If it's not Nick, then it must be Sofia. Am I right?"

Franny sighed and said, "She broke up with Brendan. I could kill her."

"Wow—they've been together for a while, haven't they? What happened?" Cookie said.

"I've only heard Brendan's side, but basically it sounds like she has no interest in marrying a firefighter and having babies."

"Really? No way," Cookie said, arching her eyebrows to show she was kidding. "And that surprises you?"

"No, but it makes me sad."

"Nobody died—" Cookie stopped, a horrified look settling on her face. "Oh, I don't believe I said that to you! I'm so sorry." Now, Cookie looked as though she might cry.

"Don't be silly. I know what you meant," Franny said. "And you're right. In this case, nobody has died. It's just—I like Brendan so much." She made a face. "And I want Sofia to find a nice guy."

"What makes you think she even *wants* a nice guy?" Cookie's hand found its way back into the box on the table. "I don't think she does. Where's the challenge for her in that?"

"You're right. The next thing I know, Sofia will be texting me about some new hottie who's panting to take her out."

Knowing that she and Cookie were capable of finishing off all the treats really meant for tomorrow's customers, Franny firmly put the top on the box and said, "What are you doing tonight? Can you come home with me now and spend the night?"

"I thought you'd never ask!" Cookie replied. "Let's pick up Chinese. I want to look at apartments online, and you can help me decide which places are worth going to see."

"Deal," Franny said. "I close in fifteen minutes!"

CHAPTER TWENTY-EIGHT

Neil was awake when the call came in, shortly before five a.m. He had stopped going to Mass since Rose had come to stay, but the habit of waking early remained. He felt it wasn't fair to leave Brid with the burden of getting both herself and the baby ready for the day without his help. He felt sure God would understand. Daily attendance at Mass had been a small sacrifice he had made since law school, but the larger sacrifice lay sleeping in the dressing room ten feet away. He would be the first to admit it was exhausting. God clearly designed humans to give birth when they were *young*, despite what science made possible today, still, he found himself enjoying having the baby with them.

He watched Brid—sprawled next to him deep in the sleep of complete exhaustion—and wondered if she would agree. Brid would be forty-seven in January. The only signs he could see were a few barely discernible wrinkles around her expressive mouth and a dusting of gray sprinkled in her dark hair. He marveled that she didn't seem burdened in the least by the gradual, insidious, thickening of middle age. And that was not due to yoga, she claimed: her daily practice—done these days with Rose in her swing at one end of the mat and Thatch sprawled at the other—was only to keep her sane. It was probably true; he knew she didn't need yoga to stay thin. No, Brid burned her calories using a metabolism fueled by nervous energy. He thought of the jogging stroller she had bought a couple weeks earlier, so that she could take Rose along while she ran. How smooth the baby's assimilation into their lives had been.

Lilah had been gone three months. Three months without a word. She could be anywhere.

"She could be dead," Brid had said flatly the previous morning as she was spooning peaches into an uncooperative Rose, who was blowing them back at her as fast as she was shoveling them in. He had been surprised—shocked, really. He had expected Lilah back in two weeks, with or without her "baby–daddy," a term he loathed. Even though she hadn't said so, he knew Brid had expected that, too. A couple times he had considered hiring a private investigator to try to find the girl, although he had not broached the subject with Brid. He was deliberating it yet again, when the cell phone on the nightstand started to vibrate.

His first thought—*Lilah!*—vanished as he snatched up the phone and saw that the caller was Brendan. Casting an anxious glance at his sleeping wife, Neil swung his legs over the side of the bed, stood up and hurried down the hall to the living room.

"What's wrong?" he whispered, trying not to wake either Brid or Rose.

"Listen carefully, Neil. I've got two minutes. Craic is on fire." Brendan's voice was all business. In the background, Neil could hear other voices urgently calling out orders. "A passing patrol car spotted the flames. The fire may have been burning for a while. I don't know. I have to go now."

Neil's heart began to race. "Des and Ronan might still be in there," he said, no longer whispering. Neil pushed the image of the old man, usually well under the influence of Bushmills by closing time, from his mind. "Are they both out?"

"I don't know. If they're not, we'll get them out. I have to go. We're rolling." Brendan disconnected the call.

Neil stood holding the phone, momentarily paralyzed as his mind processed the full impact of this news. *Focus, Malone*, he told himself as he scanned his contacts. Finding the one he wanted, he pressed it and prayed someone would answer.

"Hello," a man answered after several rings, his voice thick with sleep.

"John, it's Neil Malone. I'm sorry to wake you at this ungodly hour. We have an emergency. Craic is on fire, and we need your help."

"Just tell me what you need," John Grayson replied, awake now. Neil could hear him brief Andrea.

"Can you meet us in ten minutes in the parking lot of St. Peter's? We need you to take Rose for us."

"Of course." He paused. "Andrea says to bring the dog, too."

"Thanks, John."

Thatch, standing in the door of the living room, barked twice—two short, imperious yips—almost as if he understood the need to move quickly. In the dressing room, Rose began to wail.

"Mother of God and the Angels! I will throttle the wretched beast!" Brid groaned from the bed. "I have been up twice already tonight with that child."

"That's enough, Thatch," Neil said, not answering Brid as he stepped quickly through the bedroom, into the dressing room and to the side of the wooden crib, which had replaced the portable one. Rose had stopped crying. She lay staring, wide-eyed, at the mobile of glittery, flying dragons—a gift from Sofia—hanging over her head. Catching sight of Neil, she smiled, displaying her two new teeth.

"Good morning, Noisy Girl." Neil couldn't help meeting her smile with one of his own, despite the urgency he felt. Scooping her up, he carried her to the changing table, stripped her sleeper off and efficiently changed her diaper, nimbly avoiding her wildly-kicking feet.

"And to think that you had never touched a diaper four months ago," Brid said from behind him. "You really have become quite the expert."

Neil turned, automatically swinging the baby to his shoulder. One look at his face and she knew.

"What? Who is it? Lilah? Is she dead? Is—" She stopped. "Is it Da?"

"That was Brendan on the phone. The bar's on fire," Neil said flatly. His well-known ability to compassionately deliver bad news had deserted him. He watched his wife's face blanch as she reached behind her and grabbed the doorframe to steady herself.

"Da and Ronan? Where—?"

"Brendan knows they might still be inside. He said they *will* get them out if they are." He started to hand her the baby. "Hold her while I get dressed."

"No—I'm going now!" She pulled off her oversized T-shirt and tossed it on the floor. "You'll have to deal with her and come after." She began scrambling around for her clothes.

Gently laying the baby back in her crib, Neil followed Brid who, not yet fully dressed, was cursing as she tried to find her car keys.

Neil's hands clamped firmly on her shoulders; he swung her around to face him. "Take a deep breath and listen to me."

Still somewhat in shock and too surprised to protest, she did as she was told.

"We are all leaving together as soon as I pull my pants on. John Grayson is going to meet us at St. Peter's. We will give him the baby and the dog and continue on to Craic." He moved his hands from her shoulders and framed her face. "There is no way I'm letting you go alone—understood?"

Brid took another deep breath and nodded. "I'll get her things while you dress," she said in a shaky voice.

"Right." He headed for his closet.

In the kitchen, Brid took from the refrigerator two bottles of formula she had prepared the night before and put them into Rose's bag, already packed for the day. "Are you ready?" she called to Neil in a voice sharpened by her fear.

"Let's go," he said, appearing in the kitchen with Rose in his arms. Picking up the diaper bag, Brid called the dog over to her, snapping the leash to his collar.

The dog, happy not to be left behind, wagged his tail all the way to the car.

Neil made the trip to St. Peter's in less than ten minutes, driving as fast as he dared. On the way, Brid spoke only once, asking in an anguished voice, "What if they are still in there?"

"Brendan said they would get them out. Try not to think about it. We'll be there soon." In the distance, the lit bell tower of St Peter's beckoned them.

John Grayson's hand was on the rear door of the car as soon as Neil cut off the engine. He reached in, unbuckled Rose and lifted her into his arms. "You, too, Thatch," he said. The dog jumped out and waited. Taking the diaper bag Brid handed him, John said, "Don't worry about these guys. Good luck."

Neil nodded and began to speak, but John was already buckling the baby into her car seat, Thatch waiting patiently beside him. Neil pulled out of the lot and headed downtown.

Straining for her first sight of the bar, Brid murmured, "My mother always had a fear of fire. The building is over a hundred years old and mostly made of wood. When we did the renovations, I asked the contractor how we could make it safer and he said 'sound wiring,' but he said, because the building was so old, if a fire ever started, it would go up like a bonfire." She shivered and rambled on. "When I was a child, Mammy would make me do fire drills: out of bed, to the back door, down the stairs to the street. She would time me to see how fast I could do it."

Three blocks from the intersection of Dock and Main, two police cars, nose to nose, closed off the road. Beyond the barrier Neil and Brid could see fire equipment parked haphazardly up and down the street. Even from this distance they could smell the smoke. A camera crew from the local news station was filming the scene, held back behind a makeshift barricade.

"Sorry folks, you're going to have to turn around. We've got a pretty big fire up ahead. It's important for your own safety that you stay out of the way of the firefighters." A young police officer waved them back.

Another Lynton policeman jogged across the street toward them. "Hang on, Ryan," he called. Coming to the driver's side of the Mercedes, he leaned into Neil's lowered window. "Hi, Mr. Malone. Pull in over there, right behind that SUV. I'll take you through. Chief Hudson told me to keep an eye out for you."

Neil nodded and parked the car.

In an undertone to his fellow officer, the policeman explained, "Her father owns the bar." He walked to the Mercedes as Neil and Brid got out.

"Thanks, Jared. This is my wife, Brid Sheerin," Neil said. "Brid, Officer Jared LaPlante."

"Sorry to meet you under these circumstances, ma'am. I know it must be a tough day for you."

"How bad is it?" Brid asked as they wove their way through helmeted firefighters and large trucks.

LaPlante hesitated, looking first at Neil.

"It was a pretty bad one, burning like crazy when the men got here, but I think they have it under control now. The fire chief called in a second alarm—he was worried because of all the old, wooden buildings in this block and the condos in the old mill across the street. The crew's been soaking things for a while. The fire doesn't seem to have spread."

Coming around a large ladder truck, they got their first view of Ceol agus Craic. Brid stopped dead in the middle of the street. Neil wrapped his arm around her waist, ready to hold her up if she started to fall.

"Mother of God," she said, recoiling from the sight of the destruction.

The two long windows facing Main and Dock streets had been smashed, leaving jagged hunks of glass clinging to the frames. The beautiful oak front doors had been hacked open. The outside wall of the second floor apartment facing Dock Street was burned away, the firefighters clearly visible in the dawn light still working inside. There were no signs of an active fire.

Neil became aware of a sense of futility radiating from the men running by, moving equipment or wrestling with the long, serpentine hoses lying in the street. A tall, haggard man joined them, exhaustion and stress written in the soot on his face.

"Mr. Malone, Ms. Sheerin," LaPlante said, "this is Chief Hudson."

The chief shook Neil's outstretched hand and, focusing on Brid, said, "One of my men told me he called you. You're the owner's daughter?"

Brid nodded.

Hudson indicated the open door of a red pickup truck with a slowly flashing light on the roof of the cab. "Why don't you sit down?"

They moved to the smaller fire vehicle. Brid slipped into the passenger side and sat facing Neil, who leaned against the truck's open door. He could see her hands shaking. Hudson stood opposite them.

"Please don't tell me he's still somewhere in there," Brid said, addressing her question to Hudson. She pointed at the smoldering restaurant.

Behind them, a woman's voice pierced the background noise surrounding them. "Go ahead and try to arrest me, you asshole. I'm a lawyer, and I will sue you and your entire department."

Sofia, thought Neil.

The Chiesa sisters had pushed their way forward almost even with the pickup's cab, Franny saw Neil and joined them.

"Franny, can you give us a minute?" Neil asked, stepping in front of where Brid sat.

"Where's Brendan?" Sofia asked, before Franny could respond, searching the faces of the firefighters rushing past her.

"Who the hell are you? And how did you get in here?" Hudson demanded of Sofia.

Hearing the chief's raised voice and sensing they might be needed to assist him, two firefighters moved into the circle clustered at the pickup truck. Neil recognized them as close friends of Brendan.

"Chief," interrupted one, "she's Feeney's ex-girlfriend. The other woman is her sister. Feeney called her when we learned where the fire was. He said the sister's a close friend of the owner."

The chief sent Neil an inquisitive look, and said, "Shall I go on?"

Neil nodded.

Ignoring Sofia, the chief spoke directly to Brid.

"Ms. Sheerin, I'm very sorry. Two of my firefighters went in to get your father. The smoke was very thick, and they became separated. One of them, Brendan Feeney, made it into the apartment and was able to bring your father down the stairs to the first level. Then both of them were overcome with smoke before they could make it out. Unfortunately, it took my men a few minutes to find them. We think Feeney was sharing his oxygen mask with your father." His voice softened, and he reached for Brid's hand. "I'm so sorry, but your father didn't make it. It could have been smoke, or it may have been his heart. We have to wait for the medical examiner."

"Oh, Brid." Franny approached Brid, but halted at the look on her face.

"He was not burned? You are telling me the truth?" Brid's voice broke on the last word.

"He wasn't touched by the fire. Feeney got to him first and pulled him out of there." Hudson looked over his shoulder to where an ambulance cordoned off by yellow police tape stood. "As I said, we're waiting for the medical examiner, but you can see him if you want."

"Chief, another man, —Ronan Clougherty—lives up there, too. What about him?" Neil asked, unable to take his eyes off the burned-out apartment.

"Apparently, he was not home when the fire started. He was trying to get into the building when we pulled up. He's pretty broken up. You'll find him over there by the ambulance."

While Hudson was addressing the others, Sofia was frantically looking for Brendan in the faces of the many firefighters moving around them. "Did you say Brendan was the one who brought Mr. Sheerin down the stairs?"—her voice got more strained and anxious—"Where's Brendan now? Is he still inside?"

"Look, Miss—Feeney inhaled a lot of smoke. He was in pretty bad shape when we reached them. We got him over to St. Luke's as fast as we could." Over his shoulder, Hudson asked the two firefighters standing nearby, "They still working on him over there?"

The men looked at each other. The older one—whose name, Neil had finally recalled, was John Boucher—answered, "They've called for a life flight. It's touch and go."

"Shit," Hudson said softly, his eyes filling with tears.

Sofia began to wail.

Before Neil could stop her, Brid was out of the truck.

"Stop that right now. Or I will slap your silly face." Addressing the two firefighters, Brid asked, "Where will they take him?"

"Mass Eye and Ear," Boucher said. "They have a hyperbaric chamber there. It's his best shot."

Brid pivoted and faced Sofia, stepping in so close that they were inches apart. "You get down there. And you *do* whatever and *say* whatever is necessary to make him feel like he has something to live for. Do you understand?"

Weeping silently now, Sofia nodded.

"You go with her, Franny."

"But … " Franny looked over at the ambulance with Des' body in it.

"I'll take care of things here," Neil said, then backed up Brid's command, adding, "You go with Sofia."

"You can ride in with us; we're heading down there now," John Boucher said, putting his arm around a weeping Sofia.

"Franny," Brid called as they began to walk away.

Franny half-turned, but didn't stop walking. "Yes?"

"You make damn sure he knows how much we all love him. And call me as soon as you know something."

Franny nodded and hurried to catch up with the others.

At that moment, the helicopter lifted off the roof of St. Luke's, rising over the city before turning and heading south. On the ground around them, activity stopped, the firefighters pausing in their duties to watch it go. Neil saw several of them bless themselves as they sent a comrade on his way with a prayer.

Brid steeled herself. Straightening her shoulders, she ducked under the police tape and walked to the open doors of the ambulance where her father's body lay. Neil followed. Coming around the end of the vehicle, Brid saw Ronan leaning against the open door, standing watch, his face etched with grief.

"Ronan. Thanks be to God." She put her arms around his lanky frame.

"Ah, Brid, 'twas my fault. I wasn't here. If I had been, maybe I could have stopped it. I tried my best to get in there." His face crumpled as he spoke, his shoulders heaving with silent sobs.

"Or you could have died in there, too." Brid snapped. "You weren't hired to be his babysitter." Dropping her arms, she turned and looked down at the shrouded form on the stretcher. "He was no doubt shite-faced, the old fool. He probably put the kettle on and forgot it."

As Brid reached for the blanket covering her father's face, Neil caught her hand. "Are you sure you want to remember him like this?"

"I have to know. Or I will be haunted for the rest of my life by the thought he burned to death."

Gently, Brid lowered the blanket and stared down into her father's face. Some kind soul had closed his eyes. Neil watched the tension leave her face, replaced by sorrow. Only then could he, too, look down at the dead man. Despite an ashen color, Des looked serene. With the exception of a bruise on his temple, he was unmarked. The expression "at peace" crossed Neil's mind. Brid leaned over and rested her hand on her father's cheek. Softly she whispered, "Slán abhaile, Da." wishing him a safe passage home.

Straightening up, she surveyed the ruins of the bar. "I am glad he never had to see this. It would have killed him, if the fire had not."

She covered her father's face and, to the two men standing behind her, said, "He's my mother's problem now, God help her."

It was only then that, with a muffled sob, she stepped into Neil's open arms.

CHAPTER TWENTY-NINE

B rid perched on a sawhorse in a corner of the remains of the Snug, a well-worn leather jacket thrown over her shoulders to ward off the late October chill. The portrait of Countess Markievicz—water-stained and sooty, but still salvageable—leaned against the wall behind her. She recalled the day she had hung it.

Against her will, she wore a bright-yellow hardhat, clapped on her head by the foreman of the construction crew. He had insisted that everyone on site wear one inside the building while the demo work was going on. The abrasive screeching of crowbars attacking the fire-ravaged walls, coupled with the pervasive smell of charred wood, surrounded her. She was sick at heart and fought down the impulse to flee.

Sofia and Franny stood near her, watching the men tear out the scorched wood. Across the room, Neil and Nick were intent on discussing something with the foreman. Glancing down at her watch, she realized all the others should be on their way to work. *They should go,* she thought, and considered telling them that. She knew they didn't want to abandon her in the wreckage of what was once her father's life, leaving her with only Thatch for company. He sat next to her now, his head resting on her thigh. She twisted her fingers in his soft topknot for comfort.

But—I feel alone, she thought, despite their solicitous presence and the clamor and bustle going on around her. Yet that was not completely true. If she listened closely, Brid could hear her mother's voice, singing as she made scones in the kitchen, or her father's bellow, directed at the truck driver delivering beer out in the alley. Both her parents were gone—and yet still here, at least to her.

She winced as the construction crew dismantled what was left of the oak bar. *How proud Da was of that bar,* she thought, recalling how—to please Des—Drew had insisted that it be preserved when they had renovated the place together. *Drew MacCullough—another ghost about the place,* she thought, half-expecting him to join her on the sawhorse.

Now she watched as one of the construction workers reached down, removed a bundle from the pile of splintered wood, and handed it to Neil. Only when her husband was walking toward her did Brid recognize what he was holding.

"You might want to keep this," he said. He passed her the battered leather apron Des had brought with him from Doolin and always wore—almost as a vestment—behind the bar.

Gratefully taking it from his hand, in a voice choked with tears said, "I cannot bear any more of this. I'll be across the way."

Neil took a step toward her, but she put out her hand to ward him off. She ran the gauntlet of the makeshift door the clean-up crew had constructed of plywood and, with Thatch at her heels, crossed the street to La Boulangerie.

The familiar aroma of the French bakery greeted her; she took a deep breath and felt a moment of comfort. The early-morning crowd had thinned. Brid chose a table for four by the window so both she and Thatch could have space. She hung Des' apron on the back of her chair. Almost as soon as she sat down, a waitress placed a mug of coffee in front of her.

"Do you want something to go with this? A brioche or a muffin, maybe?" When Brid shook her head, the girl added, "You look like you could use it."

For the love of God, why is someone always pushing food at me? Brid thought. Her eyes were glued to the scene she had so recently left. Turning away from it, she smiled and said, "Thank you, this is grand."

The woman nodded. "Let me know if you change your mind."

Wrapping her shaking hands around the coffee mug, Brid continued her vigil. The plywood that initially covered the broken window facing Dock Street had been replaced by new glass; she had a clear view into the place where her father held court for most of her life. The ornate beer taps, along with the bottles that once filled the shelves behind the bar were gone. Neil had arranged for them as well as the glassware, dishes and cutlery to be placed in storage. As they continued tossing debris into the two blue dumpsters in front of Craic, the construction crew occasionally punctuated their efforts with brief conversation. She wondered what they were saying; they looked almost nonchalant. To them, none of this mattered. *They are only doing their job*, she told herself, *nothing personal*.

"I want you to eat this. You are too thin," Henry Janereau said as he slipped into the chair next to her and placed a warm brioche on the table.

"You have been telling me that for as long as I have known you." She smiled wanly at the bakery owner.

"I have, yes," he agreed. "Today it's worse than usual. You look like you're about to disappear. Eat." They both winced as a loud clang reached them from across the street. Henry nodded toward the apron on the back of the chair. "I miss him, too, you know. Underneath all that bullshit, he was a good neighbor and a good man." He sighed. "What will you do now? Sell the building?"

Brid shut her eyes. *Of course, I think I am going to sell the feckin' building—as fast as I can*, she thought. Instead, she said, "I have no idea."

Henry nodded glumly. His hand found Thatch under the table. The baker took a dog biscuit from his pocket and, slipping Thatch the treat, asked the dog, "How are you doing, my friend?"

Brid looked down at Thatch. "We should leave. If the health inspector finds him in here, there will be hell to pay."

"Well, I am the owner, and he looks like a service dog to me. Doesn't he to you? Besides, they don't show up before noon. Not like when I first opened. This bunch, they are all lazy." He looked over at the burned-out building. "Des would have been pleased with the funeral. How did you ever get the bishop here?"

She thought about the funeral. Henry was right. Des had been a

275

connoisseur of funerals, as only the Irish can be. He would have loved it—would have deemed it "a good turnout." Every seat in Our Lady Queen of the Angels Catholic Church had been taken. Mourners unable to find a spot inside stood on the sidewalk in front of the church. *Who knew the old man had so many friends?* she thought now, grinning despite her heavy heart.

Both the Ancient Order of Hibernians and the Knights of Columbus had been there in full regalia. Six bagpipers had piped Desmond Sheerin to his glory. Each one had refused to accept a penny from Neil, who, when he had attempted to pay them, got to hear six variations of the same reason, which went something like: "Des slipped me a few bucks once or twice when I needed it."

"It is hard to say who was more pleased, Da up there in heaven or Jerry McKenna down here below," Brid said. "I think it may have been the biggest funeral McKenna's has ever handled."

Henry chuckled. "Amazing, when you think there was standing room only. I knew Des had pulled a pint for a lot of people, but I didn't realize one of them was the bishop."

"He was not always a bishop," Brid reminded him. "Our Lady's was his first parish out of the seminary. Mammy was alive then, and she fed him several times a week—gratis, of course. 'Now you wouldn't be suggesting that we charge the good Father for his meal would ya, darlin'?' " She made a face as she quoted her mother. "And then Da found out 'the good Father's' family had come from Clare. They were a pair after that."

"Did you ask him to say the Mass?" Henry was still curious; it was not every day the bishop showed up.

"Me? Are you daft?" Brid snorted. "I did not. It was Father Hannigan at Our Lady's who called him."

The bishop, indeed. The assembled mourners had roared with laughter when he'd said, "I believe Des, in his career behind the bar, heard more confessions than I have. I bet he gave better penances, too."

Henry stood up. "I have to get back to the kitchen. You and the dog stay as long as you want." He pointed toward the table, adding, "Eat your brioche. I will send Sandy over with a fresh coffee. *That,*" he pointed at the cup in her hand, "is no longer fit to drink." He removed the offending beverage and headed toward the kitchen.

Moments later, the waitress placed a new cup in front of her.

"Thank you," Brid said, reaching for it with both hands. As she savored her first sip, her cell phone buzzed with a text message. A smile flickered briefly on her face as she read it. She typed a two-word response and leaned back, enjoying a rare moment of peace of mind, there had been so few since she'd learned of the fire.

Across the street, Neil was in a deep discussion with someone she could not see. From the look on his face, she knew he was listening intently. *What fresh hell is this?* she wondered.

Staring at the sad remains of the building, Brid found her thoughts turning to Drew. They had renovated the bar together almost seventeen years before. Out-dated and out of step with the gentrification taking place around it—the old customers who'd once lived in the neighborhood had long been gone—the place had become little more than a dive, with no appeal to the new people moving in. The renovation had been her idea, but it was her ex-husband's vision and money that had given the place a new life. *All gone now,* she thought, fighting back tears. She could see herself on that rainy Saturday so many years ago, watching Drew as he read her business plan. "You got an 'A' on this?" he'd laughed. "I would have given you a 'B.'"

Arrogant bastard that you were, she thought now as she sipped her coffee, *you did more than that, now didn't you? Twice.*

In the end, Drew had bankrolled the complete makeover of the place. And before it fell to fire, Craic had stood free and clear because, when he died, Drew had left her the money and a plan to retire all the bar's debt.

Brid leaned her elbow on the table and rested her forehead in her hand. Drew would want her to keep the place open. Of that, she was sure.

Beside her, Thatch suddenly stood up, his tail wagging.

She looked up to see Neil coming through the door, followed by Nick, Franny and Sofia, with Ronan and Mara—*holding hands,* she noted—bringing up the rear of the little band.

Neil patted Thatch, who immediately plopped back down under the table. Neil took the chair next to Brid as the others clustered around. Quietly, he told her, "Ronan and Mara have a proposition for you."

"Hiya, Brid," Ronan said. "Mara and I would like to talk to you about taking over the place when the repairs are done." He pulled Mara to his side. "You know I've worked with Des for the last couple of years, and I'm pretty sure I understand the running of it. And Mara has some ideas, too."

"Please say you'll think about it," Mara added, barely able to contain her excitement. "We would do an awesome job for you. All you'd have to do is collect the rent."

Brid looked across the street, not fully registering the scene of blue dumpsters and a burned-out apartment. In her mind's eye, she was back again—an inquisitive little girl, standing beside her parents on the cracked, cement sidewalk in front of a place they liked to take her to eat. In her head, she could hear her father saying, "I'm telling you now, Rosie, it's all going to be grand. Stop your worrying, woman."

With some effort, Brid pulled her thoughts back together to focus on Ronan and Mara. They *would* do a good a job with the place. Mara, she remembered, had a little girl, too, who could sit on the high barstools during the off-time, as she once had, stacking the coasters like checkers. Her parents' dream, carried across the sea with them, would live on. She felt some of the tightness she had been carrying inside her ease.

"A brilliant idea, if you are certain that is what you want to do," she said, looking from one eager face to the other.

"You'll let us give it a go, then?" Ronan asked, not quite sure he believed what he'd heard her say.

"Oh, Ronan, of course, if you want to take the place on. You know how much work it is. I would never say no." She took the leather apron from the back of her chair. "You'll need this now, won't you?"

Ronan was stunned. "But—this belonged to Des," he said.

"He would want you to have it. In fact, he would be delighted to think of you taking over the place." She glanced at Mara. "And he would have been happy about the two of you. Da always liked you, Mara. He told me your scones were almost as good as my Mammy's." *High praise, indeed*, she thought.

Blushing with pleasure at the complement, Mara said, "Did he really? That means so much to me."

"You won't be sorry, Brid. I promise we'll make both you and Des proud of the place," Ronan said, in a voice thick with emotion.

Brid looked once again across the street, surprised to find she was no longer so blue. The future seemed much clearer to her now. She smiled at Ronan. "It is settled then. You will need to talk to my lawyer. He has been in charge of all this bar business for some time now."

Her eyes met Neil's and he nodded slightly. She figured he was remembering the night he had come to her apartment two weeks after Drew died. His purpose had been to deliver an insurance policy, which Drew had taken out so that she would pay off the mortgage on the place without Des knowing the true source of the money. She had done it. She remembered thinking at the time that, when her father died, she was going to give the damn place to Neil, as she wanted nothing more to do with it. It was true then and, if possible, more true now. It was time for her to let go and move on.

Mara and Ronan took advantage of a table opening up near the door. Now that Brid had accepted their offer, they were anxious to begin planning.

Brid looked across the table at Sofia, who had slipped into a chair and was busily absorbed in her cell phone. *Probably texting Brendan,* she thought.

After the first shock of Brendan's accident had worn off, Sofia had pretty much returned to being Sofia.

Watching her, Brid wanted to shake her. *She reminds me of myself,* she thought, with a flash of insight. *Blinded by her own stubbornness to what's right in front of her.*

Brid knew, through Neil, that Sofia had made the trip every day into Boston—first to Massachusetts Eye and Ear Infirmary during the harrowing early hours when Brendan had been fighting for his life in the hyperbaric chamber and then, as he improved, across the street to Massachusetts General Hospital. Now, they were taking their relationship slowly, starting out as friends.

"How is Brendan doing?" Brid said.

Sofia looked up. "He's doing great. He can't wait to get back to work."

"That's wonderful. When does that happen?"

Sofia's smile lost some of its brightness. "Soon, at least that's what he's hoping. What he's really worried about is when he can start running again. Signs are good, though. They expect him to make a full recovery."

Brid nodded. "That's great—"

"Is that Lilah?" Franny's face was almost flat against the window. "It is! It's Lilah! She's with some guy. And they have Rose."

Brid was not the least surprised. She thought of the text she had received earlier from Andrea Grayson, who had asked if she should let them take the baby. Brid was pleased Lilah had chosen to come down to Craic right away to find them.

"Is her hair *pink*?" Nick asked, leaning over Franny, his hands resting casually on her waist like they belonged there—like they had always been there.

"She's dyed it pink, now?" Sofia was up against the window, too.

"Pink is better than purple," Brid said. "Oh, wait, that was last year." She studied the tall, slender young man walking next to Lilah. There was something about him …

Lilah and her companion paused on the sidewalk in front of the burned-out bar. Her face reflected her horror at what she saw.

Sofia left her position at the window, squeezed past Nick and Franny, and strode to the bakery entrance. Opening the door, she shouted "Lilah!" and gestured imperiously at them.

Lilah smiled. Holding Rose around the waist facing outward with her right hand, she towed the dark-haired man along behind her to the corner. As the trio waited for the light, Neil rose, ready to greet them. Suddenly Brid began to laugh, with enough of a hint of hysteria that Neil bent down slightly and looked closely at her. She was remembering Lilah insisting that Rose did not have a father. *Mother of God!* Brid was thinking. *He was here all the time. His chiseled face was right under our noses—sketch after sketch of him. And Rose looks just like him.*

They came through the bakery door.

Simultaneously, Sofia and Franny said, "Oh my God! It's Kren!"

"Actually, I'm Dave Laney." Blushing, he looked down at Lilah and then, sheepishly, at the rest of them. "I know. She drew me as one badass villain, but—honestly—I had no idea what was going on, or I would have come. Really, I would have been here. I didn't know."

"I didn't want you to feel trapped," Lilah said defensively.

Impulsively, Franny stepped forward and hugged Dave. "We're so happy to have you here now," she said. Gently, he extracted himself, clearly at a loss for words in the face of her enthusiasm.

"I'm Neil Malone." Shaking Dave's hand, Neil added, "I can't tell you what a pleasure it is to meet you." Then he reached over and pulled Lilah into a hug, being careful not to crush Rose. "And you. We've missed you."

Peeking around the curve of Neil's arm, Lilah's eyes met Brid's, sending her a silent thank-you.

Brid nodded almost imperceptibly.

As Neil began to introduce the others, Thatch came out from under the table, his flag-of-a-tail waving madly at the sight of his baby. Rose, oblivious to the fact she was surrounded by her family— created by fate and bound by love—chortled her delight, her open hands reaching joyfully for the dog's fuzzy face.

KATHLEEN FERRARI

ABOUT THE AUTHOR

Kathleen Ferrari has been making up stories since she was a little girl. Her father was so sure that she would become a writer that he built her a playhouse where she could write them.

MacCullough's Women, the first book in a series set in the fictional city of Lynton, New Hampshire, was published in 2011. *Francesca's Foundlings* was published in September 2015. Her essays have been published in **The Boston Globe** and in the **Northern New England Review.**

Her characters have a way of liking the same things she does: yoga, doll collecting, cashmere sweaters, Irish Brown Bread, Hermes scarves, persnickety cats, spoiled dogs and charming men. Like Franny MacCullough, she is always trying to lose those last ten pounds…

Kathleen lives in New Hampshire with a very charming man, a persnickety striped cat named ABoo, a Tibetan Terrier named Arleigh —also known as The Muse — and unfortunately not enough Hermes scarves.

Kathleen blogs about her writing and also what she is reading on her website: **www.KathleenFerrari.com**

She is at work on *Maggie's Girls,* the third novel in the Lynton Series planned for publication in the fall of 2016